**Adam looked up into the pale blue eyes of the mother of all those children.**

"Thank you," she murmured, her voice clear despite all the confusion around them.

"No problem," he ground out between more coughing.

"Do you always do that?" Carly asked.

"Do what?"

She crouched beside his stretcher. "Deflect a compliment. I was thanking you for saving my son from the fire. And Molly. What you did was extraordinarily brave. I don't know how I can ever repay you."

He gave her a tiny salute and muttered, "All in the line of work," then lay back down. Molly the dog was lying on the stretcher beside his, apparently playing dead except that her tail was wagging.

Adam closed his eyes.

# No Ordinary Family

### C.C. Coburn & Megan Kelly

Previously published as *Colorado Fireman*
and *Stand-In Mom*

ISBN-13: 978-1-335-69096-8

No Ordinary Family

Copyright © 2019 by Harlequin Books S.A.

First published as Colorado Fireman
by Harlequin Books in 2012 and
Stand-In Mom by Harlequin Books in 2011.

Recycling programs
for this product may
not exist in your area.

The publisher acknowledges the copyright holders
of the individual works as follows:

Colorado Fireman
Copyright © 2012 by Catherine Cockburn

Stand-In Mom
Copyright © 2011 by Peggy Hillmer

Printed in U.S.A.

www.Harlequin.com

# CONTENTS

**C.C. Coburn** married the first man who asked her and hasn't regretted a day since—well, not many of them. She grew up in Australia's Outback, moved to its sun-drenched Pacific coast, then traveled the world. A keen skier, she discovered Colorado's majestic Rocky Mountains and now spends part of the year in that beautiful state.

Currently she's living in England with her husband, as well as a Labrador retriever and three cats. Her first book, *Colorado Christmas*, received glowing reviews and a number of awards. She loves hearing from readers; you can visit her at cccoburn.com.

### Books by C.C. Coburn

*Colorado Christmas*
*The Sheriff and the Baby*
*Colorado Cowboy*
*Colorado Fireman*
*Sweet Home Colorado*

Visit the Author Profile page at Harlequin.com.

# COLORADO FIREMAN

C.C. Coburn

## Acknowledgments

Many thanks to:

Battalion Chief Neil "Rosie" Rosenberger and Captain Derek "Goose" Goossen of the Red, White and Blue for their invaluable assistance and patience with my research. It's encouraging to know our safety is in the hands of such capable men.

Remedial massage therapist Lynn Creighton for her help and insights into what is involved in massage therapy and for her amazing massages.

And my dear friends equine veterinarian Dr. Holly Wendell and horse-rescuer Helen Lacey for again patiently educating me about horses.

Any errors or discrepancies in this story are the fault of the author and in no way reflect the expertise of the aforementioned.

# *Chapter 1*

Desperate for more air, Firefighter Adam O'Malley cracked open the bypass on the regulator leading to his airpack.

The smoke inside the apartment building in Spruce Lake, Colorado, was thick and filled with lethal fumes. His helmet light shone through the gloom, barely illuminating his path as combustible materials manufactured in the seventies ensured the building burned fast and hot. Thankfully, the positive pressure inside his face mask prevented the noxious wastes from entering through its seals.

Adam heard the unmistakable whimper of a child and turned toward it.

He'd promised the mother he'd bring her toddler out alive. His vow had been the only thing that kept her from racing into the burning building to save her son.

Adam hadn't lost a victim yet and today wasn't going to be his first, not if he could help it.

Dropping to all fours, he crawled along the floor, where the smoke was less thick, toward the child. He spotted the little guy because of his diaper, a white beacon in an otherwise blackened world. He was on the floor beside his crib, hands stretched out, tears running down his chubby cheeks.

How could anyone have left a kid behind? he wondered as he ripped open his bunker coat, lifted the child into his arms and placed him inside its protection, talking to him in soothing tones. "It's okay, little guy. I've got you now. We'll see your mom in no time," he assured the child, praying their exit hadn't been blocked by falling beams or other debris.

He picked his way back out of the apartment, his body and jacket shielding the boy who clung to him, whimpering. The deafening sounds of fire consuming everything in its path—timber splintering, walls exploding, windows shattering—followed Adam as he moved down the stairs, testing each step to ensure it was still intact. Moments later, they were outside in the bright winter sunshine.

The child's mother broke from Captain Martin Bourne's hold and rushed toward them. Tears streaming down her face, she muttered incoherently as she tried to take the child from his arms. But Adam wasn't giving up his charge just yet. The paramedics needed to check him over, so he grabbed her with his free hand and directed her to the ambulances waiting nearby.

He'd just extracted the child's deathlike grasp around his neck when the mother screamed and raced back toward the building.

"Don't tell me she's got *another* kid!" Adam yelled at his captain as he ran to intercept the woman.

Then he noticed she was chasing after one of the kids they'd rescued earlier. He was running back into the building. What was it with this family?

Adam had always been quick on his feet, and in spite of the cumbersome firefighting gear he wore, he managed to overtake the mother, warning her to "Get back!" as he passed her.

He caught up with the kid, threw him over his shoulder in a fireman's hold and returned to where Martin was trying to calm the mother. The kid kicked and screamed and beat at Adam's back but the blows slid off his bunker jacket, slick with water from the fire hoses.

He put the kid down but the boy spun away, intent on running into the building. Adam reached out one arm, snagged the child and hunkered down in front of him.

"What do you think you're doing, son? We got all your family out," he said.

"M… M… Molly's in there."

Adam glanced up at the mother. "You've got *another* kid?" Sheesh, how many did this woman have? Four frightened children had been extracted from the building and she looked as if she was hardly out of her teens.

"Tiffany was babysitting my children," the mother explained. "She got my oldest *three* children out."

Served him right for making that comment about her having another kid.

"Molly is the Polinskis' dog," she said.

"How do you know she isn't already out?"

The woman indicated two elderly people being loaded into ambulances. "They'd never go anywhere without Molly."

*Except from a burning building,* Adam wanted to say.

"Mrs. Polinski told me she's still inside!" the child yelled over the sound of more parts of the building collapsing. "She wants me to get her!"

Adam closed his eyes. Some days he hated his job. There was no way he'd find the poor animal. Not until long after the fire was out...

"Son, it's too late to get her," Adam said in as soothing a voice as he could muster. What the hell were the old people thinking? Expecting a kid to go rescue their dog?

As if reading his mind, a hound of some kind howled mournfully. Another of the woman's children screamed, this one a girl of about six. "Please! Get Molly!" she cried.

Adam wished everyone would calm down and stop yelling.

"Which apartment is she in?" he asked as the dog continued to howl.

The woman pointed up to the third floor. "The one on the end, next to ours."

Adam looked into the eyes of his battalion chief and knew he was going to refuse.

"Wait till the ladder truck gets here. We'll reassess the situation then," Chief Malone said.

Adam released the boy and stood. "You know I can't leave her there, Chief," he said and, without waiting for his go-ahead, turned back toward the building.

His battalion chief's warning shout ringing in his ears, Adam sprinted up the stairs to the third level. As he did, they collapsed beneath him. He leaped the last couple of steps and landed heavily on his face, smashing his face mask and breaking the connection to his air supply. The mask filled with acrid smoke.

Ripping it off, Adam crouched down and crawled toward the sound of a dog scratching frantically on the other side of a door at the end of the hall. Adam had no idea how people could leave their precious pets behind in a fire. Or any other disaster, for that matter.

Coughing because of the smoke, he opened the door.

Inside, he found the saddest-looking dog in the world. Without wasting a second, he scooped up the basset hound, headed across the room to the window and kicked through it.

As the glass shattered onto the snow-covered ground below, he gulped fresh air into his lungs. "Ladder!" he yelled, but his voice was a harsh squawk.

Since the stairs had collapsed, the ladder truck was their only way out of the building. If it hadn't arrived, he and Molly were toast. Literally.

Irritated by the smoke, he blinked, forcing his eyes to water. A shout came from below as someone spotted him. Adam waited and prayed, sucking in huge lungfuls of air. Finally, the truck swung its ladder around toward him.

The terrified young dog squirmed in his arms. "Easy, girl," he murmured as he swung his leg out over the ledge and waited until the bucket attached to the ladder was within reach.

The smoke billowing out of the window behind him was growing thicker, choking him and the dog, who was now squirming and coughing so much he could barely hold her. He glanced back to see flames licking through the apartment's doorway. The entire building was in imminent danger of collapse.

The bucket finally reached Adam's precarious ledge and he stepped into it. "Everything's okay, girl," he said as they cleared the building. "We'll have you down in a moment."

His tone seemed to calm her and she settled in his arms, whimpering softly as they were lowered to the ground.

Once there, he was immediately surrounded by other firefighters. Molly licked his face. That small act of gratitude drained the tension of the past few desperate minutes from Adam's body. He smiled and ruffled her ears. She was grubby with soot, and the soot covering the gloved hand he was petting her with wasn't helping but he was too spent to pull off his gloves.

Exhausted, he allowed Martin Bourne to take her from his arms, then fell onto the stretcher under a triage tent set up by the EMT who was attached to their firehouse. After she'd placed an oxygen mask over his nose and mouth, she fitted another one on Molly, who lay on a stretcher beside him.

The dog was coughing pretty badly. "Look after her," Adam croaked, pushing the EMT's hand away as she began to wash out his burning eyes.

She ignored him and continued squeezing liquid into his eyes, then checked his vitals. He closed his eyes against the pain in his lungs and tried to relax in spite of his still-racing heart.

The flash from a camera bored through his eyelids. He looked up into the lens of Ken Piper, photographer for the local paper. "How does it feel to be a hero, Adam?" he asked.

Adam grunted.

"How about one of you and the dog? Smile!" Molly was lying on her back, all four legs in the air. She'd stopped coughing, so it was hard to tell if she was dead, playing dead or wanted her tummy rubbed. Ken's camera flashed again, then he melted into the crowd.

"Adam!" Hearing the familiar sound of his mother's voice, he opened his eyes again. Sure enough, his mom was elbowing her way through the crowd gathered around him and Molly.

He felt about twelve years old as he looked into his mom's piercing blue eyes and she glared down at him.

Positive that he was in for a lecture, he offered her a sheepish grin. "I got her out," he said, reaching across to rub Molly's tummy, hoping his mom would go easy on him since she was an animal lover. He didn't need a dressing-down in front of everyone.

"You sure did, darling," Sarah said, and dropped to her knees beside Adam and threw her arms around him. "I've never seen anything braver in my life."

She hugged him so fiercely the air whooshed out of his lungs, which started a coughing jag that felt as if daggers had been plunged into his chest.

"Careful, Mrs. O'Malley," his captain said. "Your son's just saved a baby, an elderly woman and a dog. Give him breathing room. There's little enough oxygen at this altitude as it is."

His mom drew back and cupped his cheek, making Adam feel like an eight-year-old instead. Why didn't she do this to any of his other brothers? Being the youngest of five boys was a curse. Since he was about to turn thirty, you'd think she'd accept that he was an adult now.

His mother's voice shook as she said, "I've never been prouder of any of my sons than I am today." Then she burst into tears.

Adam didn't know what to do. His mother rarely let

her emotions show—except when she was really angry—but now she was in all-out blubbering mode.

Luckily, Martin was good at dealing with emotional women and led his mom away, shouting over his shoulder at his men, "Find out if there's a veterinarian in the crowd to check out that dog."

Adam rubbed his eyes, unsure if his vision was blurred by the smoke or by his reaction to his mom's emotional display. Guaranteed, she'd be talking about this for a few years to come.

He'd been back in Spruce Lake less than a week and he'd had to fight his first big fire.

And then his mom had shown up. Great! Just great.

One of the reasons Adam had postponed returning to his hometown to fight fires was because of this very situation. He didn't want any of his family seeing the risks he took. His brother Matt, the county sheriff, knew full well the dangers of firefighting, but Adam had always played down the risks when discussing his job with his family.

There was another reason he'd stayed away from Spruce Lake. The reason he'd spent half his life trying to run from his hometown. Someday soon, he needed to confront that.

Adam rubbed his eyes again and started to sit up. He needed to get out of there, but found himself pushed back down as the paramedic washed out his eyes again. "I'm fine," he protested.

"I decide when you're fine," she said, placing the oxygen mask over his face again. "Breathe," she commanded. "I'll be back in a minute. I've got other firefighters to see. It's not all about you, Adam—you dog-rescuer, you." He could hear the gentle sarcasm in her voice.

"Don't hurry back," he muttered, and closed his eyes,

breathing in the cool air, feeling it surge into his lungs, restoring the O2 levels to his bloodstream. He coughed again and sat up, then removed his mask and coughed up black goop that had gotten into his lungs. He spat it out.

Only it landed on a pair of white sneakers. He looked up into the pale blue eyes of the mother of all those children.

"Thank you," she murmured.

"No problem," he gasped between more coughing. "Anything else you want me to spit on?"

"Do you always do that?" she asked.

"Do what?"

She crouched beside him. "Deflect a compliment. I was thanking you for saving my son. And Molly. What you did was extraordinarily brave. I don't know how I can ever repay you."

He gave her a tiny salute, muttered, "All in the line of work," and lay back down. He didn't want to talk to this woman. To anyone. He wanted a long shower and clean sheets. *Cool,* clean sheets.

Carly Spencer stood for a moment watching the firefighter who'd saved her son Charlie's life, knowing he'd shut his eyes to get rid of her.

She'd wept as he carried Charlie out of the burning building. She'd been so sure he wouldn't be found. Jessica, the babysitter she'd hired to care for her children after school, had been sick today and sent a friend to fill in for her.

Since today, the last day of school before the February break, had been declared a snow day, although the weather had turned unexpectedly mild, so it was actually more of a slush day, her three oldest children were home.

And since Carly had back-to-back massage appointments booked at the Spruce Lodge spa—and God knew, she needed the money—she'd had to get moving and hadn't taken enough time to run through the children's routines with Tiffany. The girl had obviously panicked and forgotten all about eighteen-month-old Charlie sleeping in the bedroom that was farthest from the living room.

"I'm so sorry, Mrs. Spencer!" she'd cried as Carly pulled up in her vehicle in front of the burning building. "There was this huge explosion and all I could think about was getting the kids out.... But then when we got down here, I remembered the baby was sleeping in the back room."

Her words had sliced into Carly's heart. Without hesitating, she'd raced into the building and collided with a firefighter who was coming out with Mrs. Polinski in his arms.

He'd handed the old woman to a colleague and grabbed Carly by the arms.

"You're not going in there!" he'd yelled through his mask.

"My baby's inside!" she screamed. "I have to get him out!"

"Which floor?"

"Third. First door on your right!"

The words had scarcely left her mouth when he released her and ran back into the building as another firefighter carried Mr. Polinski outside.

Someone grasped her by the shoulders. "Come over here away from the danger, ma'am," he said. "Adam will find your baby."

The man seemed confident of Adam's ability to find one tiny little boy in a huge inferno, but the sound of the building disintegrating and the amount of smoke billowing from the windows and doorways eroded her hope that the firefighter would get to Charlie in time.

Alex, Jake and Maddy had huddled around her, trembling with fear and shock. Carly hugged them close and waited.

She'd felt a prickle of apprehension go up her spine—as if someone was watching her. She glanced around at the crowd. *Of course people are watching you,* she chastised herself. Still, the sensation was so weird.... She searched the faces, but saw no one familiar. Shrugging it off, she put it down to her fears for Charlie.

When the firefighter returned, holding Charlie protectively beneath his coat, she'd rushed to take her son from him.

But then Alex had raced back toward the building to find Molly. Carly hadn't had time to wonder about the Polinskis leaving her behind; maybe everything had happened too quickly for anyone to think rationally. The fact that her babysitter had left Charlie behind was evidence enough of that.

The firefighter had charged into the building to rescue Molly. Carly had held her breath, fearing for his and Molly's lives. And then she'd heard the glass shattering as he'd kicked out the window. The smoke was so thick as it poured out of the window that she couldn't see him clearly. But Carly knew without a doubt it was the heroic firefighter who'd saved her son, and now he'd saved Molly.

She'd needed to thank him and had waited until he'd been checked out by the EMT before approaching. But then an older woman had come by and made a fuss over him. She'd soon realized the woman was his mom. And she was annoying her son. Carly smiled. She would've acted in exactly the same way had it been one of her children who'd acted so fearlessly.

"Adam? What the...?"

He opened one eye to find Dr. Lucy Cochrane on the other side of the stretcher.

Lucy knelt beside him, opened his jacket and put her stethoscope to his chest. The EMT had already checked his signs and was now working on some of his colleagues. Adam didn't have the energy to point that out to Lucy so he let her examine him. She was an old school buddy of his brother Matt's. Bossy, but a good friend to the family. And if Lucy was around, the woman with too many kids might leave him alone. She made him uncomfortable.

Made him yearn for things he'd denied himself for too long.

"I heard you'd come back to town. Just as well, or that dog might not have survived. Brave boy." She patted his cheek.

Adam resisted the urge to groan. His older brothers' friends still acted like he was a kid. And they all wondered why he couldn't wait to get out of town once he'd finished high school. If they'd known the truth, they sure wouldn't think he was so heroic.

Lucy listened to his chest and nodded. "Keep breathing," she said, and put the mask back on his face.

"Thanks. I intend to," Adam said with a note of gentle sarcasm as Lucy did a thorough exam under the watchful eyes of the toddler's mother. He thought again that she looked way too young to have so many kids. She resembled Meg Ryan—skinny legs, flyaway blond hair—and she seemed so vulnerable that Adam experienced an unwanted but overwhelming urge to protect her.

He wondered where all her kids were now. Had she managed to misplace one of them again? And where exactly was her husband?

Lucy departed with a promise to return again soon. Adam closed his eyes, then jumped as something wet and slimy collided with his cheek. He opened his eyes. Louella, Mayor Frank Farquar's pet pig, was standing over him. He wiped the slobber with the back of his hand. What the hell was Louella doing at a fire?

She grunted at him and went to shove her snout against his face again, but Adam pulled away in time. That was when he noticed Louella's feet. She was wearing bright red rubber booties.

"What the hell?"

"Who knew old Lou doesn't like the feel of snow between her dear little trotters?" his brother Will said from behind Louella.

"A pig in rubber boots. Now I've seen everything," Adam said. Could this day get any weirder?

"You did good, little brother," Will told him. "Lou was only showing her appreciation."

Adam groaned. Will and Louella had, in Adam's opinion, an unnatural relationship. Will didn't mind hanging out with Louella and, stranger still, she didn't mind hanging out with him.

He and Will were opposites. Will loved everyone and they all loved him. So did their animals. Adam had always found social situations difficult and preferred his own company, much like his older brother Luke, who ran the family ranch.

A camera flash went off in his face just as Louella

swooped in again. "You put that in the paper, Ken, and you're dead," Adam growled through clenched teeth.

"Hey, your ugly mug will be all over the paper tomorrow," Ken said. "Human interest, you know."

"Or porcine…" Will said with a grin.

"Go away. Both of you," Adam said. "And take her with you."

"Come on, Lou. I'm sure we can find someone who appreciates your affectionate advances."

Adam watched as Louella trotted off behind Will, her bright red boots contrasting with the snow. She paused and glanced back at him. "Don't even think about it!"

Louella snorted and turned to follow Will.

"Darling!"

It was his mom again. Adam sighed. "Spare me from women," he begged skyward.

"You don't like women?" the mother with too many kids asked. She was holding one of her kids—the toddler he'd rescued. He was perched on her hip, but looked way too heavy for someone as small as her to be carrying around.

"He comes from a family of brothers," his mother said, completely ignoring the fact that Adam was about to answer for himself. "Unfortunately, he doesn't relate to the opposite sex very well." She offered her hand to the woman. "I'm Sarah O'Malley, by the way."

Adam wasn't about to tell her he related perfectly well to women. Just not to bossy ones. Like his mom. And Lucy. And now this nosy woman with black spit all over her sneakers.

"Carly Spencer," the woman said, giving her own hand to his mom to shake.

"So nice to meet you, dear, in spite of the circum-

stances," Sarah said. "Of course I blame his father," she
continued. "The male decides the sex of the baby. After
five boys I said *enough!*"

Lucy had returned to check on Molly, since the vet
hadn't arrived yet, and chuckled at his mom's remark.
Adam saw Carly Spencer's mouth turn up in a smile.
She'd be even prettier if she smiled more often. Still, she
didn't have much to be happy about, since her home had
just gone up in flames.

"Ouch!" he yelped as Lucy reached over and prod-
ded him.

"She's only trying to help, darling," his mother pointed
out. "If you can't be more civil, you'll never find anyone
to marry you."

"Sometimes your conversation defies logic, Mom,"
he muttered through the mask. He pulled it away from
his face so she couldn't mistake his words. "And I'm not
looking for a wife," he said, hoping she'd go away. And
take the Carly woman with her.

"Oh, my God, you're gay!" his mom said, as if this
was a revelation that explained everything—his unmarried state, his aversion to moving back to his hometown,
possibly even the cause of global warming.

"Not that there's anything wrong with that, of course,"
she added quickly.

"I'm not gay."

"You've never had a relationship."

"Trust me, Mom, I've had relationships."

"With women?"

"*Of course with women!* Mom, seriously, you're acting weird."

"I just want to ensure the continuation of the O'Malley
line."

"Last count, you had seven grandkids. The O'Malley line is safe."

"But…"

Adam forced himself to sit up. "Once and for all, Mom. *I am not gay!*"

Everything seemed to freeze—the chattering of by-standers, the whine of emergency vehicles, even the sound of water gushing from the fire hoses.

Heads swiveled in Adam's direction. His colleagues, several of whom had stood down now the blaze was under control, turned toward him and stared. Louella snorted.

The television crews zeroed in on a developing human interest story. The Carly woman shifted her kid to the other hip and smiled.

Adam groaned.

His mom looked as if she wanted to argue further. Adam lay back down, replaced the oxygen mask over his face and closed his eyes.

Moments later, he heard his mother huff and go off in search of someone else to pester.

"Your mom seems concerned about you."

"She's concerned about everyone. Unfortunately, she's *insanely* overprotective of me." He wanted to assure her he wasn't gay, but what was she to him? No one im-portant. Just the mom of a kid he'd rescued. He'd never see her again after today. What did it matter what she thought about his sexuality? What did it matter what any-one thought? Even his mom.

"You're the youngest?"

He opened an eye. "How'd you guess?" He felt he had to at least try to be polite, since this woman had just lost her home. In reality, he didn't want to talk to anyone right now. Especially anyone of the female sex. Between his mom's nagging, this woman's nosiness, Lucy's brutal treatment, Molly the dog and Louella the pig slobbering on him, he'd had his fill of females for the day. What he really wanted was to take a long shower, have a beer and maybe watch a hockey game on TV with his dad. His dad rarely talked, never nagged. Mac O'Malley, patriarch of the O'Malley clan, was probably his best friend in the world. Pity Adam would never be able to talk about the night Rory Bennett died, even with Mac.

"Mothers have a special place in their hearts for the baby of the family."

Did this woman ever shut up? Adam wondered. He was so sick of being called the *baby* of the family.

"Ma'am?" Adam was thankful when his captain's voice intruded. He wanted to sleep instead of being surrounded by chattering people. Most of them women. "Your kids have all been cleared by the paramedics. You're good to go."

"Thank you. Thank you for everything," she said. Then her lip quivered.

Oh, no, here come the tears, Adam thought.

Sure enough, the woman started to cry.

"Hey, there," Lucy said, patting her back. "Your children are fine." She pulled out her cell. "Who can I call for you? Do you have family nearby or friends you can stay with?"

The woman shook her head and staggered away.

Adam had never seen anyone look so desolate in his life. And he'd seen a lot of sorrow during his years in this job.

"Oh, my goodness." His mom appeared out of nowhere and went to comfort the woman. She glared at Adam over her shoulder, as if he was the cause of her misery.

Adam strained to hear what they said to each other, then gave up. Lucy had given him the all clear, and Martin had released him from duty for the rest of his shift. It was time to head home and hit the shower. He sat up and glanced around. There were even more spectators than when he'd brought the dog down the ladder.

He could see his brother Matt conferring with the television crew. Matt was nodding his head. He turned in Adam's direction and waved. Then he smiled. Matt rarely smiled.

As a youngster, Adam had held out for praise and encouragement from his big brother. He'd come to learn that exuberance wasn't Matt's way. A wave and smile would be all the compliment Adam could expect.

He stood too quickly and stumbled, but was caught by Matt's strong arms before he hit the ground. "Hey, easy there, kid," he said. "Sit down for a bit."

Exhausted, Adam could only shake his head. "Need to get out of here. Take a shower."

Molly was still lying on her back playing dead—except her tail was wagging. Matt bent down and rubbed her tummy. She rewarded him with a squirm of pleasure.

"The television people want to interview you." Matt indicated the crew he'd been speaking to behind the police cordon.

"What for?" Adam looked away from their prying cameras. "I was just doing my job."

He felt Matt's hand on his shoulder and welcomed its warmth. "You're a hero, little brother."

He hated that word. He was no hero. "Like I said, I was just doing my job. Do you do interviews every time you arrest some bad guy?"

"You saved the life of a child and a dog. You know how this town loves dogs."

"Then tell 'em to donate generously to the pound." Adam was fed up with talking. "Where's your vehicle?" he asked. "Can you drive me home?"

Matt crossed his arms in a gesture that said he wasn't pleased. "Since you live at home, why don't you have Mom take you?"

"Because I want peace and quiet, not Mom alternating between singing my praises and getting hysterical about how risky my job is."

"Mom is never hysterical."

"You didn't see her earlier."

"Darling!"

"Speak of the devil," Adam muttered as their mother returned.

"Could you drive Adam home?" she said to Matt. "Carly and her children don't have anyone to stay with, so I've offered them the apartment over the stables for as long as they need it. Molly's coming, too."

*What am I? Chopped liver?* Adam felt like asking. Instead, he said, "In case you've forgotten, Mom, *I'm* living in the apartment over the stables."

"Yes, I'm aware of that, darling, but I'm moving you into the house so Carly and her little brood can have some privacy. You don't mind, do you?" Without waiting for his answer, she turned away and directed the Carly woman and her children toward her SUV.

Adam stared after her. "Is this the same person who, last week when I returned home, practically kissed the ground I walked on?"

"The very same," Matt said. "You know Mom can't resist a waif, and now she's got five of them to care for.

Correction—six." Matt indicated Molly being lifted from her stretcher by one of the firefighters and carried to his mom's vehicle.

"Can I stay at your place?" Adam begged. Matt and his wife, Beth, lived in a large home their brother Jack had built them in a picturesque valley outside town. Adam would love to live in that same valley one day. Someday. After he'd confronted his demons.

"Sure. I did tell you Sarah's teething, didn't I?"

"No, you didn't. Now that you mention it, maybe I *would* be better off at home," Adam said, and followed Matt to his vehicle. Although where he'd sleep, Adam had no idea, since one of his three nieces was occupying his old bedroom.

As it turned out, his tomboy of a niece Daisy was only too happy to give up her room to her "hero" uncle. So Adam slept among her animal posters and woke up during the night with a lump under the mattress that turned out to be a stirrup. He pulled it out, tossed it on the floor, coughed up more black goop and went back to sleep.

## Chapter 2

Awakened the next morning by pandemonium from the kitchen, Adam recognized the deep pitch of several of his brothers' voices and an occasional "Shh!" from his mom.

He stumbled out of bed, washed his face but didn't bother shaving and went downstairs, hungry enough to eat one of their prize black Angus steers all by himself. He'd missed dinner since he'd taken the much-wanted shower and fallen into bed, exhausted, and slept through the night.

Sunday mornings, the family usually gathered at Two Elk Ranch for breakfast. However, today was Saturday, Adam noted as he strode into the kitchen, a huge room that accommodated the family dining table. Today it was packed to overflowing with all his brothers.

"Here he is!" Celeste, his youngest niece, cried and ran to him, her arms outstretched.

Adam bent to lift Celeste the way he'd done a hundred times before, but as he did, a muscle twitched with pain. He grunted and nearly dropped her.

His reaction had most of the occupants of the kitchen rushing forward to help him. He held out a hand to restrain them and ruffled Celeste's hair. "Next time, kiddo," he said. "I must've put out something in my back."

He rubbed at the spot, but couldn't quite reach it.

"Then it's lucky Carly is a massage therapist," his brother Will said. He came around the table to clap Adam on the back, making him wince. "And in case I didn't say it yesterday, well done, little brother. Anyone who saves a dog is good people in my book."

Speaking of the dog, he wondered where she was. Adam tried not to groan as Will slapped him again.

"You should have Carly look at that," his mom said.

"I'd be happy to."

Adam glanced around and found the woman with too many children, with the littlest one perched on her hip. She seemed slightly less vulnerable than she had the last time he'd seen her. The toddler's face was covered with goo that might or might not have been oatmeal. He smiled and waved at Adam. Adam forced himself to smile back. He smiled at the mom, too—but not an overly friendly smile, since she and her kids were responsible for getting him booted out of the apartment above the stables.

He wished he could disappear. He wasn't comfortable with crowds, even if he *was* related to most of the people there. How he missed the seclusion of that apartment.

Then his eyes fell on the newspaper spread across the table and his stomach lurched. The headline, Hometown Hero, glared up at Adam, along with a photo of him carrying the child out of the burning apartment building. A smaller one showed him and Molly lying on their stretchers side by side. Unfortunately, it also featured Louella kissing him. The caption beneath read *Mayor's Pet Pig Thanks Heroic Firefighter Adam O'Malley*.

Adam hated seeing the word *hero* associated with his name. He was no hero. Heroes didn't let their friend take the rap for a fatal car accident.

His dad came forward and clapped him on the back. Like his two oldest sons, Luke and Matt, Mac O'Malley was a man of few words. Adam figured his mom more than made up for it. He didn't expect his dad to say anything, so when Adam saw tears brimming in his eyes, he nodded and let his dad pass by him and leave the kitchen.

His brother Jack came over and was about to clap him on the back, too, but Adam held up his hand and Jack dropped his. "Sore, eh, buddy?" Jack asked, and Adam nodded.

"I'm so proud of you," Jack said. Then tears welled in his eyes, as well.

Oh, jeez, this was what he didn't need, an outpouring of emotion from the O'Malley men. Although he and Jack were separated in age by only eleven months, they were pretty much opposite in temperament. Jack wore his heart on his sleeve; Adam wasn't sure if he even had a heart.

Coming back to town had been a bad idea. He shouldn't have accepted that one-month posting to Spruce Lake to cover an absence in the department. He should've gone somewhere else in Colorado. *Anywhere* else! But his mom had pressured him to take the posting, saying he was missing out on seeing his nieces and nephews growing up.

Adam had enough guilt to deal with, so he'd agreed to the job, telling himself it was only for a month. He could survive a month without having to get too close to anyone or having to care too much. And then he could return to Boulder, where no one knew anything about his past and no one ever pried into his private business.

"Thank you for saving Molly, mister."

Adam looked down into the pale blue eyes of the Carly woman's daughter. Sheesh! Her eyes were brimming, too.

He patted her on the head. "You're welcome, kid." And then to deflect the gratitude of the rest of the children who were moving in his direction, he asked, "So where's Molly?"

"She's right here, Uncle Adam." He heard Luke's middle daughter Daisy's voice from somewhere behind the crowd in the kitchen. He walked toward it and found her seated on the floor, the dog's head in her lap. Daisy had always had a way with animals.

As much as it was possible for a basset to look anything but deeply saddened by life, the dog had an expression of bliss on her face as Daisy stroked her ears.

Molly was lying on a blanket. A blanket Adam recognized from his childhood. A blanket he was very fond of.

"That's *my* blanket," he couldn't help saying, and turned accusingly to his mother.

She flapped the spatula at him and said, "You haven't used that in years. So I've given it to Molly. She needs it more than you."

"I might have *wanted* to use it," he muttered. It was the principle of the thing. He mightn't have used the blanket for more than twenty years, but it was a well-worn and much-loved childhood companion, and for some stupid reason he felt a sense of possessiveness about it. It sure as hell didn't deserve to be used as a *dog* blanket.

"It's Molly's now," Daisy piped up.

His oldest brother, Luke, who ran the family ranch, pressed him down into one of the vacated chairs at the table that occupied the huge country-style kitchen. The table easily sat ten, twelve at a pinch, and today people were rotating chairs as they finished breakfast and made way for the next shift.

He took his seat—beside Carly—and studied the occupants of the kitchen. Although heavily pregnant, Luke's wife, Megan, was helping his mom prepare and serve. Luke's oldest daughter, Sasha, was talking to Will's stepson, Nick, while Celeste, Luke's youngest, was chatting animatedly with the little girl who'd thanked him before. The two boys who belonged to Carly were bolting down second helpings of oatmeal like they hadn't been fed in a week. Maybe they hadn't, Adam decided. Their apartment wasn't exactly in the town's high-rent district.

And where was their father? he wanted to ask, not for the first time. Shouldn't *he* be taking care of his family?

"Where's your husband?" Adam blurted, before he could stop himself.

Silence descended on the kitchen and Adam wished the floor would open up.

She looked back at him with a frankness that was daunting and said, "He's dead."

Carly Spencer took grim satisfaction in watching Adam O'Malley's discomfort as he swallowed her answer and half hoped he'd choke on it. She'd already told Adam's family that her husband, Michael, was a firefighter who'd perished in a warehouse fire in San Diego. She'd been seven months pregnant with Charlie at the time.

And now she felt bad about her bald statement. She, of all people, having been married to a firefighter, should've been more circumspect. But something perverse had made her answer his question as rudely as it had been asked.

What was it with this guy? He had the nicest, most welcoming family, but he was so emotionally distant, it was almost scary.

He'd done the bravest thing yesterday, not only rescuing her son Charlie but defying his battalion chief's orders and saving Molly. Yet when she'd tried to thank him, he'd been so offhand it bordered on arrogant.

She'd wanted to call him on his behavior, but there was something in Adam O'Malley's dark brown eyes that spoke of a hurt far greater than Carly suspected he ever revealed to others. So instead of challenging him further, she asked, "Would you like some bacon?" and passed the plate to him without waiting for his answer.

His mother came up behind him and scooped scrambled eggs onto his plate, kissing the top of his head as she did.

Carly didn't miss the deep blush beneath his tan. That was interesting, the relationship between him and his mom. She got the feeling Sarah irritated him at times. Like now. She was bent over him from behind, hugging him.

"Mom. *Please?*" he murmured.

"I'm just so happy to have you home. And alive," his mom said, and kissed the top of his head again before releasing him. The guy was clearly embarrassed by his mother's display of affection. Sarah, however, seemed to revel in exasperating—if that was the right word—her youngest son, as if she was deliberately trying to provoke a reaction.

She returned with the coffeepot and poured Adam a

cup, then went to put cream in it. He took the jug from her hand and murmured, "I can do it myself, Mom."

"Of course you can, darling," she said, totally unfazed, "but you're a hero, and I intend to make you feel like one."

Carly noticed that her own sons, sitting across the table from them, were transfixed by the exchange. To diffuse their interest, she said, "I don't believe you've been properly introduced to my children. The one who caused you so much trouble yesterday is Alex and the one beside him who's eating as if he hasn't been fed in a week is Jake. My daughter is Madeleine. And this little guy," she said, indicating her youngest, sitting on her lap, "is Charlie."

Charlie, far from being grateful to his savior, chose that moment to flick a spoonful of oatmeal at Adam. Then he laughed.

To his credit, Adam didn't leap from his seat or demand an apology. Instead, he wiped the oatmeal from his cheek with his finger, then wiped his finger on his napkin. "It's gratifying to be reminded of what the public thinks of *we who serve them,*" he said, and dug into his eggs.

Will patted him gently on the back. "That's the spirit, buddy. Nothing like some creative criticism to bring you back to earth. Can't have you walking around the ranch with a head bigger than a black Angus bull."

Luke laughed from where he stood beside the kitchen range and raised his coffee mug in agreement.

Carly liked the oldest of the O'Malley brothers. Hey, she liked them all. She was trying to like Adam, too, but he wasn't exactly making it easy for her. *What's his problem?* she wondered.

He was eating in silence. Probably trying to ignore her. Well, that was fine because she didn't want to make conversation with him, either.

She sipped her coffee, savoring the richness of the blend—a far cry from the budget brand she usually drank. Various conversations flowed around the kitchen and she caught snippets of them and smiled. Maddy and Celeste seemed to have hit it off. They were both in first grade but in different classes and hadn't met each other before. Carly liked Celeste. She was an angelic-looking child with a sweet temperament and outgoing personality. Maddy was more withdrawn, but Celeste seemed to have struck a chord with her as they shared a love of drawing. The pair were presently giggling over pictures they'd drawn of Adam.

Carly wanted to see how he'd react to them and asked, "What have you got there, Maddy?"

Her daughter held up the picture. She'd given Adam curly, dark brown hair and a smiley face. Carly glanced at Adam. His hair was indeed dark brown, but cut so short, it was hard to determine if there was any curl in it.

Then Celeste held up her picture. She'd given Adam even curlier and longer hair. The child apparently knew her uncle well enough to have done that. However, instead of a smiley face, Adam's expression was angry.

"Why did you draw your uncle looking so annoyed?" she asked Celeste.

"He's not. He's thinking," the child corrected her. "He frowns when he thinks. Like he is now." Celeste indicated her uncle with a flick of her head, bit into a bagel her father had smeared with cream cheese and honey and went back to her drawing.

An odd combination, Carly thought as Celeste wolfed

it down. She turned to Adam. Sure enough, he was frowning. But he was miles away and not part of the conversation, nor had he seemed to notice the girls' drawings of him.

"A penny for them," she ventured, wanting to make friends with the man who'd saved her son's life.

"What?" he said, coming out of his reverie.

"You were deep in thought," she said. "If your back is bothering you, I'd be happy to give you a massage. It's the least I can do."

He put down his coffee cup and looked at her. "Thank you, but no." He stood. "I have to be going. There'll be a disciplinary meeting because I ignored my chief's orders," he said to the room's occupants.

"And saved Molly," Carly finished for him, knowing he'd never say the words himself. "I hope you don't get into too much trouble. If there's anything I can say to whoever you have to answer to, I will. I'll testify that Alex would have run into that building to get her if you hadn't."

"I doubt a kid would be any match for a firefighter," he said, his voice sardonic, then abruptly left the kitchen.

The rest of the adults had taken their seats at the table and were looking at her.

"I… I'm sorry, I don't know what I said to make him leave like that."

Sarah leaned over and touched her hand. "Don't pay any attention to him, dear."

She didn't go on to excuse his behavior or explain it, so Carly busied herself with clearing the table. "I wanted to thank you again…for welcoming my children and me into your home." Carly could feel her voice breaking, but she continued, hoping to find the strength she needed.

She could do it. She'd survived her husband, Michael's, accidental death. She'd survived this past year and a half without her parents' support or knowledge of how bad things were for her financially.

Her dad had suffered a stroke early last year and Carly had no intention of burdening him or her mother with her latest woes. They had enough to deal with.

She could survive the aftermath of this fire and start fresh. Just like she had before.

She'd used Michael's insurance money to pay off their house in San Diego. And to pay off his credit card debts, which had been considerable. His fascination with the latest toys—from snowmobiles to Jet Skis, Windsurfers to water skis—had been a bone of contention in their marriage. Carly hadn't realized how tangled their finances were until she opened the bills addressed to Michael after his death.

Once she'd paid off the mortgage, she'd felt more secure, knowing that no matter what, her children would always have a roof over their heads. But less than a year after doing that, Carly had wanted to get out of San Diego. Not so much to escape the memories but to escape the unwanted attentions of Michael's best friend and fellow firefighter, Jerry Ryan.

Jerry had been a wonderful support after Michael's death, but his behavior had become too familiar, bordering on obsessive, and Carly had felt trapped. She'd decided to move away from San Diego, the memories—and Jerry.

She'd rented out her home, effective January 1, intending to live off the rent and her work as a massage therapist.

Neither her parents nor Jerry were happy with her

decision to move out of the state, but Carly remained resolute.

Offered a job at a new spa hotel opening in Denver, she'd accepted. She and the children had spent Christmas with her parents, then moved to the Mile High City a week before the hotel was slated to open in the new year. She'd enrolled her children in school and paid the security deposit to rent an apartment near work. But the day before opening, the hotel was firebombed. Fortunately, nobody had died, and both police and press speculated that organized crime had been responsible.

To Carly's immense gratitude, her new landlord had been compassionate about her situation and come up with a solution. He owned an apartment building in the mountain town of Spruce Lake. In the summer it would be demolished and a new complex built in its place, but in the meantime, he had a vacancy available. If she could find herself a job in Spruce Lake, the apartment was hers. He assured her he could easily fill the vacancy in the Denver apartment she'd be leaving.

Carly had jumped at the opportunity, knowing that resort towns were often in need of massage therapists. She had her own massage table and could supplement her income by offering massages to people in the privacy of their homes.

Nearly two months had passed since that fateful day in Denver. Carly hadn't told her parents about the firebombing and her move to Spruce Lake; she hadn't wanted to worry them. Instead, she'd been upbeat in her emails and Skype calls.

And there was another reason she hadn't wanted to come clean about her move. She knew Jerry kept in touch with her folks. She didn't want him to learn where she was.

Her children had settled into Spruce Lake Elementary and were loving it. Carly liked the warmth of the community and was gradually building a client base of locals and tourists. Charlie went to daycare a couple of days a week while Carly worked. She also did a few shifts at the local spa. Finding a reliable after-school sitter for the children on the days she had to work hadn't been too difficult—until yesterday.

If she could have replayed yesterday, she'd never have left her children with a sitter she didn't know. And if Sarah O'Malley hadn't come to their rescue, Carly had no idea what she could've done. The O'Malleys were the kindest, most giving people she'd ever met.

But the raw anger, the fear and desperation she'd experienced when she realized Charlie was missing still ate at her.

"You've been so…generous…and we don't…" she started to say, but then the floodgates opened. The tears she'd held so tightly in check after the fire, the emotions she'd suppressed all through the endless night, flowed.

Conscious that she was making a complete fool of herself, Carly blubbered an apology. But warm arms enveloped her and Carly turned to cry on the offered shoulder, finding it was Mac who'd silently reentered the kitchen.

"There, there," she heard Sarah say. "Let it all out, dear. You've been holding it in, being brave for too long."

Sarah was right; she *had* been holding it in, putting on a brave face for her kids, and now that they'd left the room, she'd fallen apart.

"I'm sorry," she said to Mac, lifting her head and seeing the huge damp patch on his shirt. A wad of tissues got shoved into her hand and she tried to staunch her running nose and wipe at her eyes. Mac rubbed her back in soothing circles and said, "You lean on me all you want, Carly."

Carly sobbed at the warmth and compassion in his voice and wished her father could be there for her.

When she'd composed herself a little, she looked up into Mac's eyes and in a vulnerable moment admitted she wished her father was there. And then she wished she could take back her words, because they were too revealing. It was too much to admit to these people who until last night were strangers.

Megan hugged Mac as well, and said, "I wish I'd had a dad like Mac. I'm so glad I married Luke."

Grateful for Megan's lifeline, Carly wondered what Megan's family history had been for her to make a remark like that.

"Let's not overdo it!" When Mac finally managed to struggle out of their embrace, he was blushing. Molly got up from her blanket and came over to nudge his leg, whimpering as if in agreement. "Women!" he muttered good-naturedly, grabbed his hat and took off out the back door.

Sarah chuckled and said, "I think the estrogen overload was getting to him."

Megan smiled, dabbing at her eyes. "He needs to get used to it. He has a wife, three daughters-in-law and five granddaughters."

That broke the remaining tension in the room and the rest of the occupants laughed.

"Women!" This came from Luke and Megan's son, Cody, whom Carly had learned was the result of a holiday romance Luke and Megan had had sixteen years earlier. They'd only recently been reunited and still acted like newlyweds. Sasha, Daisy and Celeste were by Luke's ex-wife—the mention of whom had caused Sarah's lips to purse and Luke to change the subject.

Carly hadn't quite got all the family relationships sorted out, but they were gradually falling into place.

Like his grandfather, Cody grabbed his hat and headed out the back door.

"I agree with them," Luke said. "There are way too many women around here." He kissed his wife and removed his hat from the peg near the back door, then followed his father and son out to start work.

"I'd better check in with the office," Matt said, standing.

Jack glanced at his watch. "And I have an appointment with Frank Farquar. Seems the mayor wants me to build a stronger porch swing for Louella."

"Louella?" Carly asked.

"The mayor's pet pig," Will explained. "She was hanging around with me at the fire. I'll introduce you sometime."

The brothers said their goodbyes, leaving Carly and Sarah alone in the kitchen. Carly stood, ready to clean up, but Sarah indicated she should sit.

She took a seat opposite Carly, poured more coffee and said, "Now, tell me, dear, how I can help?"

"You've done so much for us already. I don't know what we would've done without you." Sarah had produced clothes and pajamas for her children last night, since they'd had only the clothes they were standing in. Carly appreciated how Sarah did everything without fuss, saving her children from any further distress. If it had been her own mother in similar circumstances, it would've felt as if Carly was swept up in a tornado. Carly's mom thrived on drama. It was one of the reasons she hadn't turned to them after Michael's death. And now that her dad was ill, there was no way Carly would even think of adding to his problems.

"Dear, I know you lost everything in that fire. I'm pretty sure the only possession you have left is your vehicle, and that got so much water damage parked where it was, it'll take a while to get fixed."

Carly nodded. She needed her minivan for work. Not that she had a job anymore since her mobile massage table was destroyed in the fire. She wished she'd had it in her van, but she'd left it upstairs because Mrs. Polinski had booked a massage after Carly's appointments at the spa. And now she'd inherited the Polinskis' dog.

Yesterday as they were loaded into the ambulance, Mrs. Polinski had asked Carly to look after Molly while they were in the hospital, but as of this morning, Molly was homeless. When Carly had called the hospital to find out how they were doing, she'd been put through to Mrs. Polinski, who'd been very upset that they'd be moving back east with their son and daughter-in-law. Apparently, their son's wife didn't want Molly coming with them. The old lady was understandably upset about Molly, and Carly promised to see what she could do. Unfortunately, Mrs. Polinski had misunderstood and thought Carly was adopting the dog.

So now it looked as if Molly belonged to her. Could her life get any more complicated? Oh, yeah, it could. Molly was due to be spayed the week after next and she'd just bet that hadn't been prepaid!

Although Carly had no possessions left in Spruce Lake, at least she had her precious children. And that was all that mattered. From what she'd been able to glean talking to the babysitter afterward, there'd been a tremendous explosion that shook the building, followed shortly after by one of the other residents screaming, "Fire!" Then all hell had broken loose.

Tiffany had grabbed the three oldest children and fled down the stairs, just as Carly had pulled up outside the building. When Carly had asked her where Charlie was, she admitted she'd forgotten all about him. Carly forced the memory of that horrible moment out of her mind and told herself, *Charlie is fine. Your children are all fine. You will get through this.*

"I have nothing left," Carly said. "I hadn't gotten around to taking out insurance on our possessions." Meager as they were, she added silently.

"I feel so overwhelmed! I don't know how I'm going to get my business going again." She fought the tears that threatened. Feeling sorry for herself wouldn't get her anywhere. She needed to find some money to buy a new massage table and start earning again. She'd resented Michael for spending their savings on frivolous toys she'd had to sell for a tenth of their value when he'd died. And now she'd been just as reckless by not insuring their possessions.

"So you don't have any savings?" Sarah asked.

Carly took a deep breath. She'd already told Sarah about her dad's stroke and how she didn't want to burden her parents.

"There've been too many bills to pay lately, what with moving costs, getting established in the apartment, paying for utilities—it all costs money."

Afraid the older woman would see her as a loser for not having saved anything, she quickly added, "But I have a home in San Diego. It's rented out. When my husband died I used the insurance money to pay off the mortgage and our credit card debts. Then…" Carly didn't want to go into why she'd decided to leave San Diego, didn't want to talk about Jerry Ryan getting too possessive of her. She'd tried letting him down nicely, but it had become very uncomfortable. In the end she'd used the excuse that she needed to get out of San Diego, to start her life anew.

"Unfortunately, the global financial crisis meant I couldn't sell the house for anything near what we paid for it. So I decided to rent it out and relocate. The rent helps with my expenses for now, but there's not much left over once all the bills are paid. In a few years, when the real estate market's recovered, I'll sell it and buy something here—if I can afford to."

Sarah's smile lit up the room. "So you like Spruce Lake? In spite of the fire?"

"I love it. My children are happy at school, even though we've been here such a short time. And Spruce Lake is delightful. It has everything I could ask for."

"I'm so glad you like our little town. I fell in love with it, too, on my first visit with Mac."

"I'd like to get established in my own business here, build up a good client base, but without a massage table, I'm going to have to cancel the appointments I had booked for next week." Carly brushed her hair back and said, "Well, I guess I'd better get cleaned up and make an appointment with the bank manager. Plead with him to lend me enough to buy a new one so I can get started again."

"That's the spirit!" Sarah said, lifting Carly's own spirits immensely. "I like the way you think, Carly."

"I don't know how to thank you. You've done so much for me. You're a godsend," Carly said. "In fact, last night

I woke up and wondered if I was dreaming. Not about the fire, but about how kind you were. How safe you made me feel."

Sarah rewarded her with another smile. "You're welcome, dear. Now, you go see if you can get an appointment today. I'll clean up here."

"Oh, no, you don't! Look at this place! It's a disaster."

Sarah glanced around. "True," she agreed. "But I like it that way. Makes me feel needed. You run along." She made shooing motions. "I'll have the girls help me clean up. You don't mind if I rope Maddy in, do you? That's how they earn their allowance."

"What a good idea. I'd get the boys to help, too, but they seem to have taken off to watch Luke with the horses." She could see her boys through the kitchen window, sitting on the corral fence as Luke worked with a horse.

"They'll get their turn," Sarah assured her. She took Charlie from Carly's arms and sat him in a high chair, then gave him a piece of toast. "He'll be fine here with me. And if you have to go into town this morning, I'll watch the children."

Carly was about to say "thank you" yet again when Sarah held up her hand. "I know. I know," she said. "Carly, it's my pleasure. I love having this house full of people. Now, off you go."

Carly went into the living room, looked up her bank's number and called using the house phone. She'd been in such a panic that she'd left her cell phone in her minivan when she'd leaped out. It was too water damaged to ever work again.

Five minutes later, Carly's hopes had been completely

dashed. After she explained the situation to her bank manager, he'd refused her a loan. Since she hadn't applied for a credit card, not wanting to be hit with high interest rates if she was late with payments and with the memory of the debt Michael had built up so easily, Carly only had a debit card. But there was barely enough in her account to buy a pair of warm winter boots for herself to replace those she'd lost in the fire. She wore clean white tennis shoes to her spa appointments, wanting to look professional and be comfortable. But tennis shoes were useless for walking in snow and ice, and since it was winter, she'd be doing a lot of that.

Carly sat on the sofa, bit her lip and forced herself not to cry. How many more things could go wrong with her life? As if sensing her melancholy, Molly waddled into the room and curled up on Carly's feet. Carly reached down to rub the dog's ears. "Poor girl, you're missing your owners, aren't you?" she asked, then jumped as a wad of money was thrust under her nose.

She stared at it, bewildered.

"Take it," Adam said gruffly.

"I... I can't do that."

"Yeah. You can. I heard your half of the conversation. You need it more than I do."

Carly shook her head and glanced up at Adam. "Thank you, but no. I'll find some way to get my business up and running again without accepting charity."

"Then give me a massage and I'll pay for it."

"I don't have a table," she pointed out.

He shrugged and proffered the money again. "So go buy a table with this and then pay me back with a massage."

Carly couldn't help smiling at his logic. "You're talking a lot of massages!"

"I've got a feeling I'll need them after I've met with my supervisors today."

Remembering the conversation before Adam had come downstairs this morning—his family was concerned about disciplinary action for disobeying his battalion chief's orders—she said, "I... I hope it goes well for you, Adam. What you did was nothing short of heroic." Her eyes filled with tears and she dashed them away. "I'm sorry I'm being so emotional. I'm not usually this weepy, but when I think of what might've happened to Charlie if you hadn't found him. And Molly, she's such a sweet dog... I...can't...help...it."

"Yeah. Well," he said, scratched Molly's head and left the room.

His sudden departure shocked Carly so much that she stopped crying. *Must get more control of emotions!* she told herself, and looked up. Adam had left the wad of notes on the coffee table.

She took them to the kitchen.

Sarah heard her entering, turned around and smiled. "How'd it go?" she asked.

"I, ah," Carly faltered, and held out the notes to Sarah.

"Goodness! That was quick," the older woman quipped. "Did he send you that through the phone line?" she asked with a grin.

"Quite the contrary. My *ex*–bank manager doesn't want anything to do with me. Adam gave me this, but I can't accept it."

Sarah's eyebrows rose. "And you told him so?"

"Of course."

"And?"

"He said I can work off the debt with massages."

"Who said that?" Megan asked, coming into the kitchen.

"Carly's bank manager won't let her have a loan to get her business up and running again, so Adam's given her an advance payment for services to be rendered. That way she can buy a massage table," Sarah explained. She rubbed her shoulders. "Hmm. I think I need to prepurchase a ten-pack of massages. Do you do discounts for friends?" she asked with a twinkle in her eye.

"You know perfectly well I wouldn't consider charging you," Carly said, and wagged her finger at Sarah.

"Then you can charge me," Megan said. "I've heard prenatal massages are wonderful for expectant moms."

"They are," Carly agreed. "But I couldn't charge you, either! You've already given me half your wardrobe," she said, referring to Megan's generous offer of clothes.

"I won't be able to fit into them for a while yet, so you're welcome." Megan brushed off her concerns. "Now, when can I book my first massage?"

"As soon as I can get a table," Carly said, shaking the money at her.

"Can you buy one locally?" Sarah asked. "If not, we could make a run down to Denver." She glanced at Megan. "After all, I have a nursery to furnish for my next grandchild, and although I like to buy locally, there are a few things I can't get up here."

"True!" Megan said, her face lighting up. "I feel a shopping trip coming on!"

Carly wished she could join in with their enthusiasm, but she simply didn't have the funds. She hadn't counted the money Adam had given her, but there couldn't be enough for a massage table, could there?

"You look worried," Sarah said. "If you can't buy a table around here, I really did mean we could take a trip to Denver."

Carly forced a smile into her voice and said, "Let me make a few calls, and if I can't buy one here today, I'll take you up on that."

Megan pulled out her cell and said, "You know, I think the other women in my prenatal class would love to sign up for some treatments with you."

"So would the ladies in my quilting group," Sarah chimed in. She, too, pulled out her cell. "Let's all meet back here in half an hour and see what we've come up with."

# *Chapter 3*

Exactly thirty minutes later, they met back in the living room. Sarah produced a list of at least a dozen names. "And more to come," she promised. Megan had an equally long list.

"Then that settles it," Carly said. "The trip to Denver is on, if you're still offering, because I can buy a massage table direct from the wholesaler."

Sarah rubbed her hands together. "I'll make sandwiches for the men's lunch. If you like, Carly, we can leave the boys here under Luke's watchful eye. I checked on them before, and he and one of the hands are teaching them to ride. I don't think you'll be able to drag them away to go shopping."

When Carly nodded, Sarah went on. "Now, we'll take Charlie and the two little girls. Daisy will want to stay here with her father. Sasha may or may not want to come with us."

"Come where?" Sasha asked as she breezed into the room.

"Shopping in Denver," her grandmother replied.

The magic word effectively stopped the teen in her tracks. "I'll be ready in five," she said, and ran back upstairs to her room.

"I'll let the guys know they're fending for themselves until we get back," Megan said as she pulled on a warm jacket and hurried out the back door.

"And I'll help make sandwiches," Carly said, her earlier enthusiasm returning.

Carly didn't think it was possible to go from feeling so completely desolate and alone to being on such a high in less than twenty-four hours.

In the past day, she'd gone from having nothing to having a new start in life, two new and already very dear friends and a measure of happiness that had been missing even before the dreadful fire that had claimed her husband's life.

Adam's money had purchased a better and sturdier massage table than she'd had before. There was even a little left over so she'd treated Megan and Sarah to coffee at a bookstore and the children to thick shakes.

They'd returned to Two Elk Ranch in high spirits, loaded down with maternity clothes for Megan, items for the nursery and new clothes for the girls and for Carly's two boys.

Sasha dashed upstairs to change into one of her new outfits, accompanied by Maddy and Celeste. Sarah disappeared into her wing of the house to find Mac, and Megan went in search of Luke to have him unpack the car, leaving Carly alone in the living room.

Only she wasn't alone for long, because Adam stalked

through the room muttering something about screaming girls.

He stopped short when he realized he wasn't alone.

"Was your trip a success?" he asked shortly, as if he
didn't care one way or the other.

Carly decided not to let it bother her. "Yes, it was.
Thanks to you. And how did your…meeting go today?"

Carly didn't miss the grimace before he got his emotions under control. "Not so good. I have to appear before a disciplinary board on Monday."

"I'm sorry. You deserve better treatment than that,"
Carly said, meaning it.

He shrugged. "Goes with the territory. I was about to
get myself a beer to drown my sorrows. Can I get anything for you…or the kid?" he asked, indicating Charlie,
nestled on her hip.

"His name is Charlie," she said, determined not to ignore Adam's "pretending he didn't care about anything"
act.

"Charlie, then," he said, and without waiting for her
answer, went into the kitchen.

Carly followed him and found him with his head buried in the fridge. "Want a beer?" he asked from the depths
of it.

"A soda would be absolutely marvelous. Thank you,"
she said flippantly, then chided herself for her sarcasm.
The man might be a Neanderthal, but he'd saved her son's
life. She needed to overlook his personality defects and
be kind and understanding.

"Kind and understanding, Carly," she muttered under
her breath.

"You say something?" he asked, holding up several
varieties of soda.

She selected one and opened it. "Nothing important," she said, noticing how he winced as he took a seat at the table. "Why don't we set up my new table and get started on those therapeutic massages I owe you?" she suggested.

He glanced up at her, eyes narrowed. "Are you really a *qualified* massage therapist?"

"What's that supposed to mean?" she snapped, at the end of her patience.

He shrugged again, annoying her even more. The guy did a lot of shrugging and she suspected it was his way of pretending nothing mattered.

Carly took a seat across from him and slammed her soda down on the table. She experienced a small sense of satisfaction when he jumped. "I asked you a question," she said. "I don't accept shrugging as an answer and I'm sure your mother never did, either."

His dark eyes bored into hers but she refused to back down. He didn't like being challenged? Well, neither did she!

"When Will said you were a massage therapist, I envisioned you working in one of those massage parlors."

Carly could feel her blood beginning to boil. She'd suspected that was what he'd been hinting at, but something perverse made her want to hear him admit it.

"Do I *look* as though I work in a massage parlor?" she demanded.

"Wouldn't know. Never been in one."

Carly released a breath. "That makes two of us. For your information, I went to the American Institute of Massage Therapy and am qualified to give both therapeutic and sports massages. And I'll accept your abject apology for being such a jerk…on one condition."

"And that is?"

"That you help me unpack my new massage table from the car and specify where you'd like me to give you your first treatment."

A few interesting images of places Adam would like Carly to give him a massage came to mind. Most of them were X-rated, so he quashed that thought, resisting the urge to shrug—Carly was right; he did it too often. He got up and said, "Lead the way."

He watched as she stood and hoisted the kid onto her hip. "Why do you always carry him around?" he asked. "Can't he walk?" He regretted the belligerence of his tone the moment the words were out of his mouth. As he half expected, Carly managed to floor him with her answer.

"As a matter of fact, he can. However, since I nearly lost him in the fire yesterday, I'm reluctant to let him out of my grasp. If you don't mind me massaging you one-handed, that would be great, because I don't want to put him down. For anything."

"Fair enough," Adam said, knowing she was baiting him. "Maybe we'd better postpone that massage until he's asleep. In a bed. Or does he sleep on your hip, too?"

He could see her muttering something under her breath, but couldn't quite hear it.

"Funny," she finally said, and threw him an exaggerated grin, which made Adam feel like a complete heel for prodding her.

Carly opened the fridge and got out some cheese slices and bread. She prepared a sandwich with one hand, then balanced the kid on the countertop as she cut the sandwich in two. She gave one half to the child, and chose a banana from the fruit bowl. Lifting Charlie onto her hip again, she said, "Let's go."

Adam found himself obediently following her through the living room and out the front door toward the car. Dusk had descended while they were inside bickering—no, that wasn't the right word. Was there such a word as *repartee-ing?* He didn't know, but it sounded...friendlier.

She opened the rear door of his mom's SUV and was about to reach inside.

"Let me get that," he said, moving around Carly.

He enjoyed brushing against her, and saw her swallow before she stepped aside to allow him access to the truck. He took out a box that looked much too small to be a massage table. "This is it?" he asked.

"Yes," she said in a reasonable voice. "It's a *portable* massage table, remember?" She turned toward the stables. "I also bought some lattes and shakes for the shopping party with the change. I hope you don't mind."

Adam could hear the mild sarcasm in her tone and ignored it. "Where are we going?" he asked.

She stopped in her tracks and he nearly barreled into her. "To the stables. I would've thought that was obvious."

"Why not the house?"

"Because Charlie is about ready for bed. His own bed. And the house will be much too noisy for you to be able to relax properly." She spoke slowly and clearly as if he were a little slow. "And one of the requirements of a good massage is to offer a zone of peace for the client."

"You sound like you're reciting that from a book."

"I am," she said, and turned back toward the stables.

As it turned out, Charlie needed a bath before bed. He'd finished the other half of his sandwich on the walk to the stables, then made a mess of eating the banana, and since there wasn't a bathtub in the apartment over the stables—*his* apartment over the stables, Adam noted, still feeling proprietary about it—Carly filled the deep kitchen sink with water and plopped Charlie into it.

Adam watched as she bathed her son. The pair seemed wrapped within a cocoon, safe together, mother humming and talking soothingly to her child.

He'd once felt safe like that, too. But years ago, something bad had happened, something he'd caused and never owned up to. Being back home was causing that memory, and the self-loathing that went with it, to resurface. He worked on pushing the thoughts away, taking deep breaths, then exhaling.

"Are you all right?" she asked, snapping him out of it. "I hope you're not suffering any aftereffects of the smoke inhalation."

Adam almost hated the concern he could hear in her voice. She sounded as if she cared. He didn't want people to care about him. Because that meant *he'd* have to care about *them*. He'd survived the past fifteen years by trying not to care.

She lifted Charlie from the sink and placed him on a towel on the counter and dried him off. "Nearly done, my little man," she cooed to the kid, then carried him to the sofa bed. "Just as well you're not too fussy yet. Otherwise, you wouldn't want to be wearing these Barbie pajamas. They used to be Celeste's," she told him as she diapered and dressed her son.

Carly tucked Charlie beneath the covers and kissed his cheek. He grabbed a rag doll, stuck it under his arm, put his thumb in his mouth and rolled over, away from the bright light in the kitchen.

When Carly flicked on a lamp in the living area and

turned off the kitchen light, the tiny apartment suddenly felt too intimate.

"He's out for the night," she whispered.

"I, ah, didn't realize it was so easy to get children to sleep," he said, for something to say, anything to break the intimacy of the room. "Celeste used to scream the house down when she was little."

"So did Maddy. But my boys have always been good about bedtime." Carly smiled as she said it and he liked the effect it had on her features. She looked younger. More carefree.

"How old are you?" he asked, needing to know.

"Thirty-two," she said, and he released his breath. "How old are you?" She opened the packaging on the massage table.

"Why do you want to know?"

"Well, duh! You asked me!"

He crouched down to help her. "I had a good reason for asking you."

"Which was?"

"Never mind," he said, straightening as they withdrew the table together. "I'm turning thirty next month."

Moments later, she had the table fitted together. "I'll get some towels and prepare the oil and then you might want to undress in the bathroom," she said.

"Undress?"

"That's how people usually have massages. Oil and clothes don't mix well."

"Um, I didn't know when I agreed to this that I'd be naked."

She put her head to one side as if considering him. "Haven't you ever had a massage before?"

Now he felt plain foolish. "No," he said honestly.

"In that case, you're in for a treat."

Adam swallowed.

"You're really uncomfortable about this, aren't you?"

"Gee, how can you tell?"

She smiled again and he wondered if he should ask to see her driver's license to make sure Carly was telling the truth about her age. "Okay, I'll put you out of your misery by telling you that you can leave your boxers on."

Adam was tempted to ask if he could keep his jeans on, as well—just this first time. But she was giving him that look again.

"Not to rush you or anything," she said, and glanced at her watch. "But I'd like to get to bed before midnight."

Visions of being in bed with Carly suddenly filled Adam's head. He fled to the bathroom.

*Strange man,* Carly thought as she wiped down the massage table and set some towels on it. Then she realized there wasn't another room for her to slip into while Adam got under the towel on the table. Some men didn't mind her seeing them in their boxers, but she had a feeling Adam wasn't one of them.

Tiptoeing to the door, Carly knocked gently. When she heard his gruff acknowledgment, she said, "There's an extra towel behind the door. You might want to wrap that around yourself before you come out."

Moments later, he emerged, wrapped in the suggested towel. Not that it did anything to cover his magnificent body, Carly decided. She'd never had such a reaction to seeing a nearly naked client before. Never. Ever.

Silently, she indicated he should lie on the table. "Face-down first," she managed to say, cursing her hoarse-sounding voice.

When he was settled, she draped an extra towel over his butt for modesty.

"I, ah, usually play calming music," Carly explained as she squirted oil onto her hands, warming it, then spread them over his back. "But obviously my CDs are history."

Observing his breathing, Carly breathed in sync with Adam, to create a better energy channel between therapist and client as she worked on warming Adam's skin and the muscles beneath, starting slowly, then concentrating on specific areas.

"Whoa!" she couldn't help saying at the same time as Adam jumped. "That is one tight trapezius. No wonder you winced when you picked up Celeste."

He grunted and Carly went to work on him, smoothing the tension in his muscles with long, soothing strokes, preparing him for some deeper work on those vicious knots she could feel beneath her fingertips.

He sighed and she smiled. Clients usually sighed inadvertently with the rhythmic motion of the effleurage strokes. As she felt him begin to relax she moved back to his trapezius, kneading the knots and the tension in his muscles, feeling them gradually ease.

Every now and then, he'd react when Carly hit a particularly sore spot.

"Why does it feel like that?" he asked.

"The knots are caused by built-up lactic acid and toxins in your tissues and muscles. Massage helps disperse them," she told him.

He grunted and she went back to working on his knots. She was just getting into a rhythm when he suddenly asked, "So do guys ever come on to you when you give them a massage?"

"That was so out of left field," she said.

"Do they?"

"Some do."

"And?"

"And I tell them the session is over. Forever."

"And if I came on to you?"

"You wouldn't."

"You sound very confident of that."

"I'm good at reading people. I had you read within two minutes of meeting you."

"Should I ask what you read?"

"You could, but I don't think you'd like the answer."

He grunted again and she moved to his legs.

Carly could tell from his posture—the unguarded moments when he hunched his shoulders—that he was protecting himself from something. She soon found some knots in his calves. "You need to stretch more," she said. "This is also caused by lactic acid. You should probably do more reps and less weights when you work out."

"So you're an exercise therapist, as well?"

"No, but I get to see the results of incorrect exercise. And then I have to fix it. You need quite a lot of fixing."

"Thank you. I'll remember that the next time I'm leg-pressing several hundred pounds."

"Oh, I *know* you'll thank me for it," she said, and kneaded a little deeper to press her point home.


Adam had no idea why anyone thought being massaged was relaxing, especially when Carly got him to roll over onto his back.

He was thankful he had two towels covering him, but he was too conscious of responding to her touch. And whatever she was doing to his toes was way too erotic!

And now she'd moved to the soles of his feet.

"What are you doing?" he asked as she pressed and stroked parts of his foot.

"A little reflexology. I can tell a few things about the state of your organs from the zones on your feet."

"Sounds like voodoo to me." Adam wanted to challenge what she'd said, but in truth, it felt strangely good.

"Not at all. It's been around a long time. The ancient Egyptians are believed to have used acupressure on the feet. For instance, when I press here..."

She pressed on part of his instep. "This area is related to your stomach. Perhaps you have an ulcer? And pressing here, on the sides of your toes, relates to your brain. Maybe you overthink things and that's led to a stomach ulcer?"

"Oh, please... You're not going to claim you can tell that from my feet." Although Adam had suffered from stomach ulcers and he did tend to overthink. Except when it involved rescuing kids and dogs from burning buildings. And if he was honest with himself, he had to admit he enjoyed having his feet massaged.

"Hmm," he murmured. "I didn't realize this is what happens during a massage. I thought it was all about long, soothing strokes."

"Depends on what sort of massage you want. Or the type of massage your therapist feels you need. Since you have no experience, I'm trying a few different things."

She moved up to his shins, working in long strokes from knee to ankle and back again. That wasn't comfortable, either. He flinched and she eased off a little on the pressure, then gradually deepened it.

"It would help if you'd relax," she said. "Try taking slow, deep breaths. Like the ones you were taking when I was finishing up with your back. You were relaxed then."

Adam wasn't aware that his breathing had revealed so much. It bothered him that she'd probably noticed a whole lot of other things about him, too.

"So when did you manage to fit in studying to become a massage therapist?" he asked.

"My husband and I married young and planned on having three children. So after Maddy, our third baby, was born I learned massage to bring in a little extra income. My home-based business was building, then I got pregnant with Charlie. I kept it up for as long as I could, but I got too fat to reach across the table."

Adam couldn't help grinning at the image of Carly heavy with child, trying to bend over a client.

Then the image of Carly heavy with *his* child filled Adam's mind. *Where did that thought come from?* he asked himself, and worked to push it from his mind.

"I went back to work when Charlie was one."

"How did you end up in Spruce Lake?"

"Long story. How about if you concentrate on relaxing and enjoying this experience instead of interrogating me?"

So, she had secrets, too, Adam surmised, judging by the way she'd cut him off. And, like him, she had a right to her privacy. He dropped the subject and did as he was told.

Oh, Lordy! Now she was stroking his thighs and it was causing him to respond to her touch in a very male way. It was far too stimulating and Adam felt in danger of embarrassing himself. Maybe he needed a male masseur? He was sure he wouldn't be reacting like this if Carly were a guy.

*"Breathe,"* she said, and deepened the pressure of the strokes.

Adam needed to say something. To apologize for his

reaction. But before he'd opened his mouth, she said, "Shh, it's okay. It happens. Just *breathe*."

Which only made him even more tense, wondering how many other men she'd massaged had gotten erections. He didn't like to think of other men responding to Carly.

He especially didn't like the thought that some of them might have tried to take advantage of her, and experienced a sudden violent need to punch out any guy who'd reacted to her like this. Bad enough that *he* was, but he knew it wouldn't go anywhere. Knew he was too much of a gentleman to take it further.

"Adam!"

Her sharp command had him opening his eyes and looking into hers.

Bad move. The room was too dimly lit. He wished the harsh kitchen light had been left on, but then the kid— Charlie—might have woken up.

She was standing over him. So close, her hips were brushing the side of his waist. Her fair hair was backlit, making her look almost ethereal. He started to sit up but she pushed him down, the warmth of her hands going straight through his shoulders.

"I need…to get out of here," he said, finding he was too weak to fight her. Man, she was strong. Had she cast some sort of spell on him, draining him of strength?

"Adam, it's okay. Don't be embarrassed."

"But I am and I want to get out of here."

"I haven't done your chest or your arms yet."

"And you're not going to." He tried to sit up again. This time she released him.

But when he sat up, he felt light-headed. He raised his knees and rested his elbows on them, his head bowed.

She touched his back and he flinched.

"I don't bite," she murmured.

He glanced at her and forced a smile. "No, you do far worse than that."

"Oh, come on! You don't mean that."

"I'm dyin' here."

"Only of embarrassment. Nothing terminal. At least nothing that your feet want to tell me about."

He stared at her.

She said, "That was a joke."

She fetched him a glass of water. He gulped it down, wanted more, but was afraid to ask. Strange how this woman scared him, had this temporary power over him.

"Like I said, I've got to go." He swung his legs over the side of the table, preparing to get off.

"Go where?" she challenged him. "Dinner won't be ready for at least an hour. Lie down on your stomach and let me do some more work on your back and arms. You'll thank me for it later."

He had to admit he'd liked her working on his back. Those long strokes were mighty soothing. Reluctantly, he rolled over.

He could hear her squirting oil onto her hands, rubbing them together, warming it. At her first touch, he flinched, hating himself for responding to her yet again.

"Is the oil too cold?" she asked.

"It's fine," he grunted, and concentrated on his breathing.

Thirty minutes later, Carly placed a towel she'd warmed by the fire on Adam's back and slowly rubbed him through the fabric, soaking up some of the oil and signaling the end of the massage.

Only Adam was snoring!

She smiled. When a session finished with the client sleeping like a baby, she knew she'd gotten that person to a point of deep relaxation.

Usually Carly had to gently wake him or her. But in this case, she didn't.

She went into the bathroom and washed the oil from her hands, looked at herself in the mirror and was shocked to see the bags under her eyes. She hadn't slept well the night before, constantly waking up to check on her kids. She could do with some meditation before they had to go to dinner.

Back in the living room, she lay down on the sofa bed beside Charlie, closed her eyes and placed her hands on her solar plexus shakra, breathing deeply and slowly. Within moments, she was asleep.

# Chapter 4

Adam woke feeling incredibly refreshed.

He was a little sore, but it was a good kind of sore. His stomach growled and he wondered how he'd missed dinner last night.

He rolled over and nearly toppled off the bed. It took him a moment to realize he was back in his apartment, but he wasn't on his king-size bed in the bedroom; he was on Carly's narrow massage table. And it wasn't morning; it was still nighttime. He could see stars twinkling through the window over the kitchen sink.

He sat up and took a moment to get his bearings. Carly was lying on the sofa bed, Charlie curled up at her side.

The last thing he remembered was Carly working on his back in those wonderful, soothing strokes. They'd felt so good, so relaxing… He must've fallen asleep. That was nearly as embarrassing as what had happened earlier when he reacted to her physically.

Nothing came close to being as embarrassing as that. Carly had said, "It happens," and she didn't seem perturbed. Hopefully, she thought he was reacting to being relaxed, rather than the erotic effect her massage was having on him. He didn't want this woman with too many kids and the most beguiling hands he'd ever encountered thinking he was attracted to her. Because he wasn't.

So why couldn't he take his eyes off her?

She moaned and stirred in her sleep and Adam wanted to lie back down on the table and pretend he was still asleep rather than get caught staring at her.

But it was too late. She opened her eyes, blinked and then fixed him with her clear, blue gaze.

She stretched and yawned, then rolled onto her side to face him, her hand coming to rest protectively on Charlie's bottom.

"Did you just wake up?" she asked.

He eased off the bed. Big mistake, because he was reacting to her again. He drew the towel around him and headed to the bathroom, saying, "I'll get changed and out of your hair."

Once the door was safely closed, he resisted the urge to beat his head against it and mutter, "Idiot! Idiot! Idiot!"

He wanted to take a shower. A cold one. Although this was *his* apartment she was staying in, he didn't feel he had the right. Instead, he dressed quickly, threw cold water on his face, dried off and emerged, trying to look as nonchalant as possible.

Carly was in the kitchen and turned to him when she heard him enter the room. "Would you like some herbal tea? I picked it up in Denver today. It's wonderful after a massage and helps eliminate toxins."

All Adam wanted to do was go take a cold shower

back at the house. But he needed to thank her for the massage before running out. "Um, okay."

She placed two steaming mugs on the kitchen table, then sat down, one leg tucked beneath her.

Adam pulled out a chair and sat, too. "Uh, I'm sorry I fell asleep. I didn't expect that to happen."

She smiled. It seemed to light up the room and warm something in his heart, something he didn't want to examine too closely.

"I'm glad you did," she said. "For a while there, you were wound up so tight I thought I might have to hit you over the head with a blunt object to get you to calm down."

"I prefer your hands working their magic on me, rather than any blunt objects," he said, and wished he could take back the words. He swallowed. "Ah, I didn't mean it like that."

"It's okay. Next time, I'll concentrate more on your back and shoulders. Since you're uncomfortable lying on your back, we'll leave that for later sessions."

Adam had no intention of there being any "later" sessions. Especially ones that involved him lying on his back!

His stomach growled again and he apologized. He glanced at the kitchen clock—9:00 p.m.! That certainly explained why he was hungry. Dinner had ended more than an hour ago.

"I wonder where the kids are," she said. "I'm surprised they didn't come and wake me."

Adam picked up the intercom phone to the house. His sister-in-law Megan answered. "Hey, sleepyhead, so you're finally awake. Is Carly up yet?"

"How did you know we were asleep?"

"Because I sent Sash over to get you for dinner and she said you were both dead to the world. I must say, you're a fast worker."

"Very funny. We were asleep in different beds."

"So she said, so I'll let you off the hook this time. Next time you're late for dinner, I'm coming over to check myself!"

He ignored her teasing. "Anything left for us?" he asked, then noticed Carly shaking her head.

"Of course. I kept a plate aside for each of you. Would you like me to bring them over?"

"Why don't we come to the house?"

"Because Charlie is down for the night," Megan said, "and you can't leave him there alone."

She was making it sound as if *he* was somehow required to stay and take care of Charlie. He needed to get out of there. Get back to the house. Put space between him and Carly. Between him…and Carly's magic hands. Him and Carly's lips, he thought, watching her sip the tea.

"I'll figure something out," he told Megan. "Just don't let Luke eat my share." He hung up and looked at Carly. "Megan's kept dinner aside for us. I…could go over and collect yours and bring it back for you." He indicated Charlie fast asleep on the sofa bed.

"That's kind of you," she said, "but I'm not that hungry. I have some crackers, and there's cheese in the fridge. If you wouldn't mind sending my kids back here for bed, I'd appreciate it."

"Done." Adam gulped down the rest of the tea. It tasted bad enough to eliminate toxins, but he didn't tell her that. He stood and said, "Thanks for the massage. It wasn't quite what I expected."

"I hope you enjoyed it enough to want more. I owe you a lot for the table."

"We'll see," he said, eager to get away from her. She looked far too sexy standing there in the lamplight.

She followed him to the door. "Good night, Adam. And thank you."

He turned to her. "What are you thanking me for? *You* gave *me* the massage."

"Thank you for giving me the chance to start my life over again. Thank you for saving my son... Molly—for everything. Good night, Adam."

She closed the door, leaving him standing on the stairs. Alone. The way he liked it.

Or at least that was how he used to like it. But now he wasn't so sure.

Adam didn't feel like facing anyone back at the house. Since he'd already slept for an hour after Carly's massage, he also didn't feel like going to bed when everyone else did. It was a good time to take a long walk in the moonlight.

Memories of that mesmerizing woman's hands and what they did to him kept intruding on his thoughts. He heard a whimper and looked down to see Molly following him.

He hunkered down, holding out his hand. "Here, girl," he said, encouraging her to approach.

She came up to him and rubbed her head against him. "What's the matter?" he asked.

He felt her feet to check if they were cold, but she'd probably only come outside for a few minutes to do her business. "Go back to the house, girl," he said.

He shoved his hands deep into his pockets to keep them warm and walked toward the paddocks.

A moment later he looked back. Molly was sitting where he'd left her. If it was possible, she seemed even sadder than before. She stared at Adam and then at the house, then back at him.

"You know your way," he said. "Scratch at the door and someone will let you in."

Still she didn't move.

Adam pulled his hands from his pockets and went over to her. "You're not seriously trying to tell me you're too tired to walk back to the house, are you?"

Molly let out a mournful howl.

"Shh! You'll have every wolf within hearing distance coming to see what's up."

She howled again.

So much for a quiet, contemplative walk. On his own. Adam knelt down, gathered Molly in his arms and carried her back to the house. She licked his face with gratitude.

"You keep this up and you'll be wearing booties like Louella Farquar," he chided her gently.

Molly settled deeper in his arms, her head on his shoulder, and closed her eyes.

From her kitchen window, Carly observed the exchange between man and dog.

She'd smiled as Adam hoisted Molly into his arms and carried her to the house.

Adam might pretend that nothing touched his heart, but Carly knew better.

## Chapter 5

When Carly woke the next morning, the countryside was carpeted in a layer of fresh snow. The snow seemed somehow symbolic, as if everything in her life had been swept clean. She and her children had a future in Spruce Lake. Carly was certain of it.

Usually her children were reluctant to leave their warm beds, but this morning they all threw back their covers and leaped out, pulling on warm clothes and boots, eager to go outside and play in the snow.

Carly dressed Charlie and by the time she'd finished, her other three children were already clattering down the stairs and heading to the ranch house to find Luke's girls.

"Slow down!" she called. "They might not be up yet!"

Carly followed them downstairs and into the stables, reached for the door and pushed it open. Her children squealed.

"Snow!"

Although it had snowed on and off since they'd arrived in Spruce Lake, the snowfalls had been meager by comparison with last Thursday's—and today's. At least two feet of fresh powder covered the ground.

Carly glanced around, looking for a snow shovel, but her children couldn't wait.

They all rushed outside and grabbed at the snow, trying to form snowballs that, due to the dryness of the air, crumbled in their hands.

She saw Adam making his way across the expanse of snow between the house and the stables, carrying a snow shovel.

"Morning," he said, and started to shovel snow away from the doorway and create a path to the house.

Carly was grateful. Although Megan had lent her a pair of riding boots to wear outside, they were no match for the depth of the snow.

"It's so beautiful," she breathed. "And quiet. So incredibly quiet," she said, referring to the complete silence of the early morning.

She looked up into the sky, which sparkled like diamonds.

"That's snow crystals," Adam explained at her smile of delight. "The air is so dry, it does that when it snows."

Shrieking, the children kicked the featherlight snow into the air. Maddy flopped on the ground and made a snow angel. So of course Alex and Jake followed suit. "Can we go sledding today, Adam?" they asked.

"Sure," he said, pulling open the back door that led into the kitchen.

Warmth gushed out, enveloping them.

"There you are!" Sarah exclaimed. "Good morning, everyone."

Molly waddled into the kitchen and greeted each of the children, sniffing their feet and wagging her tail.

Carly's kids greeted Sarah, and then the boys returned outside to play.

Molly curled up on her blanket, obviously grateful to be back on a familiar bed. Carly noticed Adam grinding his teeth as he went back out, presumably to shovel more snow.

Carly placed Charlie in the high chair. "Why does Adam pretend he doesn't care about anything?" she asked. Apart from that blanket, she almost added.

Sarah turned from the stove and leaned against the counter. "He used to be such a happy outgoing child, a lot like Will. But when he reached his teens, he changed." She turned back to the stove. "I take comfort from the knowledge that he's in a caring profession. I think the danger, the adrenaline rush, takes so much out of him that he can't allow himself to show he cares."

Carly thought it went much deeper than that, but she didn't know Sarah well enough to say anything. During Adam's massage yesterday, she'd hit an emotional trigger. She'd backed off, not wanting to cause him embarrassment. She'd hit trigger points before and ended up with grown men blubbering like babies about emotional pain they'd been carrying around for years. It was a satisfying part of her job to be able to bring forth these emotions, but she also knew that if you pressed them to bring them forward when they weren't ready, you could drive them even deeper into denial.

Carly didn't have any more time to ponder Adam and his strange behavior because the kitchen suddenly filled with the sound of Celeste and Maddy squealing their greetings to each other. Moments later, they had their heads together over the drawing pad. Daisy bounced in, greeted her grandmother and Carly, then headed out the back door, pulling on a warm jacket. "Come on, Molly!" she called. Molly lumbered to her feet and followed, her tail wagging uncertainly.

Several of the ranch dogs raced up to greet her, barking excitedly. "Shut up!" Daisy told them.

Carly grinned. The child was so no-nonsense.

Sarah had a tray of tea and crackers in her hands. "Daisy's off to see what needs to be done on the ranch today," she said. "And I'm taking this upstairs to our expectant mom. She's having a bad time with morning sickness."

"Oh, the poor thing. Please tell Megan I'd be happy to try some pressure-point massage to relieve the nausea."

"That's very kind of you, Carly. I'm sure she'd appreciate it. In the meantime, make yourself at home. The rest of my boys and their families usually come over for breakfast on Sundays, but the snow will probably prevent that. The roads in town are chaos."

Sarah left the kitchen and Carly prepared coffee for herself and hot chocolate for the children. However, Alex and Jake were having so much fun in the snow, they had no interest in coming inside for breakfast.

Minutes later, Sasha flounced into the kitchen, complaining about her "mean old grandma," and said it was way too early to be up on a weekend. Then she noticed the snow and raced outside, forgetting her jacket.

Carly was amused that even a child raised in the mountains could find so much joy in fresh snow.

"Morning."

Carly spun around to see Cody, Luke and Megan's fifteen-year-old son, wandering into the kitchen. He was rubbing his unruly mop of dark hair. "Not a morning person?" Carly said with a smile. "Would you like hot chocolate or coffee?"

"Coffee, please," he said, and sank down onto one of the chairs.

"Look, Cody! I'm drawing a picture of you being all sleepy in the morning," Celeste said, coming around the table to show him her drawing.

Cody grunted, then accepted the coffee Carly handed him. "Thanks," he said. After taking several sips, he seemed to brighten up. He glanced outside and said, "It snowed," and Carly didn't miss the note of wonder in his voice, too.

"Adam said we can go sledding today," Alex said, dashing inside. "Are we doing it here on the ranch?"

"We can," Sasha answered him as she started toasting bagels. "But there's a fantastic sledding hill in town. We'll go after breakfast and meet up with our cousin Nick. Provided the roads are cleared by then."

Daisy breezed back into the kitchen, bringing the cold with her. "Breakfast ready yet?" she asked, washing her hands. Molly rushed in behind her, glad to be out of the cold, and curled up on her bed.

Rolling her eyes at her sister's request, Sasha flipped two bagel halves onto Daisy's plate as she took a seat at the table.

Sarah came back into the kitchen, clapping her hands. "Wash up, kids, and then sit up," she said. "Carly, Megan's not well. Would you mind looking in on her?"

"Of course not," Carly said and, after getting directions to Megan's room, left the kitchen in search of her.

As she mounted the stairs and turned at the landing, she collided with Adam on his way down. She staggered backward, and lost her footing, but his strong arms caught her.

"Sorry!" they both said at once.

Carly looked up into Adam's dark eyes and repeated her apology. "I wasn't looking where I was going," she said.

"And I was coming down too fast," Adam said. He stood there, still gripping her arms.

Finally, Carly managed to say, "Your breakfast is ready and I have to go and check on Megan."

Still he held her, staring into her eyes. "You can let go of me now, Adam," she said. "I'm not going to fall."

He released her suddenly and shook his head as if he'd been in a trance, then slowly descended the rest of the steps.

Adam cursed himself as he turned into the kitchen. What the hell was that about? He hadn't been able to let go of Carly. Didn't *want* to let go of Carly. He tried telling himself he was only checking to see if she'd regained her footing, but she'd done that almost before he'd reached out to catch her.

He thought he'd be safe from running into her in the bedroom wing of the house, but no. There she was on the stairs, going up to check on Megan.

He needed to get out of this house. Go stay somewhere else. Except that both Lily and little Sarah were teething, and Will and Matt had warned him he wouldn't be getting much sleep at their houses. Jack was living in a tiny apartment in town that he'd taken over from Matt. The ranch hands had their own cabin out behind the stables, but there wasn't any spare room and they liked to smoke—Adam detested it.

Since it was peak ski season in Spruce Lake, he couldn't afford to rent an apartment short-term until his posting to the Spruce Lake fire department was over in a couple of weeks. Adam was stuck between the proverbial rock and a hard place.

He'd been contented in the apartment over the stables. He had his privacy when he needed it, ate a lot of his meals alone—the way he liked it. But now that he was in the house, there was no privacy. Certainly no quiet with his three nieces giggling and Cody stumbling around bumping into things because his body had grown so fast he wasn't used to it yet. He knew how Cody felt. He'd grown fast, too, when he'd hit his teens. When he'd been just a little older than Cody, he'd…

Adam felt the bile rising in his throat and rushed out the front door into the cold, needing it to clear his head, settle his stomach.

He sat on the porch steps with his head in his hands and breathed in slowly, trying to imitate the deep, slow breaths Carly had told him to take. By the third breath, he was feeling better. Surprisingly better. But he didn't want to go back inside the house. And he didn't want to head over to the stables where he might run into Luke or one of the hands.

He decided to take a long walk, try to exorcise his demons. Wearing nothing more than jeans, boots, a warm shirt and a fleecy vest, he set out across the yard toward the lake and the mountains beyond.

Carly frowned as she watched Adam from the bedroom window that looked out over the back of the house. He was dressed far too scantily for the weather.

"Don't worry about him," Megan said, her gaze following Carly's. "They're all used to the cold."

Carly tried to put Adam out of her mind as she went back to gently massaging Megan's shoulders, feeling the other woman relax under her touch.

They were sitting on Megan's bed. Carly had decided a shoulder rub would be the most soothing for Megan and it appeared she was right as Megan moaned softly in appreciation.

"I'm sorry you're having a hard time with morning sickness, and that it's still on so late in your pregnancy," Carly said.

"You've never had it?" Megan asked.

"Fortunately, no. Were you sick with Cody, too?"

"Yes, but it seemed much worse. I was all alone in New York. I didn't have wonderful people bringing me tea and crackers. Or giving me back rubs."

"Is Luke pleased about the baby?" Carly ventured to ask.

"He's over the moon. It was as unplanned as Cody was, so we'll have to make some decisions about *permanent* birth control when this one comes along."

Carly laughed. "Five children! That's quite a handful. You're lucky to have Sarah to help you."

"I am," Megan agreed. "But you have four children and no one to help *you*. That must be difficult."

Carly shrugged, then realized Megan couldn't see her. "To tell you the truth, I'm used to it now."

"I… I'm sorry about your husband…dying like that," Megan said, and Carly could hear the compassion in her voice.

"Me, too," Carly said a little too harshly. Lately she'd felt not only the continuing grief, which had settled into a dull ache, but anger. Anger with Michael, for dying. And for leaving her so little to fall back on financially once she'd paid the bills.

"Do they miss him?"

"Yes. I have to be careful not to show my emotions when they start talking about him. They pick up on it and then they stop. I know that's not good for them."

"The financial and emotional strain of raising four kids alone must be very stressful," Megan said. "I feel like I should be giving *you* a relaxing massage."

Carly smiled. "I actually find that massaging others, particularly when it has such good results, calms me." She finished rubbing her fingers in circles beneath Megan's ears. "How are you feeling now? Ready to face the world?"

Megan stretched and turned to face Carly. "Strangely enough, I'm starving. And I haven't felt that way in a very long time."

Carly laughed. "I'm sure Sarah's made something delicious. Shall we go?"

Carly stood, but Megan took her hand. "Thank you, Carly. Thank you for the massage and for coming to live here with your wonderful children. I hope we can become good friends."

Carly was struck by the yearning in Megan's eyes. Surely Megan had lots of friends? She seemed close to Becky and Beth, Will's and Matt's wives.

Perhaps Megan was responding to the protective shell Carly had put around herself these past two years.

She'd tended to keep to herself as an act of self-preservation. Initially, it had been because she was so busy raising her children alone. But once she sensed that Jerry Ryan wanted to be more than just her friend, she'd realized that the only way to escape him was to move out of state. After that, Carly had been so focused on getting her children settled, she hadn't had the time or inclination to make friends, to let anyone new into her life.

"Carly?"

Carly snapped out of her reverie. "I'm sorry, I was miles away." She squeezed Megan's hands. "I'd like it very much if we could be friends."

Megan's face lit up and she hugged Carly. Carly hugged her back, grateful for Megan's warmth.

By the time the two of them got downstairs, the kitchen was deserted...except for Adam. And Charlie, sitting in the high chair beside him, chewing on a piece of bagel. Molly was fast asleep, snoring way too loudly.

"Where is everyone?" Carly asked, going over to Charlie and lifting him from his chair.

"I told them if they cleaned up the kitchen, I'd take them sledding in the town park. So they cleaned it up and now they've gone to get dressed," Adam said.

"That's very kind of you." Carly was surprised by his generosity in spending a day with a bunch of rowdy children. It seemed out of character for him.

He grunted in reply and said, "Mom told me I owe my nieces some quality time."

"Then I'll keep my kids here so you can spend time alone with them."

Adam got to his feet, took his plate and coffee cup to the sink, rinsed them and set them in the dishwasher. Closing the door, he looked back at her. "It's no trouble. We're meeting up with Will and Nick."

Carly took that to mean she wasn't invited, which was fine. She was going to work through the lists of names Sarah and Megan had given her of people who wanted to book massages. The sooner she got her business up and running again, the better. "I'll go hurry my kids along, then," she said.

"No need." Adam indicated her children stomping down the path he'd shoveled earlier, occasionally kicking snow at one another.

This was accompanied by the sound of Luke's girls clattering down the stairs.

Soon the kitchen was filled with noisy children. Carly saw Molly raise her head in protest. She shushed the children, then herded them out into the living room.

Luke's girls grabbed coats, scarves and mittens, asked Alex, Jake and Maddy if they needed anything else and then they all raced out the front door, shouting their goodbyes.

"Be careful!" Carly called after them, not that anyone heard her.

"They'll be fine," Adam said, coming up behind her with several plastic sleds slung over his shoulder.

"I'm sure they will," Carly said, and shrugged. "Can't help being the anxious mom when my children try a new activity. Thank you for including them."

Adam grunted and he went out the door. Then he turned back to her, almost bumping into Carly, who'd started to follow him. "We won't be back for lunch. Will likes to take the kids to Rusty's for burgers."

"All…right," Carly said slowly. "I'll get my wallet."

Adam stopped her with a hand on her shoulder. The sensation of his touch was pleasant and unexpected. "It's our treat," he said. "Enjoy your day."

Without a further word, he strode to a big SUV, checked that all the children were belted in and drove off.

Carly hugged herself to ward off the winter chill and

watched until they were out of sight. She'd been startled but deeply moved by his kind gesture. Underneath his gruff exterior, she suspected Adam had a heart of gold. But at the moment, it was a heart full of hurt.

*One of these days, I'm going to find out what's really bothering you, Adam O'Malley,* she vowed, and went back into the house.

*Chapter 6*

By the time the children returned later that afternoon, Carly had set up nearly three dozen appointments for the coming week. Several of her regulars had managed to track her down at the ranch, as well, and booked treatments.

Carly savored a warm glow of satisfaction. She was going to get back on her feet, *and* she'd be able to pay rent on the apartment above the stables until she could find somewhere else to live.

But when she mentioned paying rent to Sarah, the older woman had told her she'd do no such thing.

Carly was out in the yard, one foot resting on a corral beam as she watched Luke working with one of his horses, when Adam's vehicle pulled up. Luke was training Cody to manage the horses and his son was doing a fine job. They both looked up and waved at her; smiling, she waved back. Thinking about the past forty-eight hours, Carly was almost thankful the fire had occurred. If it hadn't, she would never have met these wonderful people.

Then guilt filled her as she thought of the Polinskis and all the other residents who'd lost everything they owned in the fire. At least the Polinskis were safe. Mr. Polinski had suffered severe smoke inhalation and would be spending some days in the hospital. Mrs. Polinski wasn't so bad, and as the hospital had residences attached to it for the use of patients' relatives, she'd be moving in there until their son came from Miami to get them. Carly had wondered why the elderly couple lived in such a run-down apartment when both had told her on several occasions how successful their son was. Why hadn't he provided for his parents?

She smiled again as she caught sight of Molly with the ranch dogs. They seemed to have accepted her in all her oddness, since the too-short legs on too-long a body meant she couldn't keep up with them when they raced around, but at least she had sense enough to keep away from the horses' hooves.

The sound of the children piling excitedly out of the SUV distracted her from her thoughts. She turned away from the corral and went to ask if they'd enjoyed themselves. Only Carly didn't need to ask because they all talked over one another. Will and Becky's son, Nick, was with them.

He greeted Carly politely, then got swept up with the other children as they raced toward the house, calling, "Grandma!" Adam and Carly were left standing alone beside the vehicle.

He reached in the back to grab the sleds and hooked their straps over his shoulder. Carly saw him wince.

"You shouldn't be lugging anything while your back is sore," she said.

"Are you going to nag me about this?" he challenged.

"Yes," she said, putting her hands on her hips. "And I'll bet you've done even more damage to your back, because you dragged the sleds up the hill with Maddy and Celeste on them—didn't you?"

"How'd you guess?" he said, unshouldering the straps and resting the sleds against the car.

"Because although I've known you for less than two days, I can tell that you go out of your way for others. Even to your detriment. *Especially* to your detriment," she said, wondering again why this very repressed man tried so hard to hide his compassion for others. "How about coming over to the apartment and letting me work on your back?"

She noticed something flaring in his eyes. Interest in her suggestion? A yearning to have the pain in his back eased? But instead he shook his head. "I'll take some painkillers. They'll fix it."

"You can't live on painkillers! Stop being so stubborn and let me massage you."

"No, thanks," he said, and strode toward the house.

"Why not?" Carly followed him, and when he didn't answer her, she reached out for his shoulder to turn him toward her. She realized her mistake immediately as he groaned with pain.

"I'm sorry!" she apologized, contrite that she'd done the one thing she shouldn't have to someone with such an injury. "But maybe now you'll agree that your problem won't be fixed by painkillers."

"I'll go see the doc in the morning, see what he has to say."

"In case you've forgotten," she retorted, "you have that disciplinary hearing in the morning. You won't perform too well if you're in pain."

He shrugged, and she wanted to slap him. "You make me so mad!" she said, losing her cool.

"Tough." He turned back toward the house. Carly fumed that he wouldn't let her help him. Was he afraid of repeating his reaction to her last night? Why was he so intent on avoiding her?

And why did she even care?

"You care because underneath his bluster, he's a good man. A man who's hurting physically *and* emotionally," she muttered under her breath, trailing him to the house. Adam might not want to admit it, but he needed her. And not just to ease the pain in his back.

Adam went straight upstairs and hunted through the bathroom cabinet, looking for painkillers. All he came up with was an out-of-date bottle of antacid.

He cursed and tossed it in the trash.

"Looking for this?" he heard Carly say from behind him, and spun around.

Was there *no place* in this house that was safe from her?

She held up a bottle of ibuprofen. He reached for it, but she whisked it away. "You can have two, on condition that you let me massage you."

"Have you always been such a nag?" he demanded.

"It's called negotiation. It's an effective parenting tool."

"Except I'm not one of your kids," he said. "Thank God."

Carly ignored the dig. "You're sure acting like one."

She tipped two pills into her hand. "Now open wide," she said, unable to resist teasing him.

Adam set his mouth in a firm line. Then he pushed past her to get out of the bathroom.

"Where are you going?" she asked.

He pulled his keys from his jeans pocket. "To the supermarket. To buy a whole bottle of ibuprofen. All for me," he snapped.

"And by the time you get there, I could have eased some of your pain with a massage. And these." She held the caplets out again, tempting him.

Adam snatched them from her and put them in his mouth, nearly choking as he tried to swallow them without water.

"My, my, you *are* in a lot of pain," she observed. "Come with me," she said, crooking her little finger.

"No." He stopped her at the door. He didn't want to go back to the apartment. He couldn't be alone with her. He needed to be where there was noise and the possibility of discovery if she got him in the same state as she had last night. With the chance that one of his nieces might burst in on him, he could keep himself in check.

He led the way to his room. "We'll do it here," he said.

She raised her eyebrows. "I hope you're referring to the massage and not something else?"

"You wish," he muttered.

Part of Carly did wish, but she clamped her mouth shut as she returned to the bathroom. After finding a bottle of baby oil, she went back to Adam's room. He was still where she'd left him, standing stiffly by the bed, glaring at her.

"What's the problem now?" she asked.

"You want me to lie on the bed?"

"That would help."

He crossed his arms. "I don't want to."

Carly almost laughed until she remembered his embarrassment when she'd first massaged him.

"Since you're probably still a bit tender from yesterday's massage, I thought you might like an Indian head massage instead."

"And how will that help my back?" he asked.

"I'm hoping it'll relax you and diminish some of that tension you're carrying around on those broad shoulders of yours."

"Don't make fun of me."

She put the bottle of oil on the dressing table. "How am I making fun of you?"

"Talking about my broad shoulders as if there's another meaning. A sarcastic one."

Carly shook her head. "Trust me, there *is* no other meaning. You have broad shoulders." Mighty nice broad shoulders, she thought to herself. Shoulders a girl wouldn't mind leaning on. "If I'd referred to your dark eyes, would you have found something sinister in that, too?"

Adam shrugged the shoulders in question. "Guess not. So where do we do this, uh, Indian massage?"

Carly drew the tiny stool out from under the dressing table. "Right here," she said, indicating he should sit down.

He did.

"You might want to take your shirt off. There's some shoulder work involved in this and I'd hate to get oil on it," she explained.

Adam stood and started to unbutton his shirt facing away from Carly. Then something perverse in him made him turn around and finish unbuttoning it right in front of her perky little nose. So she liked his broad shoulders, did she? Then she could get a good look at them—*and* his chest.

Adam saw Carly swallow as he removed his shirt. Whether she liked it or not, the woman was responding to him. It gave him a much-needed sense of power—something he felt he had very little of when he was around her. The situation between them seemed unequal, with all the control on *her* side. Carly was so self-assured, nothing seemed to phase her—except when he challenged her and then he could see the fire in her eyes. He liked seeing that fire. But right now her eyes were focused on his chest as if she couldn't drag them away.

He cleared his throat and smiled to himself when she blinked before regaining her composure.

"I believe you were going to massage my head…not my chest," he said, teasing her, loving how flustered she got.

"I was… I am!" she said, and pressed him down onto the stool.

She was close enough that if he reached out his arms, he'd be able to clasp her butt and pull her down to straddle him.

Now Adam found himself swallowing. The thought of Carly's legs wrapped around his waist, his big hands pulling her tight little butt against him, had him reacting in exactly the way he was trying to avoid.

Carly placed her hands on his forehead. He jolted at their unexpected warmth and then he was aware of her fingertips running back through his hair in strong strokes, all the way to the nape of his neck. She left them there and, using her thumbs, rotated them below each ear as her fingertips stroked his neck.

Adam closed his eyes and sighed, then instantly regretted giving Carly any hint of the pleasure her clever
fingers were bringing him, of how much her touch affected him. She repeated the action and it was more than
soothing, it was positively erotic.

If the door to his room had been closed, he would have
drawn her onto his lap....

He wanted to open his eyes and look into hers, but was
afraid of what he'd see there. Loathing—that he could
react to her so easily? Fear—because she'd read his mind?
Ridicule—that he was so quickly seduced by her touch?

No, never ridicule. Carly took her profession seriously.
She'd never take advantage of a client. Never laugh at
anyone's reaction to her.

His fingers itched to clasp her hips, pull her close.
He sighed again and cursed himself for being so vocal,
but he couldn't help it. What Carly was doing to him
was the best thing he'd felt in a hell of a long time. Yes,
the massage last night had been great, but a lot of it had
been downright painful. This, on the other hand, was so
incredibly soothing, so unbelievably *good,* that it was
almost better than sex—

"I'll have what he's having."

Adam was torn from his erotic haze by Luke's voice.
He glanced up to find his brother lounging against the
doorjamb, arms crossed.

To her credit, Carly didn't miss a beat. She continued
the soothing movements, shaping her hands to his head
as she spoke to Luke.

"I have an appointment book downstairs on the living room table. If you'd like to fill in a time that's convenient, I'd be happy to oblige."

Adam could hear the smile in her voice. In fact, she

seemed to be teasing Luke. Flirting with him. Adam didn't like it.

"And where would we do it?" Luke asked, sounding downright suggestive to Adam. He was almost tempted to get off the stool and punch his brother's lights out. Instead, he clenched his hands into fists and forced himself to keep his anger in check.

Luke started to advance into the room, but Carly held up her hand.

"For a massage to be effective, the client needs total quiet and no distractions. Would you close the door when you leave, Luke?"

Wow. That was telling him. Luke didn't appreciate being told what to do, especially in his own house. But his brother saluted her, turned on his heel and left the room, shutting the bedroom door.

"I hope you don't mind me shooing him away like that," Carly said, her voice uncharacteristically uncertain. "But I want you to have the most beneficial treatment possible. You've got a big day ahead of you tomorrow."

Adam wanted to take her in his arms and hug her tight for caring so much. The massage was exactly what he'd needed. At least while he was thinking of seducing Carly, he wasn't worrying about the disciplinary hearing in the morning.

She stepped closer to him and increased the pressure of her fingers on the back of his head, causing his head to drop forward and rest against her midriff. She drove her fingers lower to his shoulders, kneading them, first in gentle strokes and then stronger. And just as it got almost unbearable, her hands would return to his head, soothing him, sending him into a deep sense of relaxation.

And then her hands touched his shoulders in a different movement and suddenly all the sadness and the shame he'd been holding inside over Rory began to surface. He gulped, shocked by his reaction, powerless to stop the feelings crashing in on him. Tears burned behind his eyes. Why now? Why after all these years?

And then a sob escaped his throat and, before he knew it, the tears he'd been holding back coursed down his cheeks.

With his forehead resting against Carly's chest, Adam couldn't stop the tears. Carly's touch turned soothing again, stroking through his hair. But the change in her touch only made it worse. Mortified, he raised his hands to cover his face.

"Stop. Please, stop," he begged, fighting tears, fighting the memories that kept surfacing, consuming him, threatening to drown him in all their vivid horror.

"It's okay, Adam." Carly's voice was soft.

But in his present state of mind, her words sounded patronizing to his ears. It wasn't okay. It would *never* be okay.

He sprang to his feet and caught her wrists. He read the shock in her eyes. God only knew what he must look like, a man of six-three with tears streaming down his face.

He lashed out at her verbally, trying to cover the embarrassment at his reaction to those long-ago memories. "Don't touch me. Don't *ever* touch me again!" he said, and released her so suddenly she stumbled backward.

Then he grabbed his shirt, strode to the door, tore it open and left the room.

Carly regained her footing before she landed on Adam's bed.

She hadn't expected him to react so vehemently to

her finding that trigger point. Usually a patient bawled for a bit, then admitted what had set him or her off. But not Adam. Adam was too proud, too shut down, to admit his pain.

She'd guessed she was getting close shortly before Luke interrupted. Adam had been so relaxed. When he'd sighed, she'd been pleased that he was so at ease.

And then she'd hit that trigger point and felt him tense, knew he was holding back. But she'd pressed on, hoping to help him find some release from the emotional pain. But he'd fought every one of those tears until he could fight them no longer.

Carly was sorry now that she'd pushed Adam so far. She'd embarrassed him. Their session shouldn't have ended this way. She'd never had a client grip her wrists and tell her not to touch him again!

She should recommend another massage therapist, one with whom he'd feel more comfortable letting down his guard. Only problem was, she didn't want to share Adam with anyone else, didn't want someone else to help him unlock his secrets.

Carly sat on the stool, placed her elbows on the dressing table and clasped her hands beneath her chin as she gazed into the mirror. Had she inadvertently caused him to relive some emotional damage that would affect him negatively during the disciplinary hearing tomorrow? She hoped not!

Most importantly, she wondered, what could she do to make things right between them?

One thing was for sure; Adam would be steering clear of her for quite some time.

Carly opened one of the dresser drawers, found a pen and notepad and carefully composed a note to him.

She signed it *C,* folded the piece of paper and wrote his name on the outside. Then she propped it on Adam's pillow and silently left the room.

"Damned interfering woman!" Adam muttered as he strode downstairs, pulling his shirt on and doing up the buttons with unsteady fingers. Avoiding any of the family, he grabbed his coat, wrenched open the front door and headed to his vehicle. Moments later, he peeled out of the ranch, stopping at the crossroads that led to town.

Cursing himself for what he was about to do, he turned left onto the road, headed away from town. He needed to be on his own, to think. To plan. Because he'd never know any peace until he'd confronted the biggest fear of his life.

The reason he hated himself so much.

# Chapter 7

"You and my little brother making friends?"

Carly almost jumped out of her skin. She spun around as she reached the bottom of the stairs. Luke was leaning against the wall, assessing her.

She placed her hand over her heart. "Sheesh, Luke! You scared me half to death!"

He pushed away from the wall and came to stand in front of her. "I have a feeling you don't scare too easily, but I'll make my apologies, anyway." He inclined his head toward the front door. "So what did you do to Adam to have him taking off like his butt was on fire?"

Carly had no intention of telling Luke something that was so deeply personal to Adam.

"Want to try an Indian head massage for yourself?" she said. "Then maybe you'll find out."

He cocked his head to one side. "Hmm, I don't think that

was the cause. Anyway, I came looking for you to thank you for helping Megan." He thrust his hand through his short hair. "I didn't realize that pregnancy could be so hard."

"You're talking about hard for Megan, aren't you? Not yourself?" she asked with a smile.

"Yeah. Well. It's hard for me to watch her being so sick. Apparently, she was this sick with Cody, too. I feel bad I couldn't be there for her."

Carly was touched by his concern. This morning, while Carly had given Megan her back rub, she'd told Carly how she and Luke had met, fallen in love and been separated by misunderstanding for more than fourteen years.

She put a hand on his arm and said, "You're here for her now, and that's what matters, Luke. You can't do over the past, but from what I've observed, you're a wonderful father and an attentive husband. Megan's a lucky woman."

His face brightened with a wide smile. "Thanks. You didn't have to say that, but I appreciate that you did."

"Where's Megan now?"

"Sleeping. I let her sleep as much as she needs."

"Wise man! Never get between a pregnant woman and her bed."

Luke grinned and Carly covered her mouth. "Oh, I didn't mean it to come out quite like that."

Luke grasped her shoulder and steered her toward the kitchen. "I'll tell Megan about it when she wakes up. She'll get a giggle out of it."

Carly paused before they entered the kitchen. "Luke, I wanted to let you know that my appointment book is filling up nicely. I'd like to start paying rent on the apartment, but your mom wouldn't hear of it. I called some rental agents earlier, trying to find alternative accommodation in town, but—" she shook her head "—this is high season and there's nothing available. If it's not too inconvenient, I was hoping we could stay here until something comes up."

"You're welcome to stay as long as you like, Carly. And we won't hear a word about you paying rent. It's going to be difficult enough to get back on your feet. My girls are sure enjoying having your kids around and Megan feels as if you're long-lost sisters. How could I possibly turn you out?"

Carly was so grateful, she rose up on tiptoe and placed a quick kiss on Luke's cheek. "Thank you. Megan's a *very* lucky woman to have you for a husband."

Luke scraped his boot against the floor and pretended to go all shy. "Why shucks, ma'am. You'll be givin' me a head bigger than Orion, our ol' prize-winning bull, if you keep sayin' stuff like that."

Carly dug him in the ribs. "And you can cut the country bumpkin act. I know what a good businessman and skilled rancher you are."

Luke rubbed the back of his neck. "Thank you again. But all that responsibility comes with its downside."

"Which is?"

"This crick in my neck. I didn't want to take up any of your valuable appointment times, so I thought I might prevail upon you, whenever you have a spare minute."

"Which I do now."

"You mean it?"

"Yep. Go make yourself comfortable in the kitchen. I'll run upstairs and get the baby oil." She turned to go and then looked back at Luke. "Unless, of course, you don't mind if I use olive oil?"

Luke grinned. "And walk around smelling like a salad? No, thanks!"

* * *

Two minutes later, Luke was stripping off his shirt. Carly had him straddling the chair, so she could get access to his back easily. Charlie was curled up asleep on a beanbag under Sarah's watchful eye as she started dinner preparations. Molly had her nose resting on Luke's foot.

At his first sigh of relief, Sarah smiled over at her and said, "I have a feeling, Carly, that the O'Malley clan is going to bless the day you came into our lives."

Adam pulled over when he got to the crossroads. Even now, after all these years, being here made him break out in a cold sweat. His hands shook as he let go of the wheel.

The area had changed very little, situated as it was outside the town limits. The road was still dirt beneath the snow.

He climbed out of his vehicle and froze as his gaze landed on a small memorial. The flowers were fresh. Someone had been here recently.

Adam turned and kicked the tire of his SUV. Someone a lot better than him had the guts to come here and lay flowers in memory of Rory, maybe say a prayer for him. And what had *he* done? Nothing. Nothing but stay away, far away, for the past fifteen years. Someone else hadn't forgotten who'd died here and how. But that someone didn't know the truth. Adam did. And it was eating him alive.

"I thought you said that for a massage to be effective, the client needs total quiet and no distractions," Luke griped. "So far I've had Mom nattering about what she's planning for dinner, Becky calling, Beth calling, Charlie waking up and needing his diaper changed, Daisy tearing inside to use the bathroom, Celeste wanting her hair braided and Sash and Cody fighting over what TV program they'd be watching tonight. How come Adam gets a massage in the privacy of his room and I get Grand Central Station?"

Carly slapped his shoulder playfully. She liked Luke. He had a gruff exterior, but deep down he was a big marshmallow and she liked teasing him. "Because Megan's resting and when we first came in here it *was* peaceful!"

"Someone mention me?"

Megan stood sleepily in the doorway and smiled at her husband. He reached out his hand to draw her to him. "I'd get up, honey, but Ms. Bossy Pants has me pinned to the chair. Ooh." He sighed as Carly drove her fingers back through his scalp.

"Honestly, it's been like an X-rated movie soundtrack in here," Sarah said. "That son of mine—who rarely expresses any emotion—has been moaning and groaning and sighing with pleasure for the past twenty minutes."

Megan perched awkwardly on Luke's right thigh and slipped her arms around his neck. "You must teach me some of those techniques, Carly. Seems my husband is putty in your hands."

Carly smiled. "I'd be glad to, then you can take over the orneriest client this side of the Rockies."

"Hey! That's me you're talking about," Luke protested good-naturedly.

"Sure is," Carly said, finishing off the massage on his shoulders. She placed her hands over Megan's, moving them in the same deep strokes she'd used on Luke.

Luke sighed again. "I'm glad the kids aren't here right now. This is feeling way too good."

His mother waved a wooden spoon at him. "Behave!"

"And if I don't?"

"Used to be a time I could threaten you to behave *so* easily." She shrugged her shoulders theatrically and said to Carly, "Kids, they grow up, they leave home, they lose all respect."

"Except I didn't leave home," Luke reminded her.

"More's the pity," his mother retorted with an indulgent smile.

Carly loved watching the exchange between mother and son and wondered if there'd be a time when her sons would tease her like this. She hoped so.

"You're looking wistful, Carly," Sarah said.

Carly smiled. "I was thinking how lovely it is to feel like part of your family."

"That's one of the nicest things anyone's ever said to me." Sarah wiped at her suddenly damp eyes with the back of her hand.

Carly was so touched, she went to hug Sarah, then realized she still had baby oil all over her hands.

"The next massage is for you, okay?" she said to Sarah.

Sarah nodded. "I'd like that. Thank you."

"And I thank you, too, Carly," said Luke, rising from the chair and taking Megan with him. "I'll check on the horses and round up the kids for dinner." Megan handed him a jacket; he kissed her cheek and stepped outside.

Molly lumbered slowly to her feet, following him through a doggie-door cut into the timber door that led into the backyard.

Carly stared at it. "Was that here this morning? Because I didn't notice it."

"Luke and his father made it earlier," Sarah explained.

"At Daisy's insistence," Megan said. "She blackmailed them into it by reminding them that otherwise *they'd* have to get up in the night to let Molly out."

Carly grinned. "That Daisy is one smart little girl."

"She sure is," Sarah agreed. "Daisy knows exactly which of her father's buttons to push to get what she wants."

"So does Sash," Megan said. "And Celeste is so cute, who could say *no* to her?"

"What about Cody?" Carly asked.

Megan considered for a moment. "Like his father, Cody's a man of few words. And few demands. Their relationship was a little rocky at first, but Luke treated Cody with respect, got him involved with the ranch, taught him to ride. Now they're so much in tune with each other, it's almost scary."

Carly turned to Sarah. "All your sons are so different. Was that apparent when they were growing up?"

"You don't think each of your children is different from the others?" Sarah asked.

"To tell you the truth, I've been so focused on keeping a roof over their heads, food on the table and clothes on their backs, I've had very little time to observe them closely enough. I feel bad about that."

She thought about her children. "Alex is the responsible one, Jake is a bit of a jokester, Maddy…well, she's very much like Celeste, sweet-natured, not hard to please. And Charlie…he's my easygoing baby."

"Their personalities will become more pronounced as they grow older. Just wait until they enter their teens!"

Megan nodded. "You won't know what's hit you then."

Carly put her hands over her ears. "Please, don't remind me! Alex will be a teen in a couple of years and I'm already scared!"

"Don't be," Sarah told her. "After they got over the adolescent hormone surge, all of mine, except maybe for Adam, turned into the kind of men they were as boys."

"Why not Adam?" Carly couldn't help asking.

Sarah poured glasses of iced tea—and juice for Megan—putting them on the table, then took a seat opposite Carly. "Adam was always a bit rebellious, much worse than Will as a youngster. Then, when he was fifteen, his best friend died in a car accident. Adam was the passenger, and he survived."

"That's tragic," Carly said as a thought occurred to her. Could memories of the accident have been what set Adam off earlier?

"I didn't know about this," Megan was saying.

"It's not something we ever talk about. Adam spiraled into a very deep depression. He flunked that year, and then when he finished high school, he couldn't wait to go to college, move away from the area."

Now Carly was starting to understand some of Adam's behavior this afternoon. Did he feel guilty that he'd survived and his friend didn't? Was he experiencing survivor guilt?

Until Adam dealt with it, he'd never be free of the demons that so obviously tormented him.

"That's why we built the apartment over the stables," Sarah told them. "We wanted Adam to return home. To give him his own space. But he wouldn't come. When they had a short-term vacancy at the local fire department, I had to practically blackmail him to take it."

And now, because he'd ignored his chief's orders and gone back into the building to rescue Molly, his job was in jeopardy. Possibly his career. Carly pondered the reality of that. Had Adam chosen a career that would require him to risk his life? To somehow make amends for his surviving while his friend hadn't? To save others, because he couldn't save his friend?

Carly put aside her thoughts as the kitchen filled with children, all rushing inside to wash up for dinner. They brought with them the crispness of the winter afternoon; it radiated from their bodies and had turned their cheeks red. Molly followed a few minutes later, her black nose pushing its way through the doggie-door. She eased her body slowly through the opening and waddled to her blanket. She looked so terribly sad that Carly sat on the floor beside her and massaged Molly's long spine. "Are you missing your mom and dad, sweetie?" she asked.

It was hard to tell, since Molly always looked melancholy, even when she was wagging her tail. She licked Carly's hand.

"Any news on the Polinskis?" Sarah asked.

"I called them earlier. Mrs. P. is doing fine, but as you know, Mr. P. suffered severe smoke inhalation. They're both concerned about Molly. I wish I could take her to visit them in the hospital. They're so worried about her future, even though I've tried to reassure them she'll always have a home with me."

"I think you've got more than enough dependents," Sarah pointed out.

Carly sighed. "I know. But what else could I say?"

Celeste and Maddy were the first ones back in the kitchen and, without being asked, started setting the table. Sasha and Cody still hadn't settled their argument over which television program they would watch after dinner. Since there was only one TV set in the house, this was apparently an ongoing debate. Carly wondered if she should offer to let one of them watch their program at the apartment, but Sarah must've guessed her intent and shook her head in warning.

"Neither of you will be watching anything tonight. Your father and Uncle Adam have reserved spaces on the sofa to watch the hockey game together," Sarah told them.

This news was greeted by pouting from Sasha and a grunt from Cody. The other children didn't seem to care. Carly soon found out why. Maddy had invited Daisy and Celeste to watch a Disney DVD in the apartment.

"But I'm the oldest!" Sasha protested. "*I* should get to choose what we watch."

"No, you're not. I am," Cody reminded her.

"And you're both acting like two-year-olds," Megan said. "If you don't stop pouting, Sash, and you don't stop stomping around, Cody, you can both go to bed without dinner *or* television!"

"That's tellin' 'em," Daisy said with a nod.

"Why can't we have another TV?" Sasha demanded of her father as he came in the door.

"Because there's enough noise in this house already," he said, and touched the end of her upturned nose.

"We'd be quieter if we each had a TV of our own."

"Don't even go there, Sash. You know how your mother and I feel about family time."

Sasha put her hands on her hips. "You mean the *family time* you'll be using to watch the game?"

"Uh-huh," Luke agreed.

Sasha stamped her foot.

"Before you say anything else, Sash, let me remind

you that the penalty box applies to stomping feet as well as cussing."

"Oh, you!" Sasha said, and dashed off. They could hear her yelling from the stairs, "Just you wait! I'm gonna get a job at the burger joint and save up and buy myself the biggest TV I can afford. Then I'm gonna turn it up so loud, you won't be able to hear yourself think!"

Luke went to the fridge to get a beer. "So how was the rest of everyone's day?" he asked, completely ignoring Sasha's threat and refusing to react to it.

With Sasha's departure, the room was considerably quieter. Celeste and Maddy, having finished setting the table, went to play with their dolls. Daisy produced a deck of cards and sat with Alex and Jake. She proceeded to deal the cards for Texas Hold'em, a game she'd been teaching them. Carly washed her hands after massaging Molly, then set up Charlie's high chair and warmed his supper in the microwave.

As she fed her son, surrounded by family noises in the kitchen, Carly felt a deep contentment. Even Sasha's tantrum hadn't disrupted the family routine of preparing for a meal. Her own children rarely threw tantrums and she put Sasha's down to a combination of teenage hormones and her rather dynamic personality. She'd admired Luke's handling of it and filed it away for future use.

Adam didn't return for dinner or to watch the game. Carly gathered her children together and herded them back to the apartment. Long after they'd turned in, Carly lay in bed staring at the ceiling and hoping Adam was okay, until she finally heard his SUV pull into the yard.

Relieved that he was finally home and safe and that he'd soon read her note, she slept.

# Chapter 8

The house was in darkness when Adam got home. The only sign of life was Molly struggling to her feet to join him in the kitchen. She looked at him balefully, then waddled to the back door.

She pushed her way through the doggie-door Adam was sure hadn't been there this morning.

He stepped out on the back porch to keep her company.

Minutes later she waddled back, looked at him sadly and went in through her little door. Adam stayed outside for a bit, looking at the night sky and thinking about Carly. Finally he returned inside.

He regretted missing dinner. His stomach growled as if to remind him.

He'd gone to Rusty's and downed a couple of beers before remembering he had the disciplinary hearing in the morning. So he'd sat there brooding, and nursed a beer for the rest of the night without ordering any food to go with it.

Now he was sober and hungry. He searched in the fridge, but didn't have to go far. His mom had left a dinner plate covered in cling wrap and his name printed neatly on a Post-it note.

Too hungry to bother reheating it, he wolfed it down cold. Molly watched Adam as he ate. Finally, with an enormous sigh, she rested her head on her paws and closed her eyes.

After stooping to pet her, he rinsed the empty plate and put it in the dishwasher. Adam was more than glad that he'd rescued Molly. If he had to do it over, he'd do exactly the same thing. Probably not what the disciplinary board wanted to hear, but it was the truth.

Matt had told him he'd located the Polinskis' son and daughter-in-law in Florida and the old couple would be going back there to live. As he climbed the stairs to his room, Adam was surprised by how empty he felt at the thought of Molly not being in the kitchen one morning soon.

He entered his room and, without turning on the light, stripped off, wrapped a towel around himself and headed for the shower.

Back in his room, he pulled on fresh boxers and slipped beneath the covers, looking forward to the blessed oblivion of sleep.

But something scratched the side of his face. He reached up and found a piece of paper. He was about to throw it on the floor when he suddenly needed to know what it was.

He switched on the bedside lamp and glanced at it.

*Adam* was scrawled in a neat hand on the folded sheet of paper.

He had a feeling he knew exactly who it was from. Tempted again to dispose of it, he also knew he wouldn't get any sleep without reading the contents.

He opened it.

*Adam, I'm sorry if I upset or offended you. Please know that wasn't my intention. If you need to talk, I'm a good listener.*
*C.*

Adam stared at the note. Carly didn't have to apologize; she hadn't offended him. And yeah, she probably was a good listener, but there was no way he was going to talk to her about what had upset him. He wasn't going to talk to *anyone* about that. Ever.

He'd thought that by going out to the intersection today, he'd be able to lay some of his demons to rest. But it had only served to bring back all the old memories, all the good times he and Rory had shared. Closely followed by the knowledge of how badly he'd betrayed his friend.

He needed to make amends, but how? He'd believed that by devoting himself to public service, putting his life on the line for others, would make a difference. Honor Rory's memory somehow. Rory was the one who'd always wanted to be the firefighter, not Adam.

But it hadn't made any difference. He still felt hollow. Still felt the guilt right down to his bones.

He brought the note Carly had written to his nose and sniffed it, hoping it smelled of her. But all he got was a noseful of the scent of baby oil. She sure was one hell of a masseuse. Those hands of hers should be registered as dangerous weapons, considering how easily she'd got him into a state of relaxation. And then to a state of blubbering like a baby. How had she done that?

He'd been about to pull her onto his lap, explore where the chemistry between them was going, when Luke had interrupted. By the time he'd returned to the sensuous zone he'd been in before the interruption, Carly had touched something in his shoulders, and his body had given an enormous shudder. Within moments, he was reliving the night Rory had died. Reliving the terrible dreams that had plagued him too often since. And tonight would probably be no exception.

The one night he needed a good night's sleep, he'd blown it by staying out way too late. He'd be in no condition for the hearing. Was this some self-fulfilling prophecy? Had he deliberately sabotaged himself?

He tried to push the demons aside. *Think of Carly,* his internal voice chanted. *Think only of Carly.*

He forced his breathing to slow as he lay back, hands pillowed behind his head, and pictured her. Strange how relaxed that made him feel. Then her touch… No, not good, he decided as his heart rate increased.

If he was honest with himself, Carly was his teenage fantasy come to life. Pity he hadn't met her back then.

Adam wondered what it would be like to kiss her. Make love to her. He'd had his share of lovers. Women who didn't want to probe too much, women who cared more about his body and how he could pleasure them than about Adam O'Malley, the man.

That was how Carly was different. She probed and she nagged and didn't give up until she'd made him *feel.* Until she got him so mad at her that he'd lashed out, acted as if it was all her fault that he'd lost his composure. When he knew it was quite the opposite.

He punched the pillow and tried to find a more comfortable position. He had to stop thinking about Carly or he wouldn't get any sleep. But he wanted her. More than he'd ever wanted any woman in his life.

Adam longed to throw back the covers and stride over to the stables—barefoot in the snow, if necessary—and tell her he wanted to kiss her, tell her he needed to feel her touch again.

He scraped a hand through his hair. He'd messed up so badly, in so many aspects of his life. He was damaged goods. Carly had enough to deal with; she didn't need his baggage added to her responsibilities. It would be best if she stayed a teen fantasy, rather than an adult reality.

But try as he might, he couldn't get her, or his need for her, out of his mind.

He rolled over and stared at the digital clock on the nightstand. Tomorrow already. Great. In a few hours he'd know his future. Either he still had a job or he'd lost his career altogether and would have to start over. How could he ever honor Rory's memory then? How could he ever win Carly's heart?

On Monday Carly woke before dawn. She hadn't slept well worrying about Adam and the outcome of today's hearing.

By the time she'd got the children dressed for breakfast—while they all chattered about what they'd be doing during their week off school—and herded them over to the ranch house, Adam was already walking out the front door to his vehicle.

She'd hoped to have a private moment to talk to him

before he headed out this morning, but that wasn't going to happen now. Not with her kids hanging on every word.

Adam was wearing his dress uniform. How incredibly handsome and downright sexy he looked, Carly mused, recognizing how appropriate Adam's career was for someone of such strength and fluid grace. He was born to be a firefighter.

He got to his vehicle and pulled open the door. *Look at me,* she begged silently, and was surprised when he glanced across the yard at her.

She raised her hand to wave at him and smiled. He didn't smile back, just nodded his head as if he felt he had to acknowledge her, then climbed into his vehicle and started it.

Carly couldn't let him go like this, without saying something, offering a word of support. "Go into the house, kids," she said, handing Charlie to Alex. She cut across the snow-covered yard to Adam, praying he wouldn't drive off and leave her there.

His dark eyes held hers as she neared his vehicle. He lowered the window.

"Hi," she said, feeling suddenly awkward. Ultimately she was the cause of Adam's predicament. If she hadn't left her children with an unfamiliar babysitter, if she'd been home when the fire started, she'd have gotten all her kids out and Adam wouldn't have had to risk his life saving Charlie. He'd have had more time to rescue Molly, without having to disobey his chief's orders when the fire became too intense.

"Hi," he said back.

Carly could read the pain in his eyes. Something far worse than today's hearing was tearing at his guts. She wanted to comfort him, to impart her own strength.

She lifted her hand and touched his cheek. He closed his eyes momentarily, then opened them and gazed into hers. What agony she could see in their depths. When she stroked his cheek, Adam opened his mouth and caught the base of her thumb between his lips. Carly wanted to weep. He was reaching out to her at last.

"Whatever the outcome today, Adam," she murmured, "I want you to know you're the bravest, most selfless person I've ever met."

Close to tears, she stood on tiptoe, leaned in and kissed his lips.


"Matt, what can I do to help Adam?" Carly asked when she put a call through to him after breakfast.

"Not a lot, I'm afraid. It's up to Adam to present his case, explain what he did and why. Particularly why he ignored orders."

"It won't go well, then?"

She could hear his sigh. "I'm afraid not."

"Would…would I be permitted to attend?"

"I don't see why not. Things like this are a matter of public record."

"Then I have an idea. Would you help me please, Matt?"


Adam had strictly forbidden any of his family from attending the hearing. Sarah had told Carly this over breakfast. The poor woman had been in tears.

Carly figured she wasn't *family,* so Adam's edicts didn't apply to her.

After Will had collected the older children for a day out and dropped off his daughter, Lily, with his mom, Carly told Sarah what she planned and asked her to look after Charlie until she returned. Sarah was only too happy to agree.

"Good luck, Carly. And God bless you," she said as she saw her off five minutes later. Sarah and Mac were lending her one of the ranch vehicles, an almost-new minivan.

"I'll do my best," Carly assured her, wondering if she'd be thrown out of the hearing. If not by the panel, then by Adam.

Matt met her outside the town hall. They soon found the room the hearing was being held in.

Her heart in her throat, she pushed open the door and stepped inside. Matt followed her and sat beside Carly, five rows from the front. The only people present were the members of the board, numbering seven, who sat above the rest of the room's occupants. Adam was standing at a lectern facing them.

He looked so alone. Carly wished she'd notified the paper about the hearing, have some citizens who'd support Adam turn up. But he was so intensely private, Carly knew he would've hated anyone else in the town knowing about the hearing—no matter which way it went.

The disciplinary board consisted of six men and one woman. Carly didn't spend too long pondering the sexual bias of the board; she only hoped each and every one of them had a heart a tenth the size of Adam's. If they did, then she had a chance.

Correction: *Adam* had a chance.

She recognized several officials from the night of the fire. Another man, wearing a robe with an ermine-lined collar and a huge chain of office around his neck, Carly guessed to be the mayor—the owner of the pig she'd seen at the fire and who'd had her photo in the paper, kissing Adam. She smiled at the memory and hoped his pig's affection for Adam would sway the mayor in his favor. But the mayor was obviously eccentric, so who knew how he'd react?

The lone woman looked seriously scary in a dark gray suit, glasses perched on the end of her nose and lips thinned as she listened to Adam.

Then she spoke and Carly's blood froze at her words. "We keep coming back to the same point, Mr. O'Malley. You deliberately disobeyed a direct order from your commanding officer. You could have put others' lives at risk—"

"But I didn't," Adam interrupted, perhaps a little injudiciously, Carly thought.

If it was possible, the woman's lips thinned even more, but Adam continued before she could speak again. "I don't know how many times you want me to agree that yes, I did disobey an order. And I'm sorry about that. But as I keep telling you, I knew none of the other firefighters would disobey the chief by following me in."

"You sound very sure of that," she said. "Too sure and too reckless. I don't think these are the qualities we need in a firefighter in this town. Or anywhere in the state of Colorado, for that matter."

Several other heads nodded in assent.

Carly was terrified. This wasn't looking good at all. She wanted to leap to her feet and say something in Adam's defense, but was afraid she'd only make the situation worse.

Matt's hand clasped hers. Should she speak now? Carly wondered.

The mayor cleared his throat. "Are we all finished questioning Mr. O'Malley?"

All seven heads nodded.

"Then if no one else has anything further to say, I think we should vote on whether Mr. O'Malley is stripped of his temporary position with the Spruce Lake fire department."

Carly leaped to her feet before she could think better of it. "I'd like to speak, if I may?"

Adam spun around and glared at her. Then he spotted Matt and glared even more fiercely.

Undaunted, Carly stepped forward. "May I approach the bench? I don't feel comfortable yelling from back here."

The mayor inclined his head. The woman's lips seemed to disappear altogether and she pulled herself up to sit taller, as if that would intimidate Carly.

Carly stood beside Adam and said, "You probably don't know me, but my name is Carly Spencer. My four children and I lost our home in the fire last Friday.

"If not for the courage of—" she felt her voice breaking but pressed on "—Mr. O'Malley, I would now be a mother of three children. What he did that day was nothing short of heroic. I owe my youngest child's life to him."

The woman made shooing motions with her hands. "That's all very well, but Mr. O'Malley isn't being disciplined for saving any *human* lives in that fire. He disobeyed orders to save a *dog*." She said this as if it was the most distasteful word she'd ever been forced to utter.

"I'm sorry—" Carly squinted to read the woman's name "—Ms. Wilkinson, I'm aware of the purpose of this hearing, but I wanted to point out that had Mr. O'Malley not gone to rescue Molly, my oldest son, Alex, would have.

"He would've found a way to get around all the personnel there and gone into that burning building to search for her. And I'm sure you'd agree, an eleven-year-old boy would have absolutely no chance of either finding the dog—Molly is her name, by the way," Carly said, hoping that by giving the dog's name, she might appeal to their more humanitarian sides, "or surviving the fire."

Carly shivered at the memory of Alex trying to run into that building, but she also noticed that a couple of other board members nodded in agreement.

"Molly is very dear to Alex, to all my children. I don't know about you, but the thought of an innocent animal perishing in a fire tears my heart out.

"If Mr. O'Malley hadn't ignored his chief's orders and gone to find Molly, then my children would be having nightmares for many months, perhaps years, imagining Molly's final moments."

She cleared her throat and said, "Thanks to Mr. O'Malley's bravery, my children dream of a happy, healthy Molly. He saved not only the life of my youngest child that day, but also the life of my eldest son and Molly. His selflessness, instead of being censured, should be praised—"

"This is all very emotional, Mrs. Spencer. But I'll remind you again, this is a disciplinary hearing," Ms. Wilkinson said.

"Yes, I realize it's all very emotional, but that's what life is. I won't go into the details of how difficult things have been since my husband—also a firefighter—died in a warehouse fire in San Diego. But I *will* tell you it's been incredibly traumatic for my children. By risking his life and saving a helpless animal, Mr. O'Malley has restored my children's faith in the human race and demonstrated that it's possible to salvage something precious from a fire.

"My children and I…" Again Carly had to steel herself against the tears that burned behind her eyes and bit at the back of her throat. "We lost everything we own in Spruce Lake in that fire. But what we gained in return is this. We learned that the willingness to sacrifice is part of the best of being human."

This time, everyone on the board, minus Ms. Wilkinson, nodded.

"Mr. O'Malley is a dedicated firefighter and I've since learned from his brother Matt—" she turned to smile at Matt "—that Mr. O'Malley has saved a number of lives during his career as a firefighter and been commended for it. Are you willing to risk the lives of future fire victims by not having someone of his caliber and outstanding bravery on your team?"

Carly had finished what she had to say, but she wasn't sure what to do next. Take a seat and wait for the verdict? Run from the building before she let her emotions surface and burst into tears? Grab Adam and kiss him soundly to apologize for possibly ruining his chances of keeping the job?

She was saved from making any immediate decisions by the mayor, who addressed her directly. "Thank you, Mrs. Spencer. I must say, I admire your passion and your desire to speak up for Mr. O'Malley."

He looked at her and said, "I also have to give credit to you for bringing the situation from a victim's viewpoint to our attention. I think some of us have overlooked how important that is."

Carly heard a hiss of disapproval from Ms. Wilkinson.

"If no one has anything further to add, I'd like to adjourn this hearing so the board can discuss the matter," he said, and rose from his seat, effectively ending the session.

* * *

Carly arrived back at Two Elk just as her first client of the day drove up. Kandy Mason was an energetic sixty-something woman who'd been a friend of Sarah's for many years. They'd met at watercolor classes and, along with several other women in the group, met regularly for coffee and a chat. Sometimes they also hiked into the mountains during the summer to paint.

"I was so delighted when Sarah called the other day to ask if I was interested in a treatment. She knows I love to be pampered!" the other woman told her as Carly set up her table.

"Well, I'm afraid I don't do anything except massage," Carly said, worried that Kandy might think she also offered other spa treatments like facials and manicures.

"Oh, I understand, dear. I love massage. If I had the healing touch, I probably would've studied it myself."

Carly was starting to hope the other woman wouldn't talk this much during her massage. She was feeling a little too raw after the hearing to deal with idle chitchat.

However, five minutes into the massage, Kandy was snoring softly. Carly smiled. Funny how some people were like Energizer Bunnies, talking constantly, and yet, once they were given a chance to relax, they slept like babes!

Fifty minutes later, Carly had to gently wake Kandy. "That was the best sleep I've had in ages." She stretched her arms above her head.

"I have to apologize," Carly said. "You were sleeping so peacefully I didn't want to wake you for the other side, so I just continued on your back and legs. We could do the rest some other time if you'd like."

Carly slipped behind a screen she'd set up between the kitchenette and the living room where she did the massages, so Kandy had privacy to dress.

"That would be wonderful. Can I make another appointment for tomorrow?"

"So soon?" Carly asked as she poured her a refreshing cup of herbal tea. "Do you feel you got any benefit from the massage, since you were fast asleep?"

"I feel great!" Kandy came around the screen and joined Carly in the apartment kitchenette. "I promise to try to stay awake next time." She proffered a wad of notes and said with a smile, "Keep the change, Carly. It was *wonderful*."

"Thank you," Carly said. "I've made you some herbal tea." She indicated that Kandy should take a seat at the table and sat down with her own cup.

"Don't you have another customer waiting?" Kandy asked.

"I try to leave fifteen minutes between appointments so clients can relax and rehydrate."

"That's a nice touch," Kandy told her. "Not like the big clinics where you're lucky to get forty-five minutes of a so-so massage and then you're shoved out the door, barely dressed!"

Carly laughed and sipped her tea. She liked Kandy; the woman was forthright and it was easy to understand why she and Sarah had been friends for so long.

"Now, what time can you take me tomorrow?"

Carly flipped through her appointment book. "How about the same time? Would that work? I'm afraid it's the only slot I have left."

"Perfect!" Kandy said, standing. "I'll see you then. And I'll be sure to spread the word. Sarah mentioned you had a mobile massage business. Will you be doing that again? I'm asking because I was thinking some of the ladies at the Twilight Years would enjoy it."

"That's the retirement home?" Carly asked.

"Yes, my mom's in there. They have a hairdresser and a beauty therapist who comes once a week. She's brilliant at pedicures and the like but can't do massages."

"That's a good idea, Mrs. Mason. But I won't be starting up my mobile business again until my oldest three children are back at school next week and I've got a permanent and *reliable* sitter for Charlie. I don't want to impose on Sarah any more than I already am."

Kandy patted her hand. "I understand, Carly. Just as soon as you're ready, let me know. Meanwhile, I'd be happy to bring my mom here. She always enjoys catching up with the O'Malley clan."

The rest of the day flew by with four more appointments. Two clients wanted all the details of the fire and Adam's rescue of Charlie and Molly. One talked nonstop about all her ailments, and the other about her grandchildren. As Carly wiped down her massage table for the last time and put it away and then washed up for dinner, she was completely drained.

At least all the ladies had promised to return. They'd also paid in cash and given her decent tips and the one with all the ailments said she was feeling much better than she had in a long while.

As she did her bookkeeping, Carly vowed to pace herself more carefully in the future. Five appointments back to back simply wasn't fair to her kids, or to Sarah, even though Sarah insisted she loved having a houseful of children.

If things continued to be this busy, Carly wouldn't need to do any sessions at the Spruce Lake spa to supplement her income. By comparison with her private clients, she was paid peanuts there.

Entering the kitchen by the back door, Carly kicked off her boots and put on a pair of snug slippers Sarah provided for everyone. It was a nice touch and made Carly feel even more as if she were part of the family.

The kitchen was empty apart from Molly, sleeping peacefully on her bed, her nose snuggled into Adam's blanket.

Carly made her way into the living room. Sarah glanced up with a weary smile that had Carly feeling instantly guilty. Although Lily was fast asleep, Charlie was sitting on Sarah's lap playing with her necklace.

Carly bent to pick him up. "I'm sorry. I won't stay away so long in future. You're absolutely exhausted."

"Nonsense, dear," the older woman said. "I've enjoyed every minute of looking after your little man. I'm worried about Adam. Still no word."

Carly's shoulders fell. She sat down next to Sarah, and Charlie immediately climbed back onto Sarah's lap and began to chew her necklace again. "Is no news bad news?" she ventured to ask.

Sarah lifted her shoulders. "I don't know. I've been calling his cell phone for ages and he's not answering, so then I called Matt and got told off for pestering Adam!"

Tears welled in her eyes and Carly moved to comfort her. "I'm so sorry, Sarah. I feel responsible. I hope I didn't complicate things for Adam by turning up and putting in my two cents' worth."

Sarah patted her hand. "Matt said you were magnificent. I'm sure what you did could only have helped."

"I hope so. But you should've seen the look of fury on Adam's face when he realized Matt and I were there."

Sarah smiled tiredly. "That boy is so determined to be independent. He never accepts help from anyone. I worry about him and the way he shuts himself off from everyone in the family."

"Do you expect him home for dinner?"

"I hope so. I've made his favorite—beef casserole—and the rest of the family is coming over to offer their support, whether he wants it or not."

Carly grinned. "I love how you never give up on anything."

"I'm just a stubborn old woman."

"Stubborn, yes. Old, never!" Carly found her fingers gently kneading Sarah's shoulders.

"That feels good," Sarah said. "Kandy called to say how much she liked you and how wonderful your massage was."

"She slept through most of it! But I thought she was lovely. She's coming back the same time tomorrow. Why don't I give you a shoulder rub now, before the stampede arrives? I think you need it."

"I'd love that."

"Then show me to your room," she said, hoisting Charlie onto her hip. Like Lily, he was probably ready for a nap.

In Sarah's room she placed Charlie on the bed and gave him his favorite soft toy to curl up with.

She turned to Sarah. "I think you'd benefit from a shoulder rub and an Indian head massage, so loosen your top garments and take a seat at your dressing table."

Sarah complied. At least, unlike her son, Adam's mom wasn't protesting all the way! "Now, do exactly what Charlie's done," she said. "Close your eyes and relax."

\* \* \*

Fifteen minutes later, Carly could hear cars pulling up outside. "Looks like the stampede's here," she said, finishing Sarah's shoulders.

"I feel so refreshed. Thank you," Sarah said as Carly turned away to allow her some privacy to rearrange her clothes.

The children charged through the front door, bringing the chilled air with them. "Grandma, where are you?" Carly recognized Daisy's familiar bellow.

"You rest for a few minutes. I'll take care of them," Carly said, picking up Charlie, who'd woken from his brief nap and was playing happily on the bed.

"Any news?" she asked Will as she greeted him downstairs.

Will knew exactly what news she was referring to and shook his head. "I've been texting him for hours. Nothing!"

"He's probably feeling overwhelmed if the others have been bugging him as much as we have."

"We can't help caring. He's our brother," Will said. "Hi, Mom." He bent to kiss Sarah's cheek. "You're looking gorgeous as ever."

"Always the flatterer," she said, deflecting his compliment. "Carly's given me the most wonderful massage."

Carly smiled at Sarah. Her hair was still a bit askew, but Carly knew she wouldn't waste time away from her family to preen.

"What about me?" Will asked. "I've been herding seven overeager kids all day."

"And you've enjoyed every minute of it," his mother told him. "Where's your lovely wife?"

"Right here," Becky said, coming into the living room

from the kitchen, Lily perched on her hip. "Will and the children made dessert. Better yet, I think it's edible."

"For an ex-ski bum, Will, you've certainly turned your life around," his mother remarked drily. "Of course, if your brother hadn't arrested you for vandalism and you'd never appeared before Becky in court—and had the audacity to ask her for a date—we would never have known about your latent talents. Like cooking. Have I told you lately how much I love you, my mischievous middle child?"

"Nope, don't think you have."

"Well, I do. And I'm very proud of you."

"Thanks, Ma," Will said. Red-faced, he went into the kitchen to join the children.

"Strange," Becky said. "I've never seen my husband blush before."

Sarah grinned. "That's because before you came into his life, he wasn't exactly in line for compliments on his behavior. Now I'm making up for lost time on that score."

"What score?" Matt asked, coming into the room.

"Never mind!" Sarah and Becky said at once.

"Any word?" Sarah asked.

"Nothing. And he's still not answering his cell."

Carly's heart fell. Where could Adam be? Had the outcome of the hearing been bad?

Matt tried to call him once more, but failed to make contact. When he'd disconnected, he said, "Maybe we'd better start dinner. If he comes home and finds us all sitting around staring morosely at the tablecloth, it'll make him feel worse."

Carly was all for eating. She'd been so busy, she'd missed lunch and now her blood sugar was low.

"I'll feed the kids and get them ready for bed," Sarah

said. "Perhaps by then Adam will be home, or we'll have heard from him."

"Good idea," Becky agreed. "It might be best if the kids aren't around when he gets home. The last thing he'll want is a bunch of ruffians jumping all over him."

Within moments the children were taking their places at the table. They'd apparently all agreed to watch the same thing that evening, since Will had rented a recent DVD.

Carly put Charlie in his high chair and started feeding him the casserole Becky had dished up.

"Can we watch it at our place, Mom?" Alex asked. "There's a bigger TV there."

Carly had been surprised about the size of the television in the small apartment, but Sarah had explained that Adam had brought his set with him. Carly suspected he'd done that so he could hide away from his family.

Yet he'd barely had a chance to move into the apartment than Sarah had turfed him out and into Daisy's bedroom to make room for Carly and her children. Seemed like moving back home to Spruce Lake for a while wasn't working out so well for Adam....

"Sure," she said. "As long as there's no fighting."

"No way," Alex told her. "Will got us the latest *Pirates of the Caribbean* movie."

"That might be too scary for Celeste and Maddy."

"We're not watching it, Mommy. We're gonna play dolls," Maddy said.

Carly released a breath. "Then I guess that's all right. But nine o'clock is bedtime. Okay?"

"Aw, Mom!"

"Just because it's winter break, doesn't mean you get to stay up late every night," Will cut in. "Remember, I'm taking you to look at the night sky over at the observatory tomorrow evening. We won't be home till after ten."

"You're taking them stargazing?" Carly couldn't believe what a gem Will was.

"Sure. They have a big telescope over at the science school in Silver Springs. Since I wanted to be an astronomer once, I love going over there every chance I get."

"And you didn't become an astronomer because..."

"Too much math and sitting still. I wanted to ski!"

"Figures," Becky said under her breath, and grinned at Carly.

The children were fed and given the option of eating their brownies while watching the movie.

Soon the kitchen was silent as eight adults waited, ears straining for the sound of Adam's car.

No one was in the mood to eat. Even Carly, who'd been salivating as she fed Charlie, had lost her appetite.

Instead, she sat at the table and bit her nails, then berated herself. She'd always bitten her nails when something troubled her and lately she'd been biting them a lot.

"Maybe we should go home," Beth suggested. "We might look like an execution squad if Adam walked in here and the news was bad."

"She's got a point," Jack agreed.

"Shh!" Matt got up from the table and went through to the living room.

He returned a moment later. "He's here," he whispered, although the likelihood that Adam would hear him in the yard was nonexistent. "Maybe I should go out and see him?"

"No. Sit down," his father said. "Let's serve dinner and pretend everything is normal."

"This feels almost clandestine," Beth said as she got up to help bring the mashed potatoes, peas and casserole dishes to the table.

Just as she and Sarah resumed their seats, they heard the front door open.

## Chapter 9

Adam wasn't smiling as he entered the kitchen.

Sarah opened her mouth to ask him how the hearing had gone, but Adam spoke first. "Can I see you outside?" he said to Carly, his face expressionless.

Knees shaking, Carly rose from the table. This didn't sound good.

She was about to follow Adam obediently out of the room, willing to do whatever he wanted since she'd probably helped put an end to his career.

His father stood and barred the way. "First you'll tell us how it went, son," he said.

"It's fine, Pop. I still have a job. In fact, they want me to become a permanent member of the brigade."

The collective release of pent-up breath could be heard around the table. Suddenly everyone was on their feet and rushing to shake his hand, but Adam shook his head.

"Later," he said, standing back so Carly could leave the room ahead of him.

Carly put on her coat and gloves, preparing to go outside, although nothing could stop the chill. Why would Adam want to talk to her in private? Had she caused so much damage that it'd taken him this long to convince the board she was a madwoman and that they should ignore everything she'd said?

She stepped outside onto the porch and was about to descend the few steps to the snow-covered ground when she turned back to look at him. "I'm sorr—" she began, but Adam cupped her cheeks with both hands and kissed her.

His lips were warm and caressing, exactly what she needed after the stress of the day. She closed her eyes and drank in the sensation of being kissed by a man—a man she was starting to fall for.

He broke the kiss slowly, then kissed her again. Finally, he rested his forehead against hers and dropped his hands to her shoulders.

"Thank you," he murmured, his voice hoarse.

Carly was so stunned by the kiss and how it affected her that she quipped, "You thank everyone like this?"

He drew away and she could see his smile in the moonlight. "No, just pretty women."

"I'm glad, because I'd hate to think you kissed Ms. Wilkinson like that."

His smile grew wider and Carly basked in it. "No chance," he said, stroking her face with one hand. He slipped his other hand around Carly's back and pulled her closer. "She was the only holdout in the end."

Carly inclined her head toward his palm. "Not seduced

by your charms?" Carly knew she was mumbling non-sense, but it felt so good to be touched, be held, by Adam.

"The only woman I want to seduce is you."

Carly swallowed. So did Adam.

"I guess you didn't mean to say it quite like that?" she said, giving him an out.

His eyes narrowed and he bent to kiss her again.

To Adam's relief, Carly wound her arms around his neck and returned his kiss. He hadn't intended to be so forthright, but he was glad he'd said it now, since Carly didn't seem put off by his longing to seduce her.

His lips parted and he deepened the kiss. After all the stress and anxiety of the past days, this was what he needed. Carly's kisses were as healing as her hands.

He drew back, rested his hands on her hips and gazed into her eyes. "You know when I said I didn't want you to touch me ever again?"

"Uh-huh."

"I was lying."

She tightened her arms around his neck, drawing his mouth to within an inch of hers. "That's good," she said, and kissed him gently. "Because if this isn't touching, I have to find a new definition for it."

Adam wrapped his arms around her, bringing her against him. His mouth covered hers but the sound of cheering had them springing apart.

He glanced toward the house. Silhouetted in the living room window was his family. They'd been watching every move he made on Carly and now they were voicing their approval.

He felt his face heating but Carly raised her hand to

his cheek and her touch soothed him. "I think we have a few too many chaperones," she said with a smile.

"Me, too," he agreed. "If I wasn't starving, I'd carry you to my car and get out of here, maybe take you to Inspiration Point for some serious necking."

"I'd like that," Carly murmured, and kissed his throat, sending all sorts of erotic messages to Adam's brain—and other parts of his body.

"Later?" he said, and Carly could hear the hope in his voice.

She nodded and kissed him again. "Later," she whispered. "After dinner." Her heart lifted as Adam took her hand before leading her back to the house.

Adam stopped abruptly just before opening the door. Carly bumped into him.

"I'm not one for public displays of affection," he said, as if warning her there'd be no handholding in front of the family. No more kisses.

"That's okay," she said, wanting to stroke his face as he looked so concerned.

She was about to step over the threshold ahead of him as he held open the door when she felt a prickle up her spine. She glanced back toward the darkened yard. An eerie sense of being watched filled her with the same fear she'd experienced at the fire. But this time the threat felt closer.

"What's up?" Adam asked at her hesitation.

She shrugged. "Nothing," she said too quickly, and entered the house ahead of him. It was probably the aftermath of the fire that had her so jumpy, imagining people watching her from the shadows.

Thankfully, the living room was now deserted, giving Carly a moment to compose herself before facing everyone.

She slipped out of her coat, took a deep breath and strode back into the kitchen, acting for all the world as if nothing had happened between her and Adam on the porch. But the weird feeling of being observed from the darkened yard still haunted her.

They took their places at the table. Adam had barely taken his first mouthful when the questions started. "So what happened?" Will asked.

"Matt said Carly was magnificent and probably swung the decision in your favor, darling," Sarah said. "Did it?"

"Why'd it take them so long to decide?" Jack asked.

"When can you go back to work?" Matt added.

Adam chewed and swallowed and said, "Yes. I don't know. Tomorrow at six."

The occupants of the room took a moment to process the answers and then there was a cacophony of sound as they all spoke at once.

Eventually, Adam managed to tell them that the decision had been made several hours earlier.

"So why didn't you let us know?" Sarah demanded.

"Because I needed time to think, Mom."

Adam wasn't about to tell them that the whole experience had been so shattering that afterward he'd taken a drive back to the crossroads where Rory had died. He'd sat there for hours trying to figure out what he had to do. In the end, he knew.

"What's to think about?" Will said. "You overthink everything, Adam."

"If he overthought everything, he might not have saved Molly," Jack pointed out.

All eyes turned to the dog, and Will reached out to scratch her head with his foot. She closed her eyes in bliss.

"The Polinskis' son and daughter-in-law arrive tomorrow to take them to Miami," Sarah said. "Carly told me that Mrs. Polinski thought their daughter-in-law wouldn't want a dog living with them."

"That's strange," Matt said. "Because I got a call from Mrs. Jasmine Polinski trying to confirm if Molly was a pedigreed bassett hound. She wanted her papers. I explained there was nothing left of the Polinskis' possessions after the fire. She got downright unpleasant when I asked why it mattered. I have a sneaking suspicion that she intends to sell her to a breeder."

*"What?"* Becky shouted. "No way!"

Will laughed. "I think they'll find her mom mated with something else first."

"We could tell her Molly's already been spayed and she'd lose interest in her," Becky said.

"I thought you were a judge?" Jack shook his head with a grin. "Upholder of the law and all."

"Sometimes the law's an ass," she said. "And sometimes you've got to do what you can to keep a family together."

"Then it's agreed?" Jack asked. "We'll tell them Molly's been spayed."

Becky raised her eyebrows. "And to think *you* were almost a priest."

"Obviously not a very good one," Matt said, and raised his glass to his brother.

"This will only work until the Polinskis tell their daughter-in-law that Molly's still intact," Carly told them. "She had an appointment to be spayed in a couple of weeks."

"Is it too late to call the vet and arrange to have her spayed tonight?" Will suggested.

Becky swatted him. "You can't go and have someone else's dog spayed!"

"I feel sorry for the Polinskis when they discover the daughter-in-law's evil motives," Jack said.

"Which brings us back to the problem of finding a permanent home for Molly," Will murmured. "A home that will respect her whether her lady bits are intact, or not."

"I promised I'd look after her for them," Carly admitted. "But I was sort of backed into a corner, and I didn't have the heart to say no."

Sarah said, "She's welcome to stay here until we can find her a home. But she's not a ranch dog, so I worry she'll be left behind on those short little legs of hers."

Carly chewed her lip. "How can we stop the daughter-in-law from taking Molly?"

"We could offer to buy Molly," Adam suggested. "Although I'm hoping it won't come to that because she's going to expect a lot for her."

"I wonder if her husband knows what she's got planned," Jack said. "Maybe we can appeal to his humanitarian side?"

"Spoken like an eternal optimist," Luke mumbled.

"We'll put plan A into place tomorrow morning when the Polinskis' son and daughter-in-law turn up," Will said.

"What plan?" Jack asked.

"I haven't thought of one yet."

Matt held up his hands. "Much as I want to help, you'd better count both Becky and me out. In fact, this conversation never happened."

"Good point," Will said. "Mom and I will take care of the details."

\* \* \*

The drive to Inspiration Point after dinner didn't happen.

Adam was relieved when Carly said she needed to check on her kids and might make it an early night, because during dinner he'd started having serious misgiving about taking things to the next level with Carly.

What was he thinking? Getting involved with a woman with four children had never been on his agenda. Ever. He didn't want the responsibility that came with it. Didn't trust himself. And Carly sure wasn't the kind of woman to indulge in a casual affair.

He'd been thinking with another part of his anatomy when he kissed her on the porch, and it wasn't anywhere close to his brain.

The excuse that she needed an early night since she had a lot of clients to see in the morning suited him just fine. Although he sensed that Carly was as relieved as he was when he hadn't protested.

Anything had to be better than staying at the ranch, seeing Carly every day. Wanting her... Wanting her like he'd never wanted any woman before.


Carly headed to the apartment over the stables, thankful that she had a plausible reason for not going to Inspiration Point with Adam. Lord knew what trouble she'd end up in if she did!

She'd only been with one man in her entire life. And although Adam would probably be a wonderful lover, Carly knew they didn't have a future. She had too many responsibilities; he had too many hang-ups.

Carly didn't have room for another person in her life. Another person with even more baggage than she had.

* * *

Why had he kissed her on the porch like that? Adam wondered. The woman was bewitching him, getting under his skin like no other woman ever had. What *was* it about her? She was everything he didn't need—an eternal optimist, an idealist, a woman with too many kids, too many responsibilities. And yet…she was a free spirit. He almost resented the way she could pick herself up after misfortune, the way she could smile and light up a room as if she didn't have a care in the world.

At least he'd be at work for the next two days, so he wouldn't have to talk to her, look at her, let her enchant him with those blue eyes, that ready smile.

Adam used to be attracted to girls like her in high school. But after Rory died he'd shut himself off from relationships—he didn't even attend his senior prom. He dated occasionally, but as soon as anyone wanted to make the relationship exclusive, tie him down, he was outta there. He hated that fickleness of character, but it was a way of protecting himself from having to care.

But now he *was* starting to care. He cared about Carly, her kids. Molly. He cared about his family. He worried that hearing about the night Rory died would distress them, but it was something he had to confront. No more running away.

Adam pulled up outside the mountain cabin Matt shared with his wife, Beth, and daughter, Sarah. He'd purposely waited for an hour after Matt and Beth had left the ranch following dinner. He'd given them enough time to get home, get Sarah settled. With luck Beth would already be in bed. Adam didn't want any witnesses to what he had to tell Matt.

He took a few minutes to compose himself. This was going to be one of the hardest things he'd ever done in his life and he dreaded the disappointment in Matt's eyes when he confessed the truth about what had happened that night fifteen years ago.

He climbed out of the car and made his way through the freshly fallen snow to Matt's door. His hand trembled as he raised it to knock.

Matt answered a moment later. "Adam! What are you doing here? Come on in," he said, stepping back to allow Adam to enter the house.

"Can we…talk outside?" There was no way he'd have any privacy at Matt's place. In time, he'd admit the truth to Beth, but right now he didn't want her burdened with his shame. Not until there was some resolution. The O'Malleys would have enough to endure over the coming weeks, when the circumstances surrounding Rory's death were revealed to the community of Spruce Lake.

Matt frowned, but didn't query him further. "Sure, I'll get my jacket."

Moments later, Matt joined him on the stoop and shrugged into his warm jacket. "It must be twenty below out here," he said. "What's up that you didn't want to come inside and have some tea or hot chocolate with Beth and me? Or talk about it at the ranch, for that matter?"

Adam turned away and started toward the gate leading into the property, giving Matt no alternative but to follow.

"If it's relationship advice you want, little brother, then you should be talking to Beth."

Adam spun around and said, "I killed someone and I want to make it right."

Matt stopped in his tracks and peered into his face. "Run that by me again?"

"I was the one driving the night Rory was killed."

Matt let out a long breath. "Damn," he muttered.

"I can't live with the guilt anymore, Matt. I hate being hailed as a hero, when the truth is, I'm a complete lowlife who killed his best friend and was too much of a coward to admit it."

Matt placed a comforting hand on Adam's shoulder and said, "I think we need to talk inside."

Adam shrugged him off. "I can't. I don't want Beth knowing about this yet. I can't tolerate the embarrassment. I wanted to talk to you first and find out what I have to do about turning myself in. And then… I need to talk to Rory's mom."

"Why didn't you tell someone about this when it happened?"

"You're kidding, right? I was fifteen. I was knocked out for a couple of days, and by the time I came to, the funeral was over and the accident investigators had concluded that Rory was driving. Case closed. I was scared and I didn't see any point in telling the truth—that I was in the driver's seat and thrown clear when the truck rolled. Yeah, I know it was lousy of me. Cowardly. But like I said, I was fifteen. Selfish and scared. Who do I turn myself in to?"

"Since it happened outside the town limits, me, I guess."

"How long do you get for murder?"

"For a start, it would be classified as vehicular homicide. That's a class-four felony and the usual term is from two to six years if memory serves me—"

"*Six* years?"

"You asked."

"I know. I know. On the one hand it's a shock, but on the other it seems too short a sentence for such a serious crime. So do you arrest me here or take me down to the sheriff's department or what?"

"If you'd let me finish what I was saying earlier, I would've told you that the statute of limitations on vehicular homicide in the state of Colorado is five years."

"Which means?"

"You won't be facing a jail term."

Adam let out his breath in a whoosh. "But?"

"There is no *but*. Because you didn't come forward within five years of the accident, no charges will be laid and you won't have a record."

Adam shook his head, disbelieving. "It doesn't seem right. I killed someone and I walk free?"

"You've lived with this for a lot of years.... It's torn your guts out, and I don't see that as walking free, Adam. You've led an exemplary life, saved lives in the line of duty. You've repaid your debt to society."

"Then why do I feel like crap?"

"Guilt? The knowledge that it's too late to make amends?"

"I need to talk to Rory's mom."

"And what do you think that will achieve? You'll be bringing up old memories. Maybe she'd prefer them to stay in the past."

"I need her to know that Rory wasn't responsible for his death."

When Matt was about to object, he held up his hand and said, "Yeah, yeah, everyone knows Rory was always doing daring things and everyone believed he was going to mess up his life, but Mrs. Bennett deserves the truth."

"You could be opening a whole can of worms—not the least of which is that she could sue you."

"Which would be her right."

"It could ruin your life."

"So? I've ruined hers. Mr. Bennett drank himself to death after the accident and she's been alone all these years."

"Grant Bennett was a drinker long before you were born, Adam. You can't blame yourself for his death, too."

"I can't help feeling that I contributed to it."

"For all you know, Rory could've gone down the same path as his old man. He had a blood alcohol level more than twice the legal limit, if I remember. And there's evidence that alcoholism runs in families."

"It still doesn't account for the lousy life Mrs. Bennett's led. As a result of my actions, her only son is dead."

Matt sighed. "Do you want me to come with you when you talk to her?"

Adam shook his head emphatically. "I have to do this on my own."

Matt clapped him on the back. "I admire you for coming forward, even if it is fifteen years later. It takes guts to own up to something like that."

Adam wasn't listening. "And then I need to talk to Mom and Pop."

"Oh, no! I don't think that's a good idea."

"Matt, this is going to get around town. Even if Mrs. Bennett doesn't go ballistic and sic the lawyers on me, the truth will get out. I don't want Mom and Pop hearing it from some third party."

Matt nodded. "I can see you've thought this through. I'll come with you to see our folks, then. Mom might react badly."

"I can't talk to them tonight. It'll have to wait until after my next shift at the fire station. In the meantime, can you keep this to yourself?"

Matt clasped his shoulder and turned him back toward his vehicle. "You have my word, buddy."

A half hour later, Adam parked outside the Bennett residence. It was a tiny weatherboard house that could do with a coat of paint and some repairs to the gutter and roof, he noticed.

Taking a deep breath, he stepped out of his car onto Gray Street and crossed the road to Mrs. Bennett's front walk.

He paused at the rusted gate. What was he doing? It was way too late to be visiting someone. Especially when you were bringing bad news. Reviving bad memories.

He was about to turn back to his vehicle when the front door opened and Mrs. Bennett came onto the porch.

Adam wanted to shrink into the shadows. It had been many years since he'd seen Rory's mom. She'd always been slender, but now she was painfully thin. She wrapped her arms around her against the chill of the night and called out, "Who's there?"

Now she probably thought she had a prowler. Adam didn't want to cause her any worry, so he walked through the gate and said, "It's me, Mrs. Bennett. Adam O'Malley."

"Adam! How lovely to hear your voice after all these years. Come into the light where I can see you," she said, gesturing with her hand.

On shaking legs, Adam strode up her shoveled path and onto her porch. The harsh light showed the lines on her face, but she had that smile he still remembered. Rory's smile.

"Hello, Mrs. Bennett," he said, his voice hoarse with emotion. He shouldn't have come here. He shouldn't have come to ruin this good woman's night by bringing back all the memories of the night her only son died.

"It's Jennifer, please!" she said, and hugged him. "You're much too old to be calling me Mrs. Bennett these days."

Adam hugged her back, but carefully. She felt so frail beneath his hands.

"Have you got time to come inside?" she asked, and Adam could hear the yearning in her voice, the desperation for someone to keep her company.

"Sure," he said. "I was coming to see you, anyway, but then I thought it might be too late."

She opened her door and ushered him inside. A small fire burned in the grate, barely warming the living room. "I'm sorry I don't have much of a fire. I've hurt my back and can't split enough wood to get a good fire going."

"I can do that for you," Adam offered.

"Thank you. You were always such a kind boy."

Adam swallowed down the guilt that was choking him. He wondered if he should split her wood now, before his big admission, or later.

"Would you like some hot chocolate?" she asked. "I just boiled the water."

"That would be great. Thanks." Adam knew he was being formal with her, but this was the most awkward situation he'd ever been in.

Jennifer Bennett tipped hot chocolate mix into two mugs, then filled them with hot water. She stirred them, then handed one to Adam and indicated they should return to the living room. She hastily brushed aside some newspapers opened to the crossword section so Adam could take a seat on her worn sofa.

Adam placed his mug on the coffee table. There was no way he could drink anything right now. He needed to get the words out before his courage failed him.

*Courage.* What a joke.

"Mrs. Benn—Jennifer, I have something I need to tell you and you're not going to like it."

Adam left Jennifer Bennett's house two hours later. A lot of emotions had been spent in those hours. And a friendship forged.

It astonished him how happy Rory's mom had been to see him, how she'd welcomed him like a long-lost son. And then he'd told her what had happened the night Rory died.

She'd thanked Adam for admitting the truth, praised his courage in coming to her. And then, most astonishing of all, she'd forgiven him.

They'd talked for a long time. Jennifer had gotten out photographs of Adam and Rory together and they'd remembered the good times. Then he'd split what remained of her meager wood pile.

Guessing she probably didn't have the money to get in more firewood, he told her he'd bring a truckload around when he finished his forty-eight-hour rotation and split it for her. She'd have more than enough to keep her house warm through the winter.

In the morning, he'd order a box of groceries delivered to her from the supermarket and some flowers from Mrs. Farquar, the mayor's wife. It was the least he could do to make up for all the years he'd stayed away.

As he lay in bed that night, for the first time in too many years Adam felt the weight of his guilt pressing less heavily on his chest. But he knew that in a small house on the outskirts of town, Jennifer Bennett was mourning the loss of her son all over again.

## *Chapter 10*

The next morning the Polinskis' son and daughter-in-law arrived in town.

Matt had asked them to come by his office first, before they picked up the old couple from the hospital.

And while the Polinskis' son, George, was pleasant enough and grateful for everything the fire department and rescue personnel had done for his parents, the daughter-in-law was another matter.

Jasmine Polinski's designer clothes would be the envy of many a woman in Spruce Lake, Matt surmised. But the fur coat she wore would've guaranteed her being scorned by nearly everyone.

Once settled in Matt's office, she demanded to know where Molly was.

Matt had patiently tried to explain to her—since her husband had stepped out of the office to take a call—that Molly was still suffering from smoke inhalation and probably shouldn't be moved anytime soon. He then bit his lip and hinted that Molly might not be a pedigreed basset, after all.

"They told me she was a pedigreed bassett hound!" she screeched. "Her puppies are supposed to sell for over a thousand dollars each!"

Matt did his best to hold his tongue. "If she isn't pedigreed, then any puppies she might have could be very difficult to place. In fact, my brother Will, who's an expert on dogs…" This wasn't entirely true, but Will liked dogs and they liked him, so Matt didn't mind bending the truth about Will's expertise. "Anyway, he thinks Molly's mom might have mated with another dog first. I'm afraid that, in spite of your in-laws' beliefs, Will thinks she's a mixed breed." So much for his suggestion that he and Becky stay out of the whole Molly issue. But something about this woman brought out the devil in Matt and he couldn't resist baiting her.

"You mean…she's a *mongrel?*"

The word dripped with contempt and Matt hated her for it.

"I don't believe you. I want to see her. Where *is* she?"

"At my family's ranch," Matt told her. "I can take you over there later—"

"I want to see her *now.*"

Matt had no desire to let this poisonous woman anywhere near the ranch, so he opened his cell and called his mother. "I'll have my mom bring her into town. I'm sure Carly Spencer, who was a neighbor of your in-laws' and who's now staying at our family's ranch, would love to see them before they go to Miami with you."

When his mother answered, Matt said, "Hi, Mom. Would you mind bringing Molly to my office? The Polinskis want to collect her here. Bring Carly, too, because Mr. and Mrs. Polinski will be taking his parents back to Miami on this afternoon's flight."

"What's she like?" Sarah asked. Matt stayed silent. "I see. Carly and I will be there in twenty minutes. Bye."

As it turned out, they were a good thirty minutes. Matt tried to engage Mr. Polinski's son in conversation, but he spent more time taking calls on his cell phone in the corridor than talking to Matt.

Desperate to convince them to leave Molly in Colorado, Matt searched his desk drawers for a brochure he'd received from the Twilight Years last week.

He gave it to Jasmine Polinski. "If you'd prefer, your parents-in-law could stay in Colorado," he said. "We have an excellent retirement home right here in Spruce Lake. I know they allow residents to keep their dogs there. They've just completed some excellent independent living units that would be perfect for your parents-in-law."

Jasmine Polinski sniffed with distaste. "And who do you think is going to pay for this?"

"Your mother-in-law told me they own several investment properties," Matt said. Although why they'd spend their retirement years renting an apartment in a run-down old building, he was at a loss to understand.

"They can't be sold!" she snapped.

"Why not?" Matt asked reasonably, knowing the answer. The older Polinskis had said something about the properties being tied up in a family trust. Matt had the uneasy feeling they were being used as collateral for the younger Polinskis' investments—and lifestyle.

"If your parents-in-law could liquidate some assets to help make their retirement more comfortable *and* keep

Molly with them, surely that would be a solution agreeable to all of you?"

"I told you the other day. They're coming to live in Miami, and the dog is going to be sold."

She was nothing if not forthright about her plans for Molly. Matt had gotten to the point where he'd decided strangulation would be too good for the woman.

"And do Mr. and Mrs. Polinski know that?"

"Not yet, but since they don't have anywhere else to go, they'll just have to suck it up."

"Excuse me?"

The woman leaned over Matt's desk and spoke in a low, threatening tone as she tapped a long fingernail on his blotter pad. "Listen, *Sheriff,* we're taking my husband's parents back to Miami with us. What happens to them, or their dog, when they leave this Podunk town is none of your business."

"Is it your husband's business?"

"He does as he's told!"

Matt sat back in his chair to put as much physical space between Jasmine Polinski and himself as possible. "Mrs. Polinski, I'm surprised you don't want Molly staying with them at your house. She's a lovely dog and wouldn't be any trouble."

"Because, *Sheriff,* they won't be staying in our house. They're going to the retirement trailer park!"

Bingo! "And they don't allow dogs?" Matt didn't believe that for a moment. "Then wouldn't it be preferable to have your parents-in-law move into a perfectly nice retirement home here, in a community they love?"

"Like I said, who's going to pay for it?"

"You'd rather drag them across the country and set them up in a trailer in Miami? Because it's *cheap?*"

"We all need to economize in these difficult times."

"Y…es," Matt said slowly, taking in her designer outfit and then gazing pointedly at her fur coat. "We certainly do."

When Sarah arrived with Carly and Molly, things went from bad to worse. Molly looked, and smelled, as if she'd been rolling in something unmentionable. Jasmine Polinski screeched with horror when Molly waddled in wagging her tail and rubbed her fat little body against her leg.

"Get that mongrel away from me!" she cried.

Molly growled at the insult and bared her teeth. Then she latched onto Mrs. Polinski's fur coat and, with a fierce shake of her head, wrestled it off her shoulders and onto the floor.

The behavior was so uncharacteristic of Molly that Sarah, Matt and Carly were too shocked to react quickly enough.

Jasmine Polinski lashed out, kicking Molly viciously in the ribs with the pointed toe of her expensive boots.

Molly howled in pain. Sarah kicked Mrs. Polinski in the shin and Carly dropped to the floor to comfort Molly.

"I want that dog put down!" Jasmine Polinski screamed. "And I want this woman charged with assault!"

Although Matt had been appalled at his mother's reaction, he wasn't sure he wouldn't have done the same thing.

"First, we don't euthanize dogs who bite fur coats. Second, I *could* charge this woman with assault," Matt said, mirroring the woman's tone of voice and earning a glare from his mother.

"But before I do that, I'm going to charge *you* with animal cruelty, which in this county is a far greater crime."

He picked up his phone and said, "I'm calling our animal cruelty officer to come down here and take witness statements. Then I'm arresting you."

*"You can't arrest me!"*

"I can, and I will," he said to her, and then into the phone, "Can you come to my office for a moment? I have an animal cruelty case for you."

"What's going on?" George Polinski asked from the doorway. Apparently, he'd finally found time to attend to his parents.

Jasmine dragged her husband into the room and slammed the door shut. "He wants to arrest me!"

"Your wife assaulted an innocent animal," Matt explained. "That carries a heavy penalty. I'm presently waiting for an officer from animal cruelty to come and take statements from the witnesses."

Jasmine Polinski pointed her bloodred, perfectly manicured index finger at Sarah. "That woman *kicked* me!"

"Only because you kicked Molly first," Sarah retorted. "What sort of person are you to abuse a harmless animal?"

"She's ruined my fur coat!"

"You have no business wearing the fur of a wild animal on your back!" Sarah yelled.

His office was starting to sound like a playground, but Matt was loath to stop his mother from venting her spleen. Animal cruelty was unforgivable, and his mom was more than a match for any designer-clad harpy from the East Coast.

"I'm going to make sure the animal cruelty officer knows *exactly* what you did to Molly. There's no way he'll let her leave this town with you, you lous—"

"Thank you, ladies, that'll be enough yelling for now.

If you keep it up, you'll have the prisoners over in the county jail wanting to join the fray."

"Yeah!" Sarah said. "But since she'll be there with them in a couple of minutes, they won't need to come over here."

Jasmine Polinski paled beneath her makeup. Carly concluded she must have watched some of those prison-reality programs on TV.

"Do you strip-search prisoners?" Carly asked Matt.

Obviously guessing where she was going, he nodded. "Oh, yeah."

"That's barbaric." Carly covered her mouth to hide her grin of delight.

Matt shrugged. "Gotta be done, I'm afraid. Can't tell what people have hiding on, or *inside,* them."

"But…but I haven't got anything hidden on *me!*" Jasmine insisted.

Matt grinned wolfishly, his lips pulling back over his teeth. "That's what they all say. In fact, the prisoners who protest the most are generally the ones who're hiding something. They get searched, from top to bottom…." He let the last word hang in the air. "Sometimes two, even three times."

Carly enjoyed watching the emotions on the woman's face. She'd gone from arrogant to incensed to horrified in a matter of minutes.

There was a knock at the door.

"That will be the animal cruelty officer," Matt said.

"Wait! Don't let him in yet," Jasmine Polinski demanded.

"If you want to make a full confession, that's fine, but you'll still be charged and incarcerated," Matt warned.

"Might take a while to get you bailed. Could be the judge won't give you bail. I did tell you this county looks very unfavorably on animal cruelty, didn't I?"

"*Do* something!" she implored her husband.

"Like what? Seems you're going to be locked up for the night, my dear."

Carly wanted to cheer George Polinski. Maybe he had a backbone, after all.

Jasmine bent and fished around in Matt's wastebasket and came up with a crumpled brochure for the Twilight Years. She thrust it at her husband.

He glanced at it and said, "You have to be over fifty-five to live here. I don't think it's an alternative to jail."

"For your parents, you idiot!" she snapped, then looked at Matt. "If I...*we* agree to place his parents in this place, will you drop the charges?'

"It's not my call. Animal *cruelty...*"

"*Please?*" she begged.

"It's up to your husband. Would he prefer to see you behind bars? Or his parents living out the rest of their lives—with Molly—in the Twilight Years?"

All eyes in the room swung to George Polinski.

He took a good long time making up his mind.

"George! So help me, I'll..."

"You'll what?" George asked. He clearly liked having the upper hand for once.

She stomped her expensively booted foot.

"Considering the circumstances, Sheriff," George said, returning his attention to Matt, "and the fact that our lawyer charges like a wounded bull, it would probably be cheaper to place my parents in the Twilight Years— should that be their wish—than pay to defend my wife's actions with regard to Molly." At this point he looked down at the dog for the first time and frowned. "What's that muck all over her?" he asked.

Carly scrambled to her feet and rubbed her hands on the seat of her jeans. "It's engine grease. Molly's taken to running around with the ranch dogs, but she went under a tractor—a parked one," she hastened to point out, "and got covered in engine grease. I've been trying to wash it off all morning."

"I see," he said, then looked back at Matt. "I'll call the Twilight Years, and provided they have a vacancy for my parents, I'd be very grateful if you'd drop the charge pending against my wife."

"And if they don't have space for them?" his wife demanded, and then seemed to realize that was a very stupid question, given her tenuous situation. "I mean, of course they'll have room for them. In fact, I'm sure they'd look very favorably on a generous donation to take them off our hands."

Tears of laughter had flowed down Sarah's and Carly's cheeks after they'd returned to the ranch and told everyone present what had happened in Matt's office. Will had whooped with joy as he imagined Matt lying with a completely straight face. Even Luke had cracked a smile.

"So the Polinskis are moving into their new home at the Twilight Years as we speak," Sarah said.

"And Molly's staying here for a few days while they get settled," Carly finished.

"And you're going to wash off that disgusting mix of engine grease and cow manure you rubbed all over her, Will," his mother said sternly, then smiled and patted his cheek. "Actually, that was such a stroke of brilliance, I think I'll wash her for you."

"I'll help!" said Alex.

Carly had loved watching all the children's faces as she and Sarah had related the story of pretentious Jasmine Polinski and her brush with the law—and a very dirty dog. She was only sorry Adam wasn't there to share in the fun.

Later that afternoon, Carly took a trip to the supermarket to do some shopping for Sarah. While waiting to be served in the deli section, she experienced the same weird prickle up her spine that she'd felt the day of the fire and the other night at the ranch.

She spun around and came face-to-face with Jerry Ryan.

"Carly! I wondered if that was you."

Carly was so flabbergasted, it took her a moment to regain her senses.

"What are you doing here, Jerry?" she demanded, unable to hide her shock—or her dismay.

"Is that any way to greet an old friend? Come on, give me a kiss, it's been ages!"

Without waiting for Carly to kiss him—not that she'd intended to—he took hold of her shoulders, kissed her cheek and pulled her into a hug.

Startled, Carly had remained frozen in his embrace. She needed to get out of this without spending too much time with Jerry. Certainly not enough time for him to question her about what she'd been up to and where she was living now.

She plastered a smile on her face and drew back. "It's such a surprise to see you here, Jerry. I didn't know you skied."

"Decided it was time to learn, so... I ended up here."

In exactly the same town she was living in? Carly

fought to control her racing pulse. There was no way he'd *accidentally* found her here. Carly was sure of it. She'd deliberately avoided telling him about the job in Denver. After the hotel was firebombed, she hadn't even told her parents where she'd relocated. Until last week....

"So how've you been? How are the kids?"

Carly had no intention of saying anything about the fire; he'd go all protective on her. Probably insist on taking her and the kids back to San Diego to live with him. *Not* what she wanted!

"Great! We love living in the mountains."

"You were going to email and tell me where you'd moved in Denver so I could come and visit."

She had *not* mentioned him visiting! "I'm sorry, I've been so busy with work, getting the kids settled in school…" She shrugged. "Stuff like that."

"I thought your new job was in Denver. What are you doing here?"

This was starting to feel like an interrogation. And Jerry was standing way too close. She took a step back, bringing the shopping basket up to rest in front of her, and said, "It didn't work out."

Just as she was wondering how she could get away from him before he asked where she was living now, Jerry threw her an unexpected lifeline.

"If you're not busy, we could go and have a coffee."

"Actually, I *am* busy." Carly waved Sarah's shopping list beneath his nose. "I'll have to take a rain check."

"When? Dinner tonight?"

Hell, no! Carly shook her head. "I'm sorry, I can't get a sitter on such short notice."

"I could bring takeout to your place."

Did this guy never give up? Carly could feel the walls

of the supermarket closing in on her. She had to get out of there, had to get away from Jerry.

"I don't think that's a good idea. I'm… I'm seeing someone."

She saw the glint of jealousy in Jerry's eyes before he managed to get his emotions under control. "That's great! Who is he? Maybe I should check him out for you. Don't want my best bud's widow being duped by some shyster."

"I'm old enough to take care of myself, Jerry. But thanks for the offer…."

Adam watched from a distance as Carly spoke to the other man. When she'd kissed him, he'd experienced a jealousy that went bone-deep and left his guts burning.

He'd come to the supermarket with a couple of the other guys on duty to shop for tonight's dinner. Rounding the end of the deli aisle, he'd spotted Carly and had been about to approach her when the other guy had walked up.

Curious, he'd tried to gauge the relationship between them, but finally curiosity got the better of him.

"Carly!"

Carly turned toward the voice calling her name. Adam! Thank goodness. She'd never been so relieved to see anyone in her life.

"Hi," he said, coming up to her. He looked gorgeous in his uniform, Carly thought. Real hero material. Funny how Jerry's uniform and even Michael's had never affected her that way.

"Hello, Adam," she said a little coolly, not wanting to alert Jerry to the fact that Adam was the man she was "seeing."

No one else needed to be dragged into her private affairs. She'd left San Diego behind two months ago, and as soon as she got out of this store, Jerry would be history. She refused to *ever* let him surprise her again.

"Who are you?" Jerry demanded rudely. Carly could practically see the hackles rising on the back of his neck.

Adam crossed his arms. "I'm—"

"He's the son of a good friend of mine," Carly cut in. Jerry's obsession with her gave Carly the uneasy feeling that if he knew Adam was more to her than just the son of a friend, it wouldn't end well for Adam.

Her eyes begged his forgiveness. He resisted for a moment and then backed down, offering his hand to Jerry. "Adam O'Malley. And you are?"

Jerry stared at his hand as if debating whether to shake it or put Adam in a headlock.

"Jerry Ryan. I'm a *very* close friend of Carly's from San Diego," Jerry said. "Now if you'll excuse us, we have some catching up to do," he said dismissively.

"Funny, she never mentioned you," Adam said, and Carly nearly groaned.

"Adam, you and I hardly know each other. Why would I discuss my private affairs with you?" She regretted the word *affairs* as soon as she'd uttered it.

Adam seemed about to argue.

Carly needed to get out of there and fast. The sliced roast beef she was supposed to get from the deli could wait for another day.

"It was nice seeing you both," she said. "But I have things to do." She turned to Jerry. "Have a wonderful holiday, Jerry. Bye."

Without giving him the chance to respond or swoop in for a goodbye kiss, Carly strode through the deli department, her head bent as she pretended to examine

Sarah's shopping list. She didn't take a breath until she'd gone through the checkout and was seated in Sarah's car.

Adam returned to the ranch after his forty-eight-hour shift at the firehouse, but he was acting strangely. He was avoiding her, Carly decided. Probably upset about the confrontation in the supermarket.

Seeing Jerry had unnerved her. So much so that she'd decided it would be better to keep her distance from Adam—at least until Jerry had left town. Although how long that might be, she had no idea. Like Adam, he worked a two-day-on, four-day-off cycle. He could be here another three days, or even longer, if he really *was* on vacation.

Carly's appointment book was full. One of her clients was the mayor's wife, Edna Farquar, a friend of Sarah's. She had a massage booked twice a week, mostly to work on her neck and shoulders. From what Carly could tell, much of her tension was caused by the mayor's pet pig, Louella.

Carly remembered the sight of the pig at the fire, trotting around in red rubber booties as if she owned the place. She seemed very attached to Will, but when Carly had questioned Becky about it, she'd shuddered and suggested they change the subject.

She smiled at the memory of Louella planting a wet kiss on Adam as he lay on the stretcher. Adam didn't seem too fond of Louella, either. However, Carly would be meeting her in person—so to speak—tomorrow as Will was entertaining Louella and all the children at the ranch.

Will and Becky had an interesting marriage; Will was

a stay-at-home dad, while Becky worked as a county judge. Will seemed happy to take on the responsibility of caring for Carly's children as well as his own and Luke's three daughters. He was a born nurturer and, according to Alex, had a lot of activities planned for them the following day. He was also helping the children make and wrap a special gift for their grandfather Mac's birthday. The following day, with Adam's assistance, he was taking everyone skiing.

"Can I talk to you for a minute?"

Carly jumped at the sound of Adam's voice. She'd been so absorbed in thinking about Will, she hadn't noticed Adam's approach.

"Sure," she said with a smile, trying to keep it light.

Adam, having made the request, now seemed stuck for words. He cleared his throat, then ran his hand through his hair.

"How was work?" she asked, mostly to fill the conversation gap.

"Ah, fine. No serious fires."

"Good." Carly waited.

"Um…"

"Look, if you're going to say the other night on the porch was a huge mistake, Adam, that's okay with me. I feel the same way. So let's not draw it out. You're a great kisser, but I don't want to get involved with you."

Adam looked so completely poleaxed, Carly regretted her words almost as soon as they left her mouth.

"Ah…" He shook his head. "That wasn't what I wanted to talk to you about. I was going to say I need to speak to my family in private tonight, so if you don't mind, could you make yourself and your kids scarce?"

Now it was Carly's turn to feel—and no doubt look—poleaxed.

"O…kay," she said, feeling rebuffed. Adam could be positively blunt at times, and although she was aware of his abrupt manner, it still hurt. Why, Carly couldn't say, but after feeling so much a part of his family, she now sensed that Adam was trying to shut her out.

Angry with herself for caring so much and for letting her emotions show, she shrugged and laughed it off. "No hard feelings. Like I said, the other night was probably a mistake. I think we just got carried away with the moment."

Adam stared at her blankly, and she punched his shoulder lightly. "Lighten up, Adam." She winced inwardly as she said it.

He grunted and rubbed his shoulder. Without saying anything further, he strode toward the house, leaving Carly to wonder what he had to talk to his family about that was so important.

Adam was grateful that Carly had offered to have all the children over at the apartment. What he had to tell the family wasn't fit for their ears. Cody was taking advantage of the school break to stay at a family friend's ranch for a few days.

Adam was stunned by his family's reaction to his confession about who was really driving Rory's car the day he died. The wailing he'd expected from his mom, the abject disappointment he'd expected from his dad, the loathing from his brothers and their wives—it didn't happen. None of them showed less than their complete compassion, support and forgiveness. They were so understanding that Adam suspected Matt might have prepared them for the news. But Matt was a man of his word. He'd have kept Adam's confession to himself, taken it to his grave.

Once Adam had answered their questions and assured them that he'd spoken to Jennifer Bennett, Matt said, "I'm glad we're all here. I have some worrying news."

"What is it, darling?" Sarah asked, her attention diverted from Adam for the first time that evening.

Matt stood and paced the living room floor. "Arson experts investigating the apartment building fire have discovered a link to Carly."

"Well, of course there's a link to Carly!" his mother burst out. "She *lived* there!"

"Mom, calm down," Matt said. "You're going to have to listen and let me finish. I don't want to believe what I've been told, but arson investigators and cops deal in facts, and the fact is, Carly's been linked to two previous fires."

"No!"

"Mom!"

"Sorry. Go on, dear. I'll try to control myself."

"As we all know, her husband died in a warehouse fire in San Diego."

When everyone nodded, he continued. "Her name was also flagged in relation to the recent firebombing at the Colorado Grand Hotel. A few days after that, Carly moved to Spruce Lake. Then, just weeks later, the apartment building burned."

Silence descended on the room.

"You can talk now," Matt said into the silence. Then everyone started talking at once.

"That's complete B.S.!" Will said.

"I agree!" Sarah chimed in.

"This is surely just a coincidence?" Megan said.

"How unlucky can one person be?" asked Luke.

"You're saying that Carly is an arsonist and that she *deliberately* put her children's lives in danger?" Becky asked. "That's not possible. She adores those children."

Needing to put an end to any further speculation, Adam stood. "I'm going over there and I'm asking her about this."

Matt pushed him back down into his seat. "You'll do no such thing. Leave it to the officials to deal with any questioning."

"You can't think she's truly any threat," Sarah said. "Otherwise, you'd have arrested her...or something."

"The evidence is piling up, Mom. In a day or two they'll have their answer. I wanted to give you a heads-up."

"In the meantime, she's over there in that apartment, watching our kids," Luke pointed out.

Megan, Becky and Beth couldn't help jumping to their feet and racing to look out the living room window, toward the stables.

## Chapter 11

Carly stared out the apartment window, down at the ranch house. All the O'Malleys had arrived nearly an hour ago. Carly had done as Adam requested and made herself and her children scarce. Luke's girls and Nick had wanted to come, too, and all eight children were now watching a DVD, although Charlie was dozing off, unable to stay awake past his usual bedtime.

As she filled a glass of water at the sink, Carly thought she spotted something in the yard below. A movement. Like someone snooping around. Hesistant to disturb Adam's meeting with his family, she decided to investigate it herself.

"Sash, would you and Nick mind keeping an eye on the kids while I take a walk?" she asked. "I won't be long."

"Sure," the girl said. "If we have any problems, I'll ring the fire bell."

Carly knew the stables had several fire bells installed, one of them in the apartment. "That's not a good idea. Someone might think there really is a fire."

"Nah, we use it for all sorts of things. Calling people for dinner and stuff. I'll only ring it if someone's really acting up or whatever. You go enjoy your walk."

Carly thanked her and pulled on her ski jacket, snow boots and gloves.

"Lock the door after me, would you, Sash?" she asked, then stepped outside and waited to hear the lock click into place.

A few minutes later, Carly went down the stairs and out the back door of the stables, hoping to come up behind whatever, or whoever, she'd seen moving in the yard.

She knew it couldn't be one of the ranch hands, since all three were in town celebrating Chuck's forty-ninth birthday. Beth had told her she didn't expect them back for hours. The large cabin they shared was annexed to the rear of the stables. The ranch dogs slept there, too. This evening the cabin was in darkness.

Carly walked farther across the yard, then froze in her tracks at the sight of a fox near the corrals. It stopped and gazed at her, then loped off into the darkness. She shook her head. That must've been what she'd seen from the apartment.

Since foxes didn't scare her, Carly took a moment to breathe in the crisp night air. She turned away from the ranch house, not wanting anyone inside to see her in case they thought she was spying. Not that any of the O'Malleys would think that. Only Adam. He was so closed off, so suspicious of everything!

As she trudged through the snow and out into the paddocks, a thought occurred to her. Why hadn't the ranch's dogs barked when the fox was in the yard? They usually went crazy if any wildlife was around. Luke had told her that bears often came into the area looking for food, but since the ranch had a strict policy about not leaving trash out, the bears soon moved on. However, this was winter and the bears were hibernating.

Before she had a chance to ponder the dogs' silence any further, the fire bell rang shrilly. Carly whirled around, ready to chastise Sasha for ringing the bell over some minor transgression by one of the younger kids.

What she saw turned her blood to ice. The stables were on fire!

She took off toward it, her feet barely touching the ground, her heart pounding with fear for the children inside.

Just as she made it to the rear stable doors, she saw the front door of the ranch opening and people pouring out.

She reached for the pull cord to turn on the stable lights, but nothing happened. Surely the electricity wouldn't have cut out this soon?

"Alex?" she screamed into the cavernous stables as she scrambled toward the apartment stairs. "Jake, Maddy! Where are you?"

The sound of her voice was drowned out by the screams of horses, terrified by the smoke that was filling the stables, and the sound of splintering wood.

She didn't have time to register where that was coming from. The stables were lit by a small battery-operated emergency light near the front entrance. Those doors, closest to the house, were usually left open until everyone had turned in. Only the rear doors were kept closed.

Carly got to the bottom of the stairs leading to the

apartment at the same moment the children came tumbling down. "We're here!" Alex cried. "We're all okay!"

Carly hugged and kissed them all as Sasha brought up the rear, a sleepy Charlie in her arms. The same couldn't be said for Maddy and Celeste, who were alternately screaming and crying.

Carly threw an arm around each girl and followed Alex, Jake, Nick, Daisy and Sasha to the front of the stables.

The closed doors had been thrown open, and Adam stood there framed in the moonlight, smoke billowing into his face. He held an ax. "Why the *hell* did you lock the doors?" he yelled, and then pushed past her.

"Get the children to the house," Luke said, charging in behind him, followed by his brothers. Carly could see Luke doing a head count of the kids. "Dad's called 9-1-1."

Shepherding the coughing children outside, she found Becky, Beth and Megan crossing the yard with Mac. "Come inside where it's safe, Carly," Megan said. "The fire department will be here shortly."

But Carly needed to stay and help. She passed the crying girls to Becky and Beth. Assured that all the children were in safe hands, she turned back to the stables.

"Where are you going?" Mac demanded. "Get in the house!"

Carly had never heard Adam's father raise his voice, but she didn't stop to contemplate his manner, or the strange way Megan was looking at her.

"I'll help get the horses out."

"The boys and I will do it," Mac said, but his command was lost in the sounds of whinnying horses as Matt and Jack led two of the terrified animals out of the stables, their heads covered with blankets.

Needing to feel useful, Carly reached for their bridles. "I'll take care of them," she said.

She turned and bumped into Mac.

"I'll take them," he said, and grabbed their halters.

Carly pivoted to see Will carrying one of the ranch dogs in his arms. "They've been doped, Pop," he said, and placed the dog on the snow-covered ground, out of the way of horses' hooves and any danger, if the stables collapsed.

Beth appeared and took the halters of two more horses from Luke and led them toward the house, where Mac was tethering the first horses to the railing.

Adam was nowhere to be seen. Fearing he'd been caught in the fire, Carly plunged into the stables. Through the thick smoke, she could see him way in the back, hosing down the hay in the loft, while Jack was beating out flames. The hay blazed fiercely, sending sparks dancing up to the ceiling high above them and raining down on Adam and the horses still trapped in their boxes below.

Knowing there were at least a dozen horses still to be brought out, Carly wrapped her scarf over her nose. Her eyes burned as she opened the horse box closest to her. Finding it empty, she moved on.

She jumped as a horse kicked ferociously at the box she was passing. She glanced inside and recognized one of Luke's stallions. He'd warned her this one was ornery beyond belief. And now he was so terrified she could see the whites of his eyes through the gloom.

"Careful of him," Luke said, as he hurried by, taking two more of his precious mares to safety, followed by Matt leading their foals.

"There, boy," she murmured, carefully opening the door to his box and feeling along the wall for a rope to attach to his halter. The animal reared up in alarm. "I know, I'm scared, too," she said. "How about if you come with me?" she cooed, catching his halter and clipping the end of the rope onto it.

In the distance, above the sound of wood exploding and splintering as it burned, and the horses screaming in fear, Carly could hear sirens.

At last Adam would have more people to help him save the stables. But in the meantime, she had to save this horse. The only thing was, he wouldn't move! She tugged on the rope, but he backed up hard against the back of the box as if now that freedom was offered, he didn't want it.

"Damn it!" Carly growled. "Come on!"

She yanked the rope once more and the huge animal charged out of the stall, almost knocking her over. Carly recovered her footing before she hit the floor and held his rope more firmly. She closed the door behind her. Only yesterday, Daisy had been telling her that if horses were caught in a fire, they'd often run back to where they felt safe. Carly was thankful that she and Daisy had had that talk.

The headlights of the fire trucks were trained so they shone directly into the stables. Firefighters raced past her, armed with hoses and axes.

But the bright lights startled the stallion and he reared up. Carly stepped back, but not far enough or quickly enough. His front hoof glanced off her cheekbone and knocked her to the floor. Dazed, she lay there for a moment, recovering her breath.

The stables were suddenly silent, as if someone had hit the mute button during a very noisy action movie. She could see people rushing toward her, ready to help as the stallion reared up again. Determined to do this on her own, Carly staggered to her feet, clasped the halter in her left hand, pulled the stallion's head down and punched him in the nose. Shocked, he stopped tossing his head and stared down at her, nostrils flaring, hooves stamping the ground.

"Don't you ever do that again!" she roared, then wondered why she couldn't hear herself.

Luke grabbed the reins from her. His mouth was moving, but she couldn't hear him, either. She shook her head and yelled, "What?"

He gripped her elbow and led her and the horse out of the stables. The cold, clean air made Carly gasp and cough. She tore the scarf away from her nose and coughed some more. She still couldn't hear herself.

"I think I'm deaf!" she shouted at Luke.

He nodded and passed her to his father, who led her and the stallion to the house. He tethered the horse to the veranda railing beside several others and turned toward her. His lips moved.

"What?"

He leaned closer and yelled in her ear, "I told you to go in the house!"

"No way! I couldn't leave those animals to die!"

He leaned toward her again. "You don't have to yell at *me*. I'm not deaf. You are!"

Carly blinked at him. "I am?" she asked. Almost involuntarily she raised her hand to the side of her head and hit herself, as if that would restore her hearing. Her hand came away covered in blood. "I'm bleeding," she muttered.

"And you've got a huge shiner developing under your eye."

"What?"

Mac shook his head, then led Carly up the veranda steps and handed her over to Sarah. He said something to his wife as he released Carly and hurried back to the stables.

"I have to help them," she said, but Sarah ignored her. Believing Sarah not to have heard her, she screamed, "I have to help them!"

Sarah grabbed Carly's hand when she tried to go back down the steps and held on tight. "Leave it to the men," she yelled into Carly's ear. "You're hurt. Come inside."

"I'm fine! I can help the dogs. Someone's doped them!" She indicated Becky, collecting another dog from Will's arms and carrying it away from danger.

Carly was aware that she was shouting, but she wasn't sure how much Sarah could hear above the din that was coming from the stables and the railings where the horses were tethered, whinnying in fear. Daisy and Sasha were with them, trying to calm them down, soothing them with long, gentle strokes.

The ornery stallion was behaving himself, at least. Carly didn't know why she'd punched him like that; she'd only known she had to show him who was boss. She wanted to apologize to the horse, but she'd probably end up yelling at him and upsetting him more. Maybe when her hearing returned...

A paramedic approached her. She said something. Carly shook her head and pointed at her ears. "I can't hear!"

"You need to come inside so I can examine you!" she shouted into Carly's ear.

"Not until everyone's safe!"

She glanced back at the stables. The fire seemed to be

under control. No more flames were visible, but smoke still poured from the doorway.

She saw the doped dogs lying in the snow and did a quick count. They were all there. Thank goodness Molly had stayed in the house! she thought. Still standing on the porch she saw Luke and Jack leading four horses from the rear of the stables, from the door she'd slipped out of earlier that night to investigate what she'd seen moving in the yard.

"That's the last of the horses, Grandma," Daisy yelled up to Sarah as she set off across the yard to help her father bring them in. "They're all okay!"

A couple of firefighters started picking up the dogs and carrying them to the veranda. They were completely out of it, their tongues lolling out of their mouths, eyes unfocused.

Blankets were produced from the house and they were wrapped in them and taken inside to warm up.

Luke was attending to the horses, along with Matt and Mac. Will and Jack carried the remaining two dogs into the house.

Carly glanced toward the living room window and saw her children standing there, petrified. She waved to them to let them know she was fine. She should go to them and hold them and tell them yet again that everything was going to be all right. But they'd only worry more if she started yelling at them because she was half deaf. She'd give it a few minutes and then go see them.

Worried about Adam, she scanned the yard looking for him. He was the only one from his department who wasn't wearing protective firefighting gear. Was he okay?

She raced toward Matt. "Where's Adam? Is he out? Is he safe?"

He shook off her arm. "What do you care?" he shouted at her.

"What? What are you saying? I care a lot!" she screamed back, enraged by his attitude. "I haven't seen him since he first went in there!" Bewildered by his strange remark, Carly didn't immediately realize her hearing wasn't as bad as it had been minutes ago. She could actually hear herself. A little.

She dashed across the yard, counting the number of firefighters. There were two trucks, which meant eight firefighters. The battalion chief was there, too, but no sign of Adam.

"Where's Adam?" She grabbed the battalion chief's arm.

"Adam's in there?"

"Of course he is! He was using the fire hose in the stables!"

She released him and started for the stables, but the chief's arm shot out and held her back. "Let the men go in. It's too dangerous!"

"What?"

"Leave it to us!"

"No!" she cried, and broke out of his grip, running to where the smoke poured out the stable doors.

And then she saw him. He'd emerged from the damaged structure and was walking toward her.

She ran to him and threw her arms around his neck. "Oh, God! I thought you were dead!"

She felt rather than heard Adam's gruff laugh reverberate against her cheek.

He mumbled something, but she couldn't hear him. "You'll have to yell, I'm deaf!"

He smiled and nodded. His lips moved. Those lips she loved. "I love you!" she cried, and hugged him tighter.

Suddenly they were surrounded by children and adults and firefighters, and there was no chance to kiss Adam or talk anymore.

Finally, Carly released her grip on Adam. He began to embrace Carly again, but Charlie was clinging to his leg. He hoisted the toddler into his arms and perched him on his hip.

Tears streaked down Charlie's cheeks and Adam wiped them away with a grubby finger. "It's okay, little guy. Everyone's fine."

Charlie still clung to him, his grip even fiercer than Carly's.

Adam turned to Carly and said, "I saw you hit the horse. That was brave."

"What?"

"I *said,* I saw you take charge of the stallion. That takes real guts."

Carly grinned at him. "I have no idea what you're saying," she yelled. "I'm deaf!"

"And so will we all be," said his mom. "If we don't get her checked out by the paramedics."

The group moved toward the house but Adam stayed where he was. "I need to invite my buddies in when they've finished up here," he told his mother.

"Already done, darling," she said. "Megan's making coffee and sandwiches as we speak and we'll be taking them to the guys who have to stay out in the cold to investigate the cause of the fire."

Adam didn't miss Matt and his father exchanging a

glance. Surely they didn't think Carly was responsible for this fire, too? Or *any* fire!

He'd deal with the suspicions Matt had raised earlier in the evening, but not yet. For now, they all needed to get inside and warm. Although one thing kept playing on his mind: Who had locked the stable door? He'd had to break it down with an ax.

Once inside, Charlie allowed his mother to pry him away from Adam's neck and take him into the kitchen, which was full to overflowing with dogs, people and children. Carly's kids were mute with fear. He went over to them and sat down at the table. Maddy climbed up on his lap, shaking uncontrollably. He hugged her and spoke soothingly. Carly joined them holding Charlie, who had his thumb in his mouth and a soft toy clutched in his hand. She reached out to touch the back of Jake's head and draw him against her.

Carly's children seemed to relax a little once their mom was with them, but they'd been traumatized by the fire. His nieces, however, seemed to think it was all a big adventure—apart from Celeste, who was holding on tightly to Luke. Daisy was happily looking after the horses outside, trading shifts with her father and grandfather to check on them.

Adam noticed Molly curled up on his old blanket. She was obviously confused, frightened by all the commotion. He indicated to Alex and Jake that they should go and comfort her. Both sat on the floor with her; Alex lifted her head into his lap while Jake rubbed her back. As the other dogs started to come to, Jake went to comfort them.

The boys had inherited their mother's healing touch, Adam decided, as each of the dogs gradually regained consciousness and moved to the sheltering warmth provided by the two boys.

Luke unwound Celeste's arms from his neck and gave her to Megan. The child went willingly, clinging to her stepmother.

"Once everything's settled down in the yard," Luke said, "we'll take the machinery out of the shed and set up temporary stables in there for the horses. The dogs will spend the night in the kitchen. First thing in the morning, I'll rent a couple of mobile homes for the ranch hands. I've already called Chuck and told them to stay in town for the night."

He turned to Sasha. "I'm so proud of you, honey, for handling everything so calmly when you noticed the fire and rang the alarm bell and got all the children downstairs safely." He glanced at his nephew. "You, too, Nick. I know you gave the credit to Sash, but you're equally responsible."

He kissed the top of his daughter's head and shook Nick's hand as the teenagers beamed with pleasure. Then he hurried back out to the yard, followed by Cody, Matt and Will.

Adam chugged down the glass of water his mother had given him and wondered yet again why those stable doors had been locked from the inside and where Carly was when it all started.

He leaned toward her and said, "I need to talk to you."

"What?"

Since she was still suffering the effects of being kicked in the head by the stallion, Adam decided their talk could wait until Carly completely regained her hearing.

Sarah clapped her hands, attracting their attention and stopping any further conversation. "We need to rearrange the sleeping around here. Sash is going home with Becky and Will. You can have her room, Carly, if that's all right with you."

Carly looked at her blankly. Adam knew his mother would sort everything out, and make sure everyone was happy, whether Carly could hear her or not. "Carly can have Sash's room and share it with Charlie. We have a portable crib up in the attic that Adam will bring down for him. And there are a couple of spare mattresses up there that Matt and Jack can get for the boys and put in Sash's room. Maddy can share with Celeste…"

This brought screams of excitement from the two little girls, who jumped to their feet, clapped their hands and raced upstairs without further encouragement.

"Since Daisy insists on helping out with the horses, she'll sleep on the sofa so she can be closer to them during the night. Okay, battle stations!"

Sarah clapped her hands once more and everyone sprang into action. In spite of the circumstances, Adam couldn't help smiling. His mom liked nothing better than organizing people. To her, this was like a military campaign.

He doubted that in the light of morning, when the damage to the stables was finally revealed, she'd be quite so chirpy.

"What's happening?" Carly yelled in his ear.

"Mom's rearranging sleeping quarters, and the paramedics are going to take a look at you."

They did and insisted on driving Carly to the E.R. for a scan to rule out a cerebral hematoma or any other injury, but she refused to go until Charlie was asleep and the boys and Maddy were tucked in.

Adam had dismissed the paramedics, saying he'd make sure she got to the E.R.

But now Adam could feel his frustration levels rising as she kissed each of her children good-night and patted Charlie's bottom until he'd drifted off.

Megan had said she wouldn't be able to sleep for the rest of the night with Luke reorganizing the stabling of the horses and having to keep up an endless supply of warm drinks for the workers. She'd stay in Sasha's room and keep an eye on Charlie and the boys until Carly's return.

Finally, Carly decided she was ready to leave. Adam helped her into his SUV and headed for the gates leading out of Two Elk Ranch.

As they crossed the cattle grid, he turned to face her and said, "Matt thinks you're an arsonist."

## Chapter 12

"What?"

Adam realized she wasn't questioning his statement; she still couldn't hear properly. Carly also looked sleepy. The paramedics had been wary of leaving her behind, saying if she had a concussion, they should take her to the hospital immediately. But Carly was having nothing of it. Now Adam regretted not being more insistent that she drop everything and go straight to the hospital with them.

Was he supposed to keep her awake? "Carly? *Carly!*"

"Huh?" She snapped into wakefulness. "What's wrong?"

"You were falling asleep."

She frowned.

"Stay awake!" he yelled, and went back to concentrating on the road. He wanted to floor it, but that might jostle Carly too much and cause her more injury. He wanted her awake and alert when he asked her about those locked doors. Meanwhile, he tried to make the ride into the hospital in Silver Springs as smooth as possible.

*I love you.* Carly's words echoed in his mind. Had she meant them?

He'd sure liked hearing her say those three little words. But then again, if she was suffering from concussion, she probably had no idea what she was saying.

At the hospital, Carly was given a battery of tests and scans, then kept overnight for observation. Adam hadn't wanted to leave her, but he needed to get back to the ranch, to help clean up and restable the horses.

"Hey, Matt," Carly greeted him the following morning as he entered her hospital room. "Is everything all right at the ranch?"

An uneasy feeling crept up the back of her neck. Matt wasn't smiling.

The uneasiness turned into a heavy sense of alarm, settling deep in her stomach. Sarah had sounded a little strange when Carly called the ranch earlier to check that her children were fine and to say that she expected to be discharged in the next hour or so.

"Everyone's safe," he said, his voice abrupt.

"Then why the frown?" she asked, needing to clear the air.

"I don't want to have to do this," he said, "but here goes. Carly Spencer, I'm arresting you on the charge of arson in the first degree."

"What?" Carly's hearing had been gradually returning, but now she wasn't so sure of that. "What did you just say, Matt?"

"You have the right to remain silent," he said. "You have the ri—"

"Is this some kind of a joke?"

"You have the right to an attorney."

*"What?"*

This time the query came from Adam. Carly had been so transfixed by Matt's statement, she hadn't even noticed him entering the room.

Matt took a deep breath. "I'm sorry, Adam, but I'm arresting Carly for suspected arson. Four counts."

"Oh, come on!"

Matt turned back to Carly, all business. He looked so forbidding, she felt sick to her stomach. This couldn't be happening!

"I don't want to embarrass you by having to handcuff you, Carly. Will you come quietly?"

"No, she won't!"

"Adam, stay out of this and let me do my job," Matt growled. "Carly—"

But she was already climbing out of the bed and racing for the bathroom, wishing she hadn't eaten breakfast that morning.

She stumbled into the room, gripped the sides of the hand basin and threw up. The spasms seemed to last forever as her stomach surrendered its contents, and tears sprang to her eyes. Mortified, she ran water into the basin, then reached blindly for a towel.

One was placed in her hand, and a damp cloth was applied to the back of her neck, settling her churning stomach and taking away the urge to be sick again.

"It's okay," she heard Adam's soothing voice above the sound of the running water. "Hold on to me if you feel faint."

Carly wanted to weep at his kindness.

He turned her gently toward him and wiped her face with another damp cloth.

"Rinse out your mouth and I'll help you back to the room," he told her.

Confused, grateful, Carly obeyed, splashing water over her face and using the towel Adam had handed her to dry herself. She must look a mess—she sure felt like one—but Adam's dark eyes bored into hers, reassuring her and giving her the strength to return to the room where Matt waited to arrest her.

*Arson?*

Still shaky, she clutched Adam's arm as he helped her into the chair beside the bed. He stood beside her, a reassuring hand on her shoulder.

"Is she okay?" Matt asked his brother, as if she were incapable of speaking for herself.

"I'm…" She cleared her throat. "I'm fine," Carly said, gripping the arms of the chair. "But why on earth would you think *I* set that fire last night? My children were inside the apartment!" Her voice was shrill, but Carly didn't care. Now that she felt better, she was getting downright mad at Matt and his ridiculous accusation.

Matt took a seat in the other chair. "There are a number of reasons, Carly. First and foremost, you'd locked the stable door, preventing any of us from getting in to save the children and the horses."

Enraged, Carly sprang to her feet. "Kill my children! Are you *insane?* I didn't go *near* that door! What gives you such a stupid idea?"

Matt didn't flinch beneath her fury. "Sasha said you went out for a walk about ten minutes before the fire started."

Feeling light-headed, she resumed her seat. "That's correct. So?"

"You were the only person outside at the time. The rest of us were inside the house, talking to Adam. The kids were all upstairs in the apartment watching television. The ranch hands were in town for the night."

"Matt, that doesn't even make sense," Adam said. "What evidence do you have that Carly set the fire?"

"At present, it's mostly circumstantial. But in the past two years, Carly has been present at, or involved in, four sites that were the targets of arson attacks."

"What about the dogs?" Adam asked. "You think *Carly* drugged them?"

Matt sighed. "I don't know yet." He paused. "I was starting to explain to you all last night that the sheriff's department's been investigating the fire in the apartment building."

He turned to Carly to explain. "We have a national database into which we insert the names of fire victims and cross-reference links to other fires. It's mostly set up to deal with insurance fraud, but in this instance, it flagged you on three occasions, Carly." He glanced back at his brother. "Now four. However, I didn't get to finish what I was saying last night because the stable bell started ringing and we all ran outside to find it on fire."

Numb with shock, Carly could only sit there and listen to Matt. It was true; fire seemed to follow her everywhere.

Matt counted them off on his fingers. "The warehouse fire in San Diego that killed her husband. The firebombing of the Colorado Grand Hotel in Denver the night before it was due to open—"

"What the hell's that got to do with Carly?"

Carly finally found her voice. "I was about to start work in their spa."

Adam scowled at his brother. "Oh, come on, Matt! That's got to be a coincidence."

"Then there was the apartment building in town," Matt went on relentlessly. "Last night it was the stables. Next time it could be the ranch house."

"No! How can you think I'd do such a thing? How can you even *think* I'd hurt my children or anyone else?"

Matt shrugged, not meeting her eyes. "I don't know, Carly. We're also going to request a psychiatric assessment."

*"What the hell for?"* Adam and Carly spoke at once.

For the first time since he'd walked into the room, Carly detected compassion in Matt's eyes. "Because the court's going to ask why a mother would put her children at mortal risk."

"But I didn't!"

"I don't know anything much about psychiatric illnesses, Carly. Maybe you have some form of Munchausen's syndrome by proxy?"

Carly shook her head. "I feel as if I'm trapped in some sort of terrible dream that I'm hoping to wake up from. But I suspect I'm already awake and this nightmare *is* my life."

She got to her feet and said, "The sooner you arrest me and take me in for questioning, Matt, the better. I want to clear my name and help find the real arsonist."

"Admirable, but you won't be helping us do anything, Carly. You'll be behind bars."

"I have children! I can't stay in jail! Who'll look after them?"

"Arson is a very serious offence. The D.A. will be asking the judge for a very large bail amount."

Carly slumped back in the chair. "Bail?" she muttered, staring at the floor. "I don't have a cent to spare." She stared up at Matt. "I realize you're doing your job, Matt. But do *you* honestly think I'm an arsonist?"

Matt took his time answering. "I hope not, Carly. I want to believe you aren't, but we're talking about people's lives here. Every time there's been a fire, you haven't had a viable alibi."

"Oh, Matt." Carly couldn't restrain the disappointment in her voice. In the short while she'd known him, she'd gauged Matt to be rock-steady, not the type of person to believe in hearsay and coincidence. "What alibis?"

"You claimed you were out shopping when the warehouse in San Diego went up. Yet you couldn't produce any receipts when asked."

"I didn't *claim* anything! I *was* shopping!"

"Let me finish please, Carly," Matt said. "You left your children with a sitter at your home in Denver and went out. During your absence, the hotel was firebombed.

"You told investigators you were working at the day spa in Spruce Lake the day of the fire in the apartment building, yet records show you'd left there nearly an hour earlier."

Carly opened her mouth to explain she'd gone grocery shopping, but Matt held up his hand.

"And last night, you conveniently went for a walk ten minutes before the fire broke out."

Carly's lips thinned. To think she'd liked Matt once upon a time. Now he was sounding like some sort of crazed, redneck law enforcer, ready to round up a posse and hang her from the highest tree!

"First, when Michael's superintendent told me about the warehouse fire and...and that he was missing, I dropped everything and drove like a maniac to the scene of the fire." She could feel her voice breaking at the memory. "So of course I didn't have any sales receipts! Neither did I have the items I bought. They were *dropped* somewhere on the streets of San Diego. Check your records.

"Three days after the fire and my husband's *death*—" she paused to let him absorb that "—I was questioned by the authorities as to my whereabouts at the time of the fire. It was only then that I realized I didn't have my wallet. Or my shopping. I'd driven straight to the scene, was told my husband had died and I collapsed. I was a basketcase for days afterward. People were coming and going, taking care of me and my children, so I hadn't needed to buy any food, or anything else for that matter. Once I realized what I'd done, I reported my credit cards missing and applied for another driver's license, ID and so on." She looked at him pointedly. "There'll be proof of that in the official records."

Matt nodded, but Carly wasn't sure he entirely believed her. "I was seven months pregnant, Matt. I was in so much shock, I nearly lost Charlie. The last thing I was worried about was some dumb shopping!"

Adam squeezed her shoulder and she reached for his hand, needing his touch. She smiled up at him, but Adam was glaring so hard at his brother, he missed it.

Carly returned her attention to Matt, determined to clear her name. "Second, yes, I'd left the children with a sitter while I went out to purchase some supplies in Denver. I'd be working during my older children's school hours and wanted to make up some dinners to freeze, so I'd have time to help them with their homework when they got home."

That sounded pretty thin even to her ears, yet it was exactly what she'd done.

"You moved to Spruce Lake within days of the Denver fire."

"Yes! I needed a job, since I no longer had one in Denver. The owner of the building I was living in offered me an apartment in Spruce Lake at a discounted rate, since it was slated to be demolished next summer. I wanted to get away from the city, start over in a small town, someplace where people cared about one another. I found a part-time job at the day spa, and I liked living in that apartment building. The rent was affordable, the neighbors were wonderful. I love Spruce Lake and thought I had a future here. Why would I jeopardize such an opportunity by setting fire to my home?"

"That's one of the things we're hoping the psych evaluation will tell us."

Too angry to protest, Carly could only close her eyes and shake her head. Eventually, she felt strong enough to open her eyes again and say, "I'll come quietly, Matt. But please, no handcuffs."

# *Chapter 13*

"I saw something moving outside and went to investigate," Carly said.

Matt exchanged a look with Adam.

They were sitting in the interrogation room at the sheriff's department in Spruce Lake. Carly's lawyer, Mike Cochrane, was present, as was Adam—at her request.

"I was hardly going to alarm the kids and say I thought there was a prowler in the yard, was I?"

"And was there?"

"No, it turned out to be a fox."

"What did you do then?"

"I walked away across the paddocks that are closest to the stables."

"We found your footprints in the snow," Matt confirmed.

"Then did you find the footprints of whoever set the fire?" Carly asked, hopeful.

Matt shook his head. "The snow around the stables was trampled. People have been walking all around that area, and it was impossible to distinguish one footprint from another."

"Just my luck," Carly muttered.

"So you walked away from the stables?"

"Yes, I slipped out the rear door, because I didn't want any of you seeing me from the house."

Matt's eyes narrowed in suspicion. She held up her hand. "I didn't want you seeing me and thinking I was snooping around, trying to listen in on the meeting Adam had called with his family. He'd made it seem so personal and acted pretty abrupt when he asked me to make myself scarce earlier in the day."

"I'm sorry, Carly," Adam said. "I hadn't meant to sound like that when I talked to you, but I had a lot on my mind. I needed to confess something very personal to them first."

"First?"

"I was going to tell you afterward."

"You're talking in riddles, Adam. Tell me *what?*"

"He'll tell you later," Matt interrupted. "Right now we need to get this interrogation over and done with."

Carly dragged her eyes from Adam. "Okay, then let's get it *over and done with,* so I can get back to my kids," she snapped. She rarely snapped at anyone, but this farce had gone on long enough. "I had Sasha lock the apartment door from inside. Then I went out the back door of the stables. I left it unlatched so I could get back in that way. At no time did I lock the front stable doors."

Matt nodded. "Go on."

"I noticed the fox, realized that must've been what

I'd seen, so I walked a little farther into the paddocks to get some fresh air."

"There was a fox around and you kept on walking— away from the protection of the buildings?" Matt asked, incredulity dripping from his voice.

"I'm not afraid of foxes," she said, squaring her shoulders. "And I'm pretty sure if there'd been a wolf pack nearby, I would've heard them."

"That's risky thinking," Matt pointed out.

"I wasn't intending to go far and, like I said, I wanted to get some fresh air," Carly stated. It had been the secretive way the creature had moved that had caused her to investigate. Then she'd seen the fox and, knowing they move stealthily, she'd stopped worrying about a potential prowler.

She decided it was pointless to explain that to Matt again. "I was about to turn back when I heard the bell ringing," she continued. "I saw that the stables were on fire and ran like hell. The horses were going crazy in their stalls, but right then I just wanted to get to my kids. Luckily Sasha and Nick had collected everyone and started downstairs. I met them at the bottom of the staircase."

She glanced at Adam. "It was about then that I heard someone breaking down the front stable doors." She paused. "I'd heard the noise when I first entered, but as I said, the only thing I focused on was getting to my children. Later I discovered that the sound of splintering wood was Adam breaking down the door with an ax."

She paused again. "I remember something else."

Everyone in the room leaned forward.

"Yes?" Matt prompted when she didn't elaborate.

Carly held up her hand. "I'm trying to remember exactly when I realized this. Give me a few seconds." She ran through the events of the evening, starting with the moment she'd first walked outside.

"I was in the paddock walking away from the house, when I realized the dogs weren't barking and hadn't barked while the fox was around. I know they do that when strangers or wildlife are close by because Megan warned me about it."

She glanced over at Adam. "That's the reason I turned back to the stables. I knew something was wrong. It was at that same moment that the bell began to ring."

"But someone doped the dogs," Adam said.

Carly nodded and turned to Matt. "But how did he get to the dogs to dope them in the first place without the dogs kicking up a fuss? I heard nothing while I was upstairs."

"Because whoever doped them was probably familiar to them," he said.

"And you're assuming that was me?"

He shrugged. "Like I said, the ranch hands were in town, the rest of us were in the house. You were the only adult not accounted for."

"Do you know how *stupid* and downright *irrational* that sounds?" Adam demanded of his brother.

"I can only go with the evidence."

"Yes, all of it circumstantial!" Adam sprang to his feet and grabbed Carly's hand. "Did it occur to you that it would be easy to dope a dog if you offered it a steak? The dogs were barking earlier, then they quieted. None of us went out to investigate!"

"He's got a point, Matt," Mike Cochrane said. "It wouldn't be hard to coax a dog with some meat. They'd swallow it whole."

"Let's get out of here," Adam said, pulling Carly to her feet.

Startled, Carly complied. She'd never had a truer champion. And right now, she'd rather be anywhere than here. Right now, she'd go wherever Adam wanted.

"Sit down!" Matt growled.

Carly glanced at Mike Cochrane and he nodded. Reluctantly, she resumed her seat. Even more reluctantly, she withdrew her hand from Adam's grasp.

"Adam, I'd like you to leave the room," Matt said, his voice low and threatening. "You're confusing Carly and clouding the severity of the matter. She's been charged with arson. In a few minutes we're going over to the courthouse where the D.A. is waiting to arraign her. Unless Carly can raise a substantial amount of bail, she'll be going to jail indefinitely."

"I haven't got any money for bail!"

"Then your children will be placed with protective services until your trial da—"

*"No!"* Carly cut him off. "How can you be so *inhuman?"* she demanded as tears filled her eyes.

Carly felt close to the breaking point. The past year and a half, after Michael's death, had been a living hell. The fight for the insurance payout, the decision to move from San Diego to get away from the unwanted attentions of Jerry Ryan and the peripatetic lifestyle she'd been forced to live since then—everything was all piling up, drowning her. And now to be falsely accused of arson?

"Believe me, Carly, I'm not trying to be, but I have to remain impartial. This is how we treat people who commit a serious crime and who can't pay the bail."

"I'll sell my house in San Diego!"

"I'm sorry, Carly, but posting a property bond is rarely

done. So until you can sell your house, or post a bond through a bail agent—which, by the way, will cost you a minimum of ten percent of bail and in this case, it could be around fifty thousand dollars—you'll be in jail. And your children will be taken from you."

"Dammit, Matt!" Adam sprang to his feet and grabbed his brother by the collar, his right arm raised to punch him.

Matt refused to stand, refused to react to his brother's challenge. He sat there immovable, staring at Carly.

Adam eventually released him and paced the room. "What if I can raise the bail?" Adam said.

"Can you?"

"I don't know. How much would it be?"

"A lot more than you have. Probably more than you can borrow from a bondsman."

Adam sat down again and caught Carly's hand. "Whatever the outcome, I *won't* let them take away your kids and put them in a stranger's home."

Carly wanted to kiss him. But Matt's next words left her cold.

"I'm afraid you can't prevent any of this, Adam."

"I can, if I take her kids."

Three pairs of eyes turned in his direction. Mike shook his head, Matt snorted with derision and Carly gasped with relief.

"No can do. You're not registered with the department. And the security checks and hoops you'd have to jump through to get approval would take longer than her trial," Matt said.

Adam turned to Mike for confirmation that what his brother stated was true. His shoulders fell when the attorney nodded.

Carly was sobbing and it was breaking Adam's heart. Okay, so he had no experience with kids, but neither did most men before they became fathers.

Carly's kids didn't deserve this. They'd been devastated when they lost their dad. Their lives had been turned upside down with too many moves these past few months. And they'd been completely traumatized by being caught in the middle of two fires. The one constant they'd been able to rely on was their mom. And now she was going to be taken away from them. He couldn't let her kids be thrown into foster care. Who knew what might happen to them? He guessed they probably wouldn't be placed in the same home. He also knew it could be months, maybe a year, before Carly's case came to court.

He couldn't imagine the trauma it would cause the children to be separated from one another and from their mother for that length of time. There was only one way to stop it.

"They won't be going to live with any stranger," he said to Matt, "because they'll be coming home with me."

"And I told you that can't happen."

"It can if I'm their father."

*"What?"* Carly, Matt and Mike demanded at once.

Adam turned to Carly, realizing he hadn't asked her what she thought of all this, but the tears in her eyes gave him the determination to go through with it.

Still holding Carly's hand, he stood abruptly, then bent a knee to touch the floor. "Carly, will you marry me?" he asked.

## Chapter 14

Silence filled the room.

Carly even managed to stop sobbing, but before she could answer him, Matt roared, *"Are you completely crazy?"*

Matt stood abruptly, launching into a tirade as he paced the room. "Carly's been involved in four fires in the past eighteen months, Adam. *She is going to jail.* Even if she somehow gets off, do you want a suspected arsonist living with you? Risking your life? Your home? Your family's lives?"

"That's enough!" Adam roared back at his brother, and stood, too. He kept Carly's hand firmly clasped in his.

"Carly is innocent. I'm convinced of it and I don't want to hear any more about this from you, of all people!"

Adam paused for a heartbeat, needing to get his temper under control. Unfortunately, that gave Matt the chance to further state his protests to Adam's marrying Carly.

"Adam, you're thinking with the wrong part of your anatomy. You're in lust, in thrall, in love, whatever! But you are *not* thinking straight. You can't marry Carly to save her. You can't marry her to stop her kids from being taken away. You can't marry her—"

"Excuse me?" Carly said, getting their attention. They stopped staring at each other and were now staring at her.

"Since this involves me more than it does you, Matt. I'd like to say something."

Matt nodded brusquely. Adam was so riled up, he couldn't wait to get Matt back at the ranch and give him the bloodiest nose he'd ever had.

"Contrary to what you might both think, I do have a brain and it functions independently of yours. So please don't talk about me as if I'm not here."

Carly waited while both men took that in.

She released Adam's hand and looked directly into his eyes. "Adam, thank you for the proposal. I appreciate it very much and I understand why you're doing it. I'm indebted to you for caring so much about my children that you'd make such an offer."

She turned to Matt. "I'm going to accept your brother's proposal and there's not a thing on God's green earth or in the state of Colorado that can stop me. I will do *anything* to ensure my children's safety and if that means marrying a man who doesn't love me, then I will."

"Who said I don't love you?" Adam asked.

"You've never said you do," Carly told him.

"I… I," Adam started to say, but Carly shook her head.

"It's okay, Adam. We hardly know each other. Once all this is over, we can get a divorce, move on with our lives."

"Thank you," Adam said with a smile that made her love him even more. "But what if I don't want a divorce?"

Carly's heart overflowed with something for this man, but was it love? Or gratitude? "You? One of Spruce Lake's most eligible bachelors, with a wife and four children? I don't think so."

"You got that right," Matt muttered.

Adam took a step toward his brother but Carly placed a hand on his chest. "Let's not add 'assaulting an officer of the law' to the mix. It could affect your custody of my children."

"You'd grant him custody of your kids?" her attorney asked.

"Of course I would. I trust Adam implicitly. He's proven himself to me time and time again, starting with the day he saved my son from the apartment fire. I can't see the court denying custody to a hometown hero."

Adam coughed, bringing her attention back to him.

"About that. We need to talk," he said.


At Adam's request, Matt had granted him the use of his office, posting a deputy outside the door.

Adam paced the room, not sure where to begin. Finally, he stood facing Carly, who'd sat on Matt's sofa. "I've been carrying something around with me for a very long time. It's affected my life, my relationships, everything."

"Does it have anything to do with your reaction to the massage I gave you the other day?" Carly asked.

"Everything," he said, and pulled up a chair in front of her.

"When I was fifteen, my best friend, Rory Bennett, and I went for a joyride. Rory stole a pickup truck and I drove it. Being fifteen I was full of bravado and showing off. I took a corner too fast and smashed into a tree. Neither of us was wearing a seat belt. I got thrown through the window. Rory was scrabbling around on the floor trying to find a CD he'd dropped. He was jammed in the cab, crushed to death."

"Oh, Adam," Carly said, and clasped his hands.

He bowed his head. "Please, let me finish."

"Of course."

Adam looked up; he could read the compassion in her eyes and loved her for it.

"I was in a coma for nearly a week. When I came out of it, Rory's funeral had already taken place. Because of the position of his body in the cabin of the truck, the cops concluded he'd been driving. I was a scared, stupid, cowardly fifteen-year-old and I never said a word."

"But why? Surely you were too young to be arrested?"

"I don't know about that. But my big brother was with the sheriff's department. He had his career all mapped out. How would it look if his brother was arrested for vehicular homicide? How would it affect my family, to know I'd killed my best friend? So I kept quiet."

Carly lifted her hand to his cheek. "And you've been carrying around this guilt for all these years?"

Adam leaned into her palm, needing the closeness, needing her warmth and reassurance. He wasn't sure what love felt like, but for the first time, he'd met a woman he didn't want to be parted from. A woman he wanted to spend the rest of his life with.

"I suspected you'd been holding something in that day I gave you a head massage. In fact, I suspected it when I gave you a massage in the apartment over the stables. I touched a trigger point and you flinched. I backed off. I didn't want to bring back bad memories when you were so vulnerable."

He turned his face into her palm and planted a kiss there. "You can genuinely tell that someone's holding in some deep hurt simply by massaging them?"

She nodded. "I can also help you heal."

Adam wanted to weep. He wanted so much to be healed of the guilt, to be forgiven, to be able to forgive himself.

He drew Carly into his arms.

She went willingly, surprising him as she wound her arms around his neck. He brought her closer, needing her more than he needed air.

When they both pulled back from the kiss, Carly's face was wet with tears.

Raising one hand, he traced a tear down her cheek. "I love you," he whispered.

His confession triggered a fresh surge of tears from Carly.

She eventually got herself under control. "You don't have to say that just because you asked me to marry you."

He grinned. "I know. But I want to, because I mean it. I've shut myself off from so many people—from my family especially—for too many years. But now it's time for me to start living my life. It's time for me to let others in. Beginning with you."

Carly hugged him close. "Thank you," she said, smiling through her tears.

Some time later, a knock at the door interrupted them. And a good thing, too, Adam mused as he reluctantly lifted Carly off his lap and put her back on the sofa. He grabbed one of the cushions, set it in his lap and said, "Come in."

"Darling! What have you gone and done?" his mother asked.

# Chapter 15

Carly was surprised by how noisy the courtroom was when she entered it. Louella Farquar, the mayor's pet pig, was alternately screeching and snorting at the judge—none other than Becky O'Malley, Will's wife. Finally, Becky had had enough of the pig and the noise of the courtroom audience and banged her gavel.

"Mayor Farquar, you promised me that Louella had mended her ways since you married Mrs. Farquar and moved into town a year ago. However, this is the third complaint in as many weeks that the court has heard about her. Her recidivist behavior is unacceptable and antisocial. Either you restrain her from wandering about town on her own, causing havoc with traffic and tourists, or I'll find a permanent solution," she said.

Carly was standing so close to the judge's podium, she

was sure she caught the words *bacon factory* muttered under Becky's breath.

"But, Judge, Louella doesn't like staying inside all day," the mayor protested.

"Louella is a *pig!* Why do I have to keep reminding you of that, Mayor Farquar? She doesn't belong inside all day, but she also doesn't belong downtown. I suspect half the reason you got yourself elected was in order to change the ordinance regarding the keeping of livestock within the town limits. Now, get her out of my court, and if I ever see her—or you—here again, I will personally run you *both* out of town!"

"You can't do that," he objected. "I'm the mayor!"

Becky peered over her glasses at him and said, "Try me." She banged her gavel, signaling the case was dismissed.

A whistle of approval sounded from the rear of the courtroom, almost drowning out the screeches of Louella as she was led off. "Way to go, darlin'," Will O'Malley cheered.

Becky's face looked like thunder. She obviously hadn't expected to see her husband in court. Nor the rest of his family, Carly noted as the courtroom filled with O'Malleys. How they'd gotten there so quickly, Carly couldn't imagine.

Becky picked up the file her clerk had placed in front of her and scanned it, then took off her glasses and gazed down at Carly.

She addressed the court. "Given the nature of the next case and the fact that I know the accused, I'm going to recuse myself."

A collective sigh of disappointment rose from the audience. This wasn't good. When Carly had learned that

Becky was the judge she'd be appearing before, she was hoping she'd get off with a low bail, maybe none. But if Becky recused herself, Carly's situation became even more dire.

"As it's almost lunchtime, I'm calling a recess," Becky said.

"What's this mean?" Carly hissed at Mike.

"It means the court's adjourned until after lunch."

"I know that!" Carly rolled her eyes. "I mean if Becky recuses herself, when's my hearing?"

"It'll have to be postponed until tomorrow when Judge Stevens is in session."

"But I can't stay in jail overnight!"

Cochrane stepped forward and said, "Your Honor, my client has four young children to care for. It would be cruel to expect her to wait in jail until her arraignment, simply because you've chosen to recuse yourself."

"Simply?" Becky repeated. "There is nothing *simple* about this case, Mr. Cochrane. Your client has been charged with four counts of arson. I know her, therefore I cannot preside over this bail hearing."

"I understand that, Judge. But there are extenuating circumstances. Her children—"

His explanation was halted by the appearance of Judge Stevens, who entered the court and asked if she could approach the bench. Her request was granted, and as she walked to the front of the courtroom, Carly saw Matt slip in and nod at Adam.

The two judges conferred for several minutes and then Becky said, "Judge Stevens has offered to hear this bail application in my place. We can proceed immediately if that's all right with both the prosecution and the defense?"

The D.A. and Mike agreed, and Becky vacated her

chair after saying, "In that case, I'll adjourn the court for ten minutes while my learned colleague familiarizes herself with the charges."

Carly wasn't sure whether to cheer or cry. At least she'd be able to go home to her children tonight—provided the bail wasn't too steep. Although looking at Judge Stevens, Carly suddenly wasn't feeling so confident.

Carly's worst fears were realized when the D.A. presented a very convincing case and the judge set bail on four counts of arson at four hundred thousand dollars.

Carly collapsed and had to be helped from the courtroom by the bailiff and her attorney.

Adam ignored all propriety, jumping over the low barrier separating the courtroom from the audience. Carly was aware of the judge banging her gavel, but didn't know what Adam had done until he hoisted her into his arms and carried her into the area behind the courtrooms.

"It's okay. I can walk," she said. "Please put me down."

Reluctantly, Adam did, allowing her feet to touch the floor. He held on to her until he was sure she could stand by herself.

"I didn't mean to frighten you," she apologized to the three men present. "But that was worse than I expected."

The bailiff and Mike nodded. Mike said he'd see her later, then both of them departed.

Carly wrung her hands. "Where on earth will I get that kind of money?"

"I have savings," Adam said. "Nothing like that, of course, but a bit."

Carly shook her head. "Thank you, but I can't accept it. To be perfectly honest, Adam, I can't guarantee that if I get released on bail I won't grab my children and hightail it to Canada or South America. Or Tasmania."

"I didn't hear that," another voice said.

They spun around to discover Matt standing behind them.

Adam's eyes narrowed. "I *was* going to thank you for finding Judge Stevens and getting her to court to hear the bail application, but you'll understand why I won't."

"Adam, Carly got off lightly. The usual amount of bail for first-degree arson is considerably more."

"And that makes me feel so much better," Adam muttered.

"Listen, I'd help with the bail, but all Beth's and my savings have gone into building the house. Likewise with Will and Becky."

"And believe me, we'd help if we could," Becky said. They turned to see her in a doorway behind them. Carly glanced at the office nameplate. Judge Rebecca O'Malley, it read.

Carly turned to Matt. "Do I get taken to jail now?"

"I'm afraid so," he said. "But since I'm here and it can be construed that you're in custody, we don't have to go back right away."

Matt looked up and down the corridor, then said to Becky, "Is it okay if we use your office for a while? I'd like us to meet with Mom and Pop and see what we can figure out."

Becky's face lit up. "Sure. I'll go find them. I'm not sure who's more trouble in court, Louella Farquar or a whole passel of O'Malleys."

She took off down the hallway in search of her in-laws. Matt pushed the door open and gestured that Carly should precede him into the room. Adam brought up the rear.

Adam was about to say something but Matt stopped him. He arranged three of the visitors' chairs into a small circle and indicated they should sit. Once they were all facing one another, he said, "I want to apologize to you, Carly, for having to arrest you, but I had no choice. I'm also sorry about how steep the bail is, but that's out of my control.

"What *isn't* out of my control is you two marrying right now, in order for Adam to have custody of your children." He turned to Adam. "Are you still of that mind?" he asked his brother.

"Of course," he said, reaching for Carly's hand.

"That's very sweet of you, Adam," she murmured. "But there are laws governing blood tests and waiting periods, aren't there? I could be in jail for weeks before we'd be eligible to marry."

Adam and Matt exchanged furtive smiles. "What are you two up to?" she demanded.

"I suspect," said Becky, coming through the door, followed by Adam's parents and the rest of his brothers, "that Matt hopes I'll waive the usual waiting period and marry you and Adam right here and now."

Carly's spirits lifted. "You can do that?"

"If I can run the mayor and his pig outta town, I can surely marry two people who are so obviously in love that there's no need to wait several weeks."

"Oh, that's wonderful!" Sarah O'Malley cried, and hugged her son. She smiled at Carly with tears in her eyes. "I'm so happy to welcome you to our family."

"I thought you hated me…"

"No! Never. Where on earth did you get that idea?"

"You acted strange on the phone this morning. I thought it had to do with me being suspected of burning down the stables with my children and your grand-children inside."

"Not to mention the horses," said Luke.

"And the dogs," Will added.

"Then you really do believe I'm innocent?"

"Of course we do!" they all chorused.

"There's still the circumstantial evidence," Matt re-minded them.

Luke grabbed Matt in a headlock and pretended to punch some sense into him. "Sometimes you take your job too seriously."

"He's a very serious person," said Beth, coming into the room. "What's up? Mac phoned and told us to get down here ASAP." She moved aside, so Megan could enter, too.

"Adam and Carly are getting married!" his mother said.

"So they've dropped the charges?" Megan said, and threw her arms around Carly in congratulation.

"Er, no," Adam told her. "But I'm marrying Carly so her children will be living with someone they know while she's in jail."

"Sorry, can you rewind all this? I'm totally confused." Megan patted her stomach and moved to her husband's side. "Pregnancy brain."

"Carly's bail is set at four hundred thousand dollars," Matt explained.

Soft whistles filled the room. "We could help out," Will said. "If we all pool our resources, we might be able to come up with something close to that. And if we can't, I'm sure Frank would come to the party."

"Not after this morning," his wife reminded him.

Frank Farquar was believed to be richer than Croe-sus. He was generous, but given that he was mayor of a town in which one of the fires had been set, he was unlikely to contribute to the cause. There was also the matter of Louella.

"I could offer to give him a lifetime of 'get out of court free' cards for Louella," Becky said.

"There's such a thing?"

"Of course there isn't." She smacked her husband good-humoredly. "But Frank doesn't know that."

Carly was enjoying the banter. It was what she loved about the O'Malleys, their ease with one another. But she didn't enjoy the thought of spending the night in jail, or however many nights after that. She couldn't put these people in debt to help her, though. Somehow she'd raise the bail. She'd start by selling her home in San Diego. It wasn't as if she wanted to return there anytime soon.

Ideas for raising bail money were flying around the room. Carly's head was spinning as she tried to sort one from the other. Finally, she put a stop to it by raising her hand and requesting silence.

With all eyes trained on her, she cleared her throat and said, "Thank you. All of you. You're wonderful people and I appreciate from the bottom of my heart your attempts to help me. But I have to be honest with you, if I'm released on bail, I *will* take my children and run."

There were gasps of shock, followed by a great deal of denying that Carly would do any such thing. They were finally silenced when Sarah declared, "And in your position, Carly, I'd do exactly the same thing."

"Mom!"

"Matt!" she said, mimicking him. "I would."

"And I'd go with her," Mac said.

"Well, that's a given," Will said with a smile, and dug his elbow into Luke's ribs.

"You'd run, even though you claim to be innocent?" Luke asked.

"I don't *claim* to be innocent, Luke. I am. And yes, I would, because if the case went against me, I'd lose everything that's dear to me. My only alternative is to run. I can't accept your money. But thank you all for offering."

She took a step toward Becky. "I'll be able to post bail once my home in San Diego is sold, but in the meantime, I'm resigned to going to jail. I'd very much appreciate it if you'd do Adam and me the honor of marrying us."

"Here?" Sarah cried.

"Yes, Mom, right here. Right now," Adam said. "Would you stand up for me?" he asked Jack, and all his brothers came forward.

Becky smiled and said, "We just need one of you. Now, Carly, who would you like to stand up for you?"

Carly looked at the other women in the room. "All of them. But since you're being economical…" She turned to Megan and said, "Would you be my matron of honor?"

Tears sprang to Megan's eyes and she hugged Carly.

"If all of you women don't stop crying, the wedding photo will be a mess." Will held up his camera phone.

"Glad that's settled," Becky said, giving her husband a warning glare. "Next, I need your IDs and birth certificates."

"All my papers were lost in the apartment fire. I haven't had time to replace them," Carly wailed.

"Don't upset yourself," Becky said, and sat at her computer terminal. After getting Carly's birth details, she tapped the information into the computer. Satisfied that Carly was who she said she was, she looked up at Adam, then his parents. "Do you solemnly swear that this man is your son?"

Mac and Sarah nodded enthusiastically. Mac even placed his hand over his heart.

"Carly and Adam, are you both sure this is what you want?" she said, glancing first at Adam and then at Carly, who both nodded.

"I have a distinct feeling of déjà vu," Megan murmured to her husband.

Carly turned to her in confusion.

Megan waved her concerns away. "Long story, tell you later," she said. "Hurry up and get married, you two, so we can start celebrating."

Unfortunately, her excitement fell flat as everyone realized that they couldn't have a celebration while the bride was in jail.

"I'm sorry, Carly. I wasn't thinking."

Carly gripped her hand. "We'll celebrate. But let's wait until I'm free and all the children are present."

Megan nodded. "I'll make sure it's extra special."

Five minutes later, there were hugs and handshakes all around. Carly detected a tear in Mac's eyes. More worrying was the look of desolation on her husband's face.

*Her husband.* Had she really done this? Married a man she barely knew? Carly stared down at her left hand, where Sarah O'Malley's wedding ring adorned her third finger.

"This has been a lucky ring," Sarah had said to Carly as she removed it from her finger and dropped it in Adam's hand. "I hope it'll help bring you both everlasting happiness, too."

Carly had been too choked up to reply. Adam had kissed his mother's cheek and whispered, "Thanks, Mom. I'm sure it will."

Was that just lip service, trying to reassure his mother that her ring would be lucky for them? What sort of future could they have with her in jail? They couldn't even plan a honeymoon! And soon, Carly would have to return the simple but beautiful band to its owner. She wouldn't be permitted to wear jewelry in jail.

"I think we should give these two some privacy," Matt said above the din of so many people talking at once. "I'll be waiting outside the door, so don't do anything inappropriate, okay?" he warned his brother.

"That sofa of Becky's—" Will started to say but was shushed by his wife and pushed toward the door. But Will wasn't done yet. "And don't forget the desk—"

He was cut off by the door's closing, leaving Adam and Carly alone at last.

He smiled down at her. "Are you a sofa or a desk kinda gal?" he teased.

She pretended to slap him in reproof. "If we knew each other better—the way a married couple should—you'd have the answer to that."

He rubbed his hands together. "I'm always up for some research."

"Adam, stop it!" Carly said, trying to keep a straight face. In a little while, they'd be separated for who knew how long.

"Thank you for trying to make me forget what lies beyond that door, but right now, I'm not in the mood for laughing. Or sex."

He drew her into his arms. "I know that, honey... Do you mind if I call you honey? Maybe you'd prefer darlin'? Sweetheart?"

"Carly will do. Please stop kidding around, Adam. I have a lot to tell you about the children and not much time."

Adam led her toward the sofa, sat and pulled her onto his lap. "Talk," he said, and nuzzled her neck.

"I can't concentrate when you do that!" she protested, loving every second of it.

"Okay, you have five minutes to talk and then we're going to do some serious necking."

Warmth flooded Carly. She might not know this man very well, but he was exactly what she needed. Exactly what her kids needed.

She rested her head against his chest and started speaking. "I'm instructing Mike Cochrane to make arrangements to put my San Diego house on the market."

Adam started to say something, but she silenced him with a finger placed over his lips.

"If you keep interrupting, there'll be less time for necking."

"Can you talk faster, then? I want to neck."

"Adam, this is important."

"Okay, but skip the changing diapers lesson. I already know how to do that. I also know how to cook nutritious meals."

That reminded Carly of something very important. "Hang on," she said, "Who's going to look after my children when you're at work?"

"Mom. Will. Megan. Beth. Everyone at the ranch will pitch in. Rory's mom, Jennifer Bennett, is watching them today. Mom's been in touch with her. I'd like you to meet her sometime."

"I'd like that," Carly said with a smile. She was happy Adam had reached out to Rory's mom.

"I promise you the kids will be perfectly safe and well cared for at all times, so please cross that off your list.

Can we get to the good part about being married now?"
He nuzzled her neck.

She snuggled against him and said, "I'm so scared,
Adam. I've never been to jail before."

"You're afraid it'll be like on those reality TV shows?"

"Yes." The violence between the inmates depicted on
those programs chilled her to the marrow.

Adam held her close. "Let me assure you, the county
jail isn't like that."

"And you know this how?"

"I've been there."

"You've been in jail?"

"No, Matt took me on a tour when he became sheriff.
You won't be with hard-core prisoners. Just druggies,
drunks and illegal aliens."

"Oh, wow, can we skip the necking and go straight to
jail in that case?"

Adam kissed her and she could feel his smile. He finally broke away and said, "Do you know when I first
started falling in love with you?"

Carly could feel her heart blooming in her chest. This
wasn't the conversation she'd expected they'd be having
right now. "No, when?"

"When I coughed up all that black goop onto your
white sneakers and you said, 'Thank you.' I liked the
way you took it all in your stride."

"I wasn't thanking you for spitting on my shoes. I was
thanking you for saving my son. And Molly."

"I know. But at the time, it intrigued me. It also scared
me."

"Why?"

"Because you read me so well. You asked if I always
deflected compliments. You're the only person who's

ever asked me that. Ever noticed." He brushed a strand of hair out of her eyes. "I should've known then that you'd be trouble."

She punched Adam lightly and then kissed him.

When they came up for air, he asked, "Are we officially in necking time now?"

"Not yet. There's something important I want you to do for me."

"Consider it done."

"Can you phone my parents? Speak to my mom, not my father. He's recovering from a stroke and I don't want him to hear about this. If the news service gets hold of the story and it's broadcast nationally for some reason, my dad will hear and there's nothing I can do about it. I haven't even told them about the fire at the apartment building. They were so distraught after Michael's death, I didn't want them to know how close their grandchildren came to dying."

Adam nodded solemnly.

"Now, since I'll be a guest of the county for the next days or weeks, however long we need to clear my name, I need to fill you in on what my children—"

"Let's take this one day at a time," Adam suggested. "When I think of next week and the possibility that you'll still be in jail, I feel physically ill."

"Try thinking about next month," she said grimly. "Next year."

"Why don't we concentrate on the present?" He reached for a notepad and pen from Becky's desk. "Write down your parents' details and I'll call your mom tonight. How's she going to take this?"

"Not well. But she's a strong woman. She's had a lot to deal with."

"Which highlights how little we know each other," Adam said, and regretted his words the moment he'd spoken. "Not that I'd take back marrying you," he hastened to say.

Carly touched his cheek. "I've had the same thought. I hope we can make up for lost time soon. Fill in the blanks about ourselves and our lives."

"Meanwhile, Matt will keep working to find the real arsonist." He paused and then said, "If you think of anything, Carly, no matter how insignificant you feel it is, tell him about it. He'll follow up on any lead."

"Believe me, I'll try. I haven't had time to think at all in the past week. Maybe it's a good thing I'll have time on my hands now."

"Was that supposed to be a joke?"

"A really bad one," she agreed. "I'll focus on why those fires happened when I was around." She glanced at the door. "In the meantime, can we forget about everything else for a few minutes? Except each other?"

Adam grinned, scooping her onto his lap. He pulled her close and they kissed as though it would be their last time.

# Chapter 16

Matt's soft knock at the door signaled that they'd soon be parted.

Reluctantly, Carly climbed off Adam's lap. He caught her hand and pulled her back down to sit on his knee. She slid her arms around his neck.

"Before you go," he said. "Tell me about that man you were kissing in the supermarket the other day."

"What is this? Belated jealousy?" Carly demanded, annoyed that Adam would bring up Jerry at a time like this. "For starters, I didn't kiss him, he kissed me. Couldn't you tell I wanted nothing to do with the guy?"

"He seemed pretty possessive of you."

Carly sighed and got up off Adam's knee. "Too possessive. He's the reason I left San Diego."

"Were you dating him there?"

Carly whirled around. "No! He was a colleague of Michael's. He helped me out after Michael died."

"What was he doing here in Spruce Lake?"

"I don't know. He claimed he was on vacation." Carly shrugged. "I got the shock of my life when he approached me in the supermarket. I couldn't wait to get out of there. Then you showed up and all I could think of was protecting you from him."

"Protecting *me?* Why?"

"Jerry's…obsessive. He's…scary."

"Why didn't you mention this to me?"

"I thought he was out of my life. I didn't tell him where I was moving because I didn't want him following me. Jerry got way too possessive of me and my time after Michael died. At first I assumed he was just being supportive, but then it got creepy. He was over at our house every night whenever he was off-duty, bringing food, asking me out to dinner. In the end, I decided to leave town."

"Did you tell him where you were going?"

"Of course not!"

"Is there any way this Jerry guy could know where you were planning to work in Denver?"

"He…could have. He and my mom were close," she said, then glanced at Adam. "It was the day after I told her I was about to start a job at the Colorado Grand that it was firebombed."

Adam nodded. "How do you think he found you in Spruce Lake?"

Carly hesitated, then continued, her face flushed. "I emailed my mom last week and told her I'd moved to Spruce Lake, that it didn't work out in Denver. I didn't tell her about the hotel being firebombed. She didn't need to worry about that."

Adam stood and paced the room. "Could he be obsessive enough to try to get you to return to San Diego by destroying the hotel—where you were about to start work?"

"Maybe…" Carly said slowly. "But I never made that connection because of all the media stories about how it had to be a Mafia hit or something."

"And if he knew you were in Spruce Lake…"

"Back up a bit. Are you saying *he* caused the fires in the apartment building and last night, as well? That's impossible! My children were in those buildings. He was devoted to them after Michael died!"

"Like he was *devoted* to you?" Adam said drily.

Confused, Carly searched her memory. Come to think of it, there'd been times when she'd wondered how genuinely Jerry cared for her kids. His devotion seemed a little overdone, as if he was trying to impress her.

Something else pricked at her memory.

"What's the matter?" Adam asked.

Carly explained the weird sensations she'd experienced—at the apartment fire, on the porch at the ranch and then the other day, just before Jerry had approached her in the supermarket.

"What if he *was* there on those occasions, Adam, watching me? What if he'd been there because *he'd* lit those fires? What if it was Jerry I saw lurking in the yard last night?"

There was another knock at the door, and Matt came into the room.

"I gave you both enough time to get yourselves decent," he said. "But—"

"Matt, can you check out a Jerry Ryan of San Diego?" Adam asked urgently. "He's a firefighter there."

"Whoa! What's this all about?"

As succinctly as he could, Adam detailed his discussion with Carly. "If you could check airplane records, rental cars in Denver, ascertain whether he stayed anywhere locally—anything that might link him to the fires—I think you'll find the real arsonist."

"I way Jerry Ryan could've found out where you'd moved?"

"The only person in Denver who knew where I'd gone was the owner of the apartment I rented there..."

"And he owned the same apartment complex you moved to here in Spruce Lake," Matt finished for her.

"Yes," Carly said, but her voice was little more than a squeak. Had Jerry Ryan stalked her all the way to Denver and then Spruce Lake?

"You said this guy was obsessed with you?"

Carly nodded.

"Then it's possible he was burning those places down so you'd have nowhere to work or live and have to return to San Diego—and to him."

"Adam suggested the same thing. But is one person capable of that sort of evil?"

"Hell, just this morning, I was wondering if you were."

"Yeah, thanks so much for that."

"Carly, you have to know I was only doing my job. If I didn't arrest you, then someone else would have, and it might not have gone so well for you."

"Four hundred thousand dollars is *going well* for me?"

"Well, not that part. But look on the bright side. You got a husband out of it."

Carly gazed at him, deadpan.

"Sorry, bad joke."

"No, you're right, I did get a husband out of it, so the

day wasn't a complete loss." She hugged Adam to her and kissed him soundly.

Matt strode toward the door. "I'm going to check Jerry Ryan's whereabouts on the relevant dates. Hopefully, we'll find the link we're looking for. But in the meantime, Carly, I'm afraid you're going to have to accompany me to jail."

# Chapter 17

As she'd expected, Carly didn't sleep. She tossed all night long, worrying about her kids. About Adam. Whether Matt would uncover a connection between Jerry and the fires.

She gave up on sleep shortly before dawn and lay on her bunk, hands clasped behind her head, and stared at the ceiling.

Adam was right; the jail wasn't so bad. It was new and clean and there were only two other female inmates, both illegal immigrants, on the women's side, so they each had a cell to themselves. Come the weekend—if she was still here—Carly suspected she'd be sharing with someone who'd been arrested on drug charges or for drunken behavior. She wasn't looking forward to that.

Sometime later, Carly heard a familiar voice in the corridor outside. Her cell door was unlocked and Matt stepped inside, followed by Adam. Adam smiled as he drew Carly into his embrace.

Matt's research had proven a direct link to the dates of the fires and the dates Jerry Ryan was in the vicinity. The owner of the apartment building in Denver had confirmed that a man matching Jerry's description had queried him about where Carly had moved. When he'd refused to tell him, the man had gotten downright threatening. In the end, the owner had threatened to call the cops. Jerry had left him alone after that. It wasn't until Carly had emailed her mom that he'd managed to track Carly to Spruce Lake.

"But surely this is as circumstantial as the evidence in my case?" Carly said.

Matt shook his head. "Better than circumstantial. Jerry was arrested by San Diego police as he got off a flight from Denver this morning. He fell apart and confessed to everything—including the fire at the warehouse where your husband died." Matt gave a wry grin. "Must ask them about their interrogation tactics sometime."

Carly breathed in the crisp mountain air as she walked outside the county jail to be greeted by the O'Malleys. Her children climbed all over her and she reveled in it. Charlie perched on her hip and clasped her cheeks in his chubby little fingers and kept kissing her.

"Is it true Adam's our daddy now?" Maddy asked.

Carly glanced up at him. Now that she was free, did he want to stay married to her? she wondered.

Adam looked as uncertain as she felt.

"You can have it annulled, if you want," she whispered.

Adam frowned. "Do *you?*" he asked.

"I don't want you to feel trapped because you did

something for me and my kids out of the kindness of your heart."

"I *don't* feel trapped," he said, his voice rising. "I love you, Carly."

"And that would be a *yes* to Maddy's question!" Will shouted to the gathered crowd, and they cheered. "Come on, you two, we're having a wedding breakfast at Rusty's. I'm starving!"

Adam picked up Maddy, then turned and clasped Carly's hand. "Ready to start the rest of your life, Mrs. O'Malley?"

"You betcha, Mr. O'Malley!" Carly said, and kissed him.

"That's *Lieutenant* O'Malley to you, *Mrs.* O'Malley." He pointed at the bugle on his uniform.

# *Epilogue*

Carly was curled up on the sofa, her hands wrapped around a mug of hot chocolate as she stared into the fire. Adam had lit it earlier that evening in the living room of Becky and Will's former residence in Spruce Lake.

During the summer, Becky and Will had moved into the home Jack built for them on the ranchland Will had bought years ago, when he'd been an extreme-ski movie star. He'd subdivided it into large ranchettes. Matt and Beth already lived there, and next spring, Jack would start building a home for Adam and Carly.

But right now, her children loved the old Victorian and so did Molly. She was stretched out on Adam's blanket in front of the fire, snoring gently.

After seeing how happy Molly was with the O'Malleys,

Mr. and Mrs. Polinski had decided that they wouldn't take her with them to the Twilight Years, after all. They'd asked Carly to keep her, as previously arranged. Since Molly missed hanging out with the ranch dogs now that they'd moved to town, Carly and Adam had adopted a companion for her from the pound.

Pongo was a dog of indeterminate breed, with oversize paws, floppy ears, a loud bark and a constantly wagging tail. Still a pup, he grew alarmingly each day and was completely devoted to his new family. He slept on Alex's bed every night and got up at odd hours to patrol the house, as if some instinct told him this family needed his protection.

Carly and Adam had repeated their wedding vows in the presence of all the children and Carly's parents a week after their hurried nuptials. Carly had felt blessed every day since.

"Whatcha thinking about?" Adam asked, plopping down beside her.

Carly smiled and leaned in to kiss her husband. "How much my life has changed this past year. How much better it is than it's ever been."

He kissed her back. "Mine, too."

"I don't think you thought that the first time we met."

"True. I had 'issues,' as Sash would say. But you healed me," he said.

"You healed yourself, Adam. You confronted your demons."

"You made me do it."

"Yeah, I'm good at twisting you around my little finger."

That earned her a tickle and then some playful wrestling that had Carly squealing and begging him to stop.

"The children!" she warned.

Adam sobered. "Speaking of children, would you be averse to having one more?"

Carly grinned. "*Another* O'Malley?"

"Just one."

Carly felt that having Adam's child would make her own happiness even more complete. "When can we start trying?"

"How about tonight?"

"Goodness, you *are* eager!"

"Well, you're not getting any younger," he teased.

"May I remind you, Adam O'Malley," she said, shaking her finger at him, "that I once punched out an ornery stallion. So don't mess with me."

Adam nuzzled her neck. Carly could feel her indignation abate as he moved to her mouth and kissed her. She sighed against his lips.

"Mom and Dad would be thrilled with another grandbaby."

"They're already getting two more additions to the O'Malley clan next year," Carly said, referring to Beth and Becky, who were both expecting babies in the spring. "Three in one year might be overkill."

"Never!" Adam declared. "Besides, with the birth of little Isabelle last month, Luke's said he and Megan aren't having any more kids, so Mom's been dropping hints."

"We could adopt another dog instead."

Adam laughed. "Then this place would be a complete madhouse! How about a cat?"

He reached for the latest copy of the local paper resting on the coffee table and turned to the section where the animal shelter advertised pets for adoption. "There's a litter of kittens here—"

"Hoo, boy!"

"Calm down, sweetheart. I called the shelter today and they've all been adopted. However, the mom needs a home."

Carly kissed him. "You are such a sweet man."

"I'm a firefighter, I'm not allowed to be sweet!"

"But you are, and I love you for it. Can we get her first thing in the morning?"

"Sure, the kids would have to come along, though."

"They'd want to adopt every animal there!"

"Good point. I'll go by myself and have Mrs. Farquar make up a special box, gift wrap it and I'll bring her home in that. She'll be a one-day-early Christmas present for the kids."

"You're the world's best father," Carly said. "Of kids, dogs…and cats."

"My brothers might argue with you about that, since they think they're so good at fatherhood."

"Speaking of fatherhood, what are we going to do about Jack? He'd make a fantastic dad. But we need to find him a wife first," Carly said. "I wonder what sort of woman he's attracted to?"

"Hard to say. He keeps his private life private."

"Like someone else I once knew," Carly murmured with a smile.

Adam ignored her jibe. "He had a huge crush on a really neat girl in high school, but she went off to college on the East Coast. Broke his heart."

"Is that why he entered the seminary?"

"Don't know. Not sure why he left it, either," Adam said pensively.

"You've never asked?"

"No. Now, can we forget about Jack's love life and concentrate on ours?"

"What's the holdup?" Carly said, wrapping her arms around his neck.

Adam hoisted her easily into his arms and headed toward the stairs.

Molly looked up sleepily, smiled—Carly was sure of it—then snuggled deep into her blanket and closed her eyes.

\* \* \* \* \*

**Megan Kelly** is a mom, a wife, a friend and a writer. As a shy girl, reading swept her away to places she still hopes to visit one day. Writing gives her the opportunity to experience some of those adventures (although she'd make a terrible cabin boy in disguise, couldn't possibly find clues by hiding under her blankets and never plans on doing anything more frightening than public speaking—which is scary enough). She loves hearing from readers at megankellybooks@gmail.com.

### Books by Megan Kelly

### Harlequin American Romance

*Marrying the Boss*
*The Fake Fiancée*
*The Marriage Solution*

Visit the Author Profile page at Harlequin.com.

# STAND-IN MOM

Megan Kelly

For Kimberly Killion,
whose patience and input made this book a reality.
Thanks for holding me together at a difficult time;

For my editor, Johanna Raisanen,
whose advice makes me a stronger writer;

For my kids, who make my dream of being a mother
such a joy to live;

And as always, for my husband. I wouldn't know
how to write about love without you in my life.

# Chapter 1

As Christmas parties went, it didn't suck, but Ginger Winchester would have given her left eye to be anywhere else. The ballroom in the James Brothers Hotel glittered with decorative touches to put everyone in a holiday mood. A band provided music, and she hadn't lacked for partners in the two hours since she'd arrived. But she'd rather have been home with a mug of hot chocolate and a book than dragged along by her best friend and forced to celebrate.

Until she saw *him*.

The man didn't look familiar, although Ginger didn't know all the employees at Riley & Ross Electronics, her hosts this evening. She sipped her white wine, watching him over the rim of her glass, as the band charged into an energetic version of "I'm a Believer." Even in a town the size of Howard, Missouri, she could run into a stranger. She smiled to herself. She'd like to do more than run into this guy.

He looked up then, directly at her, as though he'd heard her thoughts from fifteen feet away. Ginger didn't blush often and now was no exception. She nodded slightly. He smiled back, raising his beer bottle in a salute. His lack of a wedding ring didn't guarantee he was single.

Short brown hair shimmered with bronze highlights under the chandeliers. His dark suit emphasized his tall, lean frame. Light danced on prominent cheekbones and caressed his full lips, much as she'd like to. He looked to be in his early thirties, with lines at the corners of his eyes. Laugh lines? She liked the idea of him being a happy person. She'd been that way not so long ago. Maybe this stranger could bring some joy to *her* world tonight.

After the call from the adoption agency earlier that day, she needed some holiday cheer. She hadn't been approved as a foster parent yet, the first step of many in adopting a baby. She thought she'd have a little visitor for the holidays. Now she'd be alone. Again.

"Having fun yet?" Lisa Riley asked, appearing at her side.

"Loads." Ginger rolled her eyes for her friend's benefit, not wanting Lisa to pick up on her distress. She wouldn't ruin Lisa's holidays, nor did she want her to guess just how entertaining her fantasies of the man had been. He'd be a great distraction for her woes. Maybe she could finagle an introduction without being too obvious. "I don't know many people here, though."

"That hasn't stopped you from dancing."

Ginger forced a grin. "The band's talented. Good variety of music. There are a couple of nice single guys here."

"And a couple with not-so-nice intentions."

"Ooh, point them out." Ginger noticed the frown before Lisa turned away. Lisa and her husband, Joe, had coerced her into coming, and Ginger aimed to have a good time. If that included collecting some phone numbers or spending time with a guy in private afterward, that wasn't any business of the Rileys'.

After all, Lisa and Joe had each other, as well as her two children, Abby and Bobby. Ginger was alone now and probably would remain so.

"Do you want to introduce me to some of the nicer guys?" she asked to placate Lisa. "You'd know who's unattached with pure intentions." Not that she wanted anybody too pure of heart. Gesturing toward the mystery man with her now empty glass, she said, "What about him?"

Lisa followed her gaze. "I don't recognize him. He might be the new guy in Dylan's division."

Dylan Ross, Joe's partner, headed up the R&D department, inventing computer programs and troubleshooting existing ones. Mystery Man looked too strong and too vital to be a computer nerd.

"New guy?" Ginger tried to appear only mildly interested.

"Some genius from the South that Dylan snatched up when his company downsized. In Alabama, I think. Dylan considers hiring this guy to be a real coup."

"I can imagine." She'd consider snatching him up to be a coup, too. Strong, clean hands gripped his bottle. His lips curved in a smile in response to the blonde woman now chatting with him. Ginger wanted those hands on her, that mouth smiling at her. The rush of heat she felt just looking at him surprised her. In the past year since her ex-husband walked out, she'd never experienced such an immediate attraction.

The song ended. "We're going to slow it down now," the band leader announced. Lights lowered in the center of the room as they began playing Eric Clapton's, "Wonderful Tonight." The singer's husky baritone intensified the sexy mood in the room.

A man claimed the blonde woman and led her away.

Spotting her chance, Ginger said, "I'm going to get another drink. Meanwhile, could you find out his name?"

"Whose?" Lisa's gaze followed hers. "Oh."

"See if Joe or Dylan knows if he's single."

"Ginger."

"Don't worry, Mother Hen." She patted Lisa's arm as she moved by her. "I know what I'm doing."

"I doubt that," Lisa muttered, making her smile.

Ginger wound her way past him, not too close, but catching his eye on her way to the bar set up on the far wall. If he didn't follow, she'd go back and introduce herself. She dug through her tiny handbag for a tip. "Chardonnay, please."

"Could y'all wait on that?" a man said at her side, his Southern inflection sliding over the words like honey. The singer on the stage had nothing on this guy in the sexy voice department.

The bartender looked to her for a decision. She glanced at her mystery man and let a smile flirt across her mouth, thrilled when it drew the attention of his hazel eyes. "Why would I wait?"

"It'll be easier to dance with me if your hands are free."

"Am I dancing with you?"

His eyes locked with hers. "I surely hope so."

Her heart thrummed in her ears for a beat, then another. She spoke to the bartender without shifting her gaze. "Looks like I'll have to come back for that drink."

"Yes, ma'am."

She heard the laughter in the bartender's voice but didn't mind. She felt like giggling herself. Her new partner escorted her to the dance floor, his hand at the small of her back burning through the satin of her cocktail dress. Before she turned to him, she swallowed the lump in her throat. Pleasure, anticipation and sheer giddy attraction welled inside her.

He held her right hand and placed his other warm hand on her waist. Shivers ran across her skin as she touched his black-clad shoulder. She could feel his strength as they moved smoothly into the dance. About six foot one or two, she guessed, the perfect height for her in heels.

"What's your name?" he asked.

"Ginger."

"Unusual." He laid her hand against his chest and touched a ringlet she'd left dangling from her temple. He twirled the curl around his finger. "Because of this?"

She nodded. She couldn't actually feel him stroke her hair, but the impression of his touch tingled down her neck.

"I was born with shocking-pink hair. Picture cotton candy." She smiled when he chuckled. "My parents hoped it would calm down to a ginger shade more like my mom's, but it never did."

"It's not really red, and it's certainly more dazzling than orange. What do you call it?"

"Apricot." In the heat of his interest, she *felt* dazzling.

"That sounds about right." He picked up her hand

again but held it clasped against his chest. Her fingers stroked against the edge of his emerald silk tie.

"And you?" she all but croaked.

His mouth widened into a smile, showing beautiful white teeth. "My hair's just brown."

She laughed softly and shook her head. Up close, the bronze highlights held red and blond streaks. Lots of time in the sun, she supposed, remembering Lisa said he came from the South. *If* this was the guy Dylan hired. She only had his slow drawl and Lisa's guess to go by. "I meant your name."

"Scott."

"Nice to meet you."

"The pleasure's all mine."

"Are you new to the area?"

"How did you guess? My accent?" The corners of his lips tipped up in a rueful smile. "My part of the South has less of a twang than other places. Maybe it'll ease up some after I've been here awhile."

"Oh, I hope not." Ginger stared over his shoulder, unable to believe she'd admitted such a thing. His chuckle made her wish for the dance floor to open up, like in the movie *It's a Wonderful Life*. Her cheeks burned. Having a swimming pool to drop into sounded heavenly at the moment.

"Glad y'all like it," he murmured, drawing her closer. He led her across the floor with confidence. "But I should try to fit in here. Put some stiff Yankee talk in my conversation."

Ginger laughed. "It'd be a shame if y'all sounded like us."

"Now y'all—I mean, *you* are making fun of me." He winked at her.

She enjoyed the moment as their bodies adjusted to each other in wordless communication. He smelled of man rather than aftershave. Just strength and vitality, making her mouth water. The tan skin of his neck so close enticed her lips. She pulled back before temptation made her do something she'd regret. "Are you married?"

His hold on her loosened; his expression sobered. "Not anymore."

Hearing he was single made her pulse accelerate, although part of her wondered why any woman would let a man this adorable and sexy get away. Did he eat crackers in bed? Hog the covers? These things didn't matter to Ginger; she wasn't looking for long-term. "She must have been crazy to let you go."

He shook his head, and his gaze drifted off. *Great.* Now his thoughts centered on another woman, one he obviously had feelings for still. Ginger knew she should cut her losses and leave him to his memories. He had the look of a man recently set free—lost and hungry but too conflicted to act. Yet.

The music ended, and she sensed he would lead her off the dance floor, return her to the bar with some expression of thanks, maybe buy her that wine, but she'd never hear from him again. The first notes of "Lady in Red" sounded, and Ginger gripped his shoulder. She felt a kinship with him, although she'd long ago passed the stage of being saddened by her divorce. Maybe a nudge would lead him in the right direction. Toward her. "I'm not married, either. Not anymore."

She held his gaze as he began moving to the song, their bodies in accord.

How could she keep him with her? Judging by his reluctant withdrawal, the reminder of his wife had been a blow. Ginger recalled those first shell-shocked weeks after Kyle left her. Scott's breakup must be recent.

"I haven't done this." He gestured to their bodies with their clasped hands. "You know, been out. Not since… being single again. I didn't want to be alone tonight, but coming to a party of strangers?" He shook his head.

"It's hard the first time, but it gets easier."

The twist of his mouth expressed his doubt. Would he make the effort again? Her mood deflated. He still had a thing for his ex. She could help him over this first hurdle, but she doubted he'd be interested in trying.

Although he remained in her arms, Scott wasn't really with her anymore.

"I'm sorry." His words came out forced. "I'm not very good company, I guess."

"Don't worry about it. Let's finish the dance, okay?"

He nodded and led her to the music, dancing several steps in silence. Gradually his body relaxed. "Nice song."

His breath whispered across her temple.

"Good band."

"Exceptional partner." He laid her hand on his chest, patting it into place.

She started when she felt his left hand go to her waist. After a second, he pulled her closer until she pressed flush against his body. His hesitation must have been to test her willingness. If he only knew.

*We're in a hotel,* she wanted to say. *Test me upstairs. I'll show you willing.*

But she didn't say anything—with words. Instead she linked her hands behind his neck, letting a finger stroke against his nape. She felt his shiver.

When the song ended, Scott looked into her eyes. "Another? Or would y'all prefer that drink now?"

The intensity of his hazel eyes made her mouth go dry, but a glass of wine wouldn't alleviate the problem. A kiss from Scott might. "I'm fine here."

"This one," the bandleader said, "is for those of you who are missing family this time of year."

They began playing "Have Yourself a Merry Little Christmas," and Scott stiffened.

"Want to get out of here?" He shook his head. "No, wait. I didn't mean that the way it sounded. Outside maybe? The terrace—is there a terrace? Doesn't matter, it would be too cold."

Ginger smoothed her hand down his tie. "Wherever."

He blinked.

"We could go out and walk in the lobby for a minute." Get him away from the music and the memories.

He held her hand, dodging dancers and groups on the edge of the dance floor. Ginger avoided making eye contact as they passed. Some of these people would recognize her if they looked closely—her hair shone like neon—although few would have seen her dressed so elegantly. More likely, they knew her with paint under her nails rather than on them. Her Cinderella clothes would have to come off. She grinned, hoping for the moment to happen sooner rather than later.

She followed him out of the ballroom to the long carpeted hallway. The lights were dimmed, creating shadows for quiet conversations. Mirrors and slim tables lined the walls of the one hundred-and-fifty-year-old hotel, alternating with insets of maroon vases containing various white flowers. They strolled to a deserted area farther along, where a wide window overlooked the snow-covered grounds.

"Sorry," Scott said. "Y'all sure pulled the short straw with me."

She laughed, running her eyes over his long form. "I don't think so."

"Not literally, maybe," he agreed. "But your other partners tonight wouldn't have fled the dance floor like the room had caught fire."

He pronounced it "cot far," making her suppress a grin. And he thought he didn't have a twang?

"Hey." She tugged his hand to make him stop walking and face her. "I'm not out here with anyone else. I came out with you."

His expression softened. "I appreciate that."

Then his words caught up with her. "Have you been watching me dancing all night?"

"You're very popular."

Her chin lifted. "Then why didn't you ask me to dance earlier?"

"You're very popular."

"What does that mean?"

Scott shrugged. "I don't deal well with competition."

Had his wife cheated on him? Ginger swallowed, hoping he hadn't asked anyone about her. Since her ex-husband left her, she'd filled some of her free time with men. It irritated her that she felt guilty about it now. With Scott. That early wild streak had mellowed once she'd decided to adopt a baby on her own; still, she had to live with her choices.

He squeezed her fingers. "But you dance as though there's nothing more important than that song and that moment. Very full of life." He stepped closer. "You look like a flame with your bright hair and yellow dress. And

I wanted to be near that, to watch your green eyes light up and feel your body sway."

Scott drew her to him and she forgot guilt. She only felt admired. As a woman, by a man. A shiver ran over her.

"Cold?" he murmured.

"Not even close."

He grinned as he lowered his lips over hers, warm and persuasive. She didn't need persuading, but she appreciated the gesture as she opened her mouth to him. Scott pulled her nearer, his hands caressing her back. Her stomach clenched with need and desire burned out any chills she might have had.

He put a hand against her cheek, eyes on hers. "This is wrong. It's too fast."

She might agree, but she doubted she'd ever get another chance with him. He attracted her like a compass needle finding true North. Judging by the intensity of his gaze, desire tugged at him, too. "It doesn't feel wrong."

"No, maybe it doesn't." His thumb traced across her lips. "But I don't really do this."

"I wish you'd make an exception."

His eyes darkened before he bent to kiss her. Heat burst across her skin. His hands tightened, securing her to him, and she was grateful for the anchor as her head swam. When Scott pulled away, his face was flushed with need.

Ginger swallowed, nervous when she hadn't been in ages. "Do you want to…do something about it?"

"Is that an invitation? Like 'your place or mine?'"

She nodded. How would she bear it if he said no?

His lips brushed hers. "I'd like that. Very much."

The truth of his declaration nudged her stomach as the

kiss deepened. "So." His kiss found her cheek, then his breath was at her ear. "Your place or mine?"

No way would she let him change his mind during a car ride. "What about here?"

He tilted his head in question. She'd thrown him a curve ball.

"It *is* a hotel," she said.

"Good point." His mouth crooked, making him look endearingly nervous. "I'll go check availability."

As Scott strode to the reservation desk, Ginger pulled out her cell phone. Relieved to get Lisa's voice mail, she left a brief message. "It's 9:40. If you don't see me in the next hour, I've gotten a ride home."

If all went well, no one but Scott would see her for several hours. Or until morning.

He came toward her with a big grin and a key card. "I've never done this before. Checked in to a hotel without luggage."

She laughed. "Come to think of it, I haven't, either." It struck her that she might be leaving in the morning in her cocktail dress. "Wait."

His smile faded.

"I should retrieve my coat. In case, you know, coat check closes before we leave."

"Right. Me, too." He changed direction and marched back to the main hall. A man on a mission. The butterflies in her stomach stilled, calmed by a wave of tenderness toward him.

When they passed the gift shop, reality struck, almost making her stumble. Condoms. How could she be so stupid? Of all the nights to switch purses. She'd planned to spend the evening with Lisa and Joe, not spend the night with a guy.

"Is there anything else we'll need?" she hinted. "Unless you…?"

"Unless I what? Here we are. Do you have your coat stub?" Scott handed his to the checker then turned to her.

Damn. Joe had her coat check stub. She didn't know if mentioning his boss's name would make Scott hesitate or not. Earlier he'd seemed undecided about them being together; she didn't want to give him another reason to balk.

She stretched up to whisper in his ear. "My girlfriend's husband has it. Why don't you go to the gift shop while I get the check stub?"

"What do I need at…?" Light dawned across his face. "Gift shop, right. I'll be back in a second." He kissed her, hard. "Don't change your mind while I'm gone."

"You, either."

She spotted Joe with a group of men. He was too polite to make a scene that would embarrass her. She touched his arm to draw him aside and explained the situation.

He produced the ticket from his pocket and offered it to her, capturing her hand in the process. "If you want to call me for a ride later, I'll come."

She pressed a kiss to his cheek. "Thanks, Joe. Hopefully, this guy has enough manners to drive me home, but otherwise, I'll call a cab. Do me a different favor, though?"

"Does it involve not telling Lisa?"

"I'd never ask that of you."

"Good thing."

She grinned. "But if you could keep the news to yourself for a while, just to give me time to get out of view?"

"She won't be happy."

"She's been unhappy with me before."

He grimaced. "I wasn't referring to you."

Ginger chuckled. "Thanks."

"Sure you don't want me to talk to him?"

"Do I need your approval to date your employees?"

Being a gentleman, he didn't comment on her wording. This was as far from a date as one could get. "Make sure you call Lisa tomorrow. She'll be worried about you."

Which meant *he* was worried. Her throat tightened. "Sure thing."

Ginger claimed her coat, finally, looking over her shoulder for Scott. So much time had elapsed, he could have had second, third and fourth thoughts by now.

She spotted him as she approached the gift shop. He hovered by the entrance. Had he seen her with his boss and decided she wasn't worth risking his job? Joe would never fire him for being with her, but Scott wouldn't know that, would he?

"I thought you'd left," she said.

"No." He looked startled. "Were you hoping I had?"

"Not at all." Thank God she wouldn't have to seduce him all over again. "What are you doing in here? Did they not have what we need?"

"Got that." He patted his pocket.

Ginger laid a hand on his arm. "I have what I need, too."

Their eyes met, then his stiff posture loosened. He understood she meant him.

He exhaled a huge breath. "Okay, then. Let's go."

She laughed. "You sound like I'm going to perform a root canal on you."

"God, I hope not." He smiled and walked toward the elevators. "I'm just relieved. It took so long getting your coat, I thought y'all had come to your senses."

"Nope. How about you?"

"Not planning on being sensible for a while. It'll feel good."

"That's the plan." Once in the elevator alone, she let him push the button for their floor before she pulled him to her. She ran her hands over his chest as he bent toward her. His lips covered hers, surprising her with his passion. Maybe he didn't need warming up. She smiled against his mouth, pleased he hadn't been having second thoughts, after all.

"What?" he asked. "Do I kiss funny?"

She started to assure him otherwise but stopped. "Hmm. I'd better double-check."

"Is that a challenge?"

"You asked."

His mouth closed on hers, his lips capturing her bottom lip, then his tongue swept in, arousing, claiming, inflaming her with need. Their breathing grew erratic.

When she came up for air, she shook her head. "Not funny."

He ran his hands over her back, her hips, her breasts, sending her pulse racing. The elevator dinged as it slowed to their floor, drawing them apart. The doors opened, and they stepped out, heading toward their room. Silent, side by side, but not touching.

He stopped and drew the key card out of his pocket. The lock flashed green.

Scott opened the door and flipped on the light. "Ladies first."

He breathed in Ginger's exotic scent as she walked into the room. Something flowery but not cloying. More seductive than sweet. It made him think of hothouses, but maybe that was his overheated body. She'd done that to him, too.

The last time he'd felt an attraction this strong—Samantha, of course, and it was just wrong to think of her now. Not fair to any of the three of them. The similarities between the two women—both physically and in their "seize the day" outlooks—had drawn him to Ginger. But the way her touch made his blood burn led him here. That, and the concern in her eyes when that damned song started. He didn't need to hear about missing the ones you loved. Not tonight.

Ginger tossed her coat on a chair, drawing his thoughts back to her. Her hips swayed under that silky dress in a way that roused him. Not a chance she wore anything under there. She leaned across the desk in the corner and turned on the lamp, and his tongue stuck to the roof of his mouth. He trailed his eyes over her backside, thinly veiled by her dress and arched toward him, and he imagined things he could do to her on that desk. As she turned, he took a moment to appreciate the play of the light over her breasts, creating shadows and highlighting exposed skin.

His groin tightened to a deeper ache. She strolled back toward him and only then did he realize he stood like an idiot just inside the door. He'd been so transfixed by the sight of her, seductive and alluring, he hadn't moved.

He'd noticed her on the dance floor earlier, appreciated her from a distance, and would have been satisfied watching the party girl having fun. Until he saw her standing off to the side in an unguarded moment, watching the others, and seeming lonely and out of place. Something had stirred inside him, recognizing a kindred spirit.

Ginger caught his eye and flipped off the overhead light switch, casting the room into a dim glow. Her hands slid across his chest, up to his shoulders, and he pulled her against him, his mouth devouring hers. Hot, hard, wet.

He had to slow down. She deserved wooing—or at least some patience. Not to be attacked by a sex-starved man.

Her fingers brushed his stomach. His jacket opened as she slipped her hands inside, caressing his chest, sliding the material from his shoulders. She was undressing him, and he'd only contributed hot kisses.

Leaning back, he pulled off his jacket and let it drop to the floor, then ran his hands over her bare shoulders. He bent to taste the freckles there, then kissed his way up her neck, smiling as she shivered. His hands trailed up her ribs, fingers making lazy circles. Ginger pressed against him, her breasts prodding his chest. He let his thumbs trace slowly upward as his lips captured hers, his tongue sweeping inside her mouth. He wanted to savor her, to slow down and relish every second. Lick every inch of her warm skin until she burned as hot as he did already.

He ran the pad of his thumb across her nipple, and she moaned his name. His erection jutted against her abdomen like a heat-seeking missile. He caressed her shoulders, her arms, her breasts, his hands restless over her, learning her shape as he listened for the catch of her breath to discern what she liked. His fingers unhooked the clasp at her neck, and the top of her dress loosened. One shift had it dropping to her waist, trapped by the press of their hips. His breath caught at the sight of her breasts, all creamy skin and feminine curves, and he lowered his head to savor her.

"Scott," she moaned, pushing her hips against him.

He bent her backward, one hand supporting her shoulders, one cupping her bottom, the lushness there enticing him to caress. The soft warmth of her skin filled his mouth; his tongue flicked over her nipple. Her perfume blended with her natural womanly scent, stirring him. Little noises in her throat urged him on.

She opened his shirt and pushed it down his shoulders. Scott shrugged free of it so she could touch him, then shuddered when she did. Desire burned him. He walked her toward the king-size bed, not letting any space fall between them.

"Let's get this off," he said, peeling the dress over her hips. Tearing it off was more likely, but he called on his years of experience to slow down. Despite feeling like a teenager with his first girl in the backseat, he was a man who knew how to please a woman, and he desperately wanted to make this pleasurable for Ginger. To thank her for reminding him how good sex felt, for helping him feel alive again.

He'd been wrong; she wasn't naked under the dress. His hands revealed a tiny flesh-colored thong, sexier than bare skin. He swallowed the lump in his throat, his fingers moving on their own to his zipper as she shimmied—there was no other word for the wiggle of her body—out of the thong. Bending slightly without losing eye contact, she slipped off her high heels, then stood before him wearing only a small smile and earrings. Naked and alluring; a goddess with a most devoted worshipper.

He kicked out of his pants and his shoes, all patience gone. Heat, need, urgency took control of him. He couldn't form a coherent thought, but he knew women liked words.

"Y'all are so beautiful. I've lost my breath." His knees quivered so much, he could barely stand. His arms shook as he pulled her close again, but restrained his impulses and reined in his desire. He yearned to thrust into her, bury himself deep and hold her to him until neither could endure another moment without moving.

He encountered a bobby pin in her hair and gently removed it, then set to work on its companions. The barrette baffled him, and after a clumsy attempt, he broke the kiss. "You'll have to do it. I'm afraid I'll hurt you."

Her mouth twisted briefly before her hands rose, drawing his gaze to the outthrust of her breasts. He forgot to question her odd expression as waves of apricot hair fell to her shoulders.

She set the barrette on the table, then lay back, not taking her eyes from his, inching upward on the bed to make room. He yanked off his boxers and her gaze flickered down. Her tongue came out to lick her lips as though her mouth were as dry as his. He swelled with masculine pride, glad he could make a woman this gorgeous want him. Eyes locked on her, he slid his body over her.

He took, and she gave. She took, and he gave. He formed words, but mostly he showed his appreciation in physical ways—ways Ginger approved of with gasps and groans. She moaned when he nipped at the curve of her hip, sighed when he licked her navel, and fisted her hands in his hair when he sucked at her lush breasts.

Despite her slender body and porcelain skin, she was no china doll needing his restraint. She drew her hands and mouth over him, lingering and enjoying. When she encircled him to guide him into her, he nearly came apart. It had been a long time since he'd been touched this intimately.

She pushed at his shoulder, and he rolled with her, delighted to have her atop him with his hands free to explore. He groaned as she rode him, gritting his teeth against the intense pleasure. It almost killed him, waiting to reach his own climax until he'd satisfied her. When she shattered, he barely had a second to congratulate himself before his next thrust pushed him over the edge.

When his heart calmed and his breathing smoothed out, he rolled to the side, pulling her with him. She cuddled close, limp, and he smiled, sated and content that he'd brought her pleasure, as well.

As he drifted, lazy thoughts floated in and out of his grasp. His mind replayed the softness of her body, the textures and scents of her, the sounds of her moans. Great sex, lovely woman.

It wasn't until later that the fragments formed a cohesive thought. He'd just had the most incredible, hair-catching-on-fire sex of his life.

And he didn't know the woman's last name.

# *Chapter 2*

Ginger came awake slowly, aware of a soft prickle against her face and a crick in her neck. What had she slept on?

Realization hit and she stilled. Scott. Her eyes fluttered open. Definitely a chest under her head and curly male hair tickling her nose.

She gave an inaudible groan. She hadn't meant to actually *sleep* with him. Sex, sure, that was no problem, but she never spent the night. That led to entanglements. She must have slept like the dead not to have woken up by now. Being in his arms felt natural. A bad sign.

The slender opening in the drapes showed a black sky, but in late December that could mean midnight or nearly dawn. Light from the desk lamp she'd turned on the night before illuminated Scott's face, serene in slumber.

His arm lay under her head but didn't encircle her. Although snuggled against him, she could probably steal out of bed without his notice. Testing the theory, she inched her behind backward, then stealthily slid one foot toward the edge, watching his face for a reaction. His eyelids remained closed and his body still. She hated to wrench away from his warmth and considered waking him for a little good morning sex instead.

But the debate lasted only for a moment. She had to get away. Just *wanting* to stay longer warned her he'd breached her defenses already. He was too nice and his loneliness too touching. A guy like him—fun and kind and attentive—threatened her peace of mind.

Ginger lifted her head from his arm, freezing at a noise from him. Assured he slept on, she slid off the bed and grabbed her belongings from the floor. The bathroom provided a safe haven as she yanked on her clothes. She washed her face, grimacing at the remnants of cosmetics she left on the washcloth. Remembering why she'd gone to bed in her makeup, she smiled. Scott was a heck of a guy, seduction-wise. She scraped wet fingers through her curls, fluffing up or patting down as needed to alleviate her bed-head.

She had to skedaddle before he woke. Never had a morning-after felt so sordid, especially when the night before had been so lovely. Although they were strangers, having sex with him had been powerful and moving. Now it felt as though she'd done something to run from. She couldn't face him.

So, of course, he woke when she opened the bathroom door. The disoriented expression on his face made him look rumpled and cuddly and dangerously adorable.

"What—?" He cleared his throat. "Where are y'all going?"

"Home." She kept to the shadows of the room. His accent came thicker in his half-awake state. Why'd he have to be even cuter now? She was supposed to be leaving, firmly walking out the door without a backward glance. Had-a-great-time-thanks-see-you-around, not oh-my-stars-I-want-you-again.

"I'll drive y'all home. Hold on a minute." He threw off the covers, revealing his long tanned body as he sat upright.

Seeing him naked while she wore her cocktail dress from the night before emphasized the wrongness of the situation. "No, I'm fine."

"Oh, do y'all have a car here?"

Ginger shook her head. "I can take a taxi."

*And won't* that *cause talk if I'm seen.* She glanced at the clock. One forty-five. The Riley & Ross party crowd should all be gone by now. She hoped.

He studied her a moment longer than her composure could take. She glanced around for her purse, spotting it on the desk by the still-lit lamp. Lunging, she grabbed it and turned her back to the harsh light. She felt naked and exposed—and not in a good way.

"Thanks for last night," she said. "I had a lovely time."

His eyebrows rose. "And that's it?"

She lifted her lips in a smile. "What did you need to hear?"

Ginger cringed at her harsh phrasing, especially when he floundered, lost for words. But her statement clarified the interaction between them. They'd had great sex. Really great sex. The end.

"I don't even have your phone number," he said. "Or know your last name."

She hid her wince. "Would you really call me?"

He nodded with less assurance than he probably meant to reveal before shrugging. "I'd like to have the option."

Ginger swallowed her hurt.

"I don't have a phone installed yet, and I'll be getting a different cell number with the 816 area code. I came up this week with the movers to get the house settled and meet some of my coworkers." He ran a hand over his face. "Y'all have no idea what I'm talking about, do you? We didn't exactly exchange information."

"You work in the R&D Department at Riley & Ross Electronics. You're the new guy from Alabama."

"Atlanta, actually, and how did you know?"

Ah. Being from the most cosmopolitan city in the South explained his lack of a heavy accent. "I asked about you."

He nodded. "That would be safe."

As though she'd thought of safety. It had been curiosity, pure and simple. Well, maybe not so pure. And this was turning out to be not so simple, either.

"But I'm still pretty much a stranger around these parts," he added.

"Not to me." Ginger closed her eyes even before his surprised grunt of laughter reached her ears. How embarrassing.

"I guess that's true."

She bent over the desk and scribbled her name and phone number. "If you decide to call."

"It might be a while. I have to move more furniture in the next weeks, then get settled in."

She forced a bright, fake smile. "After the New Year, then."

"I'm serious, Ginger."

Exactly the problem. She closed the door quietly behind her. Scott was a serious guy. The kind who'd want a relationship, which, if it worked out, should lead to marriage and a houseful of kids.

Which just wasn't possible with her.

Scott rose to use the bathroom, shaking his head. Maybe Ginger hadn't had the same soul-shaking experience he'd had. To her it might have been just sex.

To him… Well, he couldn't define it. He scratched his chest and picked up the notepad containing her number, wanting to put it somewhere secure. He frowned. She'd only written her first name and a phone number. Didn't she trust him to know her full identity, even after sleeping together? Would he call the number and reach a pizza joint?

Would he even call the number to find out?

He ran a hand over his jaw as he glanced at the bed, feeling slightly sick at the warm, rumpled sheets with their scent of sex. He'd cheated on his wife. Not in actuality, considering the circumstances, but guilt churned in his gut anyway. He hadn't so much as kissed anyone except Samantha since they'd met over six years before.

He'd enjoyed the time spent with Ginger and wanted to take her to bed again. Both feelings intensified his shame.

His hand crumpled the notepaper into a ball. The next weeks' obligations made it impossible to call her anyway. First, he'd be in Georgia, packing up and trying to celebrate one last Christmas with the girls in the only home they knew. He wanted to make this year special, despite the confusion and grief and awkwardness of their changed circumstances. He'd do his best to make it seem normal, to continue the traditions he'd never paid much attention to. Samantha had always handled it, just as she had done everything where the girls were concerned.

Then he would bring his daughters to their new home with him here in Missouri. He'd just enrolled Shelby in second grade and Serena in the day care his boss's mother owned. He'd endure their tears and tantrums, and Shelby declaring him "the worst father ever" for making her leave her friends in Powder Hill. His kid had a smart mouth for a seven-year-old, he thought with a smile. No doubt her teenage babysitter, whom the girls had spent too much time with during the past several months, had been a poor influence. But that would change now. Everything would change now.

God help them, every one!

"So, who was he?"

Ginger rolled her eyes at Lisa's question, the smell of yeast making her stomach rumble. Her friend kneaded bread dough in her bakery kitchen, looking like a fifties mom in her patterned apron. She'd scraped her blond hair back into a ponytail that made her appear closer to seventeen than twenty-seven.

Lisa had made a success catering sweets and desserts for parties and special events. The kitchen she'd built in her basement declared it as a place of business: clean, efficient and utilitarian. Stainless steel appliances stood in sleek lines, but touches of Lisa's personality showed in the bright yellow walls with stenciled cherry stems.

Ginger stood on the outside of the wraparound counter and watched Lisa move with unconscious grace and skill. The question didn't surprise her; after leaving the party the night before, she owed her friend an explanation and reassurance. That didn't mean Ginger had to like it. "What makes you think there was a 'he'?"

"Joe told me."

Of course he had. Ginger had expected no less. "It was the new guy in Dylan's department. Scott."

"I figured, since that's who you'd set your sights on." Lisa punched the dough with a strong fist. "And? What's he like?"

"Really, Lisa. Comparing notes this early in your marriage? I doubt Joe would thank me for telling you."

"Don't be snotty."

"You know I don't kiss and tell."

Lisa peered at her. "Did you do more than kiss him?"

Ginger didn't speak as memories flooded her: Scott's strong, tanned hands caressing her body, his lips delighting every nerve ending, his careful tending to her needs before his and his gentle ways of loving.

Lisa stilled. "Ginger, I worry about you. It was no big deal when you took home guys you've known all your life. But this…"

"It's my own business who I go home with."

Lisa glared at her. "I'm your friend. I love you enough to make you mad at me. Even to lose your friendship if it'll keep you safe."

"I'm safe."

"I'm not talking about safe sex, although I'm glad to hear you haven't completely lost your mind."

"Gee, thanks." Ginger would be angrier if she hadn't been thinking the same thing. Especially since sleeping with Scott a few hours before. That had been a huge mistake, although she didn't regret having earth-shattering sex. But the shattering of her peace of mind since then worried her. She didn't want him to know about the guys she'd been with in the past year, trying to appease her loneliness. Being with someone occasionally had helped her get through Kyle's leaving.

They had been married, happily she'd thought, for four years. Now she was alone. If hooking up with a nice, single guy once or twice a month alleviated her melancholy for a few hours, who did it hurt?

But being with Scott changed that. She cringed to think he'd find out she'd been what her mother would call "loose with her affections." Not that she had. She'd kept a tight rein on her heart, or rather, the pieces of it she had left after Kyle rejected her.

Because she couldn't have children.

Ginger tried to suppress the constant ache the thought produced. She couldn't forget. Her infertility was as much a part of her as her arm. Sometimes when she was with a man, she could shove the reminder from the forefront of her mind. The guys she spent time with didn't care. They desired her, laughed with her and appreciated her as a woman.

She scowled at Lisa. "You couldn't possibly understand."

Lisa raised an eyebrow. "My first husband left me, in case you'd forgotten. For a younger babe he'd been sleeping with since she turned legal."

"But you have Joe now."

Her face softened. "Yes, I got extremely lucky."

"And you've got Abby and Bobby and can have more kids."

Lisa's wide gaze darted to Ginger's at the mention of another baby.

"Don't wait," Ginger said, watching her friend read her expression. It never failed—at the mention of babies, Lisa walked on eggshells around her. "I know Joe loves Abby and Bobby, but he'll want his own children."

"He's not like that. He's a great father already."

Ginger nodded. "But men like their own genes passed on. That's why Kyle wouldn't even talk about adopting."

The instant she mentioned the word, Ginger realized her mistake. Lisa would ask.

"Have you heard anything from the adoption agency?"

Ginger looked away. She knew she'd have to tell Lisa eventually, but saying it out loud would make it more real.

"Oh, no," Lisa said, obviously reading her face. "What happened?"

"I got turned down for a home visit."

"When?"

"Yesterday afternoon. Before the party." She could almost hear Lisa's thought process: *So that's why you went looking for comfort with Scott.*

"That's so unfair," Lisa said instead. "Why didn't you tell me?"

Ginger shrugged. "It's the holidays. Why should we both be depressed?"

"You weren't seriously thinking of keeping this to yourself for two weeks, I hope." She rounded the counter and hugged Ginger. "I'm so sorry. It's just not right."

"I know that and you know that." Her yearning for a child was even stronger now than when she and Kyle had gone to the fertility clinic to discuss options. "The adoption agency is concerned about me providing for a baby. The money, a sitter, the whole shebang."

Lisa's face creased into a frown. "Can they do that? I mean, I'm a mom and I have to worry about money and sitters."

"I don't know what they're allowed to do and how much of the flak I'm getting is just this woman disliking me for some reason. When you give birth, you don't have to jump through hoops to earn the right to be a mother." She gulped a breath. "I don't want to rock the boat, just in case she's playing by the book. It's better I lie low and cooperate."

"Help is available," Lisa said. "Dylan's mom would make a spot for your baby at the day care she owns. The baby would be safe and cared for during the day."

"I don't like the idea of sending a newborn to day care, even one as reputable as the Wee Care." But she'd have to. She couldn't afford to quit her job or take a couple years' leave of absence, which would be the same as quitting. She couldn't expect the school district to hold her job. Her current financial situation would only allow her to stay home during the summers.

"The adoption agency is very concerned about backup. What happens when I have a meeting at school or something comes up? You know how I'm always being assigned to some committee." She blew out a breath. "The witch at the agency was all over me about my lack of support. I don't have any family here now that Mom moved. Obviously no husband. From the drilling I endured, you'd think single people never adopt kids. Why am I different?"

Ginger studied her hands before she spoke the words that plagued her. "Do you think she can sense I'd be a bad mother?"

"That's ridiculous. You'll be fantastic. You shouldn't stand for that kind of treatment. You need to talk to someone else at that agency. Or go somewhere else." Lisa frowned. "There are other adoption agencies in Kansas City, right?"

Ginger nodded. "I might try that. Ms. Booker seems dead-set against me for some reason."

"As for help on a moment's notice—when you're not bringing the baby to Aunt Lisa, that is—Dylan's brother has eight kids and a list of babysitters when you need someone reliable." Lisa's gaze flew to hers. "Sorry, I shouldn't have mentioned Adam and Anne's family."

"I'm happy for them." Other people having kids didn't bother her, even them having eight children. Seeing pregnant women sometimes made her tear up, and envy ate acidy holes in her stomach, but she didn't begrudge anyone the kind of happiness she longed for. "It's not as though I think they got my share of kids."

When Ginger met her, Anne Ross had been near to bursting with child number eight, a beautiful girl they'd named Penelope. Dylan, the proud uncle, had brought a picture to Lisa and Joe's when Ginger had been at the same picnic. He didn't know of her condition, and she'd begged Lisa and Joe to keep it between them.

It was bad enough Ginger's own husband had found her defective. She didn't need the whole town gossiping about it. Just imagining the pity she'd receive made her blanch.

"So, this Scott guy," Lisa started, "what's he really like?"

"Are you asking as the wife of his boss or as my nosy, pushy friend?"

Lisa chuckled and washed her hands at the sink. "Both."

"He's extremely nice. Well-mannered and polite."

"Uh-huh. That was for the boss's wife. Now spill."

Ginger grinned. "He's incredible in bed. Very giving, if you know what I mean. Strong, hot body, tanned all over, except for his swimsuit lines." She closed her eyes as she recalled tracing those borders and what lay between.

Lisa giggled. "Wait. Maybe I shouldn't hear this. I'll

probably have to see him at some function, and I won't be able to block out this image."

"Sweetie, you don't know what you're missing." But Ginger was relieved not to have to think about Scott and how amazing the sex had been. Because remembering made it feel like more than sex, and it wasn't. Couldn't be.

"When do you plan to see him again?"

Ginger swallowed and tried to keep her expression calm. "What's the point? You can't improve on perfection."

"But if being with him was perfect, why not have seconds?"

Ginger lifted her lips in an artificial smile, hoping Lisa couldn't tell she'd clenched her teeth. Her friend insisted not every man would care about Ginger's barrenness, and most men would be open to adopting if that were their only option to build a family.

Ginger didn't believe it. She'd had a man, one who'd already committed his life to her. That man, with love in his heart, had found her lacking. What chance did she have making a stranger want her once she told him?

"Perfect," she said, "is an illusion. The more you try to repeat it, the more you notice flaws."

She couldn't risk seeing Scott because she wanted to so badly. He'd gotten to her, touched her in secret places that had nothing to do with sex. When he'd said he didn't want to hurt her, he'd meant by pulling her hair removing her barrette. But Ginger sensed he could seriously break her heart. And she just couldn't risk that happening again.

The New Year turned and Scott still hadn't called Ginger. He fingered the hotel notepaper in his pocket while he waited to meet his daughter's second-grade teacher. The principal reminded him more of a used car salesman than an educator, and he'd already snagged Scott to serve on a committee. Scott knew his daughter wouldn't be sent to the principal's office, though.

Shelby was a good kid, saving her smart-aleck remarks for him. Testing him, his mother-in-law assured Scott. Apparently, Shelby had been angelic when she and Serena stayed with their grandparents while he'd been here getting the house ready. Shelby could test him all she wanted; he'd always be there for her. Even without a psychology degree, he knew Shelby feared he'd leave her and her sister. Acting out and pushing the boundaries made her a normal kid, considering all she and Serena had endured.

How could he put them through anything as traumatic as seeing him with another woman?

He'd carried the paper with Ginger's phone number every day, worried he'd lose it. The crinkle and stiffness in his pocket the first days reminded him of their time together. But he'd been in Georgia then, retrieving his daughters from their grandparents' house and enduring everyone's tears. Now the paper had worn smooth, and its weight in his pocket wasn't so much physical as mental. Guilt sometimes made him consider throwing away Ginger's number, but he hadn't. Nor had he called. He couldn't bring himself to do either thing.

The office door opened and he rose, turning to meet the new teacher, who stumbled to a halt, hand on the doorknob, eyes wide and apricot hair secured in a ponytail.

His breath caught in his chest as his heart thudded. Hell of a way to find out his lover's last name.

# Chapter 3

Ginger gasped, feeling the blood drain from her face. Scott stood in Mr. Bushfield's office, apparently the father of her new midterm arrival. Her flesh felt like ice, but she couldn't blame the early January weather.

"This is Scott Matthews," Bushfield said. "He's brought in his daughter Shelby, who, as you know, is enrolled in your class."

Scott held out his hand.

*He wants to shake hands?* Ginger pressed her lips together to suppress the hysterical bubble waiting to erupt. Shake hands, after what they'd done together? After the ecstasy that hand had brought her?

Or maybe that feeling of connection had all been on her part. Maybe he'd lied to her about being married. He hadn't mentioned having a child. Had everything between them been an act? Ginger wanted to rush out, sick to her stomach.

She forced herself to focus and placed her hand in his, trying to behave as though he were any other father. Warmth zinged up her arm, raising more goose bumps. "Hello."

He nodded. "Ginger."

"You know each other?" Bushfield asked.

She snatched her hand from Scott's but couldn't tear away her gaze. His hazel eyes held none of the passion she remembered. She couldn't read his expression at all, as though he were a stranger. And really, wasn't he? "We met a few weeks ago."

"At a party." Scott's gaze trailed over her as though he'd never seen her before.

Of course she looked different, she thought crossly. She couldn't wear a slinky cocktail dress to school. Besides the kids ruining it before half an hour passed, she'd never be able to rise from the floor, where she spent much of her time. If Scott didn't like her black slacks and snowman sweatshirt, too bad.

"This is my daughter Shelby." His soft Southern accent had nearly vanished in the past weeks. Except for a slowness to his words, he sounded as hard and flat as a native Midwesterner.

Ginger peered around him as he pushed the girl forward. Dark brown eyes dominated Shelby's pale skin. Her nearly black hair had been pulled back with purple butterfly barrettes on each side of her head. She may have inherited her darker coloring and delicate features from her mother, but the scowl on her face was pure Scott.

"Hello, Shelby. I'm happy to have you in my class." She smiled, wishing the girl had a different father. One who didn't make Ginger's skin tingle. One who didn't make her stomach clench with excitement.

One who didn't know of her extracurricular activities.

"Would you like to see your new classroom?" Ginger offered. "The other children should be arriving in a few minutes." She glanced at Scott. "You're welcome to come, too. It sometimes helps for a parent to be able to visualize his child's environment."

She hid her grimace, fearing she sounded as condescending as Bushfield. She led them down the hall, overly conscious of Scott and his sullen daughter. Was the universe out to get her?

She strove for composure, but her mind had become a glaring white screen bordered by fuzzy screams she tried to ignore. Just as she tried to ignore Scott's presence at her elbow. How long before she could look up Shelby's guardian information and discover whether the night of passion she couldn't forget, the night that had changed her way of thinking about herself, was actually a night of adultery?

She pointed to the right where she heard children singing. Hopefully the playground monitors would work off some of the children's excitement about being back at school. The first day after Christmas break could be stressful. "There's the gym. The students are inside today because the weather's bad. Most mornings you can play outside. You'll also wait for the bus after school in the gym."

Neither Scott nor Shelby answered.

She could imagine the questions in his mind but wished she knew his thoughts. The woman he'd enjoyed a one-night stand with was his daughter's new teacher. Amazing bad luck.

She passed the third grade rooms and neared hers, glad the discerning eye of Cindy Grady wasn't on her at the moment. The woman stalked her every movement, waiting for a slipup. Cindy's sister had lost her teaching job at the beginning of the year. It didn't take a genius to figure out who Cindy had in mind for Ginger's replacement, as soon as she could get her dismissed.

Maybe it was unreasonable to wonder why Scott hadn't mentioned having a kid. To be fair, she hadn't mentioned being a teacher, either. They'd met too near Christmas, a time she tried to avoid all thoughts of children, even those just under her care during work hours. Adding in her bad news from the adoption agency that day, she'd been less likely to discuss children than usual.

The man she'd slept with after the Christmas party had been sweet and gentle and considerate. She couldn't believe he'd faked the loneliness she'd seen in the ballroom. Yet here he was with a child. Where was the girl's mother? He deserved the benefit of the doubt until he had a chance to explain.

"Here we are." She waved Shelby in.

The girl studied the room, not budging from the doorway. Ginger walked past them, trying to see the room as Scott might. Colorful walls, enough visuals to stimulate without overwhelming the children, and the basic white boards, with a number line, and both a print and cursive alphabet chart over them. Pull-down maps anchored each board.

"This will be your desk." Ginger tapped a finger on a desk in the second row. She'd put Shelby by two of her nicest girls. One was outgoing and would instantly declare herself Shelby's best friend; the other was quieter but just as sweet. Judging by Shelby's reticence so far,

Ginger guessed the soft-spoken Maria would be more to her liking.

Ginger glanced at Scott, who stood in the hall behind his daughter. "We have a reading corner for spare time, a library." She pointed as she named the areas. "A writing area with huge sheets of paper donated by a certain local computer firm…"

He smiled faintly.

*Tough crowd.* Still, she didn't teach incorrigible seven-year-olds because she was a pushover. "And a math center with fairly decent computers. Do you use a computer at home, Shelby?"

"My real school has a computer lab where we go to every week."

Ginger suppressed a grin. Despite the intended slight, or perhaps because of it, this girl appealed to her. Not giving an inch and putting her new teacher in her place.

Scott set his hand on her shoulder. "This is your real school, Shel."

Although she nodded, the girl's mouth firmed. She'd take some winning over. Maybe the more gregarious Jean would be closer to Shelby in attitude than Maria, after all. "Your records haven't arrived from your previous school yet. Do you have a favorite subject?"

Shelby's teeth glinted in an angelic smile. "I liked computer lab a lot."

Ginger bit back another grin at Shelby's polite rebellion. By year's end, this girl would either delight her or be her biggest headache. Glancing at Scott, Ginger decided to withhold her guess at which. His influence would be vital.

Ginger couldn't tell what Scott thought of her class-room and hated that his opinion mattered. She'd put too much of her heart in here over the past five years to view the room impartially. Hoping for an insight, she gestured the two of them in. "You're welcome to explore, Shelby."

The girl hunched her shoulders as though she didn't plan to remove her backpack or her coat. She had no intention of staying. Just then, Scott nudged her and they both entered the room. Ginger quietly exhaled her relief.

"Nice room," Scott said.

She smiled with pride.

"I'll be able to visualize you in this environment, Shelby, while I'm at work." He turned a frosty eye to Ginger. "That'll help."

Ginger narrowed her gaze as he mocked her with her own words, but she kept her calm for his daughter's sake. Not that Shelby had spared a glance for her teacher, except for the fierce scowl in the principal's office. Why had the girl taken an instant dislike to her? Had she picked up the vibes between her teacher and her father? Hard to believe, especially when Scott had treated her like a near stranger, other than his mention of them meeting at a party. Had that set the girl against her?

"The girls around you are Jean and Maria." Ginger pointed out their desks. "Harry sits in front of you and his twin brother, Ron, sits behind you."

"Ron and Harry?" Scott asked. "Like from the Harry Potter books?"

Ginger nodded and turned to Shelby. "They don't like to be teased about their names."

Shelby stared at her with her dark, depthless eyes. "Why do you think I would tease them?"

Scott stepped up beside his daughter. "Shelby doesn't make fun of other children."

*Great. Alienate the student and her father.* "I'm glad

to hear that. I'm sure you'll get along nicely then." Ginger turned her smile on Scott. "I didn't mean to imply *she* would be unfriendly."

*Just because you are.*

His jaw clenched, proving her message got through.

"I'll show you your locker so you can put your coat away." Ginger took them into the hall and indicated the girl's locker. Shelby shrugged out of her backpack, and Scott hung her coat on a hook.

He winked at Shelby. "Now I can visualize your coat in its environment."

Shelby grinned, displaying a missing tooth on the bottom row. The girl may not understand all the undercurrents, but she recognized her father had scored a hit.

Ginger had dealt with all kinds of parents through her five years teaching second grade, but she'd never had a relationship with a father interfere with her emotions before. Not that *relationship* would be the right word for what she'd shared with the insufferable man currently taunting her. It had been one night of passion. It might have been easier if they *had* dated and broken up. At least then she'd know his mind.

"May I speak to you privately, Mr. Matthews?"

"Why, of course, Ms. Winchester."

Ginger barely stopped herself from glaring, knowing Shelby watched them intently. "Shelby, go ahead and put your things in your desk."

Her student looked to her father first for his nod of approval, then dragged her feet into the classroom.

Ginger squared off with him as soon as the girl left their earshot. "One question and I only need a yes or no. Are you married?"

"No." His surprised expression was answer enough, but the spoken denial made her sag with relief.

"Okay, then. Thank you." She took a breath; it felt like the first she'd taken since recognizing him in the principal's office. "Scott, no matter what went on between us, we need to be able to speak civilly to one another for your daughter's sake."

"Why didn't you tell me you taught second grade?"

She retreated a step, taken aback by his question. Up to this point, he'd behaved as though he disliked her. Miffed, she shot back, "Why didn't you tell me you had a daughter?"

He glanced away. "Two."

It took her a moment. "You have two daughters?"

"The other is in preschool at the Wee Care. My boss's mother owns it, but you probably know that. I took her this morning. The three of us moved up after Christmas. That's why I've been too busy to call."

Ginger absorbed the news. Two daughters, no wife. "It's a good preschool. I noticed Shelby will be taking the bus there after school."

"Unfortunately." He hunched his shoulders. "I don't like leaving them for so long, but at least I can take them both to their schools in the mornings. I've already talked to Dylan about flexing my hours so I can start work later."

Ginger wanted to give him a hug of reassurance, wondering if he'd just gotten custody. The first adjustments after a divorce were hard enough without kids. Would the girls be shuttled to Georgia to visit their mother for holidays and summer vacations? Poor things. Maybe she could cut Shelby some slack.

"I'm serious about us getting along better," she said. "Especially in front of Shelby."

"I agree." He shoved his hands in the front pockets of his pants and rocked back on his heels. "I have to get to work right now, but maybe we should get together later to discuss this."

His offer sounded like a date, although *get together* gave his suggestion a casual air. Their relationship so far had been intense and intimate, if short-lived. Tempted, she steeled her resolve. She could not get involved with this man, especially now his daughter was in her class. The principal had delivered a lengthy oration—the only kind of talk he knew how to give—just that morning regarding the school district's cracking down on any hint of impropriety. She couldn't afford for the adoption agency to hear of a scandal, either. "What do we need to discuss?"

Scott blinked, some of the starch knocked out of him. "Our…"

She raised her eyebrows. "Night of passion?"

"For starters."

"Starters? That's all we have between us. Except now there's Shelby."

"So that's it?"

The bell rang and clattering children charged down the hall. "I have to go now," Ginger said. "If you want to discuss Shelby's progress in my class, you know where to find me." She snapped her fingers. "Wait, I know. You could always call me."

Turning on her heel, she marched into her classroom.

The next day, Scott waited in the school lobby to have a surprise lunch with Shelby. He'd spent the morning at the Wee Care Preschool and Day Care with Serena, making sure she eased into her new surroundings. Dylan was a heck of a guy to give him an extra day off. Scott owed the man big-time, especially as his wife, Tara, had helped ease Rena into the routine. Rena had taken pride in showing her school to him, not having attended preschool or day care back home.

He sighed, then pasted on a smile as the children from Shelby's classroom walked down the hall toward him. He spied his daughter looking at the floor as she walked, and his chest ached. Poor kid. Being older, the adjustment would be harder for her than for Serena. New school, new friends, new life.

Ginger followed the children out of the room, locking the door behind her. Scott knew when she spotted him by the way her foot stuttered, her shoulders straightened and her lips firmed. She couldn't fool him. He knew how soft those lips could be, especially pressed against his body.

Swallowing, he set down the carry-out food tray just as Shelby launched herself into his arms.

"Dad! What are you doing here?" Her smile lit his day.

Her classmates continued on, throwing questioning glances their way. "I'm having lunch with you." He looked up at Ginger. "I checked in at the office and they said to wait here."

Her eyes pierced him before her expression turned bland. "That's fine, and what a nice treat for you, Shelby."

Shelby nodded and clung to his hand.

"Why don't you show your father the way to the cafeteria." Ginger walked toward the stairs.

Scott grunted, not caring to be dismissed in such an offhand manner. As though he were just another parent. "Well, peanut, how's about you and I have some food?"

He picked up the cardboard drink tray and bags, one child's chicken pieces meal and his own more substantial fish fillet and fries. They couldn't do takeout too often, for health and financial reasons, but he wanted today to be special.

"What about the lunch you packed me?" she asked.

"Save it for tomorrow."

"Wow." Shelby hugged his waist. "We go down here, and I'll show you my table." Her brow wrinkled. "We'll have to find a chair for you."

"You have an assigned table?" He hadn't realized that nor had the office mentioned it when he'd called to find out the procedure.

"It's okay. I'll make Harry or Ron move."

"Shelby." He frowned at her as they descended. "Y'all can't kick either of those boys out of their seats."

She gave a shrug he'd seen his wife use. Samantha had always meant "we'll see" by it, and she usually got her way. He hadn't realized Shelby had picked up that particular gesture, although he'd noted other gestures of Sam's both girls had assumed. He shook his head, knowing Shelby didn't mean to be heartless.

"It'll be okay," he said. "If there aren't enough seats, you can sit on my lap."

"Daaad." She rolled her eyes.

That gesture he knew all too well meant *You're such a moron.*

As it turned out, a cafeteria monitor found him a chair while the children made envious noises to Shelby over her meal. He thanked the woman, talking for a moment to discover she volunteered at the school twice a week for lunchtime. Scott couldn't do that as the school lunch period stretched over two hours, but it put the idea of volunteering in his head. The principal had snagged him the day before to serve on a committee, but he wanted to spend time with Shelby. Maybe something in the classroom. He could flex the time he took lunch to match Shelby's schedule.

Of course, volunteering in the classroom meant seeing Ginger. He doubted Ms. Winchester would welcome him with open arms.

Which led his thoughts to when she had. He cleared his throat. Not the appropriate time or place for those images.

Shelby threw out the first names of the other children by way of introduction.

"What's a programmer do?" the boy to his left asked. Harry, Scott thought, the blond with extra large front teeth. Poor kid. Harry's twin still sported baby teeth, but Scott figured Ron would have the same appearance with his adult incisors. Wouldn't be a problem once the boys grew into them. He hoped the other kids didn't tease them in the meantime.

Scott outlined his job to the boys, who hung on his explanation as though he'd invented the internet. Shelby sighed dramatically, but then to her, he was just her father, not Mr. Wizard. Having a child interested in his work made a nice change.

"Ron," she said, "you've got jelly on your shirt."

"Oh." The boy glanced down. "Where?"

Shelby sniggered. "Made you look."

Scott shot her an admonishing glance, although the other children laughed, including Ron and Harry. The next time he came, he'd bring lunches for everyone. Would that be a problem with their parents? Did any of the kids have food allergies? He sighed. This parenting thing was harder than he'd imagined. Sharing lunch at school had been Sam's job. Now every duty was his by default.

Still, he thought as Shelby hugged him goodbye, there were rewards.

He watched her run out to the playground, her earlier doldrums forgotten, although she hadn't been pleased when he declined going outside for recess with her and her friends. Kickball or jump rope in under-forty-degree temperatures held no appeal for him. One last wave, then it was past time to get to work.

As Scott turned to the office to sign out, he noticed Ginger going into her classroom again. Awfully short lunch break. This might be the time to ask about volunteering. Perhaps she had a list of needs or a sign-up sheet.

He knocked twice, then opened her door. She raised her head, looking right at home behind the teacher's desk. A born educator.

Spotting him, Ginger masked her irritation. She should have relocked her door until it was time for the kids to come back in. Her lunch "hour" was actually forty-five minutes. Spending time with a parent shouldn't intrude, but a phone call or visit often interrupted. "Did you have a good lunch with Shelby?"

"It was very nice. Sorry." He gestured toward her desk where her lunch wrappings remained. "I didn't realize y'all were still eating."

She snapped the lid on her sandwich carrier and slipped it into her thermal bag. "I'm almost done. Do you have a question?"

"I want to volunteer. In the classroom."

Forcing her face to remain impassive, she nodded. Her fist clenched below the desk. Hadn't meeting him again yesterday been enough punishment for whatever crimes fate held against her?

"Do you have anything coming up I could do?" he asked. "Maybe before or after lunch?"

And give her indigestion? "Not that I can think of, but I'll keep you in mind."

His eyes narrowed. "Nothing? Are you sure?"

She gave him her fake smile. "Nothing that's of short duration. I'll give you the numbers of the room parents planning the Valentine's party next month." *Not that you're good about calling when you've got someone's number.* She flipped open the cabinet drawer behind her and pulled out the party folder.

"Valentine's Day? I can probably do that." His shoulders hunched.

Would the romantic holiday be hard for him this year, being suddenly single after...however long he'd been married? So much she didn't know about him, despite their night together.

"But I was hoping for something before then," he said, "to help Shelby get settled here."

"Perhaps finding her own way, without your presence, would be easier for her." *As it would be for me.*

"What about Shelby's birthday? What's normally done? Should I try to come in that day for some kind of celebration?"

He had her there. "We usually have snacks at the end of the day, just before leaving. You can send something in the morning if you have to work."

"Aren't parents allowed to come in for the party?"

"Of course." She gave a mental sigh and determined to do something kind for someone to realign her karma.

"You can bring it in around two-thirty. That gives us time to sing, serve and clean up before the bell rings."

She pulled open her desk drawer and dug out the file she needed. Extending a sheet of paper to him, she added, "Here's the list of food allergies this year. Ron and Harry West's mother will send in a special snack for them since they're sensitive to so many foods. I'll add Shelby's birthday to the list Ms. West already has."

He stepped closer and took the paper from her. His fingers brushed hers, causing her nerve endings to sizzle. Had he touched her on purpose?

Scott cleared his throat. "Food allergies. I'm glad I asked. I was thinking about bringing lunch for everyone at Shelby's table sometime."

"You'll need to keep that with you, then. It would be best to send home a note with the boys and ask Ms. West to call you. She's also in charge of the Valentine's party."

"Thanks."

He continued to stare, but she refused to fidget. He was too close, too tempting.

"Was there something else?"

Scott's lips firmed. "I guess not."

He left, taking the tension with him. Ginger retrieved Shelby's thin file, checking for her birthday. She closed her eyes. January twenty-first. Fifteen days. Not nearly enough time to prepare to see Scott again.

Curiosity conquered her better intentions, and she scanned the student information form Scott had filled out when he registered his daughter. *Sole custody.* No info filled in on the mother, but nothing flagged her as a potential threat, either. At least not as far as kidnapping Shelby went. The threat to Ginger was harder to gauge.

Memories could be more difficult to fight than a flesh-and-blood, fallible woman.

After school, Ginger went home, glad she didn't have papers to grade for once. She had lessons to prepare, of course, and reading to do—that was a given. Maybe after, she could stretch out in front of the fireplace with a novel for some escapism. What a luxury. Papers had to be reviewed for the upcoming evaluation reports, but those could wait another night.

A glance into her refrigerator reminded her of another thing she'd put off for "another night." That Scarlett O'Hara character was a bad influence. With a sigh, Ginger dragged out some questionable lettuce, a squishy pink tomato that made her long for summer, and a limp cucumber. Disgusted that she'd even consider making this into a salad, she pitched it all into the trash. Tonight, she'd take her recreational reading to a corner booth at the Panera restaurant, sitting with her back to the room so she might pass unnoticed, then force herself to the grocery store.

Scott pulled into a space in the lot at the Piggly Wiggly. Both his girls were keyed up after their first full day at school. Serena hadn't stopped chattering about Miss Tara, Dylan's wife, or Miss Betty, Rena's teacher, who was also Dylan's mom. She'd placed Serena in her class. He felt better about leaving her at the Wee Care, since he knew someone who'd been raised by the woman spending so much time with Serena. Having his boss's wife there helped, too. Not that he hadn't called the day care's references and the school district and checked into both thoroughly in December before enrolling his girls. But he appreciated the personal touch and peace of mind Dylan's family provided.

Dark had fallen two hours before, but he insisted they shop for food before going home.

Then he saw Ginger lifting a canvas tote bag full of groceries into her trunk. His stomach dropped. He couldn't make his hand turn off the engine. Seeing her today had been ridiculous. He wanted to touch her, stroke her hand, kiss her lips. Call her for a date—a real date, going out first to dinner or a movie or both.

*First.* He closed his eyes. That was the clincher. He wanted her under him, surrounding him, loving him. And then he felt sick. While he still regarded being with another woman as a betrayal of his vows to Samantha, he couldn't start a relationship.

But he couldn't seem to stay away from Ginger, either. And in a town with a population under three thousand, it was more than likely he'd run into her on occasion.

"Aren't we going in the store?" Shelby asked from the backseat.

Ginger rammed the metal shopping buggy into the cart corral and rushed back to her car, head bent against the bitter wind.

"No." He cleared his throat. "Let's wait till tomorrow. We'll drive through and get food tonight." So much for not resorting to fast food too often.

"Goody," Serena said. "I'm hungry."

"Wow," Shelby breathed. "Twice in one day?"

Scott grimaced. *Great example I'm providing.* "Let's see if this town knows how to do barbecue like home."

He pulled out after Ginger's silver Honda, smiling at her license plate: EDUK8. Her car would be easy to locate in a parking lot, except maybe at school. She turned left, and he swung in behind her.

A glance in the rearview mirror assured him neither girl noticed the wrong turn he'd taken. And why would they? Not only was this a strange place for them, they weren't old enough to know all the routes around town. Only his guilt had him checking for their reaction. Thoughts of Samantha rode shotgun.

He followed the Honda for three more turns, letting distance slide between them as the traffic thinned. He'd prefer not to be recognized in his orange Jeep Patriot, nor did he want to scare her, but his need to find out where she lived overrode any notion of abandoning the pursuit.

*What a head case.* Couldn't ask her out, couldn't leave her alone.

The Honda's brake lights shone, and then Ginger pulled into a driveway on the left. Black numbers, 927, gleamed from her white mailbox. Now, he mocked himself, if only he'd paid attention to what street this was on. Her house was a vinyl-sided two-story, about forty years old, with big front windows and a brick chimney. Nothing special. Not a princess's castle or a harem's quarters. Just a house where an intriguing, sexy woman lived.

A woman he wanted with a hunger that was as intense as fire burning down a forest.

He went back to Ginger's house Saturday night. He should have been enjoying a rare few hours of peace with the girls gone, but instead he sat in his car. Staring at Ginger's empty house, wondering where she was, who she was with, and, worse, what they were doing. It was neither an enjoyable nor a peaceful way to spend Saturday night.

Shelby had gone on her first sleepover with Maria, a sweet girl from school, who'd become Shelby's best friend. He'd talked on the phone with Maria's mother and felt as confident as he could be about the overnight. Serena had been a last-minute addition to a classmate's birthday at a tumbling party and was due to be picked up in half an hour. He'd stupidly thought he'd swing by and talk to Ginger, try to come to a decision about her one way or the other. Do her, or leave her alone.

*Do her?* He slapped the steering wheel with his palm. For God's sakes.

Since it was only—he checked his phone—seven-thirty, he doubted she'd be home soon. With a shake of his head, he turned on the ignition, letting the car warm. He'd leave now, go to the TumbleBee and watch Serena do whatever for thirty minutes, then take her home where they both belonged.

Via a detour back down Willow Lane.

He shook his head. Pathetic.

Less than an hour later, with Serena sleeping in her car seat behind him, he pulled to a stop down the street from Ginger's house and watched as she emerged from a dark pickup truck in her driveway. Watched some jerk get out from the driver's side.

Scott's hands tightened on the wheel. Ginger had gone out on a date. Bitter acid filled his mouth as she flipped on an inside light and led the guy into her house. The door shut against the dark night.

He closed his eyes. He didn't want to imagine what they'd do next. Maybe it was her brother or her cousin or her pastor. Could be another teacher discussing some school problem.

Yeah, right.

He had no hold on her. If she wanted to date other guys—hell, even have sex with other guys—he had no right to be…what?

Angry? Jealous? Hurt?

All of the above.

# Chapter 4

As a treat, Scott took his daughters to the movies late the next afternoon. While the girls were gone the previous evening, he'd cleaned, organized and finished unpacking. When he wasn't stalking Ginger's house.

Scott sighed and pulled into the movie theater parking lot. He still had quite a few to-do's on his list before he'd consider his family settled in Howard. Shelby wanted to sign up for gymnastics and dance classes. Serena needed to learn to swim. He didn't know how he'd manage transportation, let alone have any idea where to send them for instruction. He didn't want either girl subjected to a drill sergeant who would suck all the fun out of the activities. Samantha had told him horror stories of her childhood dance teachers. He couldn't imagine Shelby putting up with an instructor like that. For once, he was glad Ginger was her teacher. She wouldn't rule with too heavy a hand.

"This is so great, Dad." Shelby helped unbuckle her younger sister. "Everybody in school was talking about seeing *Whisker Puss* this weekend, but I didn't think I would get to."

"Why not?" He helped Serena down from the Jeep then shut the door.

"We haven't done much fun things lately."

*Ouch.* He nodded, taking Serena's hand. "We'll have to see about changing that. Right, Rena?" Starting with classes where his girls could make friends. He'd call Harry and Ron's mom for starters. Maybe she wouldn't know about dance classes, having the twin boys, but she might know where to sign up for swimming. Having friends would help the girls feel at home here. The sleepover and tumbling party the evening before had been a good start.

Should he encourage Shelby to have friends stay overnight? He suppressed an inward shudder, imagining high-pitched voices, sticky crafts and pink everything. Then there was Rena; could he handle even two more four-year-olds for an overnight? Would a mother let her little girl sleep at a home with a single dad?

He bought their tickets, then headed for the concession stand. The prices of popcorn and three bottled waters made him cringe. Adding the cost of admission and treats to eating out twice this week, their budget was going to need some adjustment. "Let's go find seats."

A nudge on his arm almost made him spill the tub of popcorn.

"Look," Shelby whispered. "It's Ms. Winchester."

He jerked, his gaze flying to where Shelby stared.

"No, Dad! Don't look."

Scott spotted Ginger immediately, her apricot hair a

dead giveaway. She ran her gaze around the lobby, coming back to him, then the girls. Her shoulders drooped infinitesimally before she nodded a hello.

"We have to go over, Shel. She's seen us."

"Daaad."

"It would be rude not to say hello."

As they neared, Ginger smiled but her stiff posture didn't appear welcoming. Or maybe she just didn't care to see him.

"Ms. Winchester."

"Mr. Matthews, Shelby." She turned to Serena. "Hi, I'm Shelby's teacher, Ms. Winchester. What's your name?"

Serena stared with wide, milk-chocolate eyes, like her mother's.

"This is Serena," Scott said. "She's—" He didn't want to label her as shy when Rena could hear. "She's four."

"And a half," the girl corrected.

He flashed a grin at her. "Sorry. Four and a half. She goes to the Wee Care."

"I haf school there, plus playtime. It's fun."

It seemed her shyness had disappeared. Usually, she never talked to adults she knew, let alone strangers. Must be the similarities between Ginger and Samantha easing Rena's shyness.

"I've heard that's a very nice place," Ginger said. "I'm acquainted with Miss Betty. Her son is a friend."

Serena's eyes grew larger and her plump mouth formed an O. Scott wondered how much of a friend Dylan had been to Ginger before his recent marriage, then slammed that door shut. None of his business, and he had to work with the man. Still, the tightening of his gut warned him the concern lingered, ready to flare if not contained.

"Yeah," Shelby cut in, "I got to go there, too, after school. After *real* school. And *I* get to take the bus."

Scott frowned at his daughter's self-important tone, then checked Serena, who didn't seem to register her sister's put-down. Seeking a distraction, he asked Ginger, "What are you seeing?"

She raised an eyebrow, and he realized the idiocy of the question. The Howard Cine only boasted two theaters. The other show was *The Butcher's Back in Town,* a gore fest whose commercial trailer on TV had made him slightly nauseous.

*"Whisker Puss,"* she said. "I have to keep current so I know what the kids are talking about in class."

Scott glanced at her skeptically. "Right."

She grinned. "Okay, you got me. I like cartoons."

"It's an animated feature." Shelby scowled. "Only babies like cartoons."

"I'm not a baby," Serena insisted.

Just as Scott opened his mouth, Ginger spoke. "Well, Shelby, obviously that's not true, since I like cartoons and I'm certainly not a child. And an animated feature is often a cartoon, although the description includes other forms of animation, as well." She broke off with a yawn and covered her mouth. "Excuse me."

"Late night?" Scott heard the edge to his tone. He'd bet she was tired, after having been out—or in—with that guy. How late had he stayed? All night?

"I graded papers last night so I could free up tonight for the movie."

"Graded papers. Right. The way you were *grading papers* with me over Christmas break?"

Ginger narrowed her eyes and stepped backward a few

paces, beckoning with her stare. He followed to ensure the girls couldn't hear.

"What is the matter with you?" Ginger demanded, her color high.

"I happened to drive past your house last night. I saw you go in to 'grade papers' with that guy."

Her fists landed on her hips. "If you'd 'happened by' around half an hour later, you'd have seen him leave."

He blinked, nonplused. "Half an hour?"

"Not that what I do is any of your business."

"I'm sorry." He swallowed. "I jumped to conclusions. Why?"

"Why what?"

"Why did you send him home?"

"Scott." She blew out a breath. "That's *so* not your business, either."

"No, sorry." His knees wanted to give out, to sink him to the floor in relief. "I'm glad, though. Not that it's any concern of mine," he tacked on when she opened her mouth, no doubt to set him in his place. "I get that. But still, I want you to know. I'm glad you didn't grade papers with him—or do any other schoolwork."

Her teeth glinted. "Did I say that?"

He deserved that one, he supposed, stepping back to the girls with her. No doubt she'd said it just to score a hit, and he had to admit it had. That she'd tried to wound him told him she cared about his opinion. All in all, a productive talk, giving him lots to think about.

"Would you like to sit with us?" Scott shifted, unable to believe he'd blurted out the invitation. Judging by the distress on Ginger's face, it would have been better to have restrained the impulse.

"Daaad."

Still, he should make up for Shelby's earlier rudeness over the cartoon issue. Yeah, he thought. As though that had occurred to him.

"I don't want to intrude on your family outing."

"No intrusion." He held up the tub of popcorn, forgotten until then. "I'll even share."

Ginger looked at the girls, especially Serena's watchful eyes piercing her, then nodded. "Well, then, how can I refuse? Let me get a drink and I'll meet you inside."

"We'll wait."

Ginger walked toward the counter, hearing Shelby hiss at her father. Poor kid. Nobody wanted to socialize with her teacher outside the school walls.

Seeing Scott had been a shock. She'd have to get used to the possibility of running into him. She'd hoped coming to a children's movie at dinnertime on a Sunday would lessen her chances of encountering families she knew. As well as provide her with food, she thought, paying for a medium-size popcorn of her own.

Was Scott driving by her house on purpose, spying on her? Or was the route just convenient to avoid traffic by going through the residential area? She'd have to check his address back at school. She'd denied herself a peek when temptation had struck, not needing to know Shelby's address in order to teach her. But things had changed with Scott's admission, and she'd give in to personal curiosity. How had he found out where she lived? She didn't believe in coincidences, and him driving past her house in one of the brief moments she was ever out front would be a rare quirk of fate.

They walked into the semidark theater with Ginger heading up the stairs behind Shelby. Scott helped Serena climb the stairs before him, her short legs making two steps on each stair necessary. Shelby located a nearly empty row and headed toward the center, and Ginger hesitated. Socializing was one thing; sitting by your teacher—out of the question.

"I should sit by Serena, if it's okay," Scott said, leaning closer. "Do you want to go in first?"

She noticed his uncertain glance locating Shelby, settling herself into a seat. "Go ahead of me. The girls might want to sit beside one another."

"I don't think it's supposed to be scary," he said in a lowered tone, "but you never know. And Rena can still get spooked easily."

"I understand." She waited to let him enter the row after the smaller girl, then followed.

"No way," Shelby said a little too loudly. "You guys aren't really going to sit together, are you?"

Heads turned and chuckles emerged from nearby patrons.

Scott narrowed his eyes at his older daughter, the glare momentarily still in place as he turned to Ginger. "Perhaps I should sit by Shelby. Have a heart-to-heart with her before the movie starts."

Hands full of popcorn and a pop, she nudged the back of her fingers against his forearm. "It's okay, Scott. I'm her teacher, after all. It's understandable she doesn't want us together."

"It doesn't excuse her rudeness."

She dropped her voice and made a guess. "Am I the first woman she's seen you with other than her mother?"

His mouth opened then closed before he nodded. "Hey, Rena, sit between me and Ms. Winchester, okay? I want to sit by both my girls."

Which nicely cuts me out, Ginger thought. Shelby should be appeased.

Serena scooted back into her seat, then drew her knees under her to sit on her feet.

"Do you need a booster seat?" Ginger asked. "They have them here for smaller children."

"Daddy," the girl said. "Shelby's teacher thinks I'm too little to see the movie. Can you get me a booster seat?"

Scott gave Ginger a funny look she couldn't interpret, then rose to get the seat for Serena.

"I didn't say she was too little for the movie," Ginger started when he returned and got the seat under the child.

"Did, too," Serena corrected, an earnest clarification, not arguing.

"I only asked if she wanted the booster. Not all theaters have them, and I thought this might be your first time to come here, and—"

He smiled and Ginger lost her train of thought. That smile had enticed her to get to know him at the Christmas party. It attracted her now, sending a tingle of awareness across her skin.

"It's okay, Ginger."

Serena shrieked with laughter. "You called the teacher Ginger!"

"You called my teacher *Ginger?*" Shelby's low tone conveyed her horror.

Scott winced and shot an apologetic shrug toward Ginger. "She has a first name, girls."

"That's right," Ginger added. "Teachers don't live at school, we don't eat in the cafeteria, and some of us have children or pets at home."

Serena bounced on her seat, all tension over the booster seat apparently forgotten. "Do you have a dog?"

"No, unfortunately. I had to move this past year and I can't have a dog in my new house. But I work at the Humane Society, so I get to play with the animals there."

"I thought you was a teacher," Serena said.

Ginger smiled. "I meant I volunteer with the animals. My work is teaching, of course, you're right."

The girl bobbed her head, sending her wild brown curls flying, the overhead lights catching glints of red tones. An ache pierced Ginger. If this were her daughter, she'd fasten her hair with adorable barrettes or silly cartoon character ponytail holders.

She pressed a hand to her stomach to stem the pain. Moments like this reinforced her determination to adopt. Having a son would make her just as happy as a daughter would. Her gaze strayed to Scott, and the image of a laughing bronze-haired boy struck her with longing.

All she wanted was a child to love who would love her in return, which was why she had determined to start with an infant. A baby who had never known another mother would welcome Ginger into his or her life.

She couldn't get involved with Scott or any man. Her date the evening before had been a casual dinner with no expectations on either side. Which was a good thing, as she seemed to have lost her desire for casual sex.

Again she pulled her gaze away from Scott to concentrate on the trailers for upcoming movies. Sex with him had been too much like making love. Not casual. Not just fun and forgettable.

Not going to happen again.

She needed to concentrate on being an exemplary role model and pleasing an agency into letting her adopt a baby.

Her goal set, she settled in to watch the movie, ignor-

ing the small warm body of Serena next to her and the
unsettling way the child continued to stare at her. And
definitely ignoring the tempting man on the other side
of the girl.

Ginger walked along the deserted school hallway two
nights later, mentally pumping herself up for the meeting
she'd been assigned. The Technical Advisory Committee. Jeez. She was so not the person for this. Sure, she
could use a computer, but buy new ones for the school?
Not her specialty.

Unfortunately, Marianne had broken her ankle while
sledding over the holiday, meaning someone had to replace the second teacher rep on the committee. The
principal, who wasn't any too fond of Ginger anyway, ap-
pointed her. Her inability to conceal her opinion of him as
a boob didn't help matters. Logical concerns about serv-
ing on this particular committee fell on deafened ears.

The jerk.

So here she was, giving up a Tuesday night to sit and
listen to tedious details. She put a smile on her face and a
hand on the doorknob, prepared for two hours of techno-
jargon.

And opened the door to laughter. Female laughter,
centered around…

Scott. Surrounded by a few mothers and the other female teacher, Cindy Grady. Their obvious appreciation
for his masculinity vibrated in the room the way deer in
rutting season scented the wind.

His eyes widened before he smiled, and she hoped she
didn't appear as poleaxed as she felt. Two hours of Scott
being charming? Two hours of Scott being appreciated
by those women, most of whom were married? Two hours

of Scott… She swallowed the ideas of how she'd like to have two hours of Scott to herself, in bed.

"Hi," he said as she put her folders on the table. "I didn't know you were on this committee."

"It's a good fit for you, though. Bushfield recruit you?"

He smiled. "First day I brought Shelby, before you came in."

"Figures. Our beloved principal is nothing if not focused. When he wants something or someone, that thing gets done and that person gets persuaded."

"How did he persuade you?"

Ginger gave a rueful laugh. "My paycheck."

"Ah. Do you serve on a lot of committees?"

"Ginger," Cindy Grady's voice cut in as the woman appeared behind Scott. "Have you met our newest father *already*?"

Ginger clenched her teeth at the woman's implication. Her words came off as innocuous, but her tone said, *Of course you've latched on to the most attractive man in the room.* "His daughter is in my class."

"How nice for you both," Cindy said.

"I'm glad to see a familiar face," Scott interceded. "This is my first meeting of any kind at the school. Seeing Ms. Winchester here eases some of my panic."

"Oh, I don't think you have to worry about your reception," Cindy said. "The women on this committee are more than happy to see you."

"That's so kind of you to say."

Ginger bit the inside of her cheek as she watched Scott charm the other woman. His Southern accent sounded a little heavier than usual. Did he understand Cindy's innuendoes? Most men wouldn't catch the underlying cattiness.

They took their seats while Cindy claimed the head of the table. As the former official teacher liaison, Marianne would have had to deal with the paperwork with the school district. Ginger was supposed to replace her, but if Cindy wanted the responsibility, all the better.

Scott's eyes met hers and her former thankfulness that he wasn't seated beside her disappeared. Now she'd have to watch him, two seats down and across the table, being petted and fawned over. Ugh. The poor new guy, the handsome, single male. A target for the recent divorcée on his left and the should-know-better, still-married woman on his right. Even the other man on the committee joked with Scott. Whether that was due to his relief at being with another guy in the female-dominated room, or just Scott's personality and Southern ease with people, she didn't know.

"I'd like to thank everyone for coming," Cindy said. "I'll try to keep these meetings brief. As those members from last fall know, Marianne Soball was the head of this committee, but she injured herself playing in the snow over the Christmas break."

Ginger clenched her teeth. Cindy made Marianne sound irresponsible and childish. "She was sledding with her three-year-old son," Ginger inserted in the woman's defense. "He was too scared to ride by himself. Then their steering rope broke and Marianne couldn't reach the bar. She tossed her son into a snowdrift."

"Oh, my," Julie, the divorcée, said. "I'm not sure I could lift my toddler."

"Or that I would have had the wits to bail," happily married Laurie added. "I'd have been frozen with fear. No pun intended."

"Unfortunately," Ginger continued, "Marianne couldn't

stop the sled and before she could roll off, which she said she'd intended to do, the sled hit a rock under the snow. She flew and landed badly."

"Thank you for the explanation, Ms. Winchester." Cindy's eyebrows drew together. "I'm sure everyone would like an update during the break, but I need to move this meeting along. Ms. Winchester is replacing Mrs. Soball."

"So are you in charge now?" Scott asked Ginger with bland innocence.

"No, she isn't," Cindy said.

"I'm sorry." His brows knit with—feigned?—confusion. "I thought you said Ms. Winchester was replacing the head of the committee?"

Cindy's lips drew tight as all eyes turned to her.

Ginger wanted to laugh, but the woman could be lethal. She was not an enemy Ginger wanted to incite. "I'm perfectly fine with Mrs. Grady taking over the committee now."

She cringed at Cindy's scowl. That could have been phrased more diplomatically. Offering a smile, Ginger added, "I'm really here as a teacher who has to deal with these computers every day. I'm not a computer expert, whereas Mrs. Grady has had so many more years of experience."

Oh, dear. That didn't come out right, either. She didn't mean to imply Cindy was old. The woman couldn't be more than one hundred and fifty, tops.

Ginger stifled a giggle. Scott winked at her and she nearly lost the battle. Not that her slight had been intentional, but it sure felt good.

Cindy glared then continued with introductions and brought everyone up to date. The committee had already discerned the needs of the classrooms and teachers and weeded through some possibilities. "We'd like to have a recommendation for the school district by the end of February, in order for the computers to be purchased with this year's budget and installed over the summer."

"Will it take that long to make a decision?" Scott asked.

Ginger smiled. He was new to the district's red tape and the hoops everyone had to jump through, obviously. Was the school system more streamlined in Atlanta? "Everything from our committee goes to the district's purchasing committee. The high school has a similar committee to ours."

"Y'all can't just get together and have one committee?"

"They need computers with more abilities and—" she waved her hand vaguely, since she wasn't sure of the specifics "—accessories for graphics and math and whatnot."

Scott grinned. "Accessories?"

Cindy listed computer parts and gadgets Ginger had never heard of.

"There you go," Ginger said. "That's why I'm not the head of this committee."

The other father, John, laughed. "I've only heard of some of those things myself and I work with computers all day."

"Meet me at the coffee machine later," Scott said. "We should get to know one another." He turned back to Ginger. "And does the junior high have a committee?"

Cindy shook her head. "The middle school doesn't get new computers this year."

"Is it possible to get together people from the two schools and get the same computers?"

"No," Cindy said. "The high school received a private grant, specifying the computers purchased with that money had to go to the high school only."

"Okay," Scott said. "I'm just the new guy here, but if we all bought the same computers, we might get a better discount as the number of computers purchased would be greater. They could apply their grant money to their part of the purchase, right?"

"Mr. Matthews." Cindy's smile oozed condescension. "I appreciate your enthusiasm for making the process smoother, but that's just not how a school district works."

"It should," he countered. "Does our committee have a liaison with the high school committee?"

She bristled. "As I've said, we're using separate monies and have different needs in computers. At our level, the machines don't have to be as sophisticated as they do at the high school."

"Forgive me for interrupting," Ginger said, "but Mr. Matthews is a programmer, so he knows a little something more about this than we do."

"That's the problem," Cindy said. "Mr. Matthews may know a little about it. But," she continued over the gasps of the attendees, "being new to the district, to the state for that matter, I'm afraid he doesn't understand how things work." She flashed her shark smile at Scott. "No insult intended."

"None taken. I don't wish to intrude new ideas on a system that has obviously worked well for so long."

John guffawed. "I'd hardly say our school district works well. No offense, ladies; the teaching is great. It's the politics and hang-ups like this that made me hesitate to serve on this committee."

Silence hung in the room as people avoided eye contact with Cindy.

"Well," she said, "I suppose we have a solution. Since Mr. Matthews and Ms. Winchester are of one mind, and Mr. Matthews has the expertise Ms. Winchester lacks in this area, I propose they liaise together."

Ginger held the other woman's gaze. She'd made *liaise* sound sordid. Knowing her, Ginger knew the wording was no accident.

Amidst the congratulations, Scott met her gaze.

"Sorry," he mouthed.

She shook her head infinitesimally. Her battle with Cindy Grady had been going on long before Scott arrived or Cindy's sister lost her job. She had plenty of experience enduring the older woman's innuendoes.

Now, however, Ginger worried about giving Cindy ammunition to bring her before the educational board for review. She couldn't appear to have improper relations with a parent, no matter that she hadn't known who Scott was the night they spent together. She had to keep her job.

Without employment, she had no chance of adopting a baby.

# *Chapter 5*

"Daddy," Serena said at breakfast the next morning. "Can we get a puppy?"

Scott choked on his spoonful of cereal, glad he hadn't had time to make anything hot for breakfast. Eggs would have fallen out of his open mouth and oatmeal would have gagged him. Clearing his throat, he battled back the instant negative response that sprang to mind.

Rena looked hopeful, but Shelby's gaze remained on her Froot Loops. Obviously, she didn't hold much hope for the plan. Her comment about "not doing fun things" like seeing the movie bit his conscience. He hated to disappoint her again, but what would they do with a puppy with the three of them gone all day?

His instinct to deny the request just so he didn't have to take on more responsibilities—because he knew *he'd* be doing all the cleanup, feeding and training—made him feel lower than a basset hound's belly.

"We've talked about adopting a dog," he hedged. "I thought we'd wait for nicer weather to make it easier to train him."

"I want a girl puppy," Rena insisted.

"A girl might be a good idea. They're supposed to be gentler."

Shelby's rounded eyes caught his. "You're serious? We can get a puppy? For real?"

Scott blinked. Had he agreed to that? He didn't think so. How could he say "yes" while meaning "not now"?

"We've just moved in, Shel." His heart sank as her shoulders slumped. "Do y'all really want to take on the training of a puppy now? You're—"

"Yes!" both girls called out at the same time.

"Let me finish. You're just now making friends."

"Friends like to play with puppies," Shelby countered.

"Puppies take time," he said. "You have to train them to go potty outside, and you clean up their messes when they go inside by accident."

Rena nodded, looking as though she'd given this much thought. "I think we should put the puppy in diapers and then throw away the poop like moms do with people babies."

"Dogs can't wear diapers," Shelby said.

"It's a good idea, Rena, but Shelby's right. The puppy would wiggle out of it. And puppies aren't people, so we can't expect it to wear clothes like a doll." He pictured a tiny dog in costume 24/7. Ballerina bulldog. Dolly dachshund. Tutu shih tzu. He shuddered for the poor mutt's sake. "They have to go for walks. And all puppies bite, the same way babies teethe. Are you sure y'all are ready for this? Your toys and shoes might get chewed on, as well as your fingers."

Rena crossed her chubby arms over her chest. "I don't care."

Shelby smiled. "I'll walk her, Dad, and feed her and play with her. Please? You said we could get a dog when we moved into our new house. And we're here, so isn't it time to get the dog like you said?"

He noticed the one chore she didn't claim she'd do. Unable to hold out against his daughters when reminded of his own promises, Scott gave in. "I'll check around and find a shelter or rescue program. We'll go this weekend."

Rena squealed. "Shelby's teacher works at an animal place when she isn't teaching. She tolded me so."

Scott arched an eyebrow. "Did she now? How helpful of her."

"You want me to ask her about it at school?" Shelby offered.

"No, I think I'll have a few words with Ms. Winchester myself." Like *Don't talk to my daughters about puppies. Don't make it easy for them to find a puppy. Don't even mention the word* puppy.

Despite the dire warnings he planned to give her, he couldn't help a race of anticipation through his veins at the idea of seeing Ginger again.

Scott reined himself in. He had no right to berate her about anything. Wasn't it bad enough he'd had sex with her without even knowing her last name? Or that he drove past her house at least once a week for no good reason? Or that he couldn't keep his mind off her body or his memory off how good she felt in bed with him?

No, then he had to make her work life a mess with that stupid meeting.

That crusty old nag, Mrs. Grady, had picked up on his attraction to Ginger right from the start. When he'd gravitated to her side, so damned glad to see her enter the meeting room that he couldn't stay away, he'd established his interest. When the old bat had planted her flag as head of the committee, he'd defended Ginger, once again tipping his hand.

It wasn't as though he didn't know how these committees worked. Politics, especially small town politics, were hardwired with nastiness.

He dropped Shelby off at school after breakfast. Since Rena still had to be delivered to the preschool, he had to resist the urge to see Ginger.

"*Liaise* together." He snorted in the relative quiet of his car as he left the Wee Care half an hour later. The older teacher might as well have shouted, "He wants to sleep with her."

She wouldn't have been wrong. He'd have taken Ginger on the meeting room table if they'd had privacy. Against a wall. On the floor. He wasn't picky. Seeing her soft skin and being close enough to smell the flowery scent of her again made him crazy with desire.

Would it be so wrong for her to date the father of her student?

Crap. What was he thinking? He'd seen firsthand what Ginger would be subjected to, and that was without proof of wrongdoing. Cindy Grady would have a field day if he and Ginger started a public relationship.

Not that he was ready for a relationship. *Dammit*. Ginger had him tied in knots, thinking of spreading her out on the conference table, burying himself in her warmth and softness, and just staying there for hours.

Then he'd remember why they couldn't do that. Shelby. Serena. Sam. It was way too soon for his daughters to deal with him seeing another woman. The movie outing

had proved that. A long-term relationship with someone new would have to wait. Once his heart healed, he'd
consider it.

His girls needed a mom in the house and would need
a woman even more as they grew older. They deserved
someone who would love them and care for them and just
be there. Bake them cookies. Go to school events and
watch them play sports or dance. Bandage their scraped
knees now and their scraped hearts later on.

Not that Sam hadn't been good at that. But she wasn't
here now, had chosen not to be, and he had to build a life
without her.

Could he love again? Sam had taken so much out of
him. He'd loved her with his whole heart—the part the
girls didn't claim, anyway. She'd left him to deal with
their growing up and his own broken heart.

Would he choose Ginger to replace the girls' mother
when the time came? He sensed she would be a good
mom. He already knew she was an exceptional lover.

But none of them was ready for the reality, except
possibly Ginger.

Maybe in the meantime, he and Ginger could carry
on a secret affair? If no one from her school found out…
He'd only have to face his own conscience. Did he really
want sex so badly he'd sneak around? Conduct a dirty
little *liaison* that he couldn't take public?

The organ behind his zipper screamed, *Hell, yeah.*

The organ between his ears frowned in disapproval.

The organ in his chest just ached.

Ginger looked up at the tap on her classroom door
after school. Her weariness ebbed at the sight of the man
standing there.

"I would have liked school a lot better if my teachers looked like you."

"Scott." She smiled, her skin drawing tight.

"Bad time?" He crossed to her desk.

"Not at all. Is this about Shelby?"

He shook his head.

"The technology committee?"

He perched on the edge of her desk. His study of her features made her fidget, as though he could see into her thoughts.

"That's all I can talk about here." She leaned back in her chair to create space between them.

"Are you sleeping?"

She narrowed her eyes. "I told you that's none of your business."

"No, not are you sleeping with someone, although I would like to know now that you've brought it up." He leaned forward and touched his fingertips to her cheek.

His touch heated her bloodstream like lava.

"Are you losing sleep? Is it the tech committee? Is that Grady woman giving you a hard time?"

"No, I'm fine."

He grinned and withdrew his hand. "You're a lousy liar, but I like that about you."

Ginger blew out a breath and drummed up a last thread of patience. After she'd been announced as the tech committee replacement the week before, Cindy Grady practically lived in the doorway across the hall, watching every move she made. Today her vigilance had intensified. Ginger didn't need Scott coming in her classroom, smelling like mint toothpaste and looking crisp and energetic in his ironed yellow Oxford shirt and creased gray slacks.

She visualized rumpling him up and taking advantage of that energy. Taking advantage of him.

So he thought she looked worn out. Sure, she'd had some sleepless nights, worrying over why the adoption agency wouldn't approve her to foster or adopt. What red tape or interview or referral blocked the process? What had she done wrong?

She fought the urge to smooth her hair into place. Scott had cost her a few sleepless nights, as well, as she wrestled with her attraction to him. Now here he was, making her heart jump and her skin tingle, touching her cheek with gentle concern, and making her yearn to snuggle against him. Soaking up his warmth and some of that energy would do her a world of good.

Unless someone saw them.

"Scott, I'm more than willing to discuss your daughter's progress and behavior in my class or the technology committee, but not my sleeping habits." She wished his grin didn't tempt her so. "Not anything personal."

"Okay. I have something really impersonal to discuss with you. A bone to pick, if you will."

She cocked her head as she reviewed possibilities. Shelby hadn't done anything to complain about. Her responses bordered on the smart-alecky, but nothing Ginger felt she had to curb. The girl had won a few admirers with her humor, and Ginger didn't mind giving her a little rope in order to make friends in her new town. Hopefully Shelby would use the rope to pull herself back to shore rather than the other alternative.

"You 'tolded' Rena you worked at an animal shelter."

Ginger smiled at his quotation of his youngest. "I do put in a lot of time there. I think I mentioned it—yes, I remember. We discussed volunteering versus working before the movie began."

"Well, the only part *she* remembers is you saying you'd help us pick out a puppy."

Ginger's mouth dropped open at his teasing tone as she scrambled to remember. "That's not exactly what I said."

She was pretty sure she hadn't promised that. Did Scott want a dog? Was that the bone he had to pick with her? She understood the joke in his phrasing now. She liked his sense of humor. She liked too many things about him.

"But you know about dogs," he said, "and where to get one and how to find a healthy one?"

"Well, yes, but—"

"And you wouldn't want us stuck with an aggressive dog, I'm sure."

She fought the smile that wanted to rebel. A traitorous part of her delighted that he'd go to such lengths as blackmail to have her spend time with him and his girls. "I wouldn't want you to adopt an aggressive dog, no."

But she did want to spend time with him. She shouldn't. She could list the reasons it was a rotten idea, starting with Cindy Grady, and the impact on Shelby and even Rena, and going on from there. Creating a clean slate man-wise in case the adoption agency checked—and they would. Her job, her chances at adopting, her sanity. These were reasons enough to avoid him, she thought as their eyes locked.

But, oh, how she wanted to be with him again. The clean pine scent of his soap brought to mind his luscious naked body against her. His smile made her tummy tingle.

He rose and paced away, then turned back. "Do I have

to put a dog in a crate if I adopt it at this shelter of yours? I don't like the caged look they have, but it seems all I hear about on TV or read about in the papers is crate-training dogs."

"There's no rule about training. You do what works for your family. Crates have advantages, but you can live without one. The only rule, per se, is you have to spay or neuter the animal you adopt."

He winced, and that rebel smile of hers escaped as laughter.

"It's not that bad." His skeptical grimace eased the tension that had taken up residence in her shoulders for the past several days. "Do the girls have their hearts set on a certain breed? The selection at the shelter isn't pedigree. I might be able to help you find a reputable breeder, though."

He shrugged. "So far, I've only heard it must be a girl."

"Will they accept an older dog? You'd have the added benefit of it probably being housebroken."

"I don't know. This is really bad timing for me." He ran a hand across the back of his neck. "We're still settling in. I need to get the girls in swimming and dance classes, and figure out transportation to those classes, and make sure they have friends and have rides to and from places with those friends, and now I'm supposed to train a dog not to mess in my house and chew all our furniture and shoes—" He took a breath. "And I'm whining."

"You are." And it was adorable. Jeez, she had it bad for this guy.

He grimaced. "Sorry."

"Look, I can help with the dog. If you want one." She cocked her head in question. "I've heard you say the girls want a puppy, but what about you? If this isn't a good time, if you can't give the puppy the attention it needs, wait to come to the shelter. Otherwise, you're all going to wind up miserable."

"I know. I'm not sure I'm ready, but who's ever ready when you bring someone or something new into the house? It's like bringing home a baby."

Ginger's throat tightened. She wouldn't know, but she hoped to find out soon. The reminder to be on better behavior in case Cindy was interviewed as her work contact had her straightening back in the chair.

"You prepare and organize and arrange," Scott continued on his baby theme, "but then you're home and panic seizes you anyway."

"Even with Serena, the second baby?"

A strange look crossed Scott's face that she couldn't interpret. Caution? Whatever it was, he'd closed to her, gone blank and bland and unreadable.

Then he smiled, and although it looked genuine, Ginger had to wonder what memory or emotion it covered.

"Bringing home Rena was incredible, but the dynamics changed because then we had two children. So we had two little ones to worry about, two needs to fulfill, and two children to physically care for. It was a great time, but hectic."

Her chest ached with envy. Would she be able to experience that predicament, or would her baby—if she was granted approval to adopt—be an only child?

Like the need to poke at a sore tooth, Ginger wanted to know about his wife. It would hurt, but that didn't stop her. "I'm sure you and your wife handled it just fine. What's her name?"

Scott stared for a minute. "Samantha."

"Another *s*."

"Yes."

Samantha, Scott, Shelby, Serena. Ginger. *One of these things is not like the others.*

"What does she look like? Dark-haired like Shelby?"

His gaze fell.

"I imagine Serena inherited your hair color. Brown with those red highlights. But the girls both have dark eyes." She couldn't stop probing. "Like Samantha's?"

"Look." He slid off the desk to stand rigid before her. "I don't want to talk about the girls' mother or who they got their looks from, okay? I just came about a dog."

His fists clenched and unclenched.

Ginger swallowed at the emotion the mention of his wife engendered. "Okay. Sorry."

He paced away then back. "No, I'm sorry. I just can't talk about it. Not yet."

She nodded and pushed aside her own feelings to concentrate on Scott's problem. Dog, not ex-wife. "Do you prefer a puppy or a dog? Or are you going to put off getting one until your family is more settled?"

He blew out a breath and his body relaxed. "I think we're going to do it soon. The girls have been through a lot in the past year. They need something to take their minds off…everything."

She heard what he didn't say. The girls were separated from their mother, their family down South, their house, their friends, their school. Take their minds off everything, indeed. Why had he done it? How bad could their mother be to take the girls so far away? *Sole custody,* the parent info form said.

Ginger shivered, knowing all too well the horrors a parent could visit on her child. Too many of her students over the years had been victims. "I don't have to tell you an animal is a commitment," she said instead. "Do you want me to explain it to the girls? That you're bringing another creature into your home, and you'll be responsible for it forever."

"I've tried, but no, I didn't cover forever."

"They won't quite grasp the long-term effects. I'm not even sure how much Serena will understand, but Shelby could be informed of some of the difficulties you'll have to deal with."

"No, thanks. If anyone's going to be the bad guy, it'll be me. But it wouldn't hurt for them to come visit the shelter. Just to look."

She couldn't restrain her grin.

"What? You think we can't visit without taking a dog home?"

"Let's say I'd be surprised."

"You think I'm a pushover," he accused.

Exactly. "I think you're a nice guy who loves his daughters."

"A schmuck."

She had to laugh. "Not at all."

"You'll see. You write down the address and what day you can go with us, just for a tour. And we'll go have a great time and leave without a dog."

Scott stared at the schematics on his desk, not seeing a word or line in front of him.

"What's going on?" Dylan asked at his side.

Scott jerked upright on hearing his boss's voice. "Nothing. Just thinking things through."

Dylan perched on the desk nearby. "But not about work."

Scott started to deny it, but the lack of progress today spoke the truth of the matter. "I'm sorry."

"If there's something wrong with your daughters, something you need to take care of, just say so. No one expects you to finish moving in and get settled in a month." Dylan grimaced. "I just moved across town and there are things Tara and I can't find. You moved halfway across the country."

"The girls are fine. We're moved in. If something's not where it should be, we lost it in transit."

"Ah. Is it a woman from back home?"

Scott looked around at the other desks. Empty.

"You missed break," Dylan said. "That's how I figured out something's bothering you."

Scott ran a hand around the back of his neck. "Am I that obvious?"

"Nah, I'm just a genius. So what's going on? If you need a friend to talk to, and it looks like you do, I'm available."

"It's my boss," Scott joked. "He's a real loser."

"Don't worry. I won't tell Joe you think that about him."

Scott grinned. He respected Dylan a great deal and could see them being friends. Except for that one thing. "You know her."

"Well, if she's from here, that's not surprising."

"Ginger Winchester." Scott watched Dylan's face for clues to their past.

His broad smile was less than reassuring.

"Terrific lady. So, you're seeing her?"

"In a manner of speaking."

Dylan's face hardened. "She's been through a lot lately. Her jerk of a husband walked out on her. I don't know much of that story, but I'm sure it's his fault. She's best friends with Joe's wife, Lisa. So tread carefully."

"Understood."

"Well, shoot." Dylan gave a half smile. "That's not the way I wanted to start our friendship."

"Don't worry about it. I appreciate your honesty." Scott cleared his throat. "Can I ask you one thing?"

"Absolutely."

"Did you go out with Ginger before you met Tara?"

Dylan shook his head. "I considered it, but she was too close to Joe for me to entangle myself."

"That's subtle."

"Just the way it is. Something for you to think about."

Scott stretched his neck as Dylan walked away. Thinking about Ginger, in one capacity or another, occupied most of his time these days.

The pet store was hosting an animal adoption day with the animal shelter early Saturday morning, and the place was crowded when Scott arrived with the girls. Ginger stood out, not only because of her bright hair, but because of her bright smile. He'd thought before that she looked natural behind a teacher's desk, but this was her true element. Working with and caring for animals. She glowed as she remarked on each animal to admirers, gave every furry ear a rub as she passed, cuddled and baby-talked to a couple dogs and cats that had to be her favorites, before noticing him and the girls.

"Hi," she called as she neared. Her yellow shirt set her face aglow, as if she needed the additional shine. The gloss on her lips drew his attention more than it should, which was not at all. She was his daughter's teacher. She was becoming his friend, but she'd been his lover, and his body wouldn't let him forget.

"Does everyone get to take home a pet?" Serena asked, eyeing the crowd.

"No," Scott insisted. "Some families are like us, just here to look. Just here to get an idea of what they want, of what's available."

"Right," Ginger said with a smile crinkling her eyes, laughing at him.

He didn't mind. Not when her smile and their shared humor warmed him. Not when the connection between them caught at his throat. Not when it made him want to place his hand behind her neck and bring her mouth to his.

Scott had vowed they'd come home without a dog, and he'd gotten that much right.

Horace was a monstrous, big-footed, big-hearted, floppy-eared, long-haired, five-month-old slobber machine. Already the size of a coffee table and as black as regret, the puppy was of no discernable breed.

Except maybe Shetland pony.

Many families milled around, and Horace had been admired by several different people, including his daughters. But no one else had chosen him. Probably because he looked so indefinable, a mop of all hair.

The dog had huge brown eyes that filled with love for his girls. He took to them like a long-lost brother, grateful to be located and brought home again. And the girls had latched on to him with the same fervor.

"He's a boy," Scott pointed out, futilely fighting the tide sweeping him into pet-ownership. "You want a girl dog. A *little* girl dog. Remember?"

"He's cute," Rena countered as though that settled the matter.

"We changed our minds." Shelby eyed him. "Now we'll have two girls and two boys in the house." She turned to Ginger. "Can we change his name? Will he come if we call him something else?"

"Give him a name with two syllables," Ginger suggested. "He'll get used to it, especially if you call his new name and have a treat in your hand."

"How about Floppy?" Scott offered. *Or Secretariat.*

"That's not dig, digger—digneriflied?" Shelby looked to Ginger.

"Dignified. And you're right. He needs a real name."

"Like a people name?" Rena asked.

"Maybe. That's up to you three."

"Us and Horace?" Shelby asked.

Ginger laughed. "Well, I meant you and Serena and your dad, but yeah. You should see if Horace likes his new name, too."

Serena screwed up her nose as she had all afternoon upon hearing the dog's name. "Why would anyone call him Horace?"

"I've been busy with school and haven't been here very often lately. I've only seen him once. Shall we ask?"

She called over Rob, an enthusiastic volunteer in his early twenties. His dyed neon-green hair and gawky manners made him more comfortable around animals than humans. His hunched shoulders and lack of eye contact spoke volumes.

"The people who brought him here said his former owner was a student of the classics," Rob explained. "He thought Horace sounded cool."

Ginger's jaw firmed as though she knew this story all too well.

"Unfortunately," Rob continued, "he didn't think about what would happen at the end of the school term when he returned home. According to the apartment manager, he dumped poor Horace outside his apartment before Christmas and left town."

The girls gave horrified cries and buried their faces in the puppy's fur. Horace wiggled with delight, his wet black button nose nudging their cheeks.

"I think we should go ahead and call him Horace," Shelby said after cooing for another minute. "Then he'd know we love him just like he is."

"Oh, I do, too," Rena agreed, nodding emphatically. "I love him just like he is, even with his icky name."

Scott shook his head while the three females adored the dog, rubbing its ears and neck. With the size of those feet, Horace was going to look more like "horse" before long. Forget a crate; they'd need a barn.

When Scott asked what breed or mix of breeds the shelter worker thought Horace might have in him, the other man dodged the subject. Assured of the puppy's good health, Scott thought to leave it at that.

"With those floppy ears," Rena said, "he looks like Lady in *Lady and the Tramp,* except he's all black."

"And bigger," Shelby said.

"Oh, he'll get even bigger," Rob said before clamping his mouth shut.

Scott eyed him sardonically. "I'm well aware. I saw the size of his feet. Don't worry, I'm adjusting to the idea of a big dog."

The man shifted. "He'll be an excellent guard dog.

He's not like the dog from *Lady and the Tramp*. He's more like Nana in *Peter Pan*."

"He's soft like a poodle." Ginger stroked him. "But not yappy."

"We can braid his hair," Rena said. "That'll make it pretty."

Scott rubbed the dog's ear. "Sorry, Horace. If you come home with us, your macho days are over."

Ginger placed her hand on Scott's arm, and for a moment he wished he didn't have on his peacoat so he could feel her warm touch. Her gaze stayed on the young shelter attendant.

"What else do you know about this dog, Rob?" Ginger asked. "How serious are you about him being like Nana?"

"You, uh, said you noticed the size of his feet, right? Well." He coughed. "Did you notice they're webbed?"

"No." Ginger dragged out the word in a disbelieving tone. Her wide eyes as she reached for the dog's foot made Scott nervous.

"I can't believe it," she said. Her gaze skewered Rob. "You were just going to let them leave here, not knowing? That's irresponsible, and not fair to the family or the animal."

"Not knowing what?" Scott asked as the man shuffled his feet. "Does he need surgery?"

"Is our puppy sick?" Shelby asked.

*Our* puppy. Scott closed his eyes and only hoped whatever the dog had wasn't serious. For the first time in his life, he'd be eager to hear "just tapeworms."

"He's no doubt a mixed breed," Rob hedged, "but the webbed feet indicate he's at least partly a Newfoundland."

Panic hit Scott. Those dogs stood half as high as he did. "I take it you don't mean he's Canadian?"

"Well, historically—" Rob started.

"No, that's not what he means," Ginger cut in. "This is going to be a big dog. Almost as tall as you are now, Serena. He'll be powerful." She glared at Rob. "And too much for two little girls to handle."

"We'll handle him." Shelby turned her pleading face to Scott. "Please don't let Ms. Winchester make us not get Horace."

Rena's face crumpled. "We're not getting Horace? Why not?"

"Ms. Winchester ruined it all." Shelby glared.

"Shelby." Scott laid his hand on his daughter's shoulder. "You're being rude. Ms. Winchester is only pointing out that Horace will be a huge dog. Hard for you to control. Hard to walk. He'll weigh almost as much as I do, and he'll be really strong."

"They're a gentle breed," Rob said.

"You stay out of this," Ginger instructed. The boy hung his head as she turned back to Scott. "We don't always know the breed of a rescued animal, and most dogs here are mixtures. Horace probably isn't a pure Newfie so there's a chance he won't grow as large as one."

"What's a Newfie?" Rena asked.

"It's the nickname for this kind of dog," Ginger said. "They're originally from Newfoundland, up on the east coast of Canada."

"Aww, that's cute." Rena rubbed the puppy's cheek, not seeming to notice the slobber.

Shelby didn't ease up on her scowl, although she didn't say anything else disrespectful. Scott got the lowdown on the breed from Rob and figured Horace was everything he could have asked for, except that he came supersized. Gentle and loyal, a guard dog, good with children. Since his girls had already fallen for the beast, he didn't see the point in denying them.

"What do you say, girls? Shall we take him home?"

Despite a superior glance at Ginger, Shelby only voiced positive comments.

The adoption went smoothly, although the agency's eagerness to have Horace sent to a good home made Scott wary. "Is something else wrong with the dog?" he asked Ginger. "Why is everyone relieved to see him go?"

"I double-checked. Don't worry. There's nothing wrong with Horace, except that he's supercute and lovable. And big." She shrugged. "They've all been tempted to adopt him. Dogs this large don't always find a home."

The pet store clerk loaded them up with bowls, rawhide chew bones, and a leash and collar. The special brush for long-haired dogs made Scott grit his teeth at his own stupidity—couldn't they adopt a dog that wouldn't be as much work? The clerk pointed out other items the family might need and Horace might want, and the shopping cart filled.

"No crate," was Scott's only stipulation. What was the point? A stable maybe, but a crate? Not so useful. This overgrown bundle of yarn would most likely be in someone's bed tonight anyway, taking up the majority of space. He'd have to train the girls as well as the dog. He turned to them. "How about a big pillow on the floor for his bed?"

"He should sleep in my room," Shelby claimed, "because I'm older."

"That's not fair," Rena countered. "I'm littler and I don't like to sleep by myself. Horace would keep me from being lonely."

"His bed should be downstairs," Scott told them as

Ginger's lips twitched. "He needs to be near the door." Closer to the outdoors for his nature calls. If nothing else, the dog's body would block an intruder from entering the house. Horace was too friendly to guard anything, unless he lunged at someone for a hello kiss.

Rena's eyes filled with worry. "But he'll be scared all by himself."

"He needs alone time," Scott said, although he had to admit the dog looked like a big sissy who would probably whine all night. "A place to call his own. You know when you want to play dolls by yourself and not be bothered? He'll need someplace to go when he doesn't want to play."

"We could give him his own room, Dad," Shelby said. "Where your office is."

Ginger laughed. "That's not a bad idea. Horace would have a room to escape to. During the day when you're gone, he wouldn't expect you to be where he sleeps. His pallet, or pillow, would be out of the way."

"Out of whose way?" Scott countered, making her laugh again. Even in the crowded pet store, in front of his daughters, she made him want her. Just by being herself. Her shining smile, lilting laughter and breathtaking body made him yearn to pull her close, take her someplace private, and lose himself in her.

"Can I call Grandma Baxter when we get home?" Shelby asked.

Like a shower of glacier water, Scott was jolted back to reality. The girls argued about getting to tell Samantha's mom the news while he struggled to curb his libido. He couldn't have Ginger. Not while the girls mourned their mother's absence. Not while they still missed her so much. Not now.

Not…yet?

# Chapter 6

"The coach did *what?*" Ginger glanced around the otherwise unoccupied copy room Monday morning, thankful no one else had entered. She hated to encourage Cindy Grady to gossip, but she knew Mike Reynolds, the high school basketball coach, and couldn't believe this "news." Surely someone had embellished the tale or just gotten it wrong in the first place. She'd like to curb the rumor before Cindy spread it farther than their school, for she doubted she was the first person Cindy had sought out to tell. A rumor like that could kill a teacher's career. "I don't believe it."

Cindy pursed her lips, obviously unused to being doubted. Her crossed arms communicated her stern displeasure. "I'm only telling you what I heard. After the team won the regional play-offs, Coach Reynolds gave his players an open curfew, then invited them to his motel room and provided them with beer."

Although she didn't want to antagonize Cindy, Ginger couldn't let this go unchallenged. "Where did you hear this story?"

"It's all over. One of the boys was hungover when he got home and his parents found out where he'd gotten the beer."

"So one kid, thinking to avoid trouble and shift the blame, tells this outrageous tale, and you're spreading the slander?"

Cindy's face turned red with the anger shooting from her eyes. "Some of his friends backed him up."

"Sure they did. The boys think Mike's being a coach will get him off the hook."

"Or they're telling the truth."

"That's so unlike him." Ginger had dated Mike as a teenager. He'd been a young jock, full of himself and liking to have a good time. But through the years, he had matured into a respected man. As an educator, he would know better. An idiotic move like that would cost him his job, if not put him in jail.

"How well do you know Coach Reynolds?" Cindy asked.

Ginger didn't have to see the speculative gleam in the older teacher's eyes to read her thoughts. She was tired of walking a tightrope. "Mike and I attended high school together, that's all."

"And you haven't seen him since?"

"Of course. I've seen him around town, at the games, times like that. I'm sure you've *seen* him, too." Ginger couldn't resist the dig.

"Because he's married, you know."

Ginger set her teeth, holding back a snarl and sharp comment. As soon as she could, she found an excuse to leave the copy room. No teacher would be so reckless with his career, but especially not Mike, with a wife who worked as a nurse at the middle school and two young children to consider. The ramifications would be severe.

As it turned out, the ramifications were severe for Ginger also: she had to sit through another of principal Bushfield's speeches. Within a day of the accusations and Mike Reynolds's temporary suspension "while the matter was under investigation," the district issued strict reminders to the teachers to review their Code of Conduct clause. Bushfield felt it necessary to read the statement in an "emergency" teacher assembly. So she sat crammed in the small library on a child's hard chair, feeling lucky to have a seat and not be standing along the back wall.

As the meeting dragged on, she revised that opinion. Teachers in the back were spared the sharp accusing eye of Bushfield and his pointed stare as he talked about ethics and being a role model for the children.

What had he heard? Was it only her paranoia making it seem as though everyone knew about her recent past with men and about having sex with Scott over Christmas break? He hadn't officially been a student's father then, as Shelby's enrollment didn't become active until the January return of school. Still, it didn't look good.

The teachers in the back could also fidget without seeming as though they were guilty. Ginger had to remain still as a rabbit sensing a fox nearby, appearing as though Bushfield's topic held little interest to her. Her peripheral vision picked up a smug-looking Cindy Grady, but without turning her head, she couldn't tell if Cindy's satisfaction had anything to do with her telling tales about Ginger or with Bushfield's condemning tone in general.

Guilt sheened her skin with perspiration. What could

Cindy have heard or seen and reported to the principal? For all he was a blowhard, he was their immediate supervisor, and his opinion mattered.

Scott had revealed his interest in Ginger at the tech meeting, but that wasn't against any school ethical code of which she was aware. However, it was an unspoken rule. Even teachers dating one another was frowned upon by the community, although the school district couldn't forbid it.

Cindy didn't know of Ginger's dating experiences since the divorce or if any of those dates had turned into sexual encounters. However, since Ginger was divorced, what business of it was anyone's? And since being with Scott, she'd come to her senses, repented and repined, changed her ways, turned over a new leaf, woken up and smelled the coffee, and every other cliché she could think of.

To have her mistakes come back to bite her in the rear end now would be grossly unfair.

The image of a blanket-wrapped bundle in her arms faded a little with each discouraging thought. She could almost feel the aching emptiness of her arms. Without a good job and a better reputation, she wouldn't be able to adopt.

The best course of action would be to avoid being alone with Scott Matthews. She had to. No way would she jeopardize her chance at motherhood.

That night, Ginger rushed toward the phone in the kitchen, abandoning the novel she'd been reading on the living room couch. A glance at the clock quickened her steps. At 11:00 p.m., chances increased that the call brought bad news. A metal taste washed over her tongue as fear closed her throat—Mom? Dad? Kyle? Her step faltered. Surely her ex-husband had changed his ICE contact. Wouldn't the new girlfriend be the person called in case of emergency?

Despite the sour churn to her stomach, Ginger picked up the phone. *Please, not my parents.*

Scott's "hello" filled her with momentary relief, followed closely by panic. One of the girls?

"It's the stupid dog," he assured her, as though reading her mind.

Relief made her knees weak, and she leaned against the kitchen counter. The dog. Jeez.

"I wouldn't disturb you this late," Scott said, "and I apologize, but I'm at a loss here. Is there a vet who does house calls in the middle of the night? Maybe someone the animal shelter uses?"

He muttered something about "a fortune," which Ginger could fill in for herself. "What's wrong with Horace?"

"The Horace—" he pronounced it "horse," but she didn't know whether that was due to his Southern accent or a general opinion of the beast "—has eaten something bad. I think."

"Eaten what? Do you have any idea?" Young girls played with perfumes and makeup sometimes. She searched her memory but couldn't picture Shelby or Serena glammed up like a rock star. "Was it food or maybe a part of a toy? Do they have a dollhouse?"

She rushed upstairs to her bedroom and picked up her folded jeans from the dresser. She'd planned to wear them one more time before washing, and they didn't look bad. Not too wrinkled. Perfectly acceptable for the middle of the night. This wasn't a date.

"I believe it's food-related."

The dry certainty in Scott's tone made her smile. And hesitate. He could clean up dog vomit on his own. "Is Horace in pain?"

"The Horace *is* a pain, but I shouldn't kick a guy when he's down. Yeah, I'd say he is suffering."

"What makes you think so?" She could envision all sorts of messes, none of which was dire enough for her to speed over this late at night to tend to. Or in the bright light of day, for that matter.

"You mean the way he's got his paws clutching his gut? Or his pale pasty skin tone?"

Ginger smiled at his joke.

"Other than moaning, he's just lying down. I don't know a sick dog from my aunt Patsy. The dogs down South have the good sense not to eat things that are bad for them."

All trace of humor faded as the sound of puppy whimpers grew louder. Scott must have moved closer to the dog to inspect him.

Judging by the pathetic whines, Horace needed help. Scott would require either someone to transport the dog to an animal clinic or vet's office, or to stay in the house with the girls while he did it. She wedged the phone between her chin and shoulder and stripped out of her pajama pants. Hopping and balancing, she pulled on her jeans.

"What are y'all doin'? You're puffin' like a long-distance runner. Oh." He cleared his throat. "Is this a bad time?"

She let the phone drop on the bed while she pulled her pajama top over her head and replaced it with a sweatshirt. With assumptions like that, he could just wait. After smoothing her hair back into place, she picked up the handset. "Do you mean is Monday night at nearly midnight a bad time for a phone call? Or is it a bad time to run out in the dark and cold to help you?"

"I'm sorry, honey. I didn't mean to insult you."

His accent turned the words into, "Ah'm surry," which defused her irritation. She ignored his tacking on the endearment. It was probably left over from talking to the girls all weekend and he'd accidentally let it slip. It meant nothing. It held no importance for her. She wouldn't pay it the least attention.

She'd have to pay attention to her reaction to his accent, though, and make sure it didn't buy him too much slack. Yes, it was charming and made her smile. And sent shivers up her spine, depending on what he was saying. But that was beside the point.

*Keep to the point, Ginger Pearl.* The admonishment stiffened her resolve. The man had just insinuated she was having sex with someone else. He could clean up dog poop himself. He wasn't Ashley Wilkes, too fragile to deal with the ugliness of life. But he wasn't as cavalier as Rhett Butler, either. She waffled, hating his effect on her.

"So, do you know someone I can call at this hour other than you? Someone the shelter trusts?" He hesitated and she heard the resignation in his voice. "Maybe someone who's treated Horace before."

That stopped her. She'd been about to recommend one of the vet techs who might need a couple or thirty bucks. Something in his voice indicated other objectives. Did he plan to return Horace, now that he'd proven defective? Like Kyle had rejected her? "Why do you want someone who's treated Horace? So that person would be familiar with his history?"

"Well, sure. Right. That would be why."

He sounded too relieved, too agreeable. As though he snatched at her answer like a lifeline. She hurried down the stairs and grabbed her purse, then went to the closet for her heavy coat. "That *might* be why. Or not."

He heaved out a breath. "I want someone Horace feels comfortable with, okay?"

Ginger headed to the kitchen door, touched by his concern for a puppy he hadn't intended to adopt. A big dog with a big heart, seemingly matched by his new owner. "I'll be right there."

On the short drive across town, she gave herself a stern talking to. No involvement. No dating. For sure, no sex. She had her job and her baby-to-be to consider. There wasn't an endearment or a charming accent or a sexy voice or a sexy man that mattered as much as having the adoption agency approve her application.

Anticipation coursed through her as she pulled into Scott's driveway fifteen minutes later. Despite the reason for his call, she wanted to see him. She needed to take a breath. *No,* she told herself, standing on his porch. *You're not visiting your lover. You're helping a friend. That's all.*

Scott swung open the door. She registered his grin right before—

"Oh, ick." The smell hit her. Vomit. She was glad she'd taken that deep breath already—it might be her last of the evening. "Who gave him chocolate?"

"What?"

"Someone has been giving chocolate to the dog." She knew that smell. She wouldn't be able to eat chocolate for a couple of weeks.

"What makes you so sure?" Scott took the coat from her shoulders before tossing it over a chair by the door. Boots and various shoes lay where they'd been kicked off, some in a woven basket, some on the rug, some just abandoned where they'd landed. Exhaustion marked his face; his flannel shirt and jeans had seen fresher hours. She hoped he was up to the task at hand. It wouldn't be pretty.

"We've got to take care of Horace immediately," she said. "Chocolate is toxic to dogs, and possibly fatal, depending on how much he ate. He's pretty big but he has a puppy's digestive system. It's vital to flush him out."

"Oh, sweet hell. I don't like the sound of that."

Ginger patted his arm. "Don't worry. I'll tell you how."

"Tell me? Meaning I'm on my own?" He ran a hand down his face. "Okay, let's get this nightmare started." He led her to the mudroom, which thankfully had a tile floor.

It wasn't pleasant, but it could have been worse, according to the vet tech Ginger contacted. In the past half an hour before Scott called, poor Horace had vomited out a great deal of the chocolate cake, as it proved to be. He also had diarrhea, which helped rid his body of the toxins.

"We have to keep him hydrated," she said. "The vet's assistant said Horace might be overexcited from the caffeine, too."

"Just great. A hyper thirty-pound dust mop. I didn't know chocolate cake was so bad for dogs."

Ginger couldn't believe her ears. "Did you *feed* him cake?"

"No, but he's taller than he looks."

She couldn't help but smile as she grasped his meaning. "You'll need to store food where he can't reach."

"I put it on the kitchen counter, in plastic wrap, I might add."

"Try the refrigerator next time. Or get a lockbox."

"Very humorous."

"Just hide the key up high."

Scott rolled his eyes, but his lips twitched.

"You'd better not let him see where you put it, either. He's not only taller than he looks, he's smarter than—"

Horace moaned and Scott reacted as though to a pistol shot, launching himself across the room and swinging open the door. The puppy stared at the crazy human. Then pooped on the floor.

Ginger covered her mouth but laughter escaped anyway. "What did you hope to accomplish by opening the door? Did you housebreak him already? In two days?"

Scott grimaced and latched on to the dog's collar. "Come here, you. Let's see if you can't finish your business outside."

Horace nearly bounced on his toes with glee at this new game, momentarily emptied and ready to play.

"Get him some water," Ginger called. She turned to search for whatever Scott had been using to clean earlier. Hushing the voice that said, *You're cleaning up his dog's mess while he's outside, probably fooling around with the animal,* she set about finding a plastic garbage bag. The newspapers and paper towels she used went into the bag before she twist-tied it closed. Scott could open it to reuse throughout the night as he spot-cleaned the messes.

Poor Horace. She washed her hands and looked around the room. A clothes washer and dryer, numerous shelves and cabinets and a sink lined the walls, but the floor was clutter-free and easy to clean. It wasn't a bad place for a sick dog.

The outside door opened and four muddy paws proceeded Scott's bare, wet feet into the room.

"Hold him for a minute," she said. Scott grabbed the dog's collar as she left. She located two chairs and brought one back, laying it on its side across the opening to the kitchen. Then she did the same with the second.

Scott filled the water bowl and petted Horace while the dog drank.

The room passed inspection. The man did not. "Get a towel for your feet. Where are your shoes?"

"I'm going to burn them." He didn't elaborate. He didn't have to.

"Step in it?"

"Only once, thankfully with the shoes still on. I think I know why his former owner abandoned him." He scowled, but Ginger saw the concern in Scott's eyes. "That dog is too goofy to housebreak."

Tenderness welled inside her, knowing his sour words masked his worry. She placed a hand along his jaw. "You have had a hard night, haven't you?"

"I've had worse." He kissed her palm without taking his gaze from hers. "I've had a lot better, too. Most recently with you."

"Scott," she softened her tone. "I can't tell you how *not* passionate I'm feeling at the moment."

His dimples deepened. "Let me know when that changes. Because the sight of you in that sweatshirt, with your sleeves pushed up, ready to take on all the problems of the world, is turning me on."

She uttered a disbelieving chuckle. "Really?"

"Or maybe it's because that sweatshirt smoothes over your breasts every time you move. You're not wearing anything under there but pure temptation."

She crossed her arms, mortified.

"I can see the curves you're hiding, and I remember their softness." His tone deepened and his eyes darkened. "And their taste. And their texture on my tongue."

Heat rose to her cheeks. She coughed, trying to break the spell he wove with his seductive words. Memories flooded her—the feel of his tongue on her skin, the pull of his mouth on her breasts as he sucked. The clench of need in her belly and the luxurious freedom of letting go.

Horace moaned, interrupting the moment.

Ginger had never been so glad to be in the company of a sick dog.

"Damn dog." Scott frowned and dragged the pup outside again, hopping in the cold. "Serves you right," he muttered as the huge creature in front of him not only pooped but vomited. "That's what you get for ruining my night. Try to remember this lesson."

Horace moaned and turned soulful eyes toward Scott, who gave in and bent to pet him. "I guess it's not your fault, is it, boy? Just stay off the counter from now on, okay? You want some water?"

The dog woofed and threw up on Scott's bare feet.

So much for getting romantic tonight.

Which was a damned shame, he thought as he rinsed off his feet with the water bowl he'd brought out for the dog to drink. The cold minishower did nothing to cool his libido, although he figured he might lose some toes to frostbite. He had an extrastrong case of lust, despite Horace's illness. He wanted Ginger. Her softness tempted him in the late-night intimacy. He considered locking the dog outside with a refilled bowl of water and dealing with him tomorrow. Scott had more important things to tend to.

"All better now?" he asked the dog.

Horace nudged his head against Scott's thigh.

"I'm having lustful thoughts in there, buddy. Your co-operation would mean a lot."

The dog panted, his mouth open in a smile, drool dripping in the cold night air.

"I know what you're thinking," Scott said. "You think I just want her body. And I do, I admit it. But there's more. *She's* more."

Horace's low bark sounded like agreement.

"Right. I mean, she drove over in the middle of the night, in the freezing cold." Scott rubbed his arms over his shirtsleeves. "Are you done, pal? I don't have a long shaggy coat."

They went back in, wiping their feet and paws.

"Aw, you poor baby," Ginger said, warming Scott more than a coat could have. Until he realized she was looking at the dog.

While laughing at himself, he had to admit her compassion for the sick puppy made him want her even more. Heaven help him, her nurturing the ailing animal turned him on. Which male in the room was really a sick puppy?

"Do you want to go out some time?"

She looked up from rubbing Horace's feet with a towel. "Excuse me?"

"Dinner. We kind of skipped that part before." Scott cleared his throat. He wasn't ashamed of having sex with her in December, but starting a relationship now felt awkward. Like having dessert, then going back for steak. Just as good, but in a different way. One was nutritional; one was for pure enjoyment. He wanted both.

He wanted a relationship with Ginger. They'd work with the girls, getting them used to the idea. He didn't know whether Shelby's animosity stemmed from Ginger being her teacher or Ginger's resemblance to Sam. Rena's constant staring had to be because of Ginger's appearance. Neither girl had mentioned it bothered her, but he knew. However, it had been almost a year. His life had to begin again.

"Maybe," he said, "we could go out some night this week. I think I have something Wednesday night, but other than that, I'm open."

She offered him a weak smile. "We have a tech committee meeting Wednesday night."

The reminder sobered him. He needed to check into the constraints against dating his daughter's teacher, but he sensed Ginger would evade answering if he asked her. Something was keeping her from opening herself to him, and, as they'd already been intimate, he could only think it was her job. He didn't want to push her into an impossible situation. Would she get in trouble? That other teacher, Cindy Grady, sure had a narrow view of what was allowed.

Could he date Ginger without endangering her job? Or would he have to wait until Shelby had moved on to third grade? What the hell would he do for the next five months?

Except go slowly insane.

Ginger rubbed the headache forming at her temple Wednesday night. The parents on the tech committee had batted around different wording of the Student Acceptable Use Clause for Internet Access for almost an hour.

"I think we need more stringent control."

"You can't expect the teachers in our district to safeguard each child."

"We have to protect the kids from all dangers, internet or not."

Progress had halted. No one wanted to come out and mention the allegations against Mike Reynolds, but they hung unvoiced in the room. The comments about ethics had become more pointed about fifteen minutes ago. If she chaired the committee, she'd have nipped this in the bud then. Cindy, however, reveled in the drama.

"I'm worried about the atmosphere in the district," the divorcée, Julie, said. "I've heard of teachers not acting in a responsible manner."

Her gaze darted to Ginger and away, making Ginger's spine go rigid. Did Julie mean *her?*

"We're aware of Coach Reynolds's behavior," Cindy said.

"We're aware of the *accusations* against Coach Reynolds." Ginger had had enough. She wasn't about to let Cindy malign Mike. "He hasn't been proven to have done anything wrong."

"You're right, Ms. Winchester," Cindy said. "We've just got the word of twelve boys who all said he did."

Ginger stared her down. "Have you personally heard them say this? Each of them? Telling the same story?"

Cindy's jaw bulged as she clenched her teeth. "Until the investigation is over, it would be better not to discuss Coach Reynolds."

"I agree." Ginger attempted a we're-on-the-same-side smile, but knew it fell flat. Even if it had appeared genuine—which she doubted—the recipient had to meet her halfway. Cindy did not.

"There are other teachers who display questionable practices," Julie put in. "My friend told me—"

"I think we should leave those matters be," Scott cut in. "We can't act on hearsay or unproven accusations. As a matter of fact, we can't act at all. Our job is to review the wording of this here agreement for the kids to do research on the school's computers, going out on the internet."

"I don't want to gossip, either," John agreed. "If that's where the meeting is going, I'm going, too. Toward home. So, can we get to work?"

Scott's eyes met hers. She read compassion and remorse there and gave him a brief lift of her lips in return. From now on, she couldn't even risk a smile at a man, and certainly not her student's father. And definitely not with Cindy's flinty gaze boring their way every few seconds. Not to mention the parents in the room who were ripe for signs of scandal.

For a moment, Ginger wondered if Julie's friend had told her anything regarding Ginger leaving the party with Scott in December. Plenty of people had attended; anyone could have seen them leave together. Or seen her leave the hotel later in the morning.

She swallowed down her fear. They'd been strangers. It had been a school break. Shelby's enrollment wasn't official until the beginning of the year. Ginger hadn't shown her any preferential treatment in the past few weeks that Shelby had been in her class.

She hadn't broken the morality clause, even in the past year. Bent it maybe, but that wild urge had passed.

No one had said anything yet, and surely word would have spread in whispers like brushfire if anyone knew.

Everything was fine.

# Chapter 7

"I've decided to quit using the adoption agency," Ginger told Lisa in her bakery kitchen after work on Thursday. While Lisa mixed together pale blue icing for her cookies, Ginger worked up her nerve talking about inanities. She stole pinches off an unbaked sugar cookie cut into a snowflake until Lisa scooped it off the baking sheet and onto a plate for her. Grasping the edge of the counter steadied her. She hoped support of the emotional kind would come from her friend.

Lisa set down her mixing bowl and rounded the counter. She took hold of Ginger's arms. "You can't give up on adopting. Unless you think you can get pregnant? Did you meet someone who's talked you into trying again?"

Ginger swallowed down her pain, even as the image of Scott appeared in her mind. If it was at all possible he'd accept her as she was, she'd take the chance on their relationship working. She'd take a chance on him.

But it wasn't going to happen. She couldn't conceive; she had to adopt. He already had a family. She hated to douse the light in Lisa's eyes. "No, to all those questions. This isn't about me having a baby."

"Well, I won't believe you can't until you've been through more testing. Just because you couldn't conceive with Kyle doesn't mean you couldn't with someone else."

"We had it confirmed at the fertility clinic, Lisa." It touched Ginger's heart that her best friend rooted for her happiness so vehemently that she overlooked the facts. But miracles just didn't happen in real life. "We talked to the doctors there. I'm done hoping."

Lisa crossed her arms over her chest, her expression set. "Your rat-fink ex-husband convinced you it was your fault."

"It wasn't just him saying it."

"I don't recall Kyle getting intimate with a plastic cup. His sperm could be faulty. Probably is, since the rest of him certainly is lacking."

Ginger smiled at the way Lisa spat her ex-husband's name. "I'm not able to conceive a child. I've accepted that and moved on."

"Then don't give up on adopting. You'd be a great mom. Please reconsider."

"I'm not giving up." Ginger hugged her. Lisa smelled like powdered sugar and vanilla. "I'm through with the agency route, that's all. They have these strict requirements I don't seem able to meet." She glanced at Lisa. "Do you think maybe someone found out I'd been, you know, seeing those guys since I got divorced?"

"All they have to do is talk to you for three minutes to figure out why you were doing that. I doubt it would count against you."

Ginger frowned. "What do you mean 'why I was doing it'?"

"You'd found out you couldn't have a baby, then your husband walked out on you. It's not surprising you'd be looking for reassurance from men."

Ginger couldn't believe it. There was a deep-seated reason? She thought she'd just been having a good time.

Lisa tilted her head, her eyes wide. "You knew this, right?"

Ginger opened her mouth, then closed it.

"You haven't thought about why?"

"Because I like men?"

Lisa sighed. She reached over and retrieved an undecorated snowflake cookie for each of them. "And?"

Sugary sweetness crumbled in her mouth. Vanilla and almond melted against her tongue. "I give up. What kind of reassurance did I need?"

"The feminine kind. After Brad left me for Junior Miss Gum-smacker, I doubted myself. 'Why wasn't I enough?' That kind of thing."

"Which was stupid. It was his loss."

"Absolutely. You had much more to deal with. So you sought out men to reestablish your appeal, rebuild your self-esteem. It's like hitting menopause."

Ginger laughed. "Whoa. Lost me."

"Women tie so much of our identity to the ability to have children. At some point, we need to redefine what it means to us to be a woman. That's what you did. Reassured yourself you were still desirable, if not for motherhood, then at least for sex."

"Wow." Ginger grinned, even as she acknowledged the truth of Lisa's analysis. Her friend made it so clear. "All that was going on in my head?"

"Yes, as amazing as that seems. I figured you were on a binge, like an alcoholic, and you'd come to your senses eventually. And you did."

"How come you know me so well?"

"I'm wise beyond my years. Now, go back to the adoption thing."

Ginger set aside the other revelation to ponder later. "The time frame isn't working for me. I can't wait forever, or even until Evil Witch Lady retires. I can't prove she's blocking my application, but intuition says she is."

Lisa sat on a stool at the counter. "What are you going to do?"

"Adopt privately. I've talked to my gynecologist and a family practice lawyer. You know Preston Fields, don't you? I put the word out that I'm looking." Ginger grimaced. "I don't know how else to put it. 'I'm in the market for a baby' sounds like I'm buying one. I only want to create a win-win situation for someone who's already decided she can't raise a child."

"Isn't that risky? You won't know the history of the mother."

"After I talked to Dr. Elliot, his nurse pulled me aside and said they get many pregnant women coming in, unable or unwilling to keep their babies. Elliot has helped match up pregnant women with adoptive parents." She blew out a breath. "I know it sounds like I'm taking advantage of them, but I'm going to give someone's child a good home."

"Of course you are. Anyone would be grateful to have you for their child's mother. I've often considered giving you Abby and Bobby."

Ginger laughed.

"Seriously, though," Lisa said, "going through your doctor is a brilliant idea."

"The Evil Witch at the adoption agency wouldn't let anyone else work with me at all. She had papers and interviews and all these excuses. I just can't wait any longer."

"Why not?"

Ginger blinked, taken aback. Lisa had never been anything but supportive regarding her decision to adopt. "What do you mean?"

"Why the rush?"

Ginger hesitated. She feared her attraction to Scott. Every time they were together, she discovered some aspect of his personality that made her like him more—and desire him more. Even the way he'd cared for Horace made her melt a little inside. When his dog was sick, he hadn't walked away, as Kyle had with her. Even though she tried not to compare the two men, Ginger couldn't help but wonder about Scott's reaction to her inability to conceive.

But she couldn't have a casual relationship with him. She worried about further ruining her reputation; she needed to pass the pregnant mother's approval. Something inside told her the time was near. Somewhere a woman was looking for someone like Ginger, full of love and yearning for a child to share her life with. She couldn't miss this chance, even for Scott.

She'd gone a little crazy after the divorce. Too many men, too much fun, too many late nights and regretted mornings. She understood her reasons now. Did she have to be punished for the entire rest of her life? Denied the one thing that would make her happy, that would make her complete?

"The longer it takes," she told Lisa, "the less likely I am to believe it'll happen."

"You're doing the right thing. Forget the adoption agency witch. She had a bug up her hind end about you."

Ginger chuckled. "I guess I'll have to stop swearing once I get a baby, huh?"

"Damn right." They laughed. "You'll come to us if you need a character reference, right?"

"You're first on my list."

"Abby and Bobby will swear you're the best babysitter ever." Lisa patted her arm. "They even love it when you make them work at the animal shelter. To them, it's the most fun they've ever had."

Mention of the shelter brought memories of Scott, looking at the small dogs while his daughters fell in love with the biggest animal there. Even though they'd been at a pet store rather than the shelter itself, she had a feeling the man would always be tied to the shelter in her mind. "It's an honor, helping animals, earning their trust when other humans have betrayed or abused them."

Lisa grinned. "You've already got the skewed way of presenting things down-pat. You make my kids believe they're getting a special treat when in fact you're making them clean cages. They sure don't volunteer to clean their own rooms."

"They get to walk the dogs, too," Ginger protested, feeling like a sweatshop manager. "Plus, petting an animal keeps them gentle and helps their little psyches."

"Which little psyches?" Lisa asked as she rounded the counter to take out sheets of cookies from the oven and load in more. "The animals' or my children's?"

Warmth washed over Ginger, accompanied by the

aroma of fresh baked sugar cookies. Her mouth watered. "Very funny."

"Because if you know of something to keep my kids gentle, I'll take a six-pack."

"Your children are angels."

"They've got you fooled. But, seriously, if we can do anything, let us know. Um, so…" Lisa concentrated on the coloring as she stirred icing with vigor. "I take it from your earlier comment you aren't seeing anyone? What about that guy from the Christmas party?"

Ginger watched Lisa, who didn't make eye contact. Sneaky. "What guy?"

Lisa's head jerked toward her. "The one whose daughter is in your class."

"Oh, him."

Lisa scowled, obviously blind to Ginger's sense of humor. This only made pulling her chain all the more fun. "Yes, him. How many guys did you meet at the Christmas party?"

"Well, I went to a lot of Christmas parties."

The spoon clinked in the bowl as Lisa's fists landed on her hips. "Really? And how many guys did you sleep with? A guy from every party?"

"Just the one. Jeez." Pull a chain, get a reaction.

"Exactly. And how many guys have you slept with since Scott?"

"You remember his name now?"

"Answer the question."

Ginger knew what the answer implied. She couldn't deny it—Scott had made an impression. Honestly, he'd changed the way she looked at herself, at her opinion of herself since the divorce. Kyle's desertion had been a blow. The reason for his leaving had devastated her.

Being with a man to forget that now seemed idiotic, but reasserting her femininity made sense. It had worked for a while. Until Scott.

"Well?"

"No one else." The admission cost her. Ginger felt exposed and vulnerable. "But it doesn't mean anything. I'm not starting a relationship with anybody older than one year."

Lisa giggled. "Well, if you're going to be that picky, never mind. What makes you think Scott wouldn't welcome a baby?"

"He's got his family. You should see the way he is with his daughters. They're his entire life."

"Have you talked about it?"

Ginger smirked. "We don't exactly talk when we're together. I spend the time trying to think of anything except having sex with him again."

"Maybe you should stop trying so hard. You had a good time, right?"

"I'm done being a good-time girl." If things were different, she'd like to have seen where things could go with Scott. But things were what they were. She was barren; he was devoted to his daughters and still in love with his wife.

"I've got an appointment with a prospective mom tomorrow after school."

Lisa's mouth dropped open before bursting into a grin. The stirring spoon coated with blue icing fell to the floor. "And you're just now telling me?" She looked down. "Now look what you made me do. Tell me everything you know and I won't make you clean up this mess."

Ginger smiled. She could learn a lot about mothering by watching her friend.

\* \* \*

Shelby's birthday arrived. His eldest turned eight. Even while he struggled to understand how so much time could have passed since first seeing her precious little face, Scott anticipated the school party with more eagerness than Shelby's aging warranted. He yearned to see Ginger again. Not that he wouldn't be thrilled and proud to celebrate his daughter's birthday with her at school. This year would be especially hard on Shelby without her mother to bake a cake and take care of all the little details. It was just a bonus for *him* that the woman who featured in his erotic daydreams would be there, also.

It had been two days since the technology meeting talks had hit a wall. Tension walked between him and Ginger, and he didn't like it. While he understood her need to protect her reputation, he just didn't understand why their dating would be such a big deal.

Scott signed in at the main office, juggling the tower of cupcakes Shelby had requested. After balancing his way down the hall, he knocked his heel against Ginger's classroom door, hoping someone would assist him. The door opened, and Shelby stuck out her head.

"Hi, Dad." She swung the door wider, letting out the noise of cheering as the kids saw him. Or, more probably, as they spotted the cupcakes.

A small bell tinkled and the kids subsided into their chairs, their voices cut off. He looked over to see Ginger setting the bell on her desk.

Today's pale pink top made her look soft and approachable. Gray slacks hugged her legs. She'd pulled her hair into a bun of some sort, but loose hair framed her face and softened the severity of the style.

"Thank you," she said to the class. "Shelby, you can

help your father set up, then we'll sing. The rest of you get out your cards for Shelby."

Ginger crossed to him. "Can I help you with anything?"

He spared her a wink on the side turned away from the class. "No, thanks. Shelby has it all under control."

The children sang. Shelby picked Jean to collect their cards as Shelby handed them a cupcake and Maria gave each a napkin. The kids had made the cards in class. Maria's card had twisted black paper held down by a ton of glue. "It's your new dog."

Shelby scrunched her nose. "This doesn't look like Horace."

Maria's face fell. Scott snapped his mouth closed, not wanting to reprimand her in front of her classmates.

She placed her hand on Maria's arm. "You'll have to come over and meet him. He's got big brown eyes. See?" She pointed to where Maria had glued blue paper over the end that must be the dog's face. "Will you ask your mom when you can come?"

Maria brightened and nodded. He'd say something to his daughter later about the phrasing of her invitations, but she'd saved her friend's feelings and made her feel special.

Jean pushed her card forward. "Read mine. I wrote a poem, so mine's better."

Scott looked helplessly across the room to where Ginger directed one of the boys with math he hadn't finished. The poor kid still got to eat his cupcake, but he had to work through the celebration, while the other children either hung around Shelby or talked to each other at their seats.

Were kids always this unkind? Had Jean's attitude

rubbed off on Shelby? He didn't like his daughter hanging around with mean girls.

Shelby finished reading the poem and smiled at Jean. "I like your card. Thanks for the poem. But I liked Maria's artwork, too."

Scott nodded. His daughter had some rough edges, but in her young heart lurked a thoughtful and loving girl. Parenting by himself had him second-guessing everything.

Throughout the half hour he stayed in the room, he noticed Ginger keeping away from him for the most part. He understood; a school classroom was inappropriate for necking. He grinned to himself. It was public and children lurked everywhere. Especially his.

Then the school bell signaled the end of the day and the children left, including his, as he had to get back to work. Shelby thanked him with a sticky, sweet kiss for bringing the cupcakes and left for the bus to the Wee Care.

"This was great," Scott said, throwing away napkins. "I can help wipe up the tables or sweep or something."

"Sure." She crossed to the cupboard and brought him back a spray bottle and several rags. "When your rag gets disgusting, put it in the plastic bag I have on the doorknob. That's laundry."

"You wash these rags? Why doesn't the school do it?"

"They're mine. I use a spray mix I make at home for sanitizing. It's environmentally kinder and my sensitive kids don't have a problem with it."

"Harry and Ron?" he guessed.

"And others. It's better for all of us."

She turned away and he caught her elbow to turn her back. "Hey. I've hardly gotten to talk to you."

"I'm at work, Scott. This isn't the place or time."

Frustration bit him. "Then name a place and time. I want to be with you."

Her expression grew guarded.

"I don't mean just for that." He hesitated, unable to say *sex* in their current setting, still echoing with the sound of children.

"Scott, I'm sorry. I can't."

"You're sorry that you can't? Or you're just sorry and you can't? Because there's a difference." Something like panic or betrayal welled in his throat. "Do you want to be with me? Start a relationship? See where things progress from the start we have?"

"It's not as simple as what I want. You have to understand." Her eyes misted. "I loved our night together."

"That doesn't clarify anything." He threw his hands up. "What do you want from me? I can't understand what you won't say."

She pulled away. "I'm sorry, but no, I can't be with you."

Icy crystals splintered in his chest, piercing and cold. Tossing the rag on a desk, he walked out of her classroom.

His hopes for starting a new life remained behind.

Ginger watched the door close behind Scott and put an arm across her belly, hugging herself. It hurt to let him go.

She had to pull herself together. A pregnant woman named Fiona Rawlings wanted to find a home for her baby and had set up an interview at her lawyer's office in thirty minutes. Her own lawyer, Preston Fields, cautioned against setting too much store on this encounter. Fiona had interviews with two other families that afternoon, and she'd planned to make her final decision. But the two lawyers had conferred and offered Ginger's information, and Fiona had agreed to meet with her.

Ginger swallowed down nerves as she left the building. Could this be the day she became a mother-to-be?

*Don't get your hopes up, don't get your hopes up.* She chanted it to herself on the drive over. The woman's lawyer had offices in Independence, and Ginger would just make the meeting in time if traffic wasn't too bad. Fortunately, the day was clear and the roads were dry. On an empty stretch of road, she brushed her hair. At stoplights, she reapplied her lipstick and patted on some powder to reduce the day's shine and freshen her appearance. It wouldn't do to come across as too worn out to care for an infant.

Fiona stood five foot nothing in heels. She couldn't be more than legal age, if that. Although she wasn't undernourished, Fiona's belly stuck out from a frame of small bones stretched with thin skin. Ginger wanted to feed her. She feared the woman/girl would shatter if the wind blew too hard. At least she knew from the medical reports that the girl was healthy. She was just too young to be pregnant.

After the greetings, the lawyers spent a few minutes reviewing Fiona's health care updates and Ginger's finances.

"Are you in a relationship?" Fiona asked after ten minutes passed.

Ginger managed to keep her expression calm. Why did that have to be the first question? Would it disqualify her in Fiona's mind or count as a benefit? "No. I'm divorced. So I'll be able to devote all my time to the baby."

"But you're not seeing anyone seriously? Like going to get married or anything?"

Ginger shook her head and the girl's expression shifted. Right then, she feared she'd lost her chance. She went for broke. "I can't conceive or carry a baby to term. Adopting is the sole solution for me, my only opportunity to raise a baby."

The meeting went smoothly, but Fiona had her heart set on a family. "I'm sorry," she said. "If only single women were interviewing, I'd pick you. I like the idea of a teacher being around to help my little guy or girl with her homework. But I want my baby to have a daddy, too. I'm so sorry."

Fiona's eyes welled with tears. Ginger felt the same and excused herself after wishing the girl luck.

"Ginger," Preston called. "Wait."

She pulled herself together and turned to face him on the landing. "I'm fine, Pres."

With over twenty years behind them, having met on the playground in kindergarten, he took her hand. "I'm sorry. I didn't realize it was that much of a lost cause. She never stipulated only two-parent applicants."

"It's okay. You warned me not to get my hopes up."

He cocked his head. "But you did anyway."

She shrugged. "It's going to happen soon. I feel something good is near. I believe that. This just wasn't it."

"You're not giving up?"

She shook her head. "I'm going to be a mother. I just know it. It feels…right."

He smiled. "Womanly intuition?"

She punched his arm playfully. "You just wait. We'll see who's laughing then. I bet you a quarter that I'll be a mom by the end of the year."

"A quarter?" He laughed. "Don't know that I can afford your wager, lady, but I'll be glad to come up with the dough. For once, I hope I lose."

"You will, Preston. You will."

Shelby appeared beside her desk on Tuesday. "Ms. Winchester, my dad made me ask you if you'll come help us with Horace."

Ginger clamped down on her lip to hold back her laughter. The girl's wording needed improvement. She'd have to learn to hide her feelings.

"What's wrong with Horace?"

"Nothing, but we can't train him to do anything. Dad says he has something called add."

"Ad—? Addictive personality?"

Shelby shook her head.

"Adorableness?"

The girl laughed, caught off guard. Then she seemed to remember herself and closed off again. "That's probably it. Horace is pretty cute, even when he's eating my socks. But Dad said it stood for something."

"Oh, ADD?"

"Yeah, Dad spells it, too." She shrugged. "It spells *add,* though, right?"

"Right. You've heard it called ADHD."

Shelby looked across the room and back. "Oh. Like Simon?"

Ginger nodded. The class knew of his disorder, as he experienced disastrous days when his clueless parents decided he didn't "need" his medication. The kids had seen the repercussions.

"Horace doesn't have medicine, though. And he doesn't act out, except for eating things he shouldn't. He just doesn't do what we're trying to train him to do."

"I think your dad means Horace can't concentrate on one thing long enough to learn it. It's pretty unrealistic to ask Horace to learn a behavior in a week." She grinned, knowing the answer to her next question. "What's your dad trying to teach Horace?"

"To go to the bathroom outside."

"Tell your dad to buy a book."

"So you won't come to dinner? Okay." Shelby turned away.

"Whoa." Ginger glanced at the other kids, busy drawing maps of the United States. With economic cutbacks in the district, she'd become their art teacher, as well. Today she combined geography and art, having the kids concentrate on the size of each state in relation to the others, trying to teach them about proportion. Tomorrow the class would learn about watercolors and add features like mountains and rivers, once again studying geography while learning an art technique.

No one paid any attention to her and Shelby; still, she lowered her voice. "Are you sure your dad invited me to dinner?"

"He said it would be payment for you helping us train Horace. But I'll just tell him you can't come."

The girl seemed more than happy with the outcome. While Shelby wasn't disrespectful, she'd never warmed up to Ginger the way most incorrigible students eventually did. After three weeks in her class, she might as well be marked off as a lost cause. Shelby could sense the chemistry between her father and her teacher, even if she didn't understand it. She'd seen them together on several social occasions. The girl probably saw her as a threat, trying to replace her mother. If only Ginger could explain it to Shelby, but she had trouble explaining it to herself.

She wanted Scott, ached to be in his arms again and experience the magic they'd shared the month before. If he didn't have children, she'd pursue him, working up the courage to gamble that he wouldn't reject her. His children had a mother, though, and Ginger didn't want to be anyone's second-best.

Since she'd turned away from him the week prior, after Shelby's party, she couldn't believe he'd risk asking her to dinner. Even in this roundabout way.

Guilt ate at her. She owed him an explanation.

"Shelby, tell your dad I'll be there around six-thirty." Ginger ignored the girl's crestfallen expression. "If the time doesn't work for him, just have him call me. I'll bring dessert."

At six-thirty, Ginger knocked on the Matthews' door, greeted by deep woofs. The door was opened by Serena, her two hands wrapped around the knob. Her big eyes shone a welcome very different from Shelby's usual animosity. Hair stuck out of her reddish-brown ponytail. Once again Ginger had to restrain herself from brushing the girl's tendrils into place.

The door swung wider to reveal Scott in the background, holding the collar of the wriggling black mass. He struggled to contain the dog's enthusiasm. Horace's barks welcomed rather than warned.

"Hi, Serena. Why's your dad holding the puppy?" She hung her coat on the hooks drilled into the wall.

"He jumps, but don't worry, he won't bite."

Ginger almost smiled. Horace might not. Scott, on the other hand, did bite in a most delightful way. Wait. Jump? She jerked toward Serena and frowned. "Has the dog knocked you down?"

"He doesn't mean to. He's just a puppy and don't know better."

The girl couldn't be three feet tall, and the puppy was almost two feet tall now. She could be seriously hurt. Her yellow sweater had mud spots on it that appeared to be paw prints.

Ginger squared her shoulders and held out the container of brownies. "Will you take this into the kitchen for me?"

Serena nodded and moved off with the dessert but turned in the doorway to watch.

"Hi," Scott said, voice raised over the barking. "He'll calm down in a minute. If not, I'll put him in the mudroom." He grinned. "I installed a Dutch door this weekend so we can see him while he's contained. That's where he stays during the day."

"Good idea. Now, let him go."

Scott shook his head. "Not a good idea. I'll walk him over so you can pet him. That's what he wants. A little attention."

She cocked her head. "Do you want me to help you with Horace or not?"

The puppy woofed upon hearing his name. This dog wasn't untrainable, but the family needed to take a firm approach.

"With housebreaking. I don't want him to hurt you."

"I have an idea. Let's give it a try." When Scott hesitated, she nodded once in a decisive manner. More than the puppy needed instruction. "Scott, let the dog go."

Scott released him and, as expected, Horace bounded toward her. Ginger held up one hand, palm out at waist level, and took a step forward. "No."

Horace skidded across the polished wooden floor toward her, scrabbling for purchase. His chest and chin bumped the ground, but he sat up and cocked his head at her. She bent and petted him. "Good dog."

She glanced past Scott, who stood with his jaw dropped, to locate a beaming Serena behind him. "Do you have little dog bone treats?"

The girl nodded. "I'll get him one."

"How did you do that?" Scott's eyes were wide with amazement.

Ginger smiled, still laving attention on the puppy. "I saw it on TV. The theory is you step into their planned arc and it throws them off. So they have to *not* jump while they reconfigure their launch and landing."

"That's amazing. And so simple."

"Simple if you know it already. Just step into his path. Tell him *no* in a firm voice."

Horace whined in response.

Scott grimaced. "Oh, I've been saying *no* in a firm voice quite a lot this week. It just hasn't had much effect."

"Well, my work here is done." She straightened, hiding her amusement. "Thanks for inviting me. Enjoy the brownies."

He laughed. "Hold on there. You can't leave. One, we haven't had dinner and you've definitely earned it already. Two, you haven't taught him the most important trick of all."

"Voiding outdoors is a behavior, not a trick. If you think of it that way, you'll realize it's going to take longer to train him. I'm sure the girls didn't learn in a week."

"They wore diapers. I've got to get that dog potty trained or I'll wind up buying so much cleanser, I'll go broke."

Scott patted his jeans pocket, demonstrating its emptiness. Horace bounded over and placed his paws on Scott's stomach.

"Get down, you stupid dog." He took hold of Horace's front paws and put him on the floor, getting a slobbery kiss in the process. Scott made a disgusted sound. "You fool."

Ginger laughed. "He's amazing."

"Amazingly stupid. I think he has ADD. Do they have doggie meds for that?"

"Scott, you're missing the point. He came when you called."

"I didn't call. Oh." He glanced down at Horace, who stood with his tongue out, drooling with pride. "Patting my pockets? Huh, I guess I did."

"And yes, they probably do have all kinds of medicines for dogs, given that people treat their animals as children. But Horace doesn't need Ritalin. Did you expect him to learn not to jump after one time?"

"Well, no." He shot her another grin. "But I sure hoped for it."

"Don't. It sets you both up for disappointment." She looked to the empty living room with its comfortable orange twill sofa and brown leather love seat. "Do we have time to sit down or should we go in the kitchen? I brought a book for you in my purse."

He checked his wristwatch. "We're good for another fifteen minutes."

The three of them walked over to stand by the couch. Ginger set the book on the coffee table. "Is this safe? Or will he eat it?"

"He hasn't shown an interest in books yet."

Serena came in with a dog biscuit, and Horace leaped forward.

"No," Scott and Ginger called at the same time. Horace's impetus carried him into Serena's side, bumping her arm with the treat, although Ginger thought he swerved at their command. The treat went flying, and Horace flew after it, making his action look planned. But since he came back and sniffed around Serena for more snacks, not cowering as though he'd done wrong, Ginger gave him the benefit of the doubt.

"Are you okay?" she asked the girl.

Serena shrugged, petting Horace. "That wasn't so bad. I didn't fall down that time."

"Serena." A frown formed between Scott's eyebrows as he looked around the living room. "Where did you put the pillows?"

Her gaze shifted to the floor. "They're in my room."

He glared at the dog. "What condition are they in?"

Serena ducked her head.

"It's okay," Ginger said. "Your dad is upset with Horace, not you."

"But I don't want him to go away," she appealed.

"We're not going to send him away, pumpkin." Scott sat and gestured her over. She cuddled into his side. "He's part of the family."

Ginger's knees went weak and she sank down on the cushion beside him. The tender scene stole her breath away. His words made her melt inside. He was decent and loving and gentle and kind.

She wanted him bad.

"Now, can you finish up in the kitchen while Ms. Winchester tells me what to do about Horace? Since we're going to keep him, we've got to be good to him. And I bet he doesn't like making a mess inside."

Serena's nose crinkled. "Or being home all day and stepping in it and walking it all over the floor."

"Yeah, I'm not fond of that, either."

Ginger suppressed a giggle at his dry tone.

"I'm almost done, Daddy. I just gotta spread one more bit of garlic butter." She bounded off.

Horace rose, but Scott grabbed his collar. "Not a chance, buster. You stay out of the kitchen when food is within reach." He frisked under the dog's chin. "And everything seems to be within your reach, doesn't it, you big monster?"

Ginger watched the girl leave. "Shouldn't we supervise her with a knife?"

"It's plastic. She'll be fine. I may not be Father of the Year, but I don't give my toddler a sharp knife, nor would I let her use it unsupervised."

"Of course not. Sorry. Garlic butter?" Ginger turned her attention to her nose, twitching in delight. "I thought I smelled Italian-something."

"I made lasagna. My grandma's recipe."

Good Lord on a bun. The man cooked.

Ginger wondered what time the girls went to bed.

# Chapter 8

They probably weren't going to make love tonight.

Ginger had never had sex with a man who had children in the house—or children anywhere, for that matter. She couldn't figure out how one "did it" with his daughters home. Hopefully, Scott would know.

Well, no. That wasn't a comforting thought, either.

She could hear Serena in the kitchen, singing. His other daughter remained conspicuously absent since Ginger's arrival. Was it because her teacher had come to her house or because her dad had invited a woman to dinner? "Where's Shelby?"

"She's here somewhere." He frowned. "You're right, she should have come out to greet you. I'll go get her."

Ginger placed a hand on his forearm, loving the strength emanating through the chambray, worn soft with many washings and wear. "Don't bother her. She'll come out in a few minutes anyway for dinner, right?"

He nodded.

The quiet house boomed in her ears. Unless that was her pulse, racing along with the fantasies forming in her head. "Thanks for inviting me to dinner. I felt bad, speaking to you so brusquely after Shelby's party. I had a meeting to get to."

*Where I interviewed to adopt a baby, without telling you. Even though it would change our relationship. Or end it.* A meeting where the mother wouldn't give her baby to a single woman. The coincidence of Ginger coming to dinner wasn't tied to that refusal. She suppressed a niggle of guilt. Scott had invited her. It wasn't as though she'd sought him out, needing a daddy in order to adopt Fiona's baby.

Still, she'd accepted the invitation, even though the timing stunk. If she questioned her motives, Scott would wonder, too.

"Don't worry about the manner in which you spoke." He stroked a hand down her cheek, and she closed her eyes in response, luxuriating in the gentleness of his warm touch. His lips brushed her cheek. "It was the words I didn't care for. What's going on in that beautiful head of yours right now, honey?"

She locked her gaze on his. "I'm wondering something. Have you managed to have sex without sending the girls to someone else's house? Since your wife, I mean."

His breath hitched, and his eyes darkened in instant reaction. At least he was still interested in making love with her. After Friday, she hadn't been sure.

She wanted the comfort of his arms. Being found unsuitable by Fiona had been a blow, and she had no one to console her. No husband, no baby, and Scott had ruined her for casual sex. How long would she be alone?

Not tonight, at any rate.

Old habits die hard. Losing herself in sex had been her answer when Kyle left. This felt different. This was Scott.

"I like the direction of your questions. The answer is no." He held up a finger, then placed it on her chin, slid it slowly down her throat, to the V between her breasts. "Let me rephrase. The answer is *not yet.*"

She shivered from both his touch and from anticipation. "I like the direction of your answer. And the direction of your finger."

"Are you thinking of tonight? Because I am. *Now* I am."

"I'm thinking appetizer, if I believed we could get away with it."

He laughed, husky and promising. She shivered with need.

"What time do they go to bed?" She set her mouth against his and sucked his lower lip. He tasted of garlic butter, her new favorite aphrodisiac. He must have sneaked a taste test.

"It's a school night, so eight o'clock. We're eating late." His eyes met hers. "Can you stay out late on a school night, young lady?"

"If you don't tell, I won't."

"I'll write you a note. 'Dear Mr. Bushfield, Ms. Winchester just experienced a round of hard loving, followed by a longer session of soft loving—'"

Ginger gulped.

"'And therefore didn't get home until the wee hours. Please excuse her from any physical duties today as she may not only be sore—'" he winked "'—but she must also save up her energy for future such activities.' What do you think?"

She thought it sounded lovely, like a night she'd never forget. It sounded like the beginning of a relationship, and that sounded like something she couldn't promise him. So she hedged. "I'd love to see my principal's face turn purple if he read a note like that. I can't wait for your account to come true."

A bell chimed. Scott kissed her nose. "Dinner's ready. Hold that thought."

"Daddy," Serena called from the other room, "the buzzer went off."

Was this what having a family was like? Putting the needs of the children before her own? Sneaking away for sex in stolen moments or quiet hours when the house was asleep? The idea made her smile. Millions of parents did it every day—and still managed to "do it" every day.

Ginger volunteered to take the puppy outside while the girls and Scott finished filling glasses with milk and setting out food on the dining room table while the lasagna set up. Horace danced around her, eager for play. "You're here for a reason, Horace. Go do it."

He peed then barked, making sure she noticed. She laughed and gave him a vigorous petting, praising him for being so smart.

Dinner conversation centered on the girls' activities. Shelby sat sulky and quiet unless Scott cajoled her into commenting. Serena's stares didn't unnerve Ginger as much as they usually did.

"The meal tastes like someone's Italian grandmother made it." Ginger glanced at him. "Is your grandma Italian? There's so much I don't know about you."

*Considering we've been naked together.*

"Nope." The twinkling laughter in his eyes told her he'd read her thoughts. "She was just a good cook."

After the first few delicious bites, the meal could have been one of her frozen dinners for all Ginger tasted it. Her mind locked on the coming hours, when the girls would be tucked in and she would have Scott to savor.

Even brownies didn't compete with that.

Ginger glanced around the table at this small family, solid and strong, and doing well on their own. Was it possible she—and someday a baby—could become part of the magic? Scott excelled as a father. Her adopted child wouldn't lack a dad. The girls would probably be terrific big sisters. Shelby was caring and practical when mothering her sibling, and Serena's sweet nature and loving interaction with Horace showed promise. Could Ginger bring a baby into the mix and become a vital part of this family?

She'd always believed she had to start from babyhood in order for a child to love her. The girls had known a mother's love, and in their eyes, Ginger would always be a substitute. She would have to deal with their preferring another woman, their *real* mother, for the rest of their lives. Was she strong enough?

"This is really good garlic bread, too, Serena," Ginger said to break the silence and include the little girl.

"Dad's is good," Shelby countered, "but my mom made it better."

Ginger's fork paused in midair. "I'm sure she did."

"My mom made me anything I asked for. Like pancakes for dinner sometimes. And she'd put smiley faces on them."

"That sounds fun."

"She was." Shelby's gaze bored into her. "She could do anything. Soccer and sewing and stuff. She taught me ballet 'cause she was a really good dancer. And she played with us all the time."

Serena nodded. "I remember dancing with Mommy."

Shelby shot her sister a hard look. "Of course you remember. It wasn't that long ago."

"Shelby," Scott cut in. "That's enough."

"Well, it's true. Don't *you* remember, Dad?"

"I remember everything, Shel. Now you remember your manners."

The girl sunk into her chair but said no more.

Scott offered Ginger a weak smile of apology as forks once more scraped across plates. Perhaps it was too soon for another woman in the girls' lives. She wondered if a trip home to see their mom had been scheduled. They'd only been in Missouri for one month, but time didn't rule the heart.

After dinner, Scott tucked in the girls then took Horace outside before shutting him in the mudroom. Ginger waited in the living room on the impossibly ugly orange couch, anticipation building.

Maybe she shouldn't tell him about her adoption plans, well aware he might want no part of a baby while dealing with all the other changes in his life. Since those plans were just hopes at the moment, as no one had agreed to let her adopt, she set them aside, feeling only slightly dishonest.

He came in and sat beside her, taking her hand. "I can't believe I'm nervous."

She laughed softly. "Why would you be? It isn't as though you need to seduce me."

"Yeah, and I'm thankful for that." His lips slid along her jaw. "But I'm going to anyway."

She tilted her head to allow him access, shivering as

his hot mouth found her neck. "I want this. I've thought about being with you so often since our night together."

"That feels like a different time," he said.

"Last year." Her hands smoothed over his shirt, eager for the privacy to remove it. Knowing the girls weren't yet asleep and she might have to spring apart from Scott kept her from taking his clothes off right then and there. While restrictive in one way, it freed her to explore him, as well, limiting their foreplay to fully clothed titillations. She liked the challenge of arousing him through chambray and denim, with her creativity and words, with hands, mouth and tongue. Even her teeth incited him as she pulled on his earlobe or nipped his neck.

Her breathing faltered as his hands found her breasts. Through layers of fabric, he touched and tugged, teased and tweaked, driving her crazy. She pushed against him, wanting more, needing to be closer. By the time they headed upstairs, hand in hand, anticipation had nearly robbed her of the ability to walk. Anticipation and Scott's skillful loving.

The turn of the lock on the door was the most eagerly awaited click she'd heard in her life.

A large clean room with only two pieces of furniture, almost spartan in its simplicity, lay before her. Done in grays and browns, the room needed serious livening up. Thinking of one way to energize the room, she turned back to Scott with a smile, but said instead, "You need a decorator."

"I sold my old bedroom suite."

"Oh." *Great, Ginger. Make him think of his wife.* He got the furniture and the girls? His ex must be some piece of work. Had she left and abandoned everything?

"I figured a new start should be totally new. For me.

Some of the things I kept so this would look like home to the girls, of course."

*Well done,* Ginger berated herself. *Bring his ex-wife and his daughters into the conversation—and into the room.* This wasn't working.

"Well, I'm glad it's all yours." Ginger smiled. "It just doesn't look like you." It came off as boring and mismatched.

"Why not?" He looked at the light oak furnishings as though he'd never seen them before. "I'm a guy. It works."

She stepped forward and flicked his top button open. "Who picked out that orange couch downstairs?"

"I did. Bought it with my first substantial paycheck, but I didn't realize how hard it would be to get things to coordinate with it."

Surprise shot through her. "It looks like new for being, what, ten years old?"

"A little shy of that. Usually there are green and yellow pillows, but I'm afraid Horace ate them."

She flicked open his second button, then stepped back out of reach.

He swallowed, trapping her eyes with his heated gaze. "Sam, my wife, hated that couch, but I wouldn't agree to sell it. It was a symbol of what I'd accomplished, earning money for more than rent and food, and being independent. So we compromised." He grimaced. "We kept it, but she put it in the basement with a painter's tarp over it."

Ginger chuckled. "Clever."

Scott caught her hand as she reached for his next shirt button. "I believe I'm behind."

His fingertips explored her breast, around her nipple. She shuddered in response to the tug in her belly. Heat swept through her bloodstream.

"I saw that shiver. Let's get you under the blankets."

Ginger chuckled. "I'm so far from cold, I could be in Georgia."

"It gets cold in Georgia. Not biting temperatures like Missouri, grant you. I recall a few nights in high school, with a blanket and a girl and the moonlight, where we spent more time wrapped in the blanket than rolling on top of it."

She stepped backward toward the bed without looking, and he followed. "A big warm blanket like this?"

"No, an oversize picnic blanket I borrowed from my mom." He laughed softly. "Without telling her, of course. Can't imagine explaining that one."

"Well, let's pretend." She sat on the bed. "We have moonlight shining in through the window. What did you plan to do with the girl?"

He propped a knee beside her on the bed and tipped back her chin. "Same thing I'm planning to do with you."

His mouth came down, hot and hard, tongue tickling the folds of her lips. Her mouth opened, letting him in, giving what she could in that position. The hand supporting the back of her head kept her from reclining. He held her in place, his mastery arousing, where she'd never liked such a thing before. She felt protected and conquered at the same time. Aware that he'd stop if she made the request, she held still; that he'd shift position if she whimpered her discomfort, she remained quiet; that he'd care for her and her needs, she waited.

The thick fabric of his shirt under her hands reminded her she held a man. He might yield to her. He might not. For certain, he'd pleasure her, which suited her fine. Power struggles didn't fit into tonight's game plan.

Tonight was about reuniting and rediscovering. Tonight she put aside the reasons why a relationship between them wouldn't work and concentrated on the possibilities. Tonight was about being with the man she'd come to care for. Tonight was about feeling desired.

To that end, she trailed her fingers down to the leather belt around his hips. He caught her hand.

"Not yet."

"Why? Can't take too much?" She smiled in the darkness, pleased to have such a strong effect on him. "Going to explode early like the schoolboy you remember?"

"It's not time yet." He pinched her nipple through her sweater.

She jerked and almost squirmed with longing. "What do I have to say to provoke you to do that again?"

Scott laughed and eased her down on the bed, following and settling alongside her. "We have all night. Don't be impatient."

"We have all night. Why dawdle over the first time?"

His teeth flashed in the darkness. "First time? I like the way you think. But I also like the way you look. Last time, we left the lamp on. Is it okay if I turn on a light?" He cupped her cheek. "I want to watch you when you climax."

She snorted. "You want to get an eyeful of my womanly charms."

"That, too." He rose and flipped on a light in what appeared to be a bathroom, then pulled the door most of the way closed. A strip of illumination fell across the floor and to the right of the bed, leaving most of the room in shadow.

"Your womanly charms are so charming." His accent thickened, for effect or because he was affected, she didn't know. His palm cupped her breast.

"I remember you leaning across the desk in the hotel room," he said, "flipping on that lamp. That image has replayed in my head many times. Your thin—very thin, I might add—dress curved over your backside and clung to your breasts." His hand did what his words expressed: curved over her backside just long enough to produce shudders of need, squeezed, then clung to her breast. "I thought I was going to faint."

She swallowed. "Faint? Aren't you exaggerating a little?"

"Not at all. All the blood had rushed out of my head."

She smiled.

"I wanted you like that." His voice roughened.

Mouth dry, she wet her lips. "Like what?"

"Stretched out over the desk."

"Oh."

He tilted his head. "*Oh*? Is that 'Oh, no way' or 'Oh, why didn't you say so?'"

"No. Not say so."

He nodded, his face passive.

"*Do* so."

"Oh."

She pulled his head closer, brought his mouth to hers. His whiskers scuffed across her face, prickled under her hand, tingled her fingertips. The care he took not to abrade her skin sent pools of warmth to her belly. She moaned her pleasure, unable to voice the deeper feelings she didn't want to face. Admitting she was falling in love would complicate things.

He covered her, his weight pinning her to the bed. Rising for a moment, he pulled her sweater over her head. Deft fingers played over her breasts, making her shiver with need, before unhooking the clasp of her bra.

She struggled to keep her brain working long enough to manage the rest of the buttons on his shirt, then pushed it off his shoulders. Smooth skin, coarse hair, strong muscles held in check. Her mouth found his salty skin, remembering he wasn't much of a talker, but she didn't need words. The pleasure he brought her spoke eloquently.

They freed each other from jeans and all the sundry pieces until they both lay naked. She wanted him. Not only with her body—although she certainly yearned to find completion in his arms, with him inside her—but with her heart. He'd touched her, changed her, made her want more from life than an occasional quick romp. He'd brought lovemaking back to the forefront of her mind, rather than having-sex-to-forget-her-husband's-betrayal.

For that, she'd always hold a piece of him near to her heart.

Once naked, the tempo picked up. Thoughts flew as sensations rose. It was more than sex, more than being touched and pleasured, even though she enjoyed each caress. When he parted her legs and applied his fingers and tongue to her pleasure, eagerness built inside her.

The intensity stemmed from being with Scott. Tender, ardent, adorable Scott. A valiant man raising his children alone. A man who would stand up for her at the committee meeting but step aside in order not to jeopardize her job. A man she wanted to admire her, to love her; a man she didn't want to disappoint. She sought to bring him pleasure in return for the richness he'd brought to her life.

For this might well be their last time together.

When he entered her, Ginger had to fight back tears. She didn't want to lose him. She didn't want this to be the end. Her pleasure came more from the way he touched her heart than the way he touched her body. Although he did that, superbly, building sensation, backing off, building again. The climb and climax overpowered her and she flew to pieces, held safely, holding him tightly as he followed.

Afterward, they lay together, both struggling for breath. Her head lay on the pillow near his as she curled into his side. She wouldn't ruin the moment with talk, not even of something so dear to her heart and so vital that he know about her.

It was too soon to bring up forever and family. They'd had sex twice but zero dates. She smiled wryly in the darkness. Neither had said the magic words; she wasn't sure happily ever after existed. She'd married with that ideal in her head, and look where that had gotten her.

"What are you thinking about?" he murmured.

What would he do if she said, *My ex?* She chuckled to herself. "Nothing. Everything. After sex like that, I can't gather my wits to focus on any one thing."

He hugged her closer. "Good answer."

Better than the truth, anyway.

Ginger evaded Scott's phone calls the next week as January turned into February. What could she say? *I can't be with you because being a mother is more important than a relationship with you?* No. *I can't be with you because your daughters will never accept me as their stepmother?* No. *I can't be with you because I don't want to face rejection when you find out about my infertility?* No.

But as she feared would happen when she continued to let his calls go to voice mail, Scott showed up in her doorway. Instead of her classroom, however, he came to her house. His smile weakened her resolve.

"Are you going to let me in?"

She'd have to get it over with sooner or later. She owed him an explanation. Maybe he'd be eager to adopt and build a family with her. Stepping back, she opened the door wider. "Did you see your shadow? Are we having six more weeks of winter?"

"I'm not a groundhog, honey, despite the day. I might be likened to a terrier, though, since I'm tenacious when I go after something. Or, as it turns out, that also describes a Newfie."

She smiled as he put his navy peacoat on a chair. A black cable-knit sweater stretched over his shoulders, topping an orange button-down shirt. The tigerlike colors matched his demeanor as he stalked her across the living room.

"You've been avoiding me."

"Yes." She retreated to the couch, not surprised when he sat beside her. The armchair would have been a wiser choice.

"I thought you'd deny it." His hand rested on her arm. "What's going on, Ginger? Did I do or say something wrong?"

She shook her head.

Scott grimaced. "Please don't say 'It's not you, it's me.'"

"It sounds lame, I know. I'm sorry."

The hand on her arm tightened, gripping as though reluctant to let her go but not hurting her. It was reflex. "What is it?"

"Why don't you ever talk about your wife?"

He drew back. "What?"

Ginger swallowed and forced herself to keep speaking. "Is it too painful?"

"Definitely."

Her stomach felt leaden. "Because you still love her."

"No. Well, yes. But not the way you mean. Sweet hell." His hand fisted on his leg. "She's the mother of my daughters. I married her. She was my life."

"I'm sorry."

He stood and paced away. "What do you want me to say? That I never loved her? That I don't miss her?"

The pain in his eyes as he turned back to her broke her heart.

"Of course not. I wouldn't…care for you the way I do if you were that kind of man." *I wouldn't be in danger of falling in love with you. I wouldn't be halfway there.*

"So you're fine with me still getting over my wife? Because I can't give you a timeline. It'll take as long as it takes."

How to tell him about her infertility? "I can't live up to her. I'm not perfect."

"Honey." Scott slid back onto the cushion next to hers. He put his hands on her shoulders, turned her to him. "You have nothing to worry about. Sam was far from perfect."

"I get it, no one is perfect. I just meant… I'm flawed."

His hand cupped her cheek. "What's really going on here?"

"Can you tell me something about her?" *Coward.* Dodging the subject wouldn't get her any answers.

Scott pulled back, slumping against the couch. "What do you want to know?"

Although his guard came up, he didn't refuse outright. She took that as a good sign.

"I can't live up to this image I have. According to Shelby, your wife was as magical as Houdini, cooked like Paula Deen and decorated like Martha Stewart."

Scott grinned.

"Oh, and she danced like a fairy princess."

"Look, Shelby's going to idealize her mother."

"I know. Scott, I *know*. I took enough psych courses and I've dealt with enough kids at school to understand this on an intellectual level." She couldn't meet his eyes as she bared her soul. "It's hard to be the person who comes after."

"Oh, honey." His fingers tipped her chin, bringing her gaze back to his. "You don't have to worry about that. What I felt and, yeah, still feel for Sam is only one part of me. It's my past, and, sure, I'll carry it around forever. But I'd like to think I get to have a future, too."

His lips met hers. "Do I only get one chance at happiness?"

"No. That wouldn't be fair."

He sat back again, giving her space, but also studying her. "But?"

How to start? *I can't give you children* was a little too bald, considering they hadn't discussed the future. His "wanting a chance at happiness" fell a little too short of the kind of declaration she needed if she was going to be brave enough to tell him about her barrenness. If they didn't have a future, it wouldn't matter. If they did, she could chance telling him then. Chance him walking away like Kyle had.

But letting him care for her, possibly, hopefully, fall in love with her and then telling him didn't seem fair, either. Not telling him protected only her.

Why wasn't there a book on this? *The Right Time to Tell Your Lover Some Hard Truths*. Or maybe *When to Tell, What to Tell, What to Keep Secret*.

"Ginger? Talk to me, sweetheart."

She inhaled a deep breath. "I can't be second-best."

*Damn.* Only part of the truth came out.

"What makes you think you're second-best? You're not. I'm sorry if I've done anything—"

"No, you haven't. It isn't you."

He smirked. "It's you?"

Ginger rolled her eyes. "Sorry, but yeah. I can't get past the fact you've been married, that your girls love their mother, and I'll be a substitute if we get serious."

"Whoa."

"I know, I'm rushing things, worrying about stuff that hasn't happened yet, that may not."

He placed his fingers on her lips. Then his mouth covered hers. When he drew away, he only retreated far enough to meet her eyes. "What makes you think we're not already getting serious?"

Her heart tripped.

"What do you think the other night at my house was all about? And at the Christmas party?"

"Christmas was—" She shrugged. "Loneliness. Christmas spirit. I don't know."

"No, you obviously don't. I'm not in the habit of one-night stands."

Stung, she retorted, "I'm not, either." But she had to be honest. "I mean, not anymore."

His eyes widened. "What's that mean? No, don't look away. Stay with me on this."

She wanted to look away. She wanted to run away. But she met his gaze. If he couldn't accept this, what was the point of the rest? "After my divorce, I hid out for a while and licked my wounds. Then I thought, to hell with him. I'm single. I'll go have some fun."

Scott's face was blank. "Fun with men?"

She winced, then nodded slowly. "A few."

"I see."

"I'm sorry. I didn't know I'd meet you. I didn't know it would matter." She rose and paced as he had earlier. It helped to remove herself from his scrutiny, to gather her thoughts. To not have to deal with whatever she might read in his eyes. "Why am I apologizing? This happened before I met you." She pivoted back, near to panic. "Oh, Scott, you have to know that. I haven't been with anyone else since you. Since Christmas, the night we spent together."

"Okay." His eyes searched her face, then the stiffness in his shoulders loosened. "I believe you."

"Thank you. I don't want you to think being with you meant nothing. It did. It changed me."

She eased down beside him again, wary, not of him physically, but of what he might say to hurt her. "I didn't like sneaking out after we were together. I saw myself— what I'd been doing—differently."

His lips twitched. "Having sex with me cured you of having sex? I'm not sure how I feel about that."

"It made me want to have sex only with you. You or nobody."

"That's all right, then." His hand cupped her face. "I can't say I like hearing this, but it's because you were in pain. I admit it, it bothers me you were with other guys. I'm jealous."

She frowned in confusion. "But I didn't know you yet."

"Doesn't matter."

"Well, we've both been married. You loved someone enough to propose. That's hard for me to deal with."

"Then let me tell you some things about my life to ease your mind. What do you want to hear?"

*That your ex was actually an old crone in disguise, paid a cook and housekeeper then passed their work off as her own, rubbed peanut butter in the fur of fuzzy bunnies, and when you found out, you divorced her. And she couldn't dance any better than I can.*

"Whatever you feel you can share. Maybe something about the girls? Would that be less painful?"

He thought for a moment. "Okay. Sam wasn't perfect, but it would be hard for outsiders to tell. She cooked, as you know, kept an immaculate house, ran our lives with efficient clockwork."

Ginger grimaced. "And this makes me feel better how?"

"It may not make you feel better," he warned. "You're the one who wanted to know about Sam."

She nodded. Knowing he'd been devoted to his wife, that he was the kind of man who could be, added to the reasons she was falling for him. It mattered that he had loved deeply, but it also hurt. *The one who comes after.* If only she believed he would love her with the same passion.

"You've probably noticed our names all start with the same letter. That's luck on my part, that I fit in. But she wanted the girls to have the same initials as hers."

Creepy maybe but not imperfect. "And?"

"She took the girls to classes, filling their lives with fun activities. She baked their cookies and helped with Shelby's homework and made costumes and volunteered at Shelby's school."

*Kill me now.* "She sounds perfect."

Ginger hated that she came off sounding petulant. But

jeez, the guy seriously needed to work on what constituted perfection. Everything he'd mentioned reinforced her impression of his wife.

"What did that leave me?" he asked.

"I don't understand."

"I was like a guest, Ginger. I went to work to bring home a paycheck. The girls were almost in bed by the time I finished dinner." He blew out a breath. "Her mama raised her not to let the young'uns bother the menfolk."

The humor his comment might have produced evaporated as she realized what he was saying.

"She fed them before I got home. They had baths and were in pajamas by six o'clock every night. I barely saw them on weekends, she had them so busy in tumbling and dancing and soccer classes." He exhaled. "Don't get me wrong. I loved them, all three of them, and we were a happy family, I guess. But she was unintentionally pushing me out of their lives."

Ginger digested this. Had the women's liberation movement never made it to Samantha's mother's door? Not all Southern women could be so backward in their thinking. "Wow."

"Yeah, that pretty much sums it up. So when I say she wasn't perfect, I mean it. It sounds harsh, to speak of her this way. It's not fair, when she's not here to defend herself."

His tormented gaze met hers. "She was nice. She was great, in so many ways. But if you're thinking you have to live up to Sam, don't. Believe me when I say I don't want a marriage like that again."

"Is that why you divorced her?"

His mouth dropped open.

"Oh, my God." She clamped a hand over her mouth—

too late. "I can't believe I asked that. I'm sorry. That was so rude. I'm so, so sorry."

"Stop." Scott's hands gripped hers. "Just stop."

She shook her head, appalled.

"Ginger," he said, his voice soft. "I'm not divorced. My wife is dead."

# Chapter 9

Ginger's stomach dropped. Thankfully she sat on her couch, otherwise her legs might have given out. His wife was dead? "Oh, Scott. I didn't know. I'm so sorry."

The information changed everything she knew about him and the girls. No other woman lurked in the shadows, pulling at him. Except in his memories. In his heart.

As for the girls, they couldn't run to their mother, couldn't be taken away to Atlanta or even visit their mom. They depended on their dad for total emotional support.

"I thought it would say somewhere in Shelby's school file that her mom died."

"It just says you're her sole guardian." She laid a tentative hand on his arm. He'd be thinking of his wife now, the woman he loved, the woman he'd still be with if he had the choice. "There are probably notes about your wife's passing in her file, but I didn't read them. I didn't want to invade her privacy or yours unless I had cause. Because of us, our relationship. I'm sorry."

Her mind swirled with possibilities. Car accident? Cancer? Home invasion? She didn't know anything about his life in the South. Heck, she knew little enough about his life in Howard. Since he'd introduced the subject, he'd given her permission to ask. At least, she hoped he viewed it that way. "What happened? Can you talk about it? I don't want to intrude."

"My wife had ovarian cancer. It had spread to other organs by the time we became aware of it."

Ginger covered her mouth to trap a cry of pain. How well she knew the anger and agony a woman experienced when her body betrayed her.

"We weren't thinking of having more kids, so her cycle being wonky didn't concern her. By the time she *made* time to go to the doctor after two missed appointments, it had progressed so rapidly there was little hope."

His glower spoke of his self-blame. Ginger could almost read the thoughts in his head: What if he'd pushed harder? What if he'd gone to a doctor appointment with her for support? What if he'd noticed some sign her "wonky cycle" had serious causes?

Nor had Ginger missed the sentiment about not having more kids. Did he mean at that time or ever? Did he blame himself for that? The idea being if Sam was planning to get pregnant, she'd have gone to the doctor. It wasn't as if his wife's reproductive ability or choice not to have children at that time meant she could ignore her general health. He should know that.

"When we found out, Samantha decided against chemo. She didn't want surgery or any drugs to make her sicker and weaker." His jaw flexed. "She didn't fight it at all."

"Was it that hopeless?"

He grimaced. "Pretty much."

He didn't like admitting it—it was written all over his face. His tense shoulders and tight mouth conveyed his resentment. And pain. And myriad other struggles and emotions she could only imagine.

"The drugs would have bought her time." His pent-up anguish heated to anger. "Time with Shelby and Serena. Time to say goodbye."

*Time to be with you.* The unspoken thought broke her heart. Choosing to bypass treatments and medications had cost her family, had robbed them all of time to adjust.

But Ginger empathized with Samantha, too. Quality of life meant a great deal. Not having her daughters watch her suffer would have been important. Not having her husband suffer through every hope, every setback, every treatment would have been important. Not losing her identity as the medical community turned her into "a patient" would have been important.

Ginger wanted to help Scott work through his grief and come out whole. Or at least less raggedly scarred. He'd invited her into his life only so far and their relationship was so new. What could she say, what did she have the right to say, that would help him?

She put herself in Samantha's shoes. What would more time have meant for her other than the suffering? Being with the girls—there were two sides to it. Scott only mentioned the side he saw, colored by loss.

"It would have given you time to say goodbye, yes, but time also for her girls to watch her die slowly and probably painfully."

"Right, I get that." He swung away and paced a few steps. Stopping with his back to her, his sigh was still audible. "Then she died anyway."

"Were the girls there, wherever she was, at home or the hospital?" Her heart ached.

He snorted. "She was at home."

Disgust? Pain? Ginger couldn't read him. What prompted that response? "Did you have hospice care? Or hadn't her cancer advanced to that stage?"

"No hospice yet, but we had talked to them. We had a visiting nurse. Sam didn't want a lot of people around. She would say, 'Go out, do something.' One day, she asked me to take the girls to the Georgia Aquarium there in Atlanta. We'd been putting off a trip. Never got around to it, you know how that goes."

He shook his head. "So I took the girls, and they loved it. I loved it. We laughed and ate lunch out and just took a breather. We had a great time for over two hours. I thought Sam was a genius to suggest the break for all of us. So generous." He turned to look at Ginger. "So freaking generous."

Ginger read the truth in his tortured expression. "She died while you were gone."

"She took a handful of pain meds."

Shock made her gasp as cold swept through her body. "Oh, God."

"Yeah. Exactly. She got us out of the house and downed them right away so they'd take effect by the time we got home. Took enough not to wake up and vomit them back out."

"Scott." She rose, instinct urging her to go to him, but she didn't. There was no comfort in the world for his pain. Embracing him while he spoke of his lost love felt too awkward.

"We got home and I thought she was asleep. Resting peacefully wasn't easy for her with the level of pain she was in. So I left her alone, glad—actually *glad*—she was able to sleep." He laughed harshly. "Little did I know she was resting in peace, literally."

"I'm so sorry."

"She was so damned selfish!"

Ginger started, the intensity of his anger causing her to take a reflexive step backward. Eyes wide, she watched his fists curl and release, curl and release, as he battled his rage.

"At times I hate her."

"No, you don't." He'd despise himself even more for those feelings; worse, for voicing them.

"Yes, I do. It isn't nice to admit and I know I'm a horse's ass for feeling this way." He blew out a breath. "But she left me. Abandoned our children. I can't forgive her for that."

"But think of her torment. Having to face dying. She was probably in unimaginable pain, as well."

"That was her choice. At that point, anyway. She wouldn't take her damn meds." His jaw clenched. "I didn't realize she was just hoarding them to kill herself."

He fell onto the sofa and tipped his head back with closed eyes.

She perched on the cushion next to him. He dealt with loss and betrayal, anger and love. Watching him, feeling helpless, made her throat ache with suppressed tears. "I'm sorry."

Without moving his head, he met her gaze, then gently pulled her against him. "Just let me hold you for a while, okay? I promise I'll calm down. Don't be afraid. It would kill me if you were afraid of me."

She snuggled closer, wrapping her arms around him. He must have noticed her backward step and study of his fisting hands then misread her concern for his torment as fear for herself. "I'm not afraid of you."

They didn't talk for a long time. Only held and stroked and cuddled. His trust in her at this moment of vulnerability touched her more deeply than the lengthiest declaration of love.

When Scott called a few days later, feelings of tenderness flooded Ginger. Despite her plans to carry through with a private adoption, she couldn't walk away from Scott now after finding out about his loss. The raw emotion she'd uncovered with her prodding about his wife hadn't had time to heal.

In her heart lingered the hope of becoming a family. As often as she squashed it, as often as she lectured herself about the difficulties involved in not only becoming the girls' stepmother but bringing a newborn into the mix, Ginger still fantasized about a life with Scott.

She found herself agreeing to go with him to buy dog food. Of all the lame excuses. She rolled her eyes even as it made her smile. Such an adorable man, making up a goofy reason to see her. There were worse ways to spend a Saturday.

"You really need help buying dog food?"

"You wouldn't believe how confusing it is," his voice came over the phone, into her ear, into her heart. "There are millions of brands. I don't want to get something to make a puppy sick because he's unable to digest it. As big as he is, it's hard to remember he's only a few months old. God help us, he's going to grow. You'd be doing Horace a favor."

She capitulated, as she owed him the chance to do something normal with her. To erase the lingering sadness of their last time together. Plus, she simply wanted to be with him.

And, it turned out, with the girls. Surprise swept her when she spotted them sitting in the backseat of Scott's orange Jeep. Not unwelcome, but unexpected. Shelby didn't care for her at school; Ginger dating her dad had to be on the girl's top ten list of least favorite things.

Ginger felt their eyes boring into her as they drove to the pet store. Still, she needed to spend time with them, too. If she was going to have any kind of a relationship with their father, it had to work for all of them. Even if she and Scott just helped each other through the next few months of changes in their lives, the girls couldn't be left out.

"There are cheaper places to buy food, you know." She couldn't shake feeling unnerved by the girls' silence. It didn't help that they sat behind her, out of sight, a place she'd never seat a difficult student in her classroom.

Whoever Scott dated served as a role model for the girls, since they didn't have a mother. They'd learn how to be a woman from her and how to be in a relationship. The task seemed daunting, and one she would embrace with her own child someday. But not now, with their built-in animosity of Ginger *not* being their mother but filling the role their own mother wasn't there to fill. Tension tightened her shoulders.

"The pet store is a favorite stop of ours now." Scott shot her an amused look as he drove. "We go in and look at the small dogs we might have adopted, had Horace not grabbed our hearts."

"We don't want any other dog, not even a small dog," Serena inserted, taking him seriously. "I don't care if he knocks me down sometimes. I love Horace and so does Shelby. Don't you?"

"Yeah."

Nothing more than the monosyllable from Shelby. Ginger held in her sigh. It was going to be a long day.

She turned halfway toward them, sharing the conversation with those in the back of the car. Okay, she admitted. Their staring was getting to her.

"How's the housebreaking going?" she asked anyone who cared to answer. She'd bet ten bucks it wouldn't be her student, but she doubted she'd find anyone to take that bet. Well… She studied Scott in her periphery. Did his daughter's antagonism even register with him? Or did he see Shelby's comments as normal for the circumstances—her loss combined with Ginger being her teacher out with the family? Or did he not pay attention to the girl's tone at all? Men couldn't even hear tone, whereas women—and girls of eight, it seemed—used it as a layer of communication.

Ginger had a harder time figuring out Serena's feelings. Partly because she hadn't spent as much time around toddlers as second graders, naturally, but partly because the girl stared more than talked. Not glared, just studied her. Relentlessly. Ginger felt Serena's eyes on her as though they were live things crawling across her skin. But what thoughts lurked behind the watchfulness, Ginger didn't know.

"We're successful with getting him to wait," Scott answered, "more and more often. Right, girls?"

Serena's curly head bobbed. Someone had tried to secure her chestnut waves in barrettes, but one had already inched down to the girl's chin and the other sat precariously near her ear. Another five bucks would say the girl brushed and styled her own hair. She really needed someone to take better care of the details. Her father could do it if he paid attention. Or a mother, of course, and Ginger tried to dislodge the stone pressing on her chest. She wished it could be her.

Or an older sister could manage it. Ginger eyed Shelby's sleek, almost-black hair, pulled back in a neat ponytail, with a ribbon to match her purple shirt. Maybe Serena didn't like to have her hair brushed by anyone else and that was why they didn't help her. Maybe the little girl doing it herself demonstrated some kind of independence good for her self-esteem.

Maybe Ginger was rationalizing so she didn't have to face her own yearning to mother the girl.

"So," she said, returning to the topic of the dog, "how's the other stuff coming? Serena, is Horace still knocking you down?"

"No. I talked to him about it."

Ginger blinked and turned farther around in her seat belt to face the girls. "You...talked to him?"

"Yep. Dad said Horace didn't understand that he's almost as big as me and could hurt me. That he has a big body he can't control yet, like jumping or going potty in the house. And I'm older than him and so I have to understand that he would do things but wouldn't mean them. It's like I'm a big sister."

Scott smiled, eyes on the road.

"So you talked to Horace?"

The brown head bobbed again. "Yep. I told him he

needed to stop jumping. That I could hit my head or break a bone and then I wouldn't be able to play with him. That made him sad, and he hasn't jumped on me again."

Ginger bit her lip to hold in her laughter. She could just picture this little angel having a heart-to-heart with a dog roughly her weight and size. When it was sitting. "That was clever of you to explain it to him."

Serena shrugged. "Daddy told me Horace didn't understand. Since he can't ask questions, I just had to tell him."

An image of the hairy black puppy raising his paw to ask a question, as though a student in her class, made Ginger giggle.

"Now," Scott said, "if her talks to him about potty training would take, and the ones about chewing everything in sight, I'd be a happier man."

"Doesn't he have a chew toy?" Ginger asked. "I thought you bought one or two the day you brought him home."

"We did. And dozens since then." He shook his head, clearly mystified why the dog didn't chew on them instead.

"When you catch him chewing your stuff, take it away, say no, then give him the bone or rope or whatever as a replacement.

"Shelby." Ginger addressed the girl directly, hoping to draw her into the conversation. "Where does he sleep?"

"Downstairs."

Two syllables. Progress.

"Daddy won't let him sleep in our beds," Serena said. "I promised we wouldn't fight over him, but he said Horace needs his own spot."

"You might consider giving him one of your blankets

for his bed downstairs—in the mudroom?" She glanced at Scott, who nodded. "Then he'd feel like you were with him if the blanket smelled like all three of you. Maybe use it on the couch for a week then make it his."

Serena's face scrunched up in thought. Shelby peered hard out the window, blatantly giving the appearance of not listening. Ginger remembered thinking she'd either love Shelby's spirit or the girl would prove to be the biggest headache in her class. Today it was a toss-up.

"Why?" Serena asked with her endless preschooler curiosity.

"So he can smell you and feel that you're near him," Ginger said. She tried not to form an attachment to this girl in case nothing came of her and Scott's relationship. She tried not to have a favorite between his daughters. Being an older sibling was hard enough for Shelby, worse when the younger had the charm or sweet nature or sunny disposition everyone loved.

Ginger froze. Did Shelby seek out those tendencies to be different from her sister? She'd seen it often enough as a teacher—why hadn't she thought of it before? The twins in her class, Harry and Ron, were perfect examples. One loved math, the other one was indifferent, although their grades were the same in the subject. One worked with his hands building with manipulative blocks; the other preferred writing. One played any sporting game the kids started; the other cheered from the sidelines.

Was Shelby a deliberate challenge because her baby sister was so open? Was Shelby difficult because her sister was so adorable?

Ginger put aside those thoughts for another time and answered Serena's query. "Puppies chew because they're getting stronger teeth, just like human babies. But what they want to chew on is usually something belonging to their family. Socks, shoes, toys."

"So the blanket would make him not chew up Daddy's shoes no more? Because Horace seems to like those best."

Ginger chuckled at the pained expression on Scott's face. "I can't promise that, but it might help. Replacing the shoe with a rawhide bone or some chew toy would be better because you're teaching him how you want him to behave instead of just telling him no."

"I'll try anything," Scott said. "It's getting harder and harder to find places to put things where Horace can't reach. He's pretty determined."

"Careful there, buddy." Ginger grinned and poked his arm. "You're starting to sound proud of him. Someone might mistakenly get the impression you like him."

Shelby glared at her. Ginger needed to curtail the familiarity.

"Oh, Daddy likes him," Serena assured her. "He plays with Horace all the time."

"There are no secrets in this family," Scott muttered.

"While you're shopping today, let's pick him out some new chew toys. I've heard a rope is good for a bigger dog."

"Humph" came from the seat beside her.

They pulled into the parking lot of the pet store moments later, sliding in between a car with a kennel in the backseat and a huge pile of plowed snow. Ginger noticed Shelby unbuckle Serena as though without thought, probably by habit. Shelby could be a sweetheart at times.

They pushed a cart down one aisle, both girls too big for the seat. Another point in favor of a baby—she'd be able to keep an eye on an infant while she got the hang of mothering. These two, with their impulsive interest in anything catching their eyes, could disappear at any time.

A huge bag of dry Puppy2Adult mix went in the cart, muscled by Scott.

"How long will that bag last?" Ginger asked.

"The vet said all puppies eat four times a day, so about a week." Scott shrugged. "He's not supposed to eat more than a normal dog does once he's grown. I hope the guy's right."

Serena put a box of dog treats in the cart. Shelby carried a chew toy—not a rope as Ginger had suggested—but didn't put it in the basket, despite several urgings.

"Oh, my," a woman said behind them.

They turned as though the four of them were one unit. An older woman with gray hair and as many wrinkles as a shar-pei beamed at them.

"It's so nice to see a family out together. I shop here often for my cats. Most times, I see a mom or dad running in alone. Always in a hurry, you young people."

"We're not a family," Shelby put in.

First time the girl had offered a complete sentence all day.

Scott shifted uncomfortably. Ginger smiled at the other customer. "He and I are just friends."

"I'm sorry. I didn't realize you weren't married." The woman smiled down at the girls. It seemed as though her eyes actually twinkled. "This man will make your mother very happy. I can sense these things."

"She's not our mother. He's our dad. Our mother's…" Shelby hung her head. "Not here."

"Oh, dear. My mistake. I'm so sorry for the misunderstanding."

Ginger smiled at her. "It's no big deal."

"You probably hear that a lot, that you look like a family." The woman seemed visibly relieved as she retreated a step. "I'm glad you're not upset. That could have been awkward."

"Not awkward at all, ma'am." Scott put a hand on Shelby's shoulder and one on Serena's head. "I'll claim them as mine, since they're both behaving at the moment."

She turned to Ginger. "The resemblance is much stronger with you."

"That's 'cause she looks like our mommy," Serena declared.

Ginger's breath whooshed out of her. She forgot to inhale. Her head went light, her mind blank. Instinct kicked in and she drew in a sharp breath. She looked like Samantha? Sam looked like her?

"She does not!" Shelby threw the chew toy on the floor and glared at the three adults. "Serena doesn't remember. She's just a baby. I know."

"Am not," Serena cried, cheeks flushing red with anger. Steam could have burst from her ears, she was so upset.

"Are too."

"Girls," Scott said with a stern frown.

They subsided instantly.

One word from their father calmed the swell of the tide. Ginger wished it had the same effect on her, that her heart no longer beat against the rocks, in time with her careening thoughts, ebbing and surging with bewilderment.

She looked like Sam? Is that who he saw when he kissed her? Is that what had attracted him to her at the Christmas party? A knot formed in her stomach. It couldn't be coincidence.

And she'd worried about *the girls* regarding her as a substitute.

He smiled at the woman, his eyes bleak. "I apologize for my daughters."

His accent poured out, thick as praline sauce. *Ah ah-pahlogize for mah dahters.*

The woman blushed and backed away.

"Don't you worry about it, ma'am." Scott's smile remained in place until the woman retreated, almost running the last steps in her embarrassment.

Ginger waited until he'd turned, waited to speak, waited for an explanation.

"Girls," he said, "I don't ever want to hear you argue like that in public again. Do you understand me?"

Nods.

Ginger waited for him to meet her eye.

"Now," he said. "Let's get our shopping done and get back to poor Horace. I'm sure he needs to go outside by now."

He wheeled the cart down the aisle, the girls trailing after him. Ginger stood rigid with disbelief. She'd walk home before she got in a car with him. As frozen as she felt at the moment, the thirty-degree temperatures outside wouldn't even register.

How much of his attraction to her was because she looked like Sam?

Scott turned the cart around the corner of the aisle and realized he'd left Ginger behind. Or, more correctly, she hadn't followed. He stopped and ran a hand over his face. Dammit. Why had that woman had to say anything? He'd seen it, of course, the resemblance. Who could miss another redhead coming into his life? The girls and Ginger and Sam all possessed creamy skin and heart-shaped faces. So what?

"Stay here." He waited until the girls nodded then walked the five steps back to Ginger. Her eyes looked glazed. Could a woman go into shock like this, just from words? A glance over his shoulder ensured the girls stayed close but they probably couldn't hear if he and Ginger kept their voices lowered.

Would she? Or was she a screamer when angered? Did that red hair translate into fiery outrage, like Sam's had? Lord knew Ginger had reason enough to be angry. But how and when was he supposed to have mentioned the resemblance? At their first meeting? *You look like my wife, and by the way, I want to take you to bed.* The longer he'd known her, the less he'd even thought of the similarity. Within moments, actually, all he'd seen was Ginger.

"Ginger." He fiddled with a button on his peacoat. This wasn't the place for this conversation. "I'm sorry you found out this way. Let me... I don't know. What can I do? What can I say? Except that whatever you're thinking, you're wrong."

Her eyebrows shot up.

That was stupid. "Let me pay and get the girls in the car where they'll be safe. And if you can't wait for an explanation until we get back to my place—"

Her spine stiffened and he had that answer.

"Then we can talk here. Outside or just inside the door. It won't take long, but I can't explain, I can't talk about their mother or my feelings about you, with the girls right here."

Her gaze ran over his face, traveled to the girls half an aisle away and back. Her slight nod enabled him to breathe again.

She stayed behind while he paid, loaded the girls and the dog food and toys in the car, and turned on the heater. That probably wasn't safe, but he wasn't going anywhere the car would be unsupervised. As he closed the car door, Ginger stepped out of the store and stood in front of his vehicle. If he played his cards right, she wouldn't bash in the hood.

He walked around to her, praying for the most acceptable phrasing. She'd tucked her hands in her coat pockets, and he desperately wanted to hold her hands, to make contact with some part of her.

"You do, a bit," he admitted, stopping in front of Ginger, his back to the girls in the car. "Resemble each other."

Her jaw clenched.

What did that mean? Why didn't she just say something?

"At the party," he continued, "your hair caught my eye. It caught the eye of every man there. But yeah, especially me. Sam's wasn't the same. It was a deeper red, more like rusted metal than apricots. Yours is like sunshine to her shadow."

God, was this the right thing to say? Since she hadn't turned away, or slapped him, he continued talking. "You and she have the same shape of face. So do the girls. But long before we finished the first dance, I didn't picture Sam anymore. I saw your smile, your amazing green eyes, your warmth."

Her jaw loosened. He counted that in his favor.

"I went to the hotel room with you. Not with a ghost of her. Not wishing it was her. With you and only you."

He watched her face, her body, for some softening, some sign of forgiveness. For what he wasn't sure. He had a type, obviously. He hadn't consciously picked her out because she looked like Sam. If anything, that would have been reason not to approach her, if he'd made any conscious decision at all.

Frustrated, he exhaled, watching his breath turn the air white. "You could be bald for all I care."

The wind bit his skin, but it was no colder than the fear wrapping around his heart. Why in the hell had he said something that stupid?

Then she smiled.

His panic melted like an icicle in the sun. "I'm sorry I never mentioned it. I didn't think of the resemblance past the first time I saw you. The first couple minutes, and that's all. Then you became you."

"You don't have pictures of her sitting out."

"The girls each have one in their bedrooms. There's a portrait of the four of us in the upstairs hall."

"I didn't see it the other night." Her cheeks might have colored, but as the cold had stained them ruby already, he couldn't tell.

"A right turn at the top of the stairs leads to the girls' rooms. We turned left." He waited. The polar breeze ate away at his marrow, but he wouldn't move until she gave some sign she understood. That she forgave.

"Serena's hair has red highlights," she said. "I assumed she got them from you. Shelby has no red, but her hair's so dark, I didn't expect it."

His gut tightened. Now was not the time for this conversation. Three words would straighten out the mystery, but would also introduce the need for another long explanation, which was totally beside the point. And he'd be frigging damned if he'd give another lengthy account out in the Arctic.

"Okay." Ginger met his eyes.

His heart stuttered. "Okay?"

"Okay, we'll talk about this later," she amended. "But it's enough for the moment, with the girls waiting in the car."

He shouldn't have questioned *okay,* he thought as he closed her car door and rounded the rear of the Jeep. Still, he was deeply relieved. She'd forgiven him. At least she believed him, which translated to understanding there was nothing to forgive. He hadn't actually *done* anything wrong.

Scott reassured himself of that during the entire silent ride home.

# Chapter 10

As it turned out, they didn't talk when they got back to Scott's house. Ginger just couldn't face it.

She got out of the car but didn't follow the girls up the driveway, although she did watch their small forms slip and slide across the packed snow turned icy. They giggled, the novelty of snow melting even Shelby's resentment momentarily. Ginger wished she could recapture that innocence. Instead, she dug out her car keys and, with a deep breath for courage, rounded the trunk where Scott unloaded his purchases. "I'm going home."

"No, Ginger, don't. We need to talk this out."

She had to withstand the pleading in his eyes. "I need some time to think. Time alone."

"Let me explain things first. Let me fix it. Or at least try."

She narrowed her eyes at him. "Was your wife a redhead?"

"Yes, but—"

"And she had the same shaped face. Did she, by chance, also have green eyes and pale skin?"

His mouth tightened, as irritation rushed across his features. "No, she had lovely brown eyes like the girls."

She turned away. "I'll talk to you later. Give me a couple of days."

Footsteps crunched behind her on the packed snow. "Ginger."

"Please." She faced him. "Scott, please. I need time to process this."

His jaw firmed. "I have a bad feeling about us being apart right now."

"It's better for me, and I'm going to be selfish on this one." She took a few steps backward. "Give me those days."

He didn't follow her. He stood in his driveway and watched as she drove out of sight.

She felt hollow inside. No one who crossed her path as she drove home actually died; however she wasn't sure she hadn't scared a few people. But she didn't remember any of it.

One minute she was at Scott's, driving away, watching him in her rearview mirror as he watched her; the next, she was in her own driveway.

Safe, thank God. Sound? That determination would have to wait.

Ginger didn't cry. She cleaned. Within an hour, the toilets would have passed the most rigorous military inspection. The floors sparkled, the carpet fibers fluffed, the tile shined. In the second hour, even her cabinets and refrigerator received a thorough cleaning.

All day, all night, all weekend, she stewed. The sight

of food nauseated her, even chocolate and ice cream, her old standbys. Forcing herself, she ate some cereal once or twice. She picked up the phone to call Lisa, but even her best friend wouldn't have the answers for this one. It was better to work through it on her own.

Very rationally, as she cleaned, she thought through the facts, step by step, unemotionally, from first meeting through sex and dinner and more sex, all the way to the scene at the pet store.

Scott was like Charlie Brown, the cartoon character, who liked red-haired girls. Her attempt at humor fell flat. Charlie had the good sense to like only *one* red-haired girl. Would Scott be attracted to her if she didn't share Sam's coloring? Granted, that had gotten her the first dance, but he wasn't slimy enough to sleep with her just to relive moments with his dead wife. Right?

She didn't think he was. Her aching gut said no. But then her gut was depressed and hungry and would betray her for a kind word right now.

Logic twisted her heart round and round. Could she trust his feelings for her—that they were, in fact, for her? Or was she being a fool to hang on, wanting to believe so she could stay with him?

*Aren't we all fools for love at some point?*

Love? She groaned. No way. Please, don't let it be *that* eating her insides raw.

Love was patient and kind and all that crap. Love made bad men good and good men…hotter? The first smile in a long weekend cracked her lips. It almost hurt.

Ginger didn't know what to do about seeing him again. He'd probably give her a couple of days as she requested. After that? No idea.

She picked up the cleanser and attacked the sinks.

* * *

Scott tapped his pen against his desk, staring at the monitor in front of him absently. He couldn't concentrate, so he dubbed the next ten minutes a mental holiday and went to the break room. Standing and walking did him good. Seeing his boss stretched out on the vinyl futon made him smile.

"Hey," Dylan said. "Come on in. I'm not asleep. I'm working through the fine points of a program, and I could use a break from that."

Scott opened the refrigerator and stared at the bottles and cans of refreshment. "Want anything?"

"Throw me a water." Dylan sat up as Scott sailed a plastic bottle through the air. "Thanks."

"You need some help brainstorming?" Anything would be better than thinking about Ginger. "Got a technical problem?"

"No, but thanks. This is part of the process for me. It'll become clear in a bit if I just stop looking at it so hard."

Scott popped a Coke and pulled over a hard plastic chair. Tipping his head back, he took a long swallow, the cold liquid bathing his dry throat. Maybe he had a virus coming on. "How do you people stand it being so bitter cold here?"

"We think about the coming summer and how we're going to miss the frigid temps then."

Scott didn't think that possible. "How's married life?"

Dylan grinned. "Awesome, as usual. The kids are getting along great and we've started talking about a baby."

"Yours, mine and ours?"

His boss laughed. "I suppose so, although it's hard to believe Lilly isn't really Tara's the way they take to each other. I couldn't love Jimmy more if he were my biological son. We all won when we found each other."

"That's great." Scott made himself smile at the other man's luck.

"So, what's on your mind? Something must be going on to have you asking about my home life."

"I didn't mean to intrude."

Dylan waved off his apology. "Not what I said, man. I'm more than happy to talk about my wife and kids. Heck, I've got pictures on my desk if you're really interested. But I think you're more likely just distracted."

"My project is going great. The break is for eye strain."

"Right." Dylan downed some water, watching Scott. "I wasn't asking as your boss, though. Your work is fine."

Scott didn't want to lie and screw up this tenuous new friendship, but he couldn't articulate his thoughts if he tried.

"Is it Ginger Winchester?"

Scott choked, almost spurting Coke out his nose. "Wow, that was out of left field."

"If I want to know something, I ask. Another thing the kids taught me."

"I don't feel comfortable talking about Ginger since you know her."

"Fair enough."

A full minute passed in silence as they enjoyed their drinks.

"I might want to marry her." The words were out of Scott's mouth before he thought them through. "Crap."

Dylan's hand stopped midway carrying the bottle to his mouth, but at the last remark, he lowered it, a huge grin on his face. "And how's the lady feel about that? I hope she's more receptive to the idea. Or does she think it's crap, too?"

Scott shrugged, embarrassed. "I haven't asked her yet. I'm not sure."

"You haven't been seeing each other that long. You only started here in January."

"We met in December, when I came for the initial welcome."

"I didn't realize that. So? What's the hurry?" His eyes widened.

"No—" Scott rushed in to stop Dylan's train of thought "—she's not pregnant."

Dylan's breath whooshed out.

"There isn't any hurry. That's why I haven't done anything yet." Well, he thought, not anything other than make love with her. Twice.

"But you're thinking of asking her?" Dylan smiled. "Made an impression, did she?"

"You could say that."

"How do your girls like her?"

Dylan had recently found out he'd fathered a daughter five years before. Shortly thereafter, he'd married a woman with a three-year-old son. He understood about children getting along with stepparents.

"She teaches Shelby, my second grader, which I think you know. Shelby definitely isn't teacher's pet. I think Ginger keeps her distance emotionally with me because of the classroom relationship. Shelby finds it weird to be around her teacher on a social basis."

"Hmm. I can see where that would be hard for both of them. How about your little girl?"

"Serena has trouble with Ginger resembling their mother." Scott shrugged. "Maybe Shelby does, too."

Dylan gave a soundless whistle. "Man, the hits just keep coming. And does she? Look like your wife, I mean?"

Scott shrugged again. "I guess so."

"Does Ginger know that?"

Scott nodded with a scowl. Ginger knew all right. She hadn't answered his phone calls or responded to his voice-mail messages. He could only guess at her thoughts, and nothing he came up with encouraged him to think she'd accept a marriage proposal.

"I can't imagine that her learning about that went over well."

His grunt made Dylan laugh.

"There's an understatement. She's giving me the silent treatment."

Dylan shook his head. "Women. Sorry, man. We should be nursing beers in a dark, seedy bar."

"I appreciate that. You don't have a reason to drink beer in a seedy bar, though, do you? You said everything's fine."

"Solidarity, brother. We men need to stick together." He held out his water bottle, which Scott tapped with his pop can.

"So how are you making this decision?" Dylan asked. "You going with your gut or do you have a pro/con list going?"

"Pretty much evaluating the reasons on both sides. I can't trust my gut to this. There are too many people's futures at stake."

"I'm good at logic if you want some input. Shoot."

Scott hesitated, but he missed having a friend. Dylan was solid and though it seemed early to be making this kind of connection, Scott knew he and Dylan would wind

up close friends. Since he was making lasting relationships pretty darn fast these days, he decided to go with
his instincts on this one. "Okay. On the con side, the girls
haven't accepted her yet."

"That's a tough one. How are you going to live together?"

Scott shot him a sour look before remembering the
man signed his paycheck. Dylan grinned.

"Point number two, my wife's only been dead a year."

"Or *already a year,* considering you seem ready to
move on. You're thinking of bringing another woman
into your life permanently. Does that mean you've put
the other relationship to rest—" Dylan winced "—so to
speak? Sorry. That was out of my mouth before I thought
how it sounded."

"It's okay. Fair question. Yeah, I'm ready to move on."

"That's a good thing. A counterpoint to the con. Your
wife's been gone a year and you're ready. It would be a
check mark in the pro column if you tied 'moving on' to
marrying Ginger."

"Well, if I'm going to marry anyone, it would be Ginger. Is that the same as?"

"Pretty much, yeah."

"So one con—the girls don't like her, and one pro—
I'm ready to get married and I've set my sights on Ginger."

"And they work against one another."

Scott nodded. "Very much against."

"What else do you have to tip the scales? Hold on."
Dylan consulted the ceiling tiles, coming to a decision
of some sort. He nodded and looked back at Scott. "I'm
going to ask you the only question that matters, and I

don't need the answer. You need the answer. Do you love Ginger?"

Scott stared at him.

"You answer that and you'll have your other answers. If you're not sure yet, you don't propose." He stood. "If you love her, you move those mountains, even if they look like sweet little girls." Dylan clapped him on the shoulder as he walked past. "Good luck, man. Be sure to let me know what you decide."

Well, crap. He couldn't just get married because he was in love with Ginger—if he was in love with her, and he wasn't positive. How could he even ask himself that when his daughters didn't like the woman?

Sheesh. What would he do with three females in his house, turning everything pink and talking about their feelings all the time? He and Horace would have to hide out in the garage together.

But it sure would be nice to have a mother for his girls. A bed partner for himself, which Ginger had proven to be exceptional at already. A woman to come home to, to cuddle with while watching television and while watching his daughters grow. He couldn't picture anyone other than Ginger in his arms for those activities.

That, more than anything, told him he had his answer.

On Saturday, Scott watched Ginger approach across the frozen white grass to the outdoor ice rink. His daughters had a skating lesson, and since the rink was at a park in the adjacent town, he'd figured it a neutral place away from prying eyes. He had to get them together, to get all three females past this resemblance thing. His daughters had to see Ginger for herself, not a reminder of the mom they couldn't have. No wonder they didn't send out warm and fuzzy vibes to her.

He could use some warm and fuzzy right about now, standing outside to watch the girls skate. What was wrong with these Missourians? Why didn't they put a rink in a warmly heated shopping mall like civilized people?

"Hey," he greeted as she neared. "Thanks for coming."

An emerald stocking hat covered her hair and ears, emphasizing the grass-green of her eyes. The unrelieved black of her long wool coat leached the color from her skin. Scott wanted to kiss her, just pull her close and feel her cold lips and hot breath. He glanced at the girls, pushing metal folding chairs in front of them for balance.

"They're doing well," Ginger said, also locating the girls on the ice.

"Second lesson. Believe it or not, we go from here to swimming back at the Howard Y. Indoors, thank God. I'll be sweating within ten minutes."

Ginger smiled. "Which you'll love."

"Oh, yeah. Looking forward to it." He soaked in her nearness, aching as he noticed her pale features under the tinge of pink from the cold. Maybe it wasn't the black coat. Had he done that, caused her to look so thin and drawn? "Thanks for coming."

"I wanted to talk to you."

"Can I tell you about the resemblance thing first, from my point of view?"

She nodded. "That would help."

He glanced over the skaters, spotting his girls, but not really seeing the others. The right words eluded him. What could he say that wouldn't dishonor Sam but would clue in Ginger to how he felt? Slow-talking her into marriage would take some doing, but as he'd told Dylan, there wasn't any need to hurry.

"I saw you across the room, dancing. Your hair caught my eye. Mine, and like I've said, every guy's there." He smiled at the memory. "You moved with an unconscious sensual intensity that had us all watching you."

"Did you not ask me to dance earlier than you did because I looked like your wife?"

*You look like my* future *wife,* he could have told her. Instead he shook his head, placing his palms on the waist-high wooden railing. "I liked watching you dancing and having fun. I admired you, as a man does a beautiful woman, but I didn't plan to make a move."

"No connection."

There was that word again.

"Right. Until I saw you off to the side, looking lost in the crowd of strangers. You looked like I felt, as though you wondered what crazy impulse had prompted you to attend a party."

She smiled. "I wasn't in a party mood, you're right. I'd received some bad news that day, and I want to talk to you about that in a minute. But I know what 'prompted' me to go, as you put it. My best friend is married to your boss."

His spirits lifted. Just one more way they fit together. Friends in common. "You're friends with Tara?"

"With Lisa, Joe Riley's wife."

"Ah, right. Dylan mentioned that a while back. I've had some of her desserts in the break room, but I haven't met her. So she talked you into coming."

"Lisa can be persistent."

She must be, Scott thought, to persuade his little red-head into doing something she didn't want to do.

"But," Ginger said, "back to the point. You saw the resemblance and took me to bed."

"Hell, no. Hold on." He lowered his voice when heads turned, frowns intact. "Look. I saw the resemblance, thought you were pretty. Your enjoyment on the dance floor, your love of life, drew me closer. But I took you upstairs because of *your* pull on me and your kindness when the band played that song and the way you smiled and talked about yourself. Just everything you did made me want to get to know you better." He shrugged. "I can't pretend to be sorry that getting to know you better started in bed."

"I'm not sorry, either, Scott. It was a wonderful night."

That didn't sound good. The words were right, but the underlying tone resonated with goodbye. Panic rushed through him as he sought for the words she needed to hear. With a tug on her elbow, he led her a good fifteen feet away, seeking a secluded spot. Too many parents could overhear standing around the rink's railing.

"I'm going to be blunt here. I didn't take you to bed hoping to recapture moments with my wife."

She recoiled.

"I don't see her when I look at you. I've mourned her, Ginger, and I'm ready to move on. I can't say I'm not still grieving," he conceded. "Part of me will always miss her. But she doesn't hold my heart anymore."

He searched her face. Did she understand what he was saying? That *she'd* captured his heart. If she gave him a hint of her feelings, that she was falling for him in return, he'd tell her with words. Express his love, tell her he'd like to marry her in the very near future.

Scott stomped his feet, trying to warm up. This was not the place or time for a serious, drawn-out conversation. If he wasn't worried someone might see them, he'd take Ginger to his Jeep. The added privacy would lend him the courage he needed.

A proposal didn't feel impulsive. Ill-timed, perhaps, as they stood talking about his feelings for Samantha. But not rushed or too soon. In his heart, he knew Ginger was the right woman for him. She and the girls would work through their difficulties because they fit as a family. He'd have it all, wife, lover, mother to his daughters, if only she'd give him the slightest bit of encouragement.

"I'm relieved," she said. "I'd hoped."

After a glance around at the other parents, she grimaced, then stood on tiptoe to brush her lips against his. They were as cold as he imagined, but the joy the simple kiss brought came as a surprise.

They were going to be okay.

Scott swallowed. He'd give it a minute, talk about different topics to put some distance between the conversations, but then he'd tell her she belonged in his life permanently. Maybe not a flat-out proposal, but a promise for the future. Together.

"What's with the look?" he asked. When she tilted her head in question, he expanded. "Before you kissed me. You made a sour face like you'd smelled dead catfish."

She laughed. "Ew. No. I just saw someone in the crowd, watching. She'll go home and report us being together."

"Who?" He turned, but no one's attention caught his.

"The woman in the purple parka."

"Who is she? Not the mom of a student?"

"No, but there are a few of them here. And Dylan's brother, if you want me to introduce you to him. His twins are skating."

"Yeah, I would. Later." He didn't take his gaze from the purple parka woman. "Who is she?"

"She's Cindy Grady's sister."

Scott jerked his gaze to Ginger. "You're kidding. Tell me you're kidding." He swore under his breath. Of all the rotten luck. But… "You kissed me anyway."

Ginger shrugged. "I'm tired of worrying about Cindy's opinion. I haven't done anything wrong. If our relationship could be seen as benefitting Shelby as my student, then I'd feel differently. But it's not like there's much I can do in second grade to influence her report card. She doesn't write essays up for interpretation. Her work is pretty much either getting the right answer or not."

"You kissed me anyway." He sounded like an idiot repeating himself, but the impact floored him. Maybe it wasn't too soon for that proposal after all. Ginger had just taken their relationship public.

"You said that already." Her cheeks deepened in color. "Jeez, it's not like I threw you to the ground, tore off your clothes and jumped you."

"Please don't."

She started. "What?"

"The ground is far too cold. But we can go to my car." She smiled.

"Get the heater going. Rev our engines." He winked.

"Don't be silly."

"Later?"

Ginger looked away, across the crowd to the ice. "Possibly."

He hugged her, then watched Shelby inching her weight upright, trying to skate without touching the chair, and the annoyance on her face as she had to grab for support. Serena hung on to her gray metal chair as though it were her new best friend, but she'd been smiling through-out the entire session. Her face had probably frozen that way, like his mama always warned him could happen. "We might as well go back rinkside. It wouldn't hurt for the girls to see us together."

Her hand on his arm stopped him.

"Wait." Ginger drew in a cold breath of air. "I have something to tell you, too."

"Okay. Whatever it is, we'll work through it."

"I hope so. You know about my divorce, right?"

"Just that you are. Haven't heard much about the fool who let you go, but I'm grateful he did." Please, God. Don't let her say the guy abused her. She'd been through enough with him and the girls. Maybe the jerk squeezed the toothpaste from the middle of the tube and she'd walked out, fed up.

"It's serious, Scott." She drew a deep breath. "I can't have children."

Sorrow squeezed his chest. "Oh, hell. Honey, I'm so sorry. You'd be a great mother."

"Thanks. I think so. I hope so."

He paused, caught off guard. Thank God he had the girls, right? Is that why she'd stuck with him? He pro-vided her with an instant family. Now he sounded like she had, worrying about the whole resemblance thing. But this was different.

After thinking through several ideas how this was dif-ferent, the simple truth hit him. It wasn't. She'd worried why he was attracted to her; now he worried about the same thing. But he was a quick learner. Instead of pull-ing away, he'd just ask.

"Pretty handy I have daughters, isn't it?"

Her jaw dropped and he had his answer before she

found words. For an instant, he hoped she wouldn't find words, but that was dashed by her squeal of outrage.

"*Handy?* They hate me because I look like their mother but I'm not their mother. You think that's handy? If we continue this relationship, take it forward, I'm going to have to work my butt off to make them tolerate me. You think that's the kind of relationship I'd run toward?"

He held up his hands. "Sorry. I'm sorry. I just wondered. Like you wondered when you heard you look like Sam."

The fury sagged out of her.

He touched her arm. "I just thought how convenient it was—sorry, I know it's not convenient, but you get my thought process, right?"

She nodded, then shook her head.

Women. What the hell did that mean? But her face said she accepted his explanation. Probably thought he was a fool, but accepted that, too.

"So what does your not being...?" He connected the dots. "He left you because you couldn't have kids?"

"Yeah. Thanks for announcing it."

The nearest person stood at the rink fifteen feet away, but Scott's rage might have carried.

"Sorry." Anger surged through him, along with some silent swearing. Not the place for that, with all these kids and parents nearby. Some jerk had broken her heart for something she had no control over?

The cold burned his lungs and crystallized his thoughts. "I'm sorry, honey. Sorry you were hurt."

He took her mittened hands in his. "You know it doesn't matter to me, don't you? I've already got the girls. Despite their current feelings, we can work through this and find a way to be together. I don't need you to have a baby with me. I'm happy with the children I have."

She closed her eyes for a moment, visibly gathering her emotions. "Thank you. You have no idea what it means to me to hear you say that. You're ten times, twenty, a hundred times a better man than my ex."

"I'm going to ask about your ex only one time. I figure you'd still be together if you could have kids or he could accept that you can't. You must have loved him. Are you over him?"

"He's like a dead catfish to me."

Scott laughed. "Okay, then."

This he could live with. She had an ex, a first husband, just as he had a first wife. They'd gone through good and bad with those people and both of them had dealt with their feelings for their spouses.

"There's one thing more," she said.

Holy mother. How could there be more? A scan of her features didn't scream "catastrophic" so he just nodded and waited. How bad could it be?

"I'm in the process of adopting a baby."

A hot ball of dread hit his gut, sinking to his core, spreading through him. Burning, freezing, withering the hope of a future with Ginger.

"I'd been going through an adoption agency and getting nowhere. So I started the private adoption process." Her gaze flew over his face. She rushed on. "Right now, I have two pregnant women considering me to raise their babies. We're in the last conversations. I don't think I'll get both babies." Her laugh sounded nervous. "I wouldn't mind, but it would be harder. I would actually love it. Like having twins."

She shook her head, looking thrilled at the idea. Almost vibrating with excitement.

He only stared, numb with disbelief. She stood talking about adopting two babies while a storm of denial raged through his brain.

"So, say something," Ginger said. "I know we haven't talked about a future, but we've talked around it. I'm trying to be honest here. To let you know I might come as a package, too."

She gazed at him, waiting for his response. He knew she wanted it to be enthusiastic. After all, he'd taken in the stupid dog. He obviously wasn't averse to added responsibility or growing his family.

His lips moved. "I don't want to adopt."

He heard his tone: flat, uncompromising, final. He couldn't take the words back.

Ginger flinched. "But…" Her mouth opened and closed; she appeared too upset and surprised to form words. It took another full minute. "Why not?"

He shook his head. Not going into all that. Couldn't. He'd set aside that ugliness and had no plan to revisit or rehash or reveal it all now. So he settled on half the truth. "I have children already. They're enough for me."

Her expression crumpled.

He felt like a bastard. "Can't they be enough for you, too? Can't you just love my girls?"

Tears formed in her eyes. "I want a baby."

"I'm sorry. I can't be any part of that."

# *Chapter 11*

Murphy's Law? Or was it one of those "truths universally recognized" that when you didn't want to see someone you encountered that person at every turn? Ginger ducked Scott in the grocery store the next day, and wound up sneaking out with only half the groceries she'd planned to pick up. Then she drove to the discount store to finish shopping for the school party on Monday and pulled out of the parking lot as his Jeep pulled in. Their eyes met before he very deliberately turned down an aisle away from her.

The Valentine's party would be hell. She checked the list the room mom, Mrs. West, had given her, and Scott was in charge of some of the food. He was also bringing a music CD he'd put together to play on the computer. Incredibly ironic that she didn't want to see the man she loved on Valentine's Day.

Then he didn't show.

She couldn't believe it. He'd come in before school and left the food in the refrigerator the cafeteria kept for school events. He put the music disk in her mailbox. The coward. It didn't matter that she didn't want to see him and he obviously didn't want to see her. It didn't matter that Shelby seemed accepting of the excuse that her dad had to work. It didn't matter that he'd broken her heart and she despised him.

He should have shown up.

So after school, when everyone was gone and everything was clean, Ginger drove to Riley & Ross Electronics to tell Scott what a jerk he was.

"Hey, Ginger," Dylan said, seeing her in the hall.

"Oh, hi." She'd been directed to Scott's area, but it turned out to be a huge open room with large desks, multiple monitors, miscellaneous parts, architectural plans, computer plans, myriad papers and plenty of drink cups. She'd been peering into the room, trying to locate Scott to flag him over. This wasn't the place for the conversation she had planned.

"What's going on?" Dylan asked. "Oh, you're here to see Scott, of course."

She nodded. "If I'm not interrupting. I know he's not off yet."

Dylan flipped open the phone on his belt holster. "Half an hour. It doesn't matter. We're not that strict about punching the clock. Plenty of times he'll be working late on a project. You want me to call him?"

"If you wouldn't mind."

A piercing whistle emitted from his lips, which then formed a grin as she winced. "I can teach you to do that, if you want. Might come in handy in the classroom when the kids get unruly."

Heads had turned, then ducked again when they didn't recognize Ginger. One pair of hazel eyes focused on her in disbelief.

"Yo, Matthews," Dylan called. "Get your butt over here and talk to your lady."

"Oh, it's, ah, not like that." Ginger felt the heat in her face.

Dylan shrugged. "That's between the two of you. But if you want my advice—"

"She doesn't," Scott said as he arrived.

His boss just laughed. "You can take off if you need to, Scott. Otherwise, the break room is empty till people wander in to collect their lunch bags." He studied Ginger's face. "Unless you want to use my office? I don't need to be in there for the next however long."

She laid her hand on his arm. "Thanks, but no. The break room will be fine."

Scott's jaw shifted. Too bad if he didn't care for her making any arrangements with his boss. He should have come to the party as promised.

Partly for spite and partly because Dylan was so considerate, she stretched up and kissed his cheek. "Thanks."

"Hey, more than my pleasure. You let me know what else I can do for you. I'm always available for that kind of thank you." Dylan clapped Scott on the shoulder. "You're a lucky man. Don't screw it up."

They both watched Dylan walk away, Ginger the more amused and entertained of the two. "Which way?"

Scott turned and led her to the break room, the size of her classroom and just as bright and welcoming. Tables and chairs filled most of the middle floor, while sofas, futons, cabinets and refrigerators lined the walls. Several microwaves and even a stove supplied the need for warming food.

"Coffee?" Scott asked, his Southern hospitality fully active despite the displeasure on his face. "There's always a fresh pot brewing."

He indicated four industrial-size coffeemakers.

"No, I'm fine." She frowned at him. "I'm full of candy and cupcakes and punch."

"Oh, yeah, the party. Did y'all have a good time?"

Ginger set her teeth. "Shelby missed you."

"She understood I wouldn't be there."

She waited.

"I thought it would be better for all three of us not to be in the same room. You and I aren't dating now, and I didn't want to send the wrong signals."

"You and I never dated."

"True." He nodded acknowledgment, propping his back against the counter and crossing his arms. "So why are you here?"

"I want to talk. I want to understand."

"There isn't anything to understand. You want to adopt. I don't."

Ginger took off her coat and tossed it across a chair.

Scott scowled. "Now, don't do that. There's no need. You won't be here that long."

"Maybe I have some things to say." She perched her behind on a table three feet away and crossed her arms, mirroring his stance.

"Dylan really needs to start stocking beer in here," he muttered. "Okay. Shoot."

*Don't tempt me.* "What do you have against adoption?"

"Not a thing."

That threw her. "Then why won't you talk about adopting a baby with me?"

His eyebrows rose. "I didn't realize we'd been talking about adopting a baby together. You just told me your plans. Did I miss a proposal?"

Her teeth clenched even as embarrassment swamped her. He hadn't proposed. They hadn't talked about forever. Damn him.

"You said you wanted me. That you were over Samantha." What else had he said? He'd been implying a future.

"But you're adopting a baby," he said. "You want more than me and my girls. I can only offer you the three of us."

Aha. She knew by the flush of his skin and the tightening of his lips that he hadn't meant to admit to any offer.

"So I can be part of the family if I don't adopt?"

"I didn't say that." He shot her that annoyed look again as she waited him out. "Okay, I might have hinted at that. But it's a moot point, right? You want a baby."

"I do." *And I want you. And the girls.* Not that she could say that.

"I've done the baby thing. Serena was no piece of cake and I don't want to go through that again. Been there, changed those diapers."

He did it again. Talked about Serena as a baby, just as he had once before. "Was Shelby not a difficult baby?"

His mouth opened then closed. Shutting his eyes for a second seemed to help him come to some decision. He blew out a long breath. "Sit down."

He pulled out a chair for her and sat beside her. "Shelby isn't mine. Biologically, anyway. But she is my daughter."

Ginger lost the ability to speak, picturing the girl's almost black hair, the color of rich coffee. "She's adopted?"

He shook his head. "She's Samantha's. Shelby was one year old when I met Sam and less than two when we married. She doesn't know."

"You adopted Shelby, but you won't accept me if I adopt?" She heard her voice rise, wanted to rise to her feet with it, wanted to raise her hand to his face. But she wasn't a hitter, and slapping a man was melodramatic.

Besides, it couldn't come close to repaying him for his betrayal.

"Sam got pregnant in high school. The dad signed away all rights, but he was a minor. About the time Sam was pregnant with Rena, he came back, wanting those rights. Shared custody. He took us to court."

"I'm sorry." She subsided, ready to listen, trying to understand. Pain laced his words and she couldn't ignore it.

Scott rubbed a hand over his face. "He lost. Proved to the court he was still irresponsible and would provide a negative environment in which to raise a child. The guy didn't even have a decent place for a baby to visit, let alone live. Thank God."

Scott took a breath. "I'm her legal father now. The judge agreed Beau had signed away his rights to Shelby."

"Beau?"

"Beauregard Sheldon Abernathy."

"Sheldon and Shelby?" It couldn't be coincidence.

"Sam was feeling sentimental after the birth, and she regretted the name afterward. So we named the new baby with an *S,* too. Sam wanted it that way. I didn't care."

"Serena."

"I talked her out of 'Serenity.' She claimed our lives would be smooth sailing with serenity surrounding us. So I countered with it being serene waters, and it stuck. Poor kid."

"I still don't get it." She stood before him and squeezed his hand. Time neared when his coworkers might wander in. "If you understand about adopting a child, about that child bringing love into your heart, why are you trying to block me from experiencing that?"

"I'm not blocking you, Ginger. I'm just not going through it again." He shook his head. "I told the story too fast, made it sound too easy. We went through hell for almost a solid year, worrying about losing Shelby to that…loafer. I really worried the stress would make Sam miscarry."

"Was there reason to worry?"

"She was under her doctor's eye. Nausea related to her stress had her vomiting so much she became dehydrated, and neither she nor Rena got the nutrition they should. Her blood pressure rocketed. There was the fear of an early delivery." He shook his head. "Then of course, the fear of losing Shelby on top of it all. That man almost took everything from me, both my daughters, and he endangered my wife's health. Because he changed his mind."

"That's just one case, Scott. Your experience with adopting soured you, but—"

"Soured me? Soured? That's way too mild. I was incensed and sick and panicked. I can't go through that again."

"But I won't be pregnant when I adopt. Can't be, so we wouldn't have that worry of me miscarrying."

"Are you sure you can't? I mean, you went through all the tests?"

"Kyle, my husband, ex-husband, wouldn't donate his sperm, but by the time they tested me he didn't have to. I couldn't have a baby."

"Why?"

"Why? What do you mean?"

"What did the doctor tell you? The diagnosis."

She knew he wanted an easy answer. Something fixable.

"Is the cause of your infertility too embarrassing to discuss with me?"

"Just useless. My fallopian tubes are blocked. I've been taking fertility drugs to deal with the pain and cramps and such, but there's not much hope of conceiving, even with the aid of the drugs."

"I'm sorry." He squeezed her hand. "Surgery?"

She shook her head, too choked to speak. She'd wanted a baby so badly. Not being able to carry Scott's baby cut more deeply.

She loved him to an extent she'd never loved Kyle.

"There are complications to the treatments and surgery available to me. Few would likely kill me, but the chances of us having a child were low even with treatment."

"Could we, you and I—" Scott's smile trembled. "Try in vitro fertilization? I have good sperm."

"I bet you do." Tears ran down her face. She leaned over and kissed him, putting her heart into it. "Serena is proof of that. But no. It's no use. I can't carry a child to term."

"Is that something your doctor confirmed or does that come from your ex, too? Because if he didn't get tested you can't be sure the problem wasn't partly him." He smiled weakly. "Maybe your body knew what a jerk he'd turn out to be and sent out toxins to kill his sperm."

She chuckled, liking the idea. "Scott, trust me. If we could have found a way, we'd be parents now."

"If there's anything I can do to help you get pregnant—" He grinned. "You know I'd be more than happy to try." He sobered. "But I can't go the adoption route again. Even for you."

She swallowed her tears and sadness. "I see."

"It was pure hell, Ginger. Time and money are only the start of the cost. Our emotions were yanked all over the place. I'm not doing it again."

"Not everyone regrets giving up a child for adoption."

"Can you guarantee me that whoever this is you're talking with won't come back in a couple of years, after we've fallen in love with this baby and considered it our own, and try to take him or her away? Or a member of this person's family won't? Because that happens, too."

"You know I can't guarantee that."

"Then I can't risk it. I'm sorry, honey."

He didn't love her as much as he needed to in order to overcome his fear of a remote possibility.

It hurt. There weren't words to describe her pain.

"You can't let my girls be your girls?"

The girls that hated her? She didn't think so. "I want a baby."

Stalemate. Maybe he thought she didn't love him enough to take them all into her heart. But that wasn't it. She loved him too much to make his daughters miserable, to put him in the middle of their unhappiness and hers. Shelby and Serena deserved a woman they could accept as a mother.

Scott stilled. "These pregnant women you're talking to. Is either a minor?"

She nodded.

He grimaced. "Both? Because, if you're going to do

this, I'd urge you to pick someone who's old enough to sign a legal document and make it valid."

"I will." She glanced at the clock. Five-twenty. "Where is everyone?"

Scott shrugged and stuck his head out in the hall. "Come on in, Jerry. You don't have to wait in the hall."

"Most of us went home," the bald man said. "I just finished up a second ago."

"I have to go," Scott told Ginger. "I can meet you later, but I have to get the girls from the Wee Care. If I leave now, I'll just make it."

Ginger smiled faintly. "What happens if you're late? They don't keep the girls and lock the doors, do they? Take them home to their houses?"

"No, I just get fined. Tara, my boss's wife, will be waiting."

Ginger put on her coat. "Call her. Tell her it's my fault."

She was screwing up everything lately, she thought as she got in her car. Her marriage died because she couldn't conceive. Her relationship with Scott was over because she couldn't *not* adopt. Nothing was going right these days.

"Which means your luck's bound to change," Lisa said, handing her a shortbread cookie at her cheery kitchen table.

The whole sorry story had spilled out over cookies and iced tea. Ginger felt lighter for having shared her burden, but they hadn't come up with any solutions. There was no middle ground on which a compromise could be negotiated.

The back door swung open into the kitchen. Lisa's husband, Joe, came in with her children, Abby and Bobby.

"Hi." Joe leaned over and kissed Lisa. The kids yelled their greetings on the way through. "Should you be drinking this?" he asked.

"It's decaf."

Ginger looked at Lisa consideringly. No caffeine?

"Okay, then," Joe continued. "I've got some homework to do with Bobby, but I'll be down in a bit to fire up the grill. Ginger, you want to stay for dinner?"

"Can't tonight, thanks. I have homework of my own."

"Make a date with Lisa. We don't see you often enough."

Ginger watched him go after one more caress of his wife's arm. His wife who was pink cheeked and avoiding her eyes.

A smile worked its way to Ginger's face and came out as laughter. "You're pregnant."

Lisa's mouth opened then shut. She nodded.

"Oh, sweetie." Ginger rose and embraced her friend. "That's terrific. How far along?"

"Almost three months."

"And you didn't tell me?" She sank back into her chair. "You didn't feel you could. I'm sorry about that."

"No, I'm sorry. I should have known you'd be happy for us."

"Of course I am."

"Deep down, I knew you would be," Lisa corrected. "I was afraid you'd also be sad or hurt or something. I'm sorry I didn't tell you."

"How long have you known?"

"We've been trying since Thanksgiving. Decided it was time after the last year had gone so well. The kids have adjusted to Joe and him to them."

"And if you could find Brad and get him to give permission, Joe could give them his name."

Lisa waved a hand. "That doesn't matter. I think they're ready to call him dad without the legal stuff settled. They love him."

"And he loves them back."

"Like his own." Lisa covered her mouth. "Oh, I'm sorry. I didn't mean to compare our situation to yours with Scott's girls."

"It's okay. Stop walking on eggshells." It hit her then, how often Lisa had danced around the topic of babies. "I was urging you to have a baby with Joe not too long ago. Did you already know then? How are you feeling?"

Lisa's gaze met hers. "Are you sure you want to talk about it?"

"It would hurt me more if we couldn't. You're my best friend."

"I've been sicker than a dog." Lisa smiled.

Ginger thought of poor Horace. "That's awful."

They talked about the pregnancy and the coming baby. Ginger wound up staying for dinner, soaking in the good vibes of a happily blended family.

It hurt just a little, but not enough to override her joy for her friend.

Ginger kept an eye on Shelby the next week, watching for clues to what was going on at her home. The girl said nothing and acted no differently. She was probably glad her teacher had stopped hanging around her father.

The art project at the end of February centered on family roots. With a nod to Black History Month and Presidents' Day, the intent was to make all students proud of their heritage.

"I finished my report, Ms. Winchester," Harry called.

"That's good, Harry. Please remember to raise your hand."

"That's not fair," Jean said, shooting her hand up as she spoke. "Ron and Harry only did one report between them."

Ginger stared her down. "Jean, have you finished your report?"

The girl held up a page of writing. "I talked to my grandma on the phone and got more information about my family. But it's not interesting."

*Interesting* to the class meant pirates and killers, heroes and leaders. Part of the lesson helped the students understand the importance of everyday people making a difference.

Ginger stopped by Shelby's desk. Mentioning family gave her an odd feeling. She knew more about Shelby's family than Shelby did. Keeping the secret felt almost like lying, although she didn't see how Shelby would benefit by knowing. This was Scott's decision, after all.

"How's your family tree coming along, Shelby?"

The girl shrugged. "Okay, I guess. You think I should call my grandma for more facts about my mom's side of the family?" She pointed at her notepaper filled with scribbles and a few connecting arrows. "It's got some holes. Are you going to mark me down for stuff I don't know?"

"I'll be grading the effort on everyone's paper," Ginger addressed the class. "Howard wasn't always the thriving community it is today." She held in her laughter. *Thriving* was pushing it. "If your family has always been here, it might have been farmland when they came. Farming was a vitally important and sometimes dangerous job."

"Ms. Winchester." Shelby's hand went up. "I just got here."

"Ask your dad what his family did down South. Many people worked two jobs to feed their children and pay for their homes."

Some of the children nodded, familiar with this in their lives.

One eye on the clock assured her she only had two more hours until she met with Emma, a pregnant college student. Ginger mentally crossed her fingers. This was her third meeting with Emma. She had a feeling the young woman would make a decision today, one way or the other.

The bell sounded at last, and Ginger rushed the children on their way. Just a quick tidy-up and she had to go, too. This interview might change her life. She couldn't let herself think otherwise. She'd lost Scott and the girls. A baby was her last hope for a family.

Ginger doubted she could endure one more difficulty in her life, but the next time she looked up from scrubbing glue off a desk, fate decided to test her.

Cindy Grady loomed in her doorway, a cruel gleam to her smile. "I hear you've been seen out in public with the dad of your new student."

Ginger clenched her teeth against the urge to scream at the woman. It was just too much. But she restrained herself. "I saw your sister. I figured she'd come tattling to you."

"It's not tattling if it's true."

"Yeah, Cindy, it still is." Ginger ran the rag across the art table, satisfied. She would not be goaded into an argument.

"My sister would never engage in improper conduct with a student's father if she had your job."

"Just what did she claim we were doing?"

Cindy's lips tightened. "You were on a date."

Ginger shook her head. "Nope."

"Yes, you were. She saw you together."

"She saw Scott, and she saw me. We did talk to one another." Ginger smirked. "Does that constitute a date in your sister's book? She must not get out much."

"Don't talk about her that way. Everyone saw you at the skating rink. There's no use denying it."

"Then I won't bother. It doesn't happen to be true, but you and your sister don't care about truth. Or decency."

Cindy sucked in a breath. "What did you say? You're using the word *decency?* After the way you've behaved since your divorce?"

"Is it 'decent' to try to oust someone from her job? To spy? To spread rumors about the coach, when you had no idea what the truth of the matter was? Is it 'decent' to make up lies?"

"My sister doesn't lie. It's no wonder Kyle left you. I know him, and—"

"You know nothing. Not about me or my marriage."

"But I know what you've been up to since it ended."

Ginger doubted it, and she'd had enough of Cindy's fishing. "And just what is that?"

"Sleeping around."

"Prove it." Sheer bravado pushed her on, especially since Ginger's heart was racing, but Cindy didn't know that. "Names? Dates? Photos? What have you got?"

"I wouldn't stoop so low."

Ginger dug her nails into her palm to keep the relief from showing. "That's a surprise. You've done nothing

but ride me for two years, even before my divorce. I'm
not responsible for your sister losing her job, and she can't
have mine. So get off my back."

Silence pulsed in the room. Ginger waited for the explosion.

Cindy sneered. "Maybe we'll just see what Mr. Bushfield thinks about you dating the father of a student."

"Since I have never been on a date with Mr. Matthews,
Cindy, you go right ahead and tell him. I'm tired of you
hovering like the Grim Reaper, waiting to end my career.
We'll see what Mr. Bushfield thinks of a teacher with no
regard for the truth. You know how he feels about being
role models for the students."

The other woman went pink.

"And," Ginger continued, "while we're on the subject,
there's nothing in our contracts that says we can't date
the single fathers of students. So I'd advise you to walk
carefully back to your own room, Cindy, before I have
you brought before the principal on harassment charges."

Cindy stepped back, then turned on her heel and
marched to her own classroom. Ginger felt as though
she'd shed twenty pounds of stress.

The irony didn't escape her, though. Now she could
date Scott without worrying about Cindy, and he didn't
want her.

Scott met Dylan at Jesse's, the bar in the James Brothers Hotel. It wasn't seedy, as Dylan had joked a few days
before. It was expensive and no TV in sight. He wouldn't
have expected this to be Dylan's kind of place. If the
guy preferred refined, one-hundred-year-old-plus oak
surroundings over a loud sports bar, who was Scott to
judge? The beer tasted the same.

Walking in the hotel reminded him of the night he'd met Ginger at the Christmas party. They hadn't come to the bar then, just the ballroom and one of the guest rooms.

He missed her.

"Are you happy here?" Dylan asked.

Scott looked at the man who was his boss as well as his friend seated on the bar stool next to him, and wondered which was asking. "We're settling in. The girls are making friends."

"How about you? Are you making friends?"

Scott tapped his beer bottle against Dylan's. "Other than you?"

"I haven't heard you talk about anyone except me and Joe. And Ginger."

"Low blow, sneaking her into the conversation like that."

Dylan shrugged.

"You know how to harvest a peach?"

Laughter and curiosity lit Dylan's face. "Can't say that I do."

"First you wait. If you pick it too soon, the fruit is hard and not very juicy or sweet."

"The pits."

"Exactly. If you shake the tree, like you would with pecans, the peaches get bruised and mushy. Also not good to eat."

"Okay. So wait and don't shake the tree."

"Right."

Dylan laughed long and loud. "Are you telling me you're a peach?"

"I'm telling you, as your new friend, if you want information, you should wait until I'm ready to tell it. Don't push me or shake me down."

"Got it."

Scott drank from his beer, embarrassed at his vehemence but gratified to have made his point.

"So how's it going with Ginger?"

Scott eyed his friend. So much for making a point. "It's not."

"That's a damned shame. She's a fine lady. Can't understand why her husband left her."

"Not my story to tell."

"Wouldn't want you to," Dylan agreed. "Just hoped you wouldn't be the same kind of horse's ass."

Scott coughed out some beer with his laughter, caught off guard. "Gee, thanks. Ginger would probably claim I'm a different kind of ass."

"I'm counting on you to do the right thing by her." Dylan took a long pull of his beer. "Do you know why I pushed to hire you?"

"I was desperate and would work for peanuts?"

"Other than that."

Scott shook his head, curious.

"I'm hoping you're trainable to be my second. Fill in for me."

Scott's eyebrows shot up even while his heart sank. "You're going somewhere? I thought you were a partner? I can't take on any financial obligations right now."

"I am and I'm not." Dylan grinned and shook his head. "I guess I should say, I'm not and I am."

"Do I have to shake a straight answer out of you?"

"Hey, I'm no peach."

Scott smirked. "You shake the pecans."

"Well, I'm not a nut, either. I'm not leaving R&R. However, I just got married. I have two kids and we're looking at having some more. I can't be travelling off-site to troubleshoot for long periods anymore."

Scott shook his head. "You've got the wrong man. I'm sorry. I can't leave my daughters for long periods, either."

"I was afraid you'd say that. I still need someone here as my second anyway. We'll have to find someone else to travel."

"Charley?"

Dylan frowned. "She has kids, too. We'll work it out. Even if you can't travel, I'm thinking you might fit as an assistant manager."

Surprise shot through him, gratified at having proven himself so soon. "Thanks, Dylan."

"I haven't had an assistant before, but we get along well. We think the same. I've been watching your solution process when you hit a snag. I think you'll do fine at handling my job. Joe's thinking of doing the same thing, getting an assistant, and actually Charley might be better with him, though I'd hate to lose her from Development."

"I don't know everyone as well as you do, of course, but I'll keep an eye out. And I hear what you're not saying. Nothing's official yet, so I'll keep my mouth shut."

"That's true, but it's not all I'm not saying."

Scott drained his beer, sure he wasn't going to like whatever came next.

"I'm also not saying you need to stop being an idiot. Figure out a way to make that relationship work with Ginger Winchester. She's going to give you the stability you need to raise your children."

Scott was right. He didn't like hearing it. Not from Dylan and definitely not from his heart.

He drove home, thankful to have Tara's neighbor watching the girls. Kim was seventeen and wanted to be an elementary school teacher. He often considered setting her up to talk to Ginger, to get the lowdown on the behind-the-scenes, nitty gritty aspects of teaching. Since Ginger didn't even talk to him these days, nor had he contacted her since their last talk, he didn't see that meet happening.

Another thing to feel guilty about. He should just give his babysitter Ginger's number. But he was holding back, he admitted. Maybe he'd use Kim as an excuse to call Ginger. Just to hear her voice, to make a connection.

He missed her. Every day. Every night.

He opened his front door, met Horace halfway and bent down to pet him. The dog hardly ever jumped anymore. Ginger's influence again.

"Daddy."

Scott looked up in time to see—and catch—Rena as she launched herself toward him from the fourth stair up. His heart pounded with fear until he had her in his arms. "Don't do that, pumpkin."

He gave her an extra squeeze and set her down. He'd have to enroll her in some gymnastics class to funnel her energy. "Did you have dinner?"

She nodded. "Kim made chicken. But Shelby wouldn't come eat it."

He raised his eyebrows at the teen coming into the room. Today her spiky hair was tamed into black and orange curls. What did his mama call them? Pin curls? Like Shirley Temple's only skinnier. He wanted to grin but wasn't sure how Kim would take it. "I left money for pizza, Kim. You didn't have to cook. Thank you, by the way, for picking up the girls after day care."

She grimaced. "No problem."

Scott waited, as her face and words sent different messages. No doubt more was coming. And no doubt it had to do with his absent daughter who wouldn't eat Kim's chicken.

"Shelby's in her room," Kim confirmed as though reading his mind. "She was unhappy about something the entire evening, right after she got off the phone, but when I tried to talk to her, she was disrespectful."

"She told Kim to shut her big mouth," Rena clarified, swinging back and forth from the newel post. "Then she wouldn't say sorry."

"I sent her to her room, Mr. Matthews. I didn't know what else to do with her."

"She was screaming," Rena added.

"That's enough tattling, Serena. What does she mean, Kim?"

"She was swearing at me." Her gaze went to his little girl. "I'd rather not repeat what she said."

"Swearing? Shelby?" He'd never heard it from her and instantly felt guilty. He knew where she must have learned to swear—straight from him.

He took off his coat, grim clear down to his boots. "Can you stay, Kim? Until I can talk to Shelby and get her calmed down. I'll have her apologize to you."

Kim nodded. "But I do have an eleven o'clock curfew."

Scott stopped midstride then glanced back over his shoulder. It was ten to seven. Kim's grin had him smiling. Kids were so darned resilient. He'd probably get upstairs to find Shelby lost in a book, all former misery forgotten.

But when he got to her room and jimmied open her lock, she was gone, a note propped in the arms of her old teddy bear.

She'd run away.

# Chapter 12

Scott read the note for the fourth time. It still didn't make sense that Shelby would run away. What did she mean nobody loved her? Which friend would hurt her so deeply? Even if she didn't have friends, she had him and Serena. She'd probably talked to that mean girl, Jean. And the bit about wanting to go back to Georgia? "Back home" as she called it. He swallowed down panic. She wouldn't be trying to make it to some kind of transportation center, would she? She knew full well how far away "home" was. Hell, they didn't even have that house anymore. Where did she think she was going?

Kim and Rena were in the living room, crying. He'd grilled the babysitter on everything she could remember, any hint Shelby might have given since leaving day care.

Everything Kim related sounded normal. "Shelby was quiet on the ride home. She was on the phone then came downstairs in a bad mood."

"I think she was crying," Rena put in.

They both looked at her. "Why do you think so?"

Kim's forehead furrowed. "I didn't notice. Are you sure?"

Rena nodded. "Her eyes were red and sad."

"Why didn't you say something?" Kim asked.

"Shelby and me cry a lot. Our mommy died before we moved here. It makes us hurt inside."

Scott swallowed his guilt. He'd known, but he'd hoped it would ease. Crying was part of the grieving process, so he hadn't wanted them to feel they shouldn't. Maybe moving the girls away from both sets of grandparents had been a mistake. Despite his talk with Dylan earlier about becoming his assistant, he might have to move his girls back to Atlanta.

He'd have to think about that later. Right now, he had to find Shelby.

"Shelby said mean things to both of us," Kim continued, "then stomped upstairs to her room. About twenty minutes later, she came down to take Horace out again, even though I'd taken him out when we got home."

"She said," Rena inserted, "it was her job and at least Horace loved her."

"At least?" Scott questioned.

The teenager wiped away her tears and met his gaze. "I'm sorry, Mr. Matthews. I thought it was normal. She's never happy to have me over because that means you're gone. I get that a lot with kids." She shrugged, looking helpless. "I didn't put any added importance on it today."

They hadn't seen Shelby since nor had she responded to calls for dinner. Her door was locked; her music turned up.

Kim blamed herself. Scott tried hard not to.

He needed a plan. Tearing through papers on his desk, he searched for the phone number list of her classmates. Jean. Maria, or was it Marie? Harry and Ron. Who would she turn to? Who did she know?

And God, how would she get there? He swallowed, picturing his little girl in the dark, in the cold, walking alone. Please, Lord, let her still be alone. Safe somewhere.

Terror seized every muscle and organ in his body. How long before he called the police? Would they act before twenty-four hours passed since she was so young?

Remembering he'd left the phone list in the kitchen while making plans for the Valentine's Day party a couple weeks before, he surged into the room, trying not to look as frantic as he felt. No need to scare Rena or Kim as much as he was scared. He yanked open the junk drawer, thumbed through the file he kept on Shelby's school. Finally spotted the paper sticking out of the residential phone book where he'd highlighted the numbers of her friends that he didn't want to lose.

His cell phone rang, and he snatched it from his pocket, heart pounding. *Let her be found. Let her be safe.*

"Shelby's here."

Scott's knees buckled on hearing those words and recognizing the voice. He closed his eyes and sank against the counter. Ginger. "Thank God. What is she doing there? Where are you? Home? School? I'll come right away. I'm putting on my coat."

He matched action to his words in an instant, flying to the front door. With a hand over the speaker, he turned to Kim and Rena. "She's okay. She's with a friend."

Kim's tears tracked mascara down her cheeks in black rivers. She hugged Serena close, rocking them both as they cried out their relief.

"Wait," Ginger's whisper came in his ear.

"Wait? What are you talking about? I can't wait. Why would I? I'm coming right now. To your house, right, not the school?"

Considering the time of night, he'd go to Ginger's whether she confirmed or not. It was closer anyway.

*Wait*? What kind of B.S. was that?

"Don't come yet," she urged, still in a whisper. "I wanted to let you know she's okay. She's in the bathroom, so I only have a minute."

"Ginger, that's just not going to happen. I'm on my way."

"I'm trying to get her to tell me what's going on. Why she ran away. I don't want her to do it again, so if we can get to the bottom of it now, when she came someplace safe, maybe she won't run away again. And if she does, she'll know she can trust me."

He closed his eyes, processing. He wanted to deny her logic, wanted to rush over and get his baby girl in his arms.

He put his forehead against the front door, ignoring Horace's whine at his side. The important thing was Shelby was safe. That's all he wanted. He took a deep breath. "How long?"

Ginger's breath whooshed through the phone. "I don't know. It would be best if she called you, but if I can't get her to do that, I'll call you myself. No more than an hour."

"Forget that. I'll give you half an hour, but then I'm on your porch."

"Whatever you think is best for Shelby." She disconnected.

He scowled at the phone before putting it back in his pocket. That last shot was underhanded.

And probably smarter than his plan. Not that he had a plan, per se, other than driving over and holding Shelby so tight he'd likely crush her. Then spanking her to within an inch of her life—did parents still spank kids? He didn't think so. She was definitely grounded forever. First, of course, he had to give her something to be grounded from other than school and lessons.

He put a smile on for Kim and Serena. "She's safe. I'm going to go get her in a little bit."

He hoped they called soon.

Kim sagged in relief. "I can stay here with Serena. I wouldn't charge you."

"No."

His reflexive answer whipped the girl like a lash. She flinched and dropped her gaze, nodding her acceptance into her lap.

"It isn't your fault, Kim. I'll have you back to babysit."

Probably. If he ever went out again.

"It's just that I need to be with the girls, both of them, right now. You understand that, right? It has nothing to do with you."

The girl bought it and rallied. She wouldn't accept payment for the night, and Scott didn't push it. She felt guilty enough losing his kid.

He sat on the couch, hugging Rena close, and watched the minutes tick by. Half an hour had never passed so slowly.

Ginger handed Shelby a shortbread cookie, glad she'd taken some home from Lisa's house. The girl had done wrong and didn't deserve a treat, but on the other hand, Ginger had never seen anyone more in need of a cookie and a hug than Shelby. Since the girl wouldn't accept a hug from her, Ginger offered what she could.

She pulled out a chair and sat facing her across the small dinette table. "You want to talk about it, Shelby?"

The girl shook her head.

Ginger smiled gently. "I don't blame you. Whatever happened must have been terrible to make you run away."

"I don't belong anywhere." Anguished eyes met Ginger's. "I called my Grandma Baxter, like Jean did. My mom's mom."

Ginger's chest ached. She had a bad feeling she knew what was coming.

"I asked about how my mom met my dad. I mean, Dad has told me the story before. The guy I thought was my dad." Tears started down her face. She sniffed. "I'm adopted."

Not thinking, Ginger opened her arms. Surprise hit her as Shelby catapulted into her embrace. Standing by Ginger's chair, the girl buried her face in Ginger's shoulder, hot tears wetting her blouse.

Ginger rocked her, stroking her hair. "Go ahead and cry. Let it out, sugar."

Shelby took her at her word and cried herself dry. It only took about five minutes, as the girl had been crying for most of the evening before knocking on Ginger's door. Running away still had to be discussed, but it was way down on the list.

The girl sank back onto her chair, palming tears from her face. Ginger retrieved a dish towel right before the girl's sleeve swiped her nose. With a sheepish grin, Shelby used it instead. Taking another cloth, Ginger wet it with cold water and handed it to Shelby.

"Press it against your face. It helps."

She did so, then nodded and handed it back. "Sorry I had to come here. I don't know where anyone else lives close by."

Ginger gaped. She lived a good three miles from Shelby's house. She couldn't imagine walking that far at night when she'd been eight. Getting lost on all the different streets and scared by dogs would have had Ginger turning back for home after two blocks. "How did you know where I live?"

Shelby crumbled her cookie. "Dad... I mean *Scott,* drives past here all the time. He thinks we don't know why, but I saw you in your car once."

"Oh." More to think about later. Or not. After all, she and Scott were at an impasse. Essentially, their relationship was over. As soon as her love for the man faded, he'd just be a memory.

Since he was due at her house in roughly twenty minutes, she'd have to put off getting over him for another day.

"Shelby, you know your dad loves you. And yes, I mean the man you've called Dad since you could talk."

The girl's eyes went round. "Did you know?"

Oh, crap. Ginger took a breath and put her hand on Shelby's. "Your dad told me last week. Sugar, what did your grandma say?"

She broke her cookie into bits. "I kind of lied. I told her I'd already talked to Dad, to *him* about the project. Sometimes me and Serena hear the same stories over and over, and I know them already. So I thought if I said that, she'd tell me something interesting, something new."

The irony hit Ginger. The woman had obviously told her something Shelby hadn't heard before. But why? "How did it come up?"

Shelby pursed her lips. "I told her Dad—Scott—wanted me to call. That there was stuff she knew, stuff about my ancestors and about my mom and me, stories from when I was a baby, that he didn't know."

The girl lifted wounded blotchy eyes to Ginger. "I didn't know that was true. I just wanted to hear something nice about my mom because I miss her so much. I didn't really care about the homework."

Ginger patted her arm. "It doesn't matter right now."

Shelby hung her head for a moment. "Grandma said, 'Oh, he told you why he wasn't around?' I didn't know what she meant because Dad, you know who I mean, he doesn't travel for work like Maria's dad does. But maybe he did years ago so I said, 'Yeah, he told me.'" Her shoulders came up to her ears, just as Scott's did when he was unhappy with reality.

"I'm sorry." Ginger was relieved. At least it had been an innocent misunderstanding on the grandmother's part, even if there were serious repercussions.

"Everyone knew but me." Her jaw set with the stubborn expression Ginger had seen too many times. "Grandma said Dad loves me like I was his own. As much as he loves Serena."

Tears fell down her cheeks again.

"Shelby, your dad does love you. That's why he adopted you instead of just being your stepdad."

Shelby scrubbed at her tears as her face turned thoughtful. Obviously that hadn't occurred to her.

"That's right. He didn't have to adopt you when he married your mom. He wanted to. He wanted *you*." Ginger took a fortifying breath. "I know something about that myself. About wanting a baby, loving it even though you didn't..." Oh, dear. Not the birds and the bees. She really was stepping on Scott's toes tonight. "Didn't physically bring it into the world."

"Are you adopted, too?"

"No, but I'm adopting a baby. I can't have one, get pregnant and all that, even with a husband." Hopefully, this wouldn't turn into a chat on how an unmarried woman could have kids.

*Hurry, Scott.*

"You want a baby that's not yours? On purpose?"

Ginger nodded. "You know some adopted kids, don't you?"

"Well, yeah. I guess. I just thought… I don't know."

"It wasn't important to you when you found out about them."

Shelby nodded. "Right."

"It doesn't matter whether you're born into a family or adopted into one, sugar. And you know your mom gave birth to you, right? Your grandma explained that?"

Shelby shook her head. "I didn't ask."

Ginger took her hand. "I can't have a baby the regular way. I'll love the adopted baby no differently than if it were born out of my body. I'm sure that's how Scott, your dad, feels."

Shelby's small face scrunched in concentration. Then she nodded. "You don't think, now that my mom's gone, he'll, like…return me?"

Ginger's heart ached. "No. Not for one second. Your dad loves you. He wouldn't stop loving you no matter what. He's your *dad,* Shelby, not just a guy who married your mom and sometimes took care of you. It's forever."

The girl nodded and drew patterns across the Formica tabletop with her fingertip. "I didn't like you at first."

Ginger suppressed a smile. "Really?"

A quick glance darted her way. "Not at first. Because you look a little bit like my mom. And my dad—" Shelby swallowed, but didn't correct herself calling Scott that. Progress. "He liked you. I could tell at school on my first day."

"I like him, too."

"I could tell that you did. I didn't like it. Because you're not my mom."

"No one can take her place, Shelby. Even if, and it won't be me, but even if your dad gets married again, it's because his heart grew bigger and he made room for someone. Not because he replaced your mom."

The girl tipped her head. "Can that really happen?"

The science teacher in her vied with the romantic. She compromised, supplying the truth. "Love grows."

"I guess so."

"You didn't know you had a place for Horace in your heart until he was already there."

Shelby sat up with a smile. "I had a dog place in my heart?"

"Sure seems like it. You never know how much you can love someone until you love them. You love your dad, right?" Ginger held her breath, fearing she was pushing it.

But Shelby nodded.

"So does that mean you don't have room to love your little sister?"

"Of course I love Serena. I mean, she's my sister."

"See what I mean? It's a family thing. That's how your dad feels, too."

"So, say you got married," Shelby started. "And say the guy had kids already…"

Ginger shook her head. "I'm not discussing that with

you, sugar. Now, here's something you do need to know. Your dad will be here in about five minutes."

She grinned, thank the Lord. "You called him?"

"He's very eager to see you."

Shelby sighed. "He's going to spank me."

"Maybe."

"I guess I deserve it."

"I guess you do. Why don't you wash your face and brush your hair."

She nodded and stood, then threw her arms around Ginger again.

Ginger's chest nearly burst with love as she hugged her in return.

The knock on the door came as little surprise. With a quick primping of her own, Ginger went to the front to let him in. Serena accompanied him.

"Where is she?"

"Upstairs, cleaning up for you. She's fine. But, Scott, she knows."

He shut his eyes.

"Knows what?" Serena asked.

"That I'm adopted," Shelby called from halfway up the staircase.

Scott turned. Their eyes met and his arms opened. Shelby leaped, as though they were a circus family, used to doing this every day. He hugged her close, face buried in her neck.

"Don't ever run away again."

"I won't."

"You need to talk to me, Shelby. About everything. I love you."

"I love you, too, Daddy."

Serena tapped Ginger's leg.

She looked down at the girl through tear-blurred eyes. "What's she mean, she's adopted?"

Scott set Shelby down but kept a hand on her shoulder. "You and I will talk later." He looked at Ginger. "Do you mind if we all sit down for a minute? This discussion will be easier if I'm not driving."

She nodded and took his and Serena's coats, then hung them on the hall tree. Not sure she had enough cookies for the reunion, Ginger edged toward the kitchen to check.

"You, too, if you wouldn't mind," Scott said. "You're a part of this anyway."

He sat on the couch with a daughter on either side, holding them close. Ginger sat across from them, amazed at how well-adjusted they looked. Just a family discussion. All they lacked was Horace. It hurt a bit that they were complete without her.

"I'm going to say this once." Scott broke off and grinned. "And then I'm going to repeat it until you believe it. I love you, Shelby. Just as much and just the same as I love Serena."

Both girls beamed at him.

He looked at Serena. "You and Shelby have the same mom, but not the same dads. I'm your biological father. That means you and I might look something alike. Shelby has a different biological father, but I'm her real dad just like I'm your real dad. Because I raised her, and I love her."

He turned to Shelby. "When your mom was in high school, she thought she fell in love with this boy. Turned out she didn't really love him, but by then you were on your way."

Ginger smiled. Nice way to smooth over that birds and bees discussion.

"So she gave birth to you, but she didn't want that boy to be your dad. Because he's nice but he wasn't the one she wanted to marry."

"She wanted you," Shelby said.

"She didn't know me yet, but, yes, she wanted to be able to give you the right dad when she met him. When she met me."

Rena made dots on his leg and stared at the denim for a minute. "So the mom or dad you have isn't the right mom or dad?"

"Most of the time they are. But sometimes the right dad is out there, like I was, waiting."

"Like Ms. Winchester," Shelby put in. "Waiting for a baby to adopt."

Scott stared at her, then at Ginger.

Ginger shrugged. "We had quite a conversation."

"But, Daddy." Serena pulled his attention to her. "If you were the right dad for Shelby, what about me?"

He hugged her close. "I'm the right dad for both of you. I got lucky that way. I'm so grateful your mom found me to be a daddy to both of you."

Rena nodded. "Yeah, Mommy was pretty smart to pick you."

Shelby tilted her head in question. "Do I have to meet my other dad?"

"No." Scott hesitated. "Unless some day you want to. But he's really just a guy your mom knew a long time ago."

It hit Ginger then how young Samantha would have been when she died if she had Shelby while in high school. Seventeen or eighteen when she got pregnant— she wouldn't have seen twenty-seven.

"How old were you," she asked Scott, "when you met Shelby?"

"Twenty-two. Their mom was almost twenty and the baby peanut—" he tickled Shelby and made her giggle "—was just shy of a year old."

"Dad's thirty." Shelby helpfully did the math.

"Thanks." His mouth twisted wryly.

"But he hasn't had his birthday yet, so he'll be thirty-one."

"And now that that's settled," he said, "is everyone okay? Should we head home? Or do you have more questions that don't concern my age?"

The girls giggled.

"Is Shelby going to get in trouble?" Serena asked.

"You bet."

Shelby ducked her head but didn't argue.

"Hey," he said, "come to think of it, what's this about you swearing at the babysitter? You owe Kim an apology, for that and for running away while she was watching you. You know better."

"I'm sorry. I'll tell her."

"And the swearing?"

"I learned it in class."

Ginger jerked upright. Scott raised his eyebrows. "Really?"

"From Jean."

Ginger relaxed, while making a mental note to talk to the girl. "What did Jean teach you?"

"About being a bastard. It was in our homework."

Ginger opened her mouth, paused, then closed it. "Not technically," she told Scott. "We did a unit on our ancestors. Jean is quite the researcher."

"You did a unit on family trees?" *And didn't tell me?* his eyes accused her.

"We do it every year."

Scott shook his head. "Look, Shelby, you're not to use swear words."

"I was saying I was one, not that Kim is."

"Doesn't matter. I mean, yes, it does. I'm glad you weren't swearing at her. But you're still too young to understand the impact words can have."

"So when will—?"

"Shel."

She grinned at his warning. "Just kidding. *Dad.*"

He hugged her. Ginger had a feeling he'd be falling for that trick for a while to come.

They put on their coats. Shelby hugged her. "Thank you, Ms. Winchester. I'm sorry I haven't been very nice to you."

"Let's put it behind us, sugar. Tomorrow morning we'll start fresh."

"Bye." Serena tugged on her hand until she bent over, then she kissed Ginger's cheek. "Thanks for taking care of Shelby."

They turned to their father.

Scott grinned and pulled Ginger close. His hug smothered her. "God, yes. Thank you, thank you for being here."

For a minute, he just held on to her. Then he kissed her, right in front of the girls. His kiss held gratitude and longing, remembered terror and relief.

Serena's laughter bubbled out, as though this were the silliest thing she'd ever seen. Shelby groaned. "Daaad. That's my teacher."

But she grinned at them when they broke apart.

"Come on, girls," he said. "Let's get home."

Ginger stood and watched the Jeep back out of her driveway, waving at the toot of their horn. Everyone was fine. Everybody back where they belonged.

Tears stung her eyes as Scott drove away with the girls.

Scott couldn't believe what an ass he was. His second grader was smarter, he thought, tipping back a beer as he sat on his couch. Shelby described it to a T. While he'd been explaining how it felt to be her dad, she'd already pegged Ginger as the perfect mother.

"Like Ms. Winchester," Shelby had said. "Waiting for a baby to adopt."

All Ginger lacked was that baby, just as he'd needed Shelby to enrich his life. Then Serena.

His obstinacy and fear stood in the way of her adopting a baby with him. He'd seen how much the girls had both come to care for her and she for them. If she needed a baby, too, he shouldn't be such a coward about it. His fear kept them from being a family.

He rubbed his eyes tiredly. He'd gotten them home while Shelby related her conversation with Sam's mom. Damn all the luck that the words had made sense to each of them, even though neither was talking about the same thing. There was a phone call he dreaded. Not that he blamed Sarah Baxter. She would never intentionally hurt either of the girls.

Scott took a long swallow of the beer turning warm in his hand.

He'd removed Shelby's door from its frame until he could figure out some worse punishment. Turned out he couldn't spank her. She'd been slashed up inside. He wouldn't add to that. It was tempting, though, just to prove he loved her enough to punish her. So he'd removed her door and told her more was coming. That uncertainty had shut off any complaints she might have made about her lack of privacy.

He worried over Ginger. What if no pregnant woman approved her because she lacked a husband?

He was selfish. He was tired. And, he admitted, tonight would have been a good night to cuddle up with Ginger and celebrate their family being whole again.

Except it wasn't whole without her.

Ginger opened her door to Scott the next evening, sure he was on her porch to read her the riot act. She should have warned him about the ancestry project, but she didn't know Shelby hadn't told him. Besides, she'd listed it on the handout she sent home at the beginning of the month, before he'd told her about Shelby being adopted.

Which were just rationalizations, she admitted as she took his coat. She'd owed him a follow-up phone call when the project started. They'd just "broken up," if that was the right term for people who'd never officially had a date.

"Sit down, okay?" he said.

She took the chair. Scott scowled as he sat, then stood and finally sat again. This was going to be bad.

"Is Shelby okay?" she asked.

"Fine. Both girls are fine. Did I thank you properly for taking care of Shelby last night?"

"She was afraid you'd spank her."

"I should have. I just didn't have the heart after all

she'd endured alone." He met her eyes. "But she wasn't alone. She came to you."

"I was surprised."

"Now that I've had time to think about it," Scott said, "it makes absolute sense. She recognized it before I did."

Ginger's heart beat harder at the warmth in his gaze. "Recognized what?"

"You're like I was, a natural parent, waiting for a child to love."

"I am." She smiled.

"And I'm selfish to deny you a chance to adopt."

Ginger moved to the cushion at his side, taking his hand. "No, you have to do what's right for you, and for the girls."

"Yes, I do. That's why I want you to marry me."

Shock dropped her mouth open. "You want… What?" She gathered her wits even as her heart shattered. "No. Scott, no. You're just grateful. You're still getting over Shelby running away, coming here. You'd propose to Lizzie Borden if she'd been the one to comfort Shelby."

He laughed. "Give me some credit."

"She only axed her parents, not any husband or kids."

"Because she didn't have a husband or kids. But I meant give me some credit over knowing what's real and what's gratitude." He grinned. "I might have been thankful Lizzie showed my daughter some kindness, but I wouldn't mistake being in love with her. I love you, Ginger."

She couldn't speak. Tears of sadness and joy and regret closed her throat. Scott loved her? The warmth of his eyes radiated sincerity. He believed it, anyway. For now, when it was easy.

"I wish I…" She started again. "Thank you. That means the world to me."

He frowned. "But?"

"I can't marry you."

"Of course you can. You're the mom my girls need. Just like I was right for Shelby. You proved that last night."

She nodded and pulled her hand free. She stood and walked two steps away before turning to face him, hands clasped at her waist to still their trembling.

"I'm going to be a mother."

His gaze shot to her stomach, then back to her face.

"No, I'm adopting. I heard yesterday."

He surged to his feet with a grin. Grabbing her up, he swung her in the limited space of the living room.

"That's terrific." He set her down again. "Honey, that's fantastic. What a roller-coaster day for you yesterday must have been."

She stared at him. Did he not get it? She'd just done the one thing he objected to the most. Fully aware her action would keep them apart forever, she'd put her needs first. Ahead of him, ahead of Shelby and Serena.

She waited for him to understand. He smiled at her like the village idiot.

"Scott. I can't marry you."

His brow furrowed in a frown. "Is it a condition of the adoption that you raise the child alone?"

"Of course not."

"Do you not love me?" He swallowed. "Do you need some time? I never did court you properly. I can do that. I *want* to do that."

"I'm adopting a baby."

"I heard you the first time."

"You don't want to adopt."

"Ah." He took her hand. "Come sit down with me for a minute, honey. While I tell you a little story."

She didn't see what difference words would make. The deed was done.

Nevertheless, they sat, facing one another and still holding hands. "Once there was a man who was an absolute fool."

She smiled. "I like this story already."

"I thought you might. This man met the ideal woman for him. And he was stupid enough to let her go. She wanted a baby and he was afraid. Afraid of a baby, can you imagine?"

Ginger shook her head, entranced. No wonder she'd fallen in love with him.

"But to him, that baby meant risking heartache. Instead, he should have been thinking of the joy and love the baby would bring. The joy and love the woman already filled his heart with."

He raised her hand and kissed it. "I'm sorry I was a fool, honey. You were wonderful with my girls last night. Even Serena kissed you goodbye. If you need a baby, and since there's one on the way—" He grinned. "Then we get a baby. And if you want to adopt a fourth and a fifth and a sixth, we'll do that."

She laughed. "Whoa."

"I understand that you don't need a husband to adopt, but I hope you need me. Some lucky pregnant woman was smart enough to recognize you as the perfect mom for her child.

"And," he continued, "I think the four of us could be the perfect family for that baby. My family isn't complete without you, Ginger. I realized that last night."

"I come as a package deal."

"As long as you love me."

She kissed him, long and sweet and full of passion. "From the first. You changed my life."

"I love you. You've made my life richer, even when you were driving me crazy."

She scowled at him. Then she relented and cupped her hand against his jaw. Tears filled her eyes. "I bet my attorney I'd be a mother by the end of the year. I just didn't know I'd be the mother of *three* children."

He marveled at her. She would love his children as much as she loved any they adopted. Ginger was as ideal for his girls as she was for him, and he'd almost lost her. "I'm a fool," he said. "But marry me anyway."

\* \* \* \* \*

SPECIAL EXCERPT FROM

*Love Inspired.*
SUSPENSE

*A K-9 cop must keep his childhood friend alive
when she finds herself in the crosshairs of a
drug-smuggling operation.*

*Read on for a sneak preview of*
Act of Valor *by Dana Mentink,*
*the next exciting installment in the*
True Blue K-9 Unit *miniseries, available in May 2019
from Love Inspired Suspense.*

Officer Zach Jameson surveyed the throng of people congregated around the ticket counter at LaGuardia Airport. Most ignored Zach and K-9 partner, Eddie, and that suited him just fine. Two months earlier he would have greeted people with a smile, or at least a polite nod while he and Eddie did their work of scanning for potential drug smugglers. These days he struggled to keep his mind on his duty while the ever-present darkness nibbled at the edges of his soul.

Eddie plopped himself on Zach's boot. He stroked the dog's ears, trying to clear away the fog that had descended the moment he heard of his brother's death.

Zach hadn't had so much as a whiff of suspicion that his brother was in danger. His brain knew he should talk to somebody, somebody like Violet Griffin, his friend from childhood who'd reached out so many times, but his heart would not let him pass through the dark curtain.

"Just get to work," he muttered to himself as his phone rang. He checked the number.

Violet.

He considered ignoring it, but Violet didn't ever call unless she needed help, and she rarely needed anyone. Strong enough to run a ticket counter at LaGuardia and have enough energy left over to help out at Griffin's, her family's diner. She could handle belligerent customers in both arenas and bake the best apple pie he'd ever had the privilege to chow down.

It almost made him smile as he accepted the call.

"Someone's after me, Zach."

Panic rippled through their connection. Panic, from a woman who was tough as they came. "Who? Where are you?"

Her breath was shallow as if she was running.

"I'm trying to get to the break room. I can lock myself in, but I don't… I can't…" There was a clatter.

"Violet?" he shouted.

But there was no answer.

*Don't miss*
Act of Valor *by Dana Mentink,*
*available May 2019 wherever*
*Love Inspired® Suspense books and ebooks are sold.*

www.LoveInspired.com

LISEXP0419

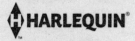

# Reward the book lover in you!

Earn points on your purchase of new Harlequin books from participating retailers.

Turn your points into **FREE BOOKS** of your choice!

Join for FREE today at
**www.HarlequinMyRewards.com.**

Harlequin My Rewards is a free program (no fees) without any commitments or obligations.

MYR18

# Love Harlequin romance?

## DISCOVER.

Be the first to find out about promotions,
news and exclusive content!

f Facebook.com/HarlequinBooks

🐦 Twitter.com/HarlequinBooks

⭕ Instagram.com/HarlequinBooks

P Pinterest.com/HarlequinBooks

ReaderService.com

## EXPLORE.

Sign up for the Harlequin e-newsletter and
download a free book from any series at
**TryHarlequin.com.**

## CONNECT.

Join our Harlequin community to share
your thoughts and connect with other
romance readers!
**Facebook.com/groups/HarlequinConnection**

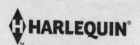

**HARLEQUIN®**

**ROMANCE WHEN
YOU NEED IT**

HSOCIAL2018